Kingdom's End is a work of fiction. Names, characters, places, and incidents are either the product of the author's imagination or are used fictitiously. Any resemblance to actual persons, living or dead, locations, or events is entirely coincidental.

2021 First Edition

Cover by Anthony Celli

Published in the United States by John Bachkosky through Amazon Kindle Direct Publishing services.

ISBN: 9798985813029

This book is dedicated to Phil. Thank you for working with me through nearly every narrative problem I had and for helping to make *Kingdom's End* as good as it could be.

Chapter One
The Cave

The sun was low, making General Mai and her horse appear to the gate guards as a black silhouette against the red-streaked sky. She sat straight as an arrow, hand and hook gripping the reins as she approached. Without stopping, she nodded to the closest guard, a younger boy she did not recognize, and passed under the massive stone arch. After the rebellion's assault on the capital, King Gjanion had enacted a curfew with knights patrolling the streets for suspicious activity. Once the sun set, the gates were closed and barred. Mai could hear the clamoring of the knights behind her preparing to close the entrance off for the evening as she directed her steed up the cobblestone path towards the castle.

The multi-spired fortress loomed over the surrounding city, scraping the darkening pink clouds and catching the last of the sun's light in its many glass windows, making it appear as though a fire engulfed its

2

insides. Mai's mind felt similarly aflame. Her ride back from The Cave had given her time to think, and for the first time in her life she felt truly conflicted. She was the general. She stood at the top of the mountain and could see everything. She had reached her peak. All was below her save for the throne, yet something inside her stirred unhappily. A feeling that all she had wasn't as it seemed. She kept trying to push it away, that feeling, but she knew what it was. Mai knew why she felt this way.

Saros.

That goddess-forsaken town had been the impetus for all of her troubles. Meeting Mara, the last wizard in the entire kingdom, had caused a chain reaction that led to Mai losing her arm and being framed as a traitor. *Of course, if I hadn't attacked Reg when he had recognized me…no. None of this is my fault. Long was supposed to kill off the last wizards. He failed, and I suffered.*

Mai rode up to the castle gate and steered her mount through a door meant for the comings and goings of smaller parties. The massive iron gate remained shut as a knight of the royal guard opened the smaller side door for the general and her horse. Mai dismounted and handed the reins to a waiting stable boy, then marched across the shadow-streaked courtyard and into the castle.

She strode swiftly across the castle's main hall, passing quickly under the watchful eyes of the portraits of past kings. Her burgundy cloak flapped behind her as her long legs made short work of the walk to the throne room. The riding boots she wore were still caked in mud, but she wanted to waste no time in delivering the crucial information she had gathered. Her scouting mission to locate the rebellion's hideout had proven fruitful and she knew she had to report back to Gjanion or he would have her head.

Don't slow down. Don't think.

As the battle in the throne room had reached its end in the death of the man she had correctly assumed was Gant's brother, Mai took the opportunity to disappear from the fray and position herself to follow the group back to their base as they fled. She trailed them for the better part of three days before they suddenly disappeared. Knowing they couldn't have gone far, Mai followed tracks and other clues until she came to a dead end: the rocky side of a hill. Hidden in the rock were small gaps just big enough for people to squeeze through, as well as trails worn into the dirt leading to each crack, indicating they were being used regularly. Mai staked out the area for two days and observed the comings and goings of several people, one of which was Gant.

On the second day, Gant had emerged from one of the openings in the side of the hill and disappeared into the woods, returning an hour later with some roots that Mai didn't recognize. In that moment, Mai suppressed the urge to reveal herself and express her sympathies for his loss, surprised that she felt the need to do that at all. Worried by this internal development, she decided to leave for the castle, removing herself and returning focus to her mission.

4

Now, as she stood at the door of the throne room carrying knowledge that could end the war that had lasted over a decade, she paused. Her hand hovered inches from the door.

Just go in. Why am I hesitating?

The alchemist had done nothing but help her. He helped track down General Long when the now-dead general had framed Mai as a traitor, he saved her life, and he had a versatile and unique weapon made for her when she lost her arm after her duel with General Long. Gant's daughter, Mara, had only revealed her powers to defend Reg, the man that Mai had attacked outside the inn. After Gjanion left Mai in Saros, none of the townspeople had ever raised a weapon against her.

Are these people so bad? They'd been living peacefully until I arrived.

Emotions rolled around inside Mai like a stormy sea. The people of Saros had simply been defending themselves. The battle that had transpired there wasn't their choice. Gjanion himself had ridden in with a small army.

Mai shook her head. "I've worked too hard to feel this way," she said to herself as she stared at her boots. She had what she wanted—she was the general of the Gjanion's army and his right hand woman.

I earned this.

Throwing it all away now would mean throwing away all of her hard work. Besides, Gjanion was on the verge of victory, how could she abandon the winning side? If nothing else, it was safer to be where she was.

Mai looked down at her left arm. Her riding hook glinted in the light of the setting sun that streamed through the high windows. She pushed all of her thoughts away and opened the heavy wooden doors.

~~~

"You can do this, my rose."

"I can't. I can't do it," Mara cried, looking for her grandmother. All she saw was black.

"You are strong, you are brave. Be who they need you to be." Fiona's ethereal voice seemed to come from all directions.

Mara's eyes opened to the sound of someone knocking on her stone hut's door. She sat up and realized that she had been crying in her sleep. Using her tunic, she wiped away the tears that her dream had brought forth.

"Mara?" Rylan knocked on the door of the small stone hut, but there was no answer. She tried again. "Mara, come on." Rylan sounded exasperated.

"I'm sorry, now isn't a good time." Mara's tone made it clear she had no intention of opening the door.

After Zhira's death in Gjanion's throne room, Mara, along with Rylan and the rest of their small team, narrowly escaped the castle under the protection of Dazel, the goddess of magic. Dazel's brilliant appearance above Zhira's body distracted Gjanion long enough to provide cover for their getaway. Mara and
~~~

Gant managed to lead their team of rebels out of the capital safely and into the woods beyond. Three days later they arrived at The Cave, where Rylan learned that her great grandfather, Radion, was still alive and leading the rebellion. Since Radion was alive, they now understood that Gjanion was not the reincarnated god he claimed to be—he was nothing more than an extremely accomplished alchemist.

An alchemist that Mara had nearly lost to, despite the advantage her magic gave her.

Upon returning to The Cave, Mara immediately locked herself away and had yet to address anyone in the week that followed. The loss of her father, as well as the near-defeat at the hands of the tyrannical king of Kyros, was too much.

"I'm not leaving until you talk to me," Rylan replied.

"Then you'll be here awhile," Mara said through the closed door.

"You're already talking to me, why not just get it over with?" Rylan challenged her.

Mara did not respond. She did not want this, but after turning away her father and others so many times, she was tired of saying no. After a moment, she used her magic to open the door, tilting her head slightly to push it open. Sitting with her back to the entrance, Mara listened as Rylan ducked into the dome-shaped abode and sat down.

"Care to tell me why you've been avoiding everyone?" Rylan asked her.

"I just need to be alone." Mara did not turn around to face her.

"How is that working out for you? Feeling better?"

Mara just grunted in response. She felt no better, but she wasn't going to tell the princess that. *Why is she here? Of all people?*

"You don't have to deal with this by yourself," Rylan said. "We are all here for you, we all want to help you."

"You can't help me, you didn't lose your father." Mara's flat tone verged on annoyance.

"I may as well have."

Mara could feel the princess's golden eyes boring into her. She felt stupid. *Of course Rylan is hurting. Her father is the impetus for our entire situation. Is that why she is here?* Mara had not considered that in choosing to side with the rebellion, Rylan had essentially lost her father as well. Mara's shoulders dropped and she turned around, locking eyes with Rylan. The two sat in silence before Rylan broke the moment and hugged her.

"I'm so sorry, Mara." Rylan started crying.

Mara was unsure of what to say. What did Rylan have to be sorry for? Why was this girl she barely knew hugging her?

Why does this hug feel so nice?

Mara had not realized how much she needed this. Unable to hold up the facade of strength, Mara broke down crying.

"I'm the one who should be sorry," Mara responded through her own tears. Her guilt for the losses everyone had suffered began to overwhelm her. After a moment, the two separated and looked at each other. "I've ruined so many lives, including yours. You left your family and your whole life behind because of me."

"You didn't ruin my life, Mara. You saved it. If it wasn't for you, I never would have stood up to my father. I wouldn't be here with you and Kei and everyone else who wants to make our kingdom a better place to live. I won't deny it hurts, but I'm definitely better off now."

Who is this girl? Mara thought. *Why is she so open? Does she really think so highly of me after all of this…chaos I've caused?*

Despite her overflowing feelings and many questions swirling about in her head, Mara just stared at Rylan; the blonde haired princess suddenly looked like an entirely different person to her than the one she had met in the dungeons of the castle. That girl was gone and in her place was a far more confident and slightly intimidating woman. Mara could see it in her eyes: the conviction and resolve were apparent. She felt bad for uprooting Rylan's life, and could not bring herself to be proud of the things Rylan spoke of, no matter how the princess spun it.

"Because of me, you've lost your family and the life you knew. Because of me, my father has lost his mother and his brother…all because I couldn't protect them…I wasn't ready." Mara put her head in her hands; Rylan put a comforting hand on her knee.

"You can't protect everyone. We know the risks," Gant said, appearing in the doorway. "Your grandmother would be proud of you. Zhira too." He choked up slightly as he mentioned his brother's name.

Mara lifted her head at the sound of her father's voice. He looked just as exhausted as she felt.

"Stop holding yourself accountable for everyone else's actions. You are not the one killing them. It's not your fault," Gant said firmly.

"Then why does it feel like it?" Mara asked them.

"Because you care. That's why people risk their lives *with* you, not *for* you. You're inspiring. Gjanion strives to rule without a care for any of those around him. He uses people as a means to an end. That day you stood up to Mai without thinking about protecting your secret, you did the exact opposite," Gant said, sitting down next to her.

"I endangered everyone that day. I didn't think about what would happen to them," Mara said, wiping a fresh stream of tears from her face.

"You saved Reg from Mai. That's what you were thinking about," Rylan explained. "My father does not save anyone unless it serves him. He is a monster…you are a hero."

"Your father is a king, isn't that how it works? People die for their kings all the time," said Mara.

"A king who doesn't care about the people who die for him is no king worth dying for," Rylan said somberly. "I am sure he loses no sleep at night over the deaths of knights in his army. I doubt he'll lose much sleep over my betrayal either."

"We need you, Mara. Come back to us. You are driven by love, Gjanion is driven by power," Gant said, offering her a purple handkerchief.

"I know, I just…I don't know if I can do this," Mara replied quietly.

"Do it for them—for Zhira and your grandmother." Gant put a hand on her shoulder.

Mara sat in silence. She was overwhelmed by the compassion being shown by Rylan and her father. The two people she thought she had hurt the most were here comforting her and trying to help her get back on her feet. For the first time in what felt like years, she smiled.

"I'll do it for *everyone*. Nobody else needs to feel this pain." She put her hand on her father's.

Rylan gave her another hug. "Welcome back."

That night, Mara finally slept well. She emerged from her dome the following morning still feeling drained, but better than she had in days. She stretched her back as she stood up fully and went to find Kei. Her father and Rylan's visit had been uplifting and made her feel much more at peace with everything that had happened, but Mara had not seen any sign of Kei since they arrived at The Cave. He had not come to try to console her once, and she was worried. Deep down

Mara thought she knew why: she was dangerous. People died when they were around her. Her grandmother, Zhira, and other citizens of Saros had all met their untimely ends on account of her.

Mara walked in between the small stone houses as quietly as she could. She had no idea what time it was; the consistent soft glow of the ferrosols, glowing yellow stones in the walls of The Cave, made it impossible to determine time. At the end of the pathway was a large opening in the wall that led to The Cave's main hub. Mara emerged to find Gladys talking to Forbin.

"Good morning!" The rebel commander addressed her. "About time you joined us."

"Morning Gladys," Mara said with a smile. As she continued on towards the forge.

The rebellion's forge was cleverly hidden. To prevent the subterranean base from being clouded in smoke, the blacksmith vented the flames up through a chimney into the rock above. The chimney let out in a small hut that doubled as a lookout's post, which was cleverly disguised as a hunting cabin, the chimney of which was an extension of the forge's below. Two lookouts could be posted there armed without arousing suspicion should anyone come across the small log building.

Mara walked over to where the blacksmith, Jerra, was working on a large piece of armor. Mara wasn't abnormally tall, but she stood almost two heads above Jerra. The blacksmith was surprisingly skinny given her profession of choice, though nobody ever questioned her strength. She was roughly the same age as Gant, her dirty blonde hair was always pulled back in a bun, and her many freckles made it look like she was covered in ash.

"Good morning, Jerra, have you seen Kei?" Mara asked her. Kei was a blacksmith by trade, so she figured the forge was as good a place as any to find him.

"No, sorry love. I haven't seen him," Jerra replied, putting her hammer down. "It's still early, maybe he ain't up yet."

"All right, thanks." Mara gave her a soft smile, making a mental note that it was, in fact, early in the morning.

"Glad to see you up and about. You seem to be doing better," Jerra said, smiling softly.

"I'm trying," Mara replied, returning the smile as she turned away.

Walking down The Cave's main path, Mara passed Radion's hut and heard her father's voice.

"So I just add some of this and…" Gant's voice was cut off by a muffled explosion.

"Not that much!" Radion replied in a frustrated voice.

Mara pushed open the door and found the two of them covered in a red powder.

"What happened here?" she asked, grinning at her father.

"A very eager alchemist didn't wait until I was done with my instructions," Radion answered as he brushed off his grey tunic, clearly flustered.

"Sorry," Gant replied as he too de-powdered himself.

"What are you attempting to make?" Mara inspected the remaining contents of the small black cauldron on the table.

"It's an invisibility powder," her father explained.

"It's *supposed* to be. I have been working on it for years, but haven't managed to get it quite right," said Radion.

"Ideally it works under the light of the moon. Certain plants, most notably the moonflower, glow under its light. If we can find the right combination of ingredients, we could reverse the effect and use it to become less visible," Gant explained.

"Your father is a smart man. He has done his research. I didn't even think to use something's trait against itself. Something mixed with moonflower should produce the desired effect, but we haven't found the right catalyst," Radion mused.

"Don't use a moonflower, use a ferrosol," Mara suggested.

"What?" Gant asked, confused.

"One of the rocks here in The Cave—they glow no matter what. Grind that up with darkpowder and you don't need to worry about the moon. The darkpowder will reverse the glow like it does at Sari's shop back home and it will be constant no matter the time of day."

Gant and Radion stared at each other, then at Mara.

"I thought *you* were the alchemist," Radion said jokingly to Gant.

"I'm glad to see she paid attention all those years," Gant replied.

"Gant, grab a rock from the wall," Radion instructed.

"Just… out of your wall?"

"Yes, yes, they're just rocks." Radion was eager to try Mara's suggestion.

Gant pried a rock from the wall and placed it in another small cauldron with some darkpowder.

"Mara, would you mind speeding up the process a bit for us?" Gant asked her.

"Happy to!" Mara stared at the mixture and twirled her pointer finger counterclockwise. The rock and powder broke up as if crushed by an invisible pestle and settled into a light gray powder with a hint of blue mixed in.

"Now what?" Gant asked them.

"Now we try it!" Radion exclaimed, grabbing a small ceramic jar from the ledge behind him.

"What's that?" Mara asked.

"Just water. I'm turning some of the powder into a paste we can spread onto Gant to try."

"Me?!" Gant asked, clearly not keen on being the test subject. "What if it's permanent?"

"Then we will know it worked!" Radion scooped some powder into the jar and shook it up until Mara could no longer hear the water sloshing around.

Gant took the jar and spread some of the paste onto his left forearm, covering it from his wrist to his elbow. All three of them waited with bated breath until Gant's forearm disappeared, making his hand look like it was levitating in front of him.

"Goddess above!" Radion exclaimed.

"It worked," Gant said, shocked.

"I wonder for how long," Mara pondered.

"Hopefully long enough to be useful," said Radion.

Mara sat with her father and the old king for a while, helping them mix ingredients and watching them work with various concoctions. It brought her back to the days in Saros when she would sit and watch her two fathers work in the kitchen; they would mash berries and mix potions while she toyed with her magic. She missed her father, but for the first time since their arrival at The Cave she smiled at the thought of him. He had died trying to save her, and thanks to her conversation the night before with Rylan and Gant, she no longer felt guilty. She felt loved. She felt safe.

~~~
~~~

Mai pushed the door open and walked into the cavernous throne room. Purple drapes hung from the walls, depicting the king's crest: a moon with a lightning bolt across its face. The stained-glass windows glowed brilliantly in the light of the setting sun, except for one that was boarded up to be repaired. The marble floors had been repaved quickly after the brawl between them and the rebels, but there were still signs of the struggle in the stonework on the walls and pillars lining the room. Mai glanced at the crack in the column that Commander Hearth had been thrown against when Gjanion had learned of his traitorous ways.

"Well, General? What have you found?" King Gjanion addressed Mai from his throne. His purple robes had gold trim that glowed in the light of the flames as they danced in their braziers. Sitting to the right of Gjanion was Commander Tren, whose face still sported the yellowish remnants of a bruise from his bout with Commander Hearth the night of the assault on the throne room. His dark hair was pulled up in a top knot with a dark blue band that matched his armor.

Mai looked at the two of them and made her decision. "The rebellion is hiding in a cave network no more than three or four days' ride due east from here."

"Three days?" Gjanion asked, more surprised by her revelation than confused.

"Yes sir, they've been right under our noses the whole time," Mai explained.

"Tell me about this base," the king commanded as he leaned back on his throne.

"I observed them coming and going from cracks and openings in the side of a hill for two days. Some of the assailants we fought in the throne room were among them. It's well hidden. Easy to miss if you don't know where to look."

"Your Majesty, if I may," Tren spoke up, earning him a sharp look from Mai. He continued when Gjanion nodded. "The location of the outpost General Long and I found would be logical in relation to where the general claims this cave hideout is. I'm willing to bet there are several concealed outposts that surround this secret base, which would give them ample time to hide from any undesirable confrontations."

Mai did all she could to keep herself from smiling. Tren was suddenly siding with her, and she knew why. After Hearth had revealed himself to be the traitor, Tren realized he had been wrong about Mai all along. He had tried to sell her out before Long got the chance, with Hearth supporting him to protect his own cover. But now here he was, faced with the truth: Mai had been loyal and he had been wrong.

"If what you both say is true, then there are two options." King Gjanion leaned on his arm in his throne as he processed this new information. Mai was slightly surprised at the calmness in his voice after what she had told him. Learning the rebellion had been within spitting distance all this time must be a hard thing to hear.

"My king, I think we should—"

"SILENCE," the king interrupted Tren, who immediately clammed up. Gjanion's voice returned to normal and he continued. "We either run a full and immediate assault on their hideout or we give them a taste of their own tactics: infiltrate them as they did us."

"Given that there are probably several outposts we don't know about, like the commander said, I believe we would be at a disadvantage in either scenario," Mai replied. She chose her words carefully, sensing the anger the king was hiding.

"Do you have another suggestion, General?" the king leaned forward; he did not like to be contradicted. Mai knew this, but took the odds that his desire to win this war outweighed his pride.

"I do." Mai's stoic face gave way to a slight grin.

Chapter Two
Retaliation

Gjanion sat in a plush high-backed chair cradling his newborn son while across the room, his wife slept soundly for the first time in two weeks. He stared down at Karbalion, who had come into the world screaming and with a full head of black hair.

This child will secure my legacy. He will teach me about who I am when I am reborn.

According to the book Gjanion had discovered that held his family's lineage, the cycle of Knorr's reincarnation had been lost and rediscovered every few generations. Gjanion was determined not to lose the knowledge again, and that meant passing it on to his son. What he had learned was too important. Gjanion believed that he was Knorr, the god of power, who was banished by the goddesses Dazel and Eres for abusing his powers. The banishment doomed Knorr to an eternal life without magic, being reincarnated every other generation and always as a man.

Gjanion wrote down all he knew and ensured that there was a male heir to carry on the line and steward the knowledge he needed in his next life. He dared not think what would happen should he have no son. Would Knorr cease to exist? Would the line end?

Gjanion's mind drifted as the quiet night enveloped him. He walked over to a window that overlooked the courtyard and trees beyond it, illuminated by the half moon. A lone stryx, a large, brown, creature reminiscent of an owl with an elongated neck and two tendril-like tails soared over the castle and out over the woods, gliding as silently as its shadow. The creature began tracing large circles over the trees, looking for food.

Rylan was out there somewhere. She had betrayed him and was now helping the rebellion, the same group that had killed her mother.

Where did I go wrong?

He had loved her, raised her, taught her to ride and use alchemy, and been the best father he could while also being king. When he had told her the truth about who he was, it had broken her.

How could she not be so honored to help me continue my true destiny as a god?

Despite his best efforts, he had raised an ungrateful, selfish child ready to betray him over a single lie. Rylan didn't see the glory in helping him in his next life, she was only concerned with what she couldn't have. Gjanion looked down at his son. Would this innocent child betray him too?

No, he thought, *Rylan was manipulated by the wizard.*

Karbalion would have no such outside influence. Gjanion would see to that. He would keep Karbalion safe. Gjanion smiled as his son, his heir, his future scrunched his face at something in his dream.

"What are you dreaming of?" Gjanion asked his son softly.

Gjanion turned his back to the window and, with Karbalion sound asleep in his arms, left his wife to sleep and meandered down towards the main hall. He paced the massive atrium that served as a pictorial archive of those that preceded him. He looked up at the portrait of his father. He had few memories of the man, but by all accounts he had been a good king to his people. His grandfather's likeness hung beside his father's. Radion, the savior king who tossed out the entrenched and corrupt regime of wizards and reclaimed the throne for their family. Radion's aged face looked down on him from its spot on the wall as if waiting to see how Gjanion's war would play out.

Will I live up to his legacy? Gjanion smiled up at his past life. Radion had been a king for the people. His conquest had seen the dethroning of magic itself—by someone with no magic, either. Gjanion was still unsure of how his grandfather had managed such a feat, but it didn't matter. *No wonder I am succeeding. I have done it once before.*

The smile faded from his face as he wandered into his throne room, still holding the swaddled, sleeping prince. The fight that had taken place here had shaken him. Only by wielding all three relics, powerful artifacts imbued with old magic, did he match the power of Mara's own magic, and even then it was a stalemate.

Am I really succeeding?

He had to get the sword back, but where was it? Thanks to that aetherial entity that had saved the rebels' hides at the last moment, the rebels had managed to escape, likely with the sword. Gjanion audibly scoffed at the cowardly way they had fled, calling upon some brilliant distraction and stealing the body and the sword away with them into the woods.

"That sword will be mine again," Gjanion said confidently to his sleeping son. "And so will this kingdom."

~~~

Rylan sat up and looked around, not recognizing her surroundings. Tall gray-trunked trees stood at random intervals, peppering the landscape and sporting a mix of red and purple leaves. Blue grass flowed in the light breeze, resembling the surface of a lake disturbed by wind. Confused, Rylan stood up and began to wander around the unfamiliar landscape. As she walked, she realized there was no sun, yet the sky was painted in gold streaks and the clouds were pink and orange.

Thinking that this had to be a dream, Rylan walked for a while until she came across a strangely shaped structure. The building was made of a light grey
~~~

stone and looked like a crescent moon on its side. Each curved side reached up into the sky higher than any man-made structure she had ever seen, apart from the castle she had grown up in. As she approached the building, she heard a scream that made her blood curdle. Her instinct told her to flee but her feet wouldn't move. The building moved closer to Rylan while she stood in place until she was suddenly standing in front of the door. She reached out to turn the handle and the door disappeared suddenly in a cloud of smoke, leaving a black archway.

Rylan took a deep breath and walked forward, entering the crescent-shaped building. As soon as she passed through the arch, a scene appeared in front of her that made her want to cry, though no tears came. Laying on the floor and writhing in pain was Zhira, a gaping hole in his chest where her father had stabbed him. The sword was nowhere to be seen.

Relax. A soothing and familiar voice seemed to come from the walls.

Rylan's head whipped around trying to find the source of the voice. Nobody else was in the room besides her and Zhira. She looked down at the writhing alchemist. Zhira did not seem to notice she was there; Rylan reached out and touched his chest, right where the hole was. As soon as she made contact with him, he stopped and looked up at her, staring at her so intensely that she couldn't bring herself to even blink.

Rylan shot up, nearly hitting her head against the ceiling of her dome. She looked around, recognizing her stone hut and the small glowing stones embedded in the walls. Zhira's face remained embedded in her mind's eye. Shaken, she got up and went to go find Mara. As Rylan walked through the tunnels distracted, she thought about what she had seen.

Why would Zhira be in my *vision?*

As she approached Mara's hut, Kei came walking up looking nervous.

"Looks like we both have business with the wizard," Rylan said in a sarcastically formal voice.

Kei smiled halfheartedly. "What are you here for?"

"Oh, I just…" Rylan began, but trailed off as Mara emerged from her stone abode.

"Hey guys, what's up?"

"Uh…why don't you go first," Kei said to Rylan, taking a step back.

Rylan gave him an odd look, then turned her attention to Mara, whose gaze was on Kei, standing awkwardly away from them. Rylan felt the tension between the two of them and decided her vision could wait. Mara had complained to her that Kei had not been around once to console her since they had reached The Cave. Judging by his body language, Rylan figured that he must be here to apologize.

"Actually, I just remembered. I was supposed to talk to Radion…about…a…family thing." Rylan began to back away, and gave Mara a comforting smile before turning and disappearing through the tunnel she had come from.

~~~

Mara and Kei stood a few paces apart for what felt to Mara like several hours. Eventually, Kei broke the silence.

"Hi."

"Hey," she replied.

"So I…just wanted to…" Kei stumbled as he began to speak; Mara said nothing, encouraging him to continue. "I'm sorry. I should have been there for you."

"Yes you should have," she said, not unkindly.

"Death scares me. It makes me so uncomfortable. I don't know what to say or do whenever someone dies. It feels so unnatural. I've never lost someone, so I can't relate. I can't sympathize. I feel like a don't belong in those situations, like I have no place to offer comfort and—"

Mara interrupted him with a hug. She wrapped her arms around him, and put her head on his shoulder. Kei said nothing. He put one arm around her and stroked her hair with the other.

"I'm sorry," he said again, tears in his eyes.

"It's okay. I'm glad you're here now," Mara said, realizing she had never been angry at him; she'd missed him.
~~~

After a minute, she separated from him and looked up. His dark skin made his light colored eyes stand out in the glow of the rocks in the walls.

"So you haven't been avoiding me because I'm dangerous?" Mara asked him.

"Dangerous? What do you mean?" Kei sounded genuinely confused.

"Wherever I go, people die. I know it's not my fault but I certainly don't help their odds…" she trailed off.

"So you thought I've been distant because you're some harbinger of death or something? Mara, I'd rather die fighting by your side than live by hiding from danger…no matter where it comes from," he smiled.

"That's good to hear," Mara replied before kissing him.

"Rylan is cute though, and far less dangerous…" Kei said, jokingly.

"Stop it." Mara smiled and kissed him again.

"I guess this is long overdue, but…are you okay?" Kei asked her.

"I am now, thank you," Mara said as she stood wrapped in his arms, strong from his work at the forge.

After a moment, Kei pulled away and retrieved something from his waistband.

"My knife?" Mara asked, confused as to how he had gotten it.

Kei handed it to her. "I wanted it to be as useful as possible. Back in the capital, it was the best I could do. Now that we are here and I have access to a forge, I…finished it."

Mara unsheathed the knife and examined the now sharpened blade, which had been dull and slightly rusty before. The sleek, almost mirror-like weapon in her hand looked completely new. The handle was wrapped in a fresh leather binding, the amethyst was more tightly secured in the end of the hilt, and the blade now tapered to a deadly point. Not only could she conduct magic with it like she had that night in the castle, but now in a pinch, she could wield it for its original purpose.

"This is perfect," said Mara, giving the knife a few swings. It even felt more balanced than it had before.

~~~

"You want to do what?" Tren asked, dumbstruck.

"I want to force them out," Mai replied. She had asked the king for a day to detail her plan for dealing with the rebel presence so close to the castle. In reality, she used the day to find a way to suppress her sudden sympathetic feelings towards the rebels. Gant may have helped her, but that didn't make the whole of the rebellion good. She sat down next to Tren in the council room with a map rolled out in front of them.

"That's bold," said Tren. "Why not try and sneak up on them? Gain an element of surprise and give them no time to prepare?
~~~

"Because they're in a cave network that they know and we do not. We need to get an army to their base and surround them, which will limit their movements. They'll know we are there, and it will put pressure on them. I want to smoke them out. Make them come to us. We don't know what waits for us in those caves, so I'm not going to risk sending our knights in blind. The rebels will not want to be trapped in their hideout, and even if they're prepared for a siege, we can wait them out. Eventually, they'll begin funneling people out through their most trusted and most secret passages. If we are properly set up around their base, we can pick them off slowly as they appear and close in on exits, increasing the pressure until they panic. They'll have nowhere to go but through us."

Tren looked over the map, covered with battle plans. Mai could see that he was impressed with her strategy.

"This is assuming we know all of their entry points, or will be able to find them. What if they slip away?" Tren's concern was valid, but Mai was ready.

"Wide perimeter. Have teams within earshot of each other, but spread them thin. We may not get every rebel, but if they see us everywhere, they'll panic. They can't get everyone out through one exit."

"I'll circle back to my original point: why not just rush them? Give them no time to prepare and catch them by surprise? Sure we'd probably lose a few knights to booby traps and things we haven't scouted in the caves, but—"

"No. I'm not wasting lives. These knights are people. Gjanion may want to throw bodies at every problem, but he isn't out there leading the army. If I do something that brash, I lose the trust of every knight we have. Besides, this way we control the battlefield. Remember, Gjanion wants Mara most. We can't lose her," Mai explained.

"You really have thought this through. I think this could work," Tren lauded her.

Mai didn't see through his flattery. "You can stop with the puffery. I know you tried to paint me as the traitor."

Tren sighed, as if he had been expecting this moment. "General, I am truly sorry. I was only trying to protect Kyros, and the evidence seemed overwhelming. Hearth played me, I'll admit. It was easy to think I was correct in my accusations with him and others validating me." Tren's sincerity spoke to Mai more than his words.

"I will never fault a knight for acting in the best interests of his kingdom," Mai responded.

"Do you think the king will go for this plan?" Tren asked.

"I think he'll do whatever it takes to end this war and get rid of the last wizard." Mai rolled up the map and walked with Tren out the door and towards the throne room.

Mai pushed the door open and set the map out in front of her king. Gjanion said nothing as Mai laid out her plan for flushing out Mara and the rebels. When she finished he stared at the map for a moment before looking up at her and Tren.

"You think this will work?" the king asked.

"Yes. It's very well thought out and gives us an advantage," Tren replied immediately. "Especially with Varyn recently declaring its independence. The rebellion will likely flee east, if we don't destroy them completely. That will leave them with their backs to the sea and we will be able to finish them."

"Varyn…" Gjanion growled. "How dare they denounce me? I am their king! They do not get to choose otherwise. I want to see that city burn. Begin preparations immediately. I want to give the rebels as little time as possible. They'll think we are still reeling from their assault, but we will use that energy against them. Revenge is a powerful ally. We will destroy them and then continue on to Varyn. This war ends now."

Mai and Tren turned to leave, but Gjanion called out to Mai.

"Yes, sir?"

"Capture that wizard, kill her if you must. If she escapes, she could rally more to her cause. The kingdom still thinks I am the last wizard. I can't have her undermining me," Gjanion explained, a hint of worry in his voice that surprised Mai. After a moment, he added, "And bring my daughter back. Alive."

"Yes, sir." She turned on her heel and followed Tren.

~~~

The next morning, Gjanion stood on a balcony that overlooked the castle square. The sky melted from orange to blue as the sun rose higher into the sky. Row after row of knights dressed in shining silver armor and purple shields stood at perfect attention waiting to hear what their king had to say. Gjanion stood in a bright red tunic with black gloves, black boots, and his sapphire-emblazoned crown shining in the sunlight. He clutched the emerald staff in his left hand and his belt sported a golden-hilted iron sword, a placeholder for the relic sword that had disappeared after the battle in the throne room.

"Today is a glorious day for our kingdom!" Gjanion held both of his hands up high. "As you know, our General Mai has ascertained the location of the rebels' secret base we have sought for so long!" A wave of cheers rose up from the crowd as Mai took her place next to Gjanion. She sported a black tunic with gray boots and a purple cape draped over her left shoulder.

"In their attack on our beloved city, many of our knights…your brothers and sisters…lost their lives defending us. I call upon each and every one of you to take up arms and go hunt these villains down in their names! Avenge those who defended you. Let their deaths not be in vain, but instead let it fuel you. Go forth and destroy their home like they tried to destroy yours!"
~~~

More cheers rose up from the knights, angrier and more energized than the last wave. Gjanion and Mai looked over the army with satisfaction, though something deep inside Mai stirred again and kept her from fully enjoying the moment. She buried the feeling and refocused.

"Go and take your revenge!" Gjanion commanded.

The mass of knights moved from the square like a silver flood. Hundreds of metal-clad men and women marched in perfect unison down the Magic Mile and out through the main gates. Mounted cavalry rode on each side of the formation, and at the rear were several carts full of supplies pulled by massive three-horned oxen.

"I will send a pigeon when we have reached our position," Mai said as she turned to follow her troops out.

"I believe a more trustworthy form of communication will be needed here. Take this with you." King Gjanion turned to an advisor Mai had not previously noticed. Sitting on one of the young man's arms was a brilliant nighthawk standing at perfect attention like one of the knights. Its eyes were as black as midnight with feathers to match save for their tips, which were traced in silver, matching its beak.

"Thank you sir," Mai said as the hawk climbed from the advisor's leather glove to her shoulder.

"This will be a far faster and more efficient way to communicate. Nighthawks are special creatures. They do not require sleep and draw energy directly from the stars, travelling faster at night as a result. They are virtually invisible against the night sky."

"A significant upgrade from pigeons," Mai remarked, staring at the beautiful bird.

"Indeed. General, I have an additional request. I need you to once again retrieve the sword for me. It was taken after the fight, and likely resides at this base."

Mai nodded. "I'll find it, sir."

"You'd better. I had them on their heels…not even Mara can withstand the old magic of the three relics together."

Gjanion saw a look of confusion run across Mai's face. "If you are a god, why do you need the relics?" she asked.

"Those relics predate our kingdom by hundreds of years. They were created by wizards of the old world…the product of archaic rituals that bestowed upon each object an immense power that, when wielded together, gives the user vast magical powers," Gjanion explained. "As a banished god, I have no innate abilities that I have discovered thus far. I am hoping to change that. In the meantime, the relics do nicely."

"So anyone can use them?" Mai asked.

"Technically, yes. Though I made sure that Rylan never tried. I told her that only a god could wield them…and only a god will," Gjanion clarified to his general.

"Yes, of course sir, I apologize. Do not confuse my curiosity with desire. I have no interest in such things. I prefer the tried and true methods." Mai patted her left arm. "I've trained all my life to be the best swordswoman there is. That is enough for me."

Gjanion relaxed and leaned on the staff. "Hopefully it will be enough to finish off the rebellion for good."

Mai nodded and bowed without another word, exiting the balcony to lead her troops into battle.

~~~

"I need to go get dad's books." Mara spun her finger, which turned a pestle that helped to grind up more invisibility powder. She sat on the counter of the table in her father's rather large hut. Radion had offered Gant the abode next to his on the main road so they could easily work together on potions and alchemical research.

"I know, but we have no idea if Saros is safe," Gant replied as he chopped up vegetables for their dinner.

"If only we had something that could help me sneak in and out undetected!" Mara said sarcastically, gesturing to the large cauldron of invisibility powder.

"It lasts for an hour, you think you can get in and out that fast?"

"I do, and we don't even need to really go into town, just back to the house." Mara's brain began to grind out a plan while she ground the powder. "It's
~~~

simple. I ride over, hide the horse, apply the paste, and go get his things. It shouldn't take more than a day each way."

"You're not going to be able to do this alone, you can't carry all the books by yourself," Gant replied, frowning.

"Dad?"

"Yes?"

"I'm a wizard."

"So you're just going to casually float the books home the whole time? What if someone sees you? What if you have to do other magic? Come up with a plan that works and I'll gladly bite my tongue."

"What if I shrunk them down and then made them full size when I got back?" Mara suggested.

"Do you know how to do that?" Gant questioned her knowingly.

"No, not yet…but I'm sure I can figure it out!"

"When you do, you can use that plan. For now, you need a partner."

At that moment, Rylan appeared in the doorway of Gant's hut. "Mara, can I talk to you?"

Gant smiled. "Well that's convenient."

"Sure," Mara said, hopping down from the counter and stepping outside with the princess, leaving Gant to his work. "I could use your help as well."

"Oh, really? With what?"

"Are you a decent rider? I'm assuming that being part of the royal family, you were taught all sorts of—"

"I'm a great rider!" Rylan interrupted her excitedly. "When I was little my father and I…"

"What?" Mara asked.

"Nothing, it's just…my father and I used to go riding all the time, and he would teach me how to use various potions and things out in the fields surrounding the castle…but yes, I am a good rider," Rylan said, trying to sound peppier than Mara was sure she felt.

"Okay, great, because I need someone to help me retrieve my dad's notes and charts back in Saros," Mara explained, trying to keep the conversation moving away from Rylan and her father.

"Sure, I can help. When do you want to leave?"

"How about first thing in the morning?"

"I'll be ready!" Rylan said confidently.

"Great! And bring that staff of yours. Never know when we are going to need to mount another escape like back at the castle."

"Oh, right. Yeah sure, no problem," Rylan said, her tone softening once again.

"Sorry, did Gjanion teach you that too? Your skills are really impressive…" Mara said, feeling awkward.

"Thanks. Mai taught me, actually," Rylan replied, then seeing Mara's surprised face, added, "She may be the enemy now, but for most of my life, she was the only real woman I had in my life. After my mother died, she did her best to teach me things she thought would be useful, including how to defend myself. She's not all bad. She cares."

Mara didn't know what to say; she had not been expecting an answer like that. She knew that Rylan's life was going to be a complicated whirlwind from now on, but she did not expect it to manifest so soon. The silence between them grew uncomfortable, so Mara took a shot at breaking the tension. "Well, whatever she taught you, it helped get us out of there alive."

Rylan smiled halfheartedly. "Glad I could help."

"So what did you want to talk to *me* about?" Mara asked, suddenly remembering why Rylan was there in the first place, and happy to move on from their conversation.

Rylan instantly looked excited, yet nervous. "Well I had this dream…"

Chapter Three
Return to Saros

"I still can't thank you enough for taking Neela when you left the castle." Rylan patted her blue-eyed horse on the neck as she talked to Mara.

"You're welcome, but again I didn't know it was your horse. She just seemed the strongest and fastest, so I hopped on. She didn't put up a fight either, she just let me ride. It's as if she knew what was happening."

"Either way, there is no horse I'd rather be on, right girl?" Rylan lifted the saddle onto Neela's back.

Commander Hearth came over holding the reins to a jet black stallion. "This is the fastest horse in The Cave. He'll get you there and back in no time at all."

"I bet he can't keep up with Neela!" Rylan bragged.

Mara's stallion seemed to understand Rylan; it whinnied and stomped the ground. Mara chuckled.

"Thank you, Commander Hearth," she said as she took the reins.

"Of course, madam. Best of luck on your excursion. Oh, Rylan?" Hearth turned his attention to the princess.

"Yes?" she replied as she bridled Neela.

"Please be careful. I am not sure what sort of directions your father gave any knights out there looking for you. I can't imagine they'll treat you kindly for betraying him." Hearth handed her a spear.

"Thank you for your concern, Commander." Rylan took the spear from him and tied it to her back. "Should we run into any trouble, I'll be glad I have a wizard with me." She gave Mara a comically affectionate look. Mara grinned awkwardly, caught off-guard in the moment.

"Be careful, princess," Hearth replied.

"I am a princess no more, Commander. Just Rylan will do," she said with a soft smile.

As Rylan and Hearth talked, Mara turned to Kei, who had come to see them off. "Are you sure you don't want to come with us?"

"I'm sure. You two need to travel fast and I'm not a great rider. Besides, it would be hard to not detour and go see my family. Stick to your plan and come back safe." Kei gave her a kiss and walked over to help Hearth with the door.

Together he and the overweight commander pulled a pair of ropes that opened the door leading out into the woods. On the outside it was covered with rocks and grass to blend into the hillside.

"Good luck!" Kei called after them as they sped off into the woods.

Mara was barely balanced on the saddle of the unfamiliar horse. She and Rylan wanted to get away from the exit as fast as possible, in case they were being watched, but Mara couldn't hold the speed for long. Once they were safe, they slowed to a trot so Mara could get acquainted with her new mount.

"So, uhm…" Mara began, still feeling some residual awkwardness from their last conversation.

How do I talk to someone going through so much? Her world has been turned on its head. Her father is her enemy now, Mara thought as they rode in and out of the sun poking through the leaves.

"What's wrong?" Rylan asked. "Are you okay?"

"I…yeah. I'm fine, it's just…I don't know what to say. You're going through so many complicated changes, and while you claim that they're good changes, I still feel a weird responsibility for—"

"If you say 'I feel bad for what I did to you' again, I am going to take off and leave you in these woods alone. I didn't come along to listen to that nonsense again," Rylan replied seriously, then cracked a grin. "And I definitely *could* leave you out here alone…"

"Is that a challenge?" Mara asked, gripping her reins a little tighter.

Rylan's grin grew into a full-blown smile and without even so much as a crack of the reins, Neela took off at a full sprint. Mara laughed in relief and urged her stallion to pursue Rylan. She caught the princess quickly, though Mara suspected that Rylan had allowed her to do so. Once they were neck and neck, Rylan began to pull away again.

The two of them dodged between the trees as they barreled towards Saros. Just ahead, Mara could see Rylan's curly blonde hair whipping around wildly behind her. Mara was in awe of the way Rylan rode so gracefully and effortlessly. She was perfectly synchronized with Neela's gallops; never had Mara seen someone so in their element. Eventually, Rylan began to put some distance between them.

"Alright, let's see what you're made of," Mara said to her stallion as she whipped the reins and urged him on. The horse responded and chased after Rylan and Neela at breakneck speed. Mara felt like a kid again as they weaved through the forest and jumped over the underbrush. Riding alongside Rylan made her feel giddy for the first time in what seemed like ages. The weariness that had set in after the last few weeks was gone, and there was nothing but the two of them and their horses.

After a while, the two of them gave their horses a break and settled into a comfortable trot. The trees were almost completely bare, save for a few leaves that were hanging on as long as they could. The ground was painted red and orange by their fallen comrades, which muffled the sounds of their horses' hooves

"You really are a natural," said Mara after a while.

"I had a lot of practice and a really good teacher," Rylan responded, not smiling.

"Your father?" Mara guessed, bracing herself for another round of this topic.

Rylan nodded. "Yes. For all of the horrible things he has said and done, he wasn't all bad as a father. I turned out okay, so he must have done some things right."

"Nobody is all bad," Mara said in solidarity. "Everyone who does bad things usually has a reason for why. Your father was driven by the death of your mother."

"No, my father's actions and militant lust for control are why my mother is dead. If he had been a better king, a better leader, maybe someone wouldn't have tried to take his life that night. Maybe my mother would still be alive."

"Was your father really so horrible before the war?" Mara asked.

"As far as I understand, yes. Though I am hazy on the details. Leading up to the war, he ruled with an iron fist. If anyone crossed him in any way, be it late tax payments or messing with soldiers, he would punish them harshly. Too harshly. People began to resent him. My father is not merciful, nor is he forgiving. Two qualities that I think are important in a good leader. My father demanded perfection, but nobody is perfect. When he didn't get what he expected, he lashed out."

"You seem to have a much better grip on leading than he does," Mara observed. "Being able to acknowledge his flaws is an impressive step on its own, let alone that you have a completely different set of morals. Are you sure you're his daughter?" Mara laughed.

"Ha, yeah I guess the apple really did fall far from the tree, didn't it?" Rylan replied.

"You'd make a far better leader than he is," Mara said in support. She was proud of Rylan for not being more hateful than she had every right to be.

Rylan smiled softly, "I don't know that the throne is for me…but thanks."

The two of them rode on in comfortable silence for a while. Mara watched the shadows of the nearly-barren branches get longer as the sun began to sink towards the horizon. Thee sky slowly turned from blue to gold, with the scattering of clouds reflecting the sun's rays in vibrant pinks and oranges.

"This sky looks almost the same as the one from my vision the other night—the one with your father."

"But you said there was no sun?" Mara clarified.

"Yes. It was weird, and a clear indication to me that it was a dream."

"I still can't figure out why you have a connection with Dazel. I can use magic to search peoples' minds, yet I can't connect to her or Zhira. You do it accidentally!" Mara frowned in thought.

"I don't know what to tell you. I didn't ask for it, and I can't make it happen on my own." Rylan was equally confused.

"Was your mom a wizard or something?" Mara asked the princess.

"Not that I know of. You'd think I'd have shown some sort of ability by now if I had magic," Rylan suggested without much confidence.

"Maybe you are a wizard, but your abilities are suppressed somehow…or you just have different magical powers than I do. Who's to say that we'd be the same?"

Both women sat in silence for a moment as their horses cantered side by side through the woods. They realized that neither of them could come up with a single plausible explanation for the princess's connection with the goddess, so they decided to leave it and focus on the task at hand. As they rode on, the orange rays of the setting sun shone through the bare branches and engulfed the woods in a fiery light.

"Should we make camp?" Rylan asked Mara.

"No, we're almost there. Besides, it'll be easier to hide the horses and sneak around in the dark," Mara replied, nudging her black stallion to move a little quicker.

Rylan had Neela keep pace. "Aren't we going to be invisible?"

"Yes, but the horses won't be and we'll still make noise. Plus anything we grab will look like it is floating."

"Good point."

As they approached the cabin, the woods became increasingly familiar to Mara. They navigated their horses to a secluded spot outside the town.

"We'll be back. Behave and be quiet," Rylan said to Neela as she stroked her horse's face. Neela seemed to almost nod in understanding. The black stallion too was looking at the princess.

"You really have a connection with her," Mara observed.

"It has always felt natural. I like to think she can actually understand what I say after all this time," Rylan replied.

Mara went to a nearby stream and collected water into two small glass bottles they had brought. She mixed the invisibility powder into the water and gave one of the bottles to Rylan.

"Rub it all over your clothes. Be thorough," she said as she began to take the grayish paste and spread it all over her tunic.

"I can't get my back," Rylan's floating head said to where Mara's legs and left arm stood unattached.

"I got it," Mara's left arm scooped some paste out of her bottle and spread it on the princess's dark gray tunic between her shoulder blades, "Can you get mine too?" Mara turned around to reveal the still visible back of her maroon top.

"Sure." Rylan returned the favor.

Once the two of them were convinced they were invisible, they set off in the direction of Mara's cabin.

"Ouch!" Rylan exclaimed as Mara bumped into her.

"Sorry, I can't see you," Mara replied.

"How do we make sure we don't lose each other?" Rylan asked.

"We can still hear each other, and I can see where you are standing in the grass."

Mara looked down at where they both were standing, then back at where they had walked and realized a small error in their plan: the paste was rubbing off as the grass brushed past their feet. Small strips of their boots were exposed while some of the grass appeared to be missing where the paste had rubbed off on it. If she hadn't known to look for it, she wouldn't have noticed the grass. Their boots were another problem and she pointed this out to Rylan.

"If anyone sees a couple pairs of boots walking around, they'll know something strange is...afoot," Rylan said with a small giggle.

"Dear goddess," Mara rolled her eyes.

"But in all seriousness, what should we do?" Rylan posed the question.

"Be efficient, and hope we don't come across anyone anyways. We didn't bring any more paste and what we do have will wear off," Mara replied. "We need to keep moving."

The two of them eventually came upon the cabin, which was sitting quiet and deserted in the rising moonlight. They approached the wooden building and its central stone tower and went around the side.

"The front door creaks. If anybody is here, that'll alert them. We'll go through the window in the kitchen."

Mara opened it silently and climbed over the sill into the cabin; she held out her hand to help Rylan through before she realized the princess couldn't see it. Once Rylan's boots had landed next to hers, they crept over to the stone tower in the center of the living space.

"So this is where you grew up?" Rylan asked her.

"Shh! Later," Mara shushed her. "We don't know if anyone is here."

Mara wiggled her fingers on her right hand and unlocked the door to the tower. Rylan started to ask if Mara had done that, but Mara shushed her again. Creeping up the stairs, Mara pushed the door open slowly and entered the cold empty room.

The only light came from the moon peeking through the window. Mara stood in the middle of the room and looked around, overwhelmed by the fact that Zhira had been the last person here. This was exactly as he had left it, and Mara did not want to disturb it in any way. It felt wrong, like disturbing a shrine. Rylan's boots moved towards the lever that opened the roof hatch.

"Stop," Mara commanded.

"What is it?" Rylan asked, startled.

"That lever opens the ceiling. It's loud and obvious, and we don't want to attract any unwanted attention," she said sternly.

"Right, sorry!" Ryan whispered.

Mara rolled her eyes at Rylan's childish curiosity as she reluctantly gathered some of Zhira's books and scrolls into a bag she found on his desk. Rylan watched the floating bag stretch as Mara shoved the last book into it.

"Okay, that's what we came for. Let's go while we're still invisible." Mara started walking towards the door.

"The bag isn't invisible, though," Rylan observed.

"A risk we'll have to take. We have no more paste, remember?"

The two of them walked back down to the kitchen and hoisted themselves through the window. As they ran into the woods across from the cabin, a thought stopped Mara in her tracks.

"Rylan, wait." Mara called to her.

"What is it?" Rylan's voice sounded worried.

"My grandmother…I never got to say goodbye." Mara's voice was barely above a whisper. She had promised Kei she would stick to the plan, but knowing they were so close to the graveyard, it was hard to not go and say goodbye herself.

"Oh…well then we should go change that." Rylan fumbled for Mara's shoulder and eventually placed her invisible hand on it.

The two of them made their way around the edge of town, staying deep in the trees until they came upon the cemetery. Rylan said nothing as she followed what little she could see of Mara. The paste was beginning to wear off, but nobody was around. For the moment, they were safe.

Mara wandered amongst the tombstones until she came across the one that displayed her grandmother's name. Moonlight filtered through Mara and Rylan's translucent forms, giving them both an ethereal look as they stood over the headstone.

"I'm sorry," Mara whispered to Fiona's grave as she stood over it. "I truly am."

A single tear ran down Mara's face and fell to the ground. She fell with it, dropping to her knees. Without hesitation, Rylan quietly sat down beside her. For a few minutes, they stayed there under the stars. The woods surrounding them were quiet and still; the crisp late autumn air had driven most of the bugs and frogs into their winter sleeps. A bit of frost graced the top of the headstone, crowning it with crystal that shimmered in the light of the moon. It was a simple and beautiful sight that made Mara smile.

"Are you okay?" Rylan asked her quietly.

"Yes, I am." Mara reached out and touched Fiona's name. "Like I said, nobody else needs to feel this pain."

As Mara's fingers graced the stone, a scream pierced the air.

"GHOSTS!"

The two of them whipped around at the sudden outcry. They saw a knight standing petrified with two others at the edge of the cemetery. The knights quickly turned around and bolted back towards Saros.

"What was that?" Mara asked, confused. "Where are the ghosts?"

"I think he meant us! I can see through your whole body!"

Mara looked down and sure enough, her body was returning to its natural visible state. She watched as the paste wore off and her arm went from see through to solidly visible. Looking up, she could no longer see the trees behind Rylan's head.

"Rylan, your face," Mara said, pointing with her slightly visible hand.

"They'll come back to investigate. We need to go! " Rylan exclaimed.

"Carefully. We didn't see anyone on the way in, we probably won't on the way out either. Don't panic," Mara said, reassuring the princess.

But before the two of them could depart the graveyard, two of the knights returned with Sari and Keylon in tow.

"Ghosts, you say?" Keylon asked the knights as they came upon the rows of tombstones. Mara's heart leapt at the sound of her voice. She was relieved to know that Keylon was okay, or at least that she sounded okay. Mara and Rylan ducked down quickly before anyone saw them.

"I don' see nothin'," Sari observed as he lifted his torch higher and walked the first row of graves. Mara was almost giddy to know that he and Keylon were so close by. She wanted to run to them.

"They were there!" The first knight pointed towards Fiona's grave.

Sari gave Keylon a subtle look and slowly meandered over to the grave of their friend.

As Sari approached Fiona's grave, Keylon suddenly cried out, "There! I think I saw something!"

She pointed away from Sari towards the opposite side of the cemetery and walked away with the two knights.

Sari did not turn around but instead poked his head behind Fiona's tombstone and found Mara and Rylan crouched down out of sight.

"Wha' in the name of Dazel are you doin' here?" he asked, genuine shock crossing his face.

"I never got to say goodbye," Mara said solemnly to the blacksmith.

"Honestly Mara, if you don' go now we'll be sayin' goodbye to you!" Sari replied.

"I find that unlikely," Mara said confidently.

"I wasn' talkin' 'bout yerself! If they think we're harborin' you, we're as good as dead!" Sari scolded her. "Who is that?" he pointed to Rylan.

"Oh, sorry, I'm—"

"She's one of the rebels that helped me escape the castle!" Mara cut her off, earning herself a confused look from Rylan.

"Thank goddess that you did!" Sari exclaimed, addressing Rylan.

Rylan smiled back but side-eyed Mara. Mara did not return her gaze.

"Keylon can only hold the knights' attention for so long. You need to go." Sari returned to the matter at hand.

"But we can help…" Rylan was defiant.

"We're holdin' our own, surprisingly enough. King Gjanion made sure a garrison was set up here, but 'tis fairly thin. I suppose he didn' think much of our small town," Sari remarked.

"Well then I won't stay, I don't want to draw any attention and cause more problems than you already have to deal with," Mara stated, already turning to leave.

"Mara, wait!" Rylan stopped her, grabbing her now fully visible arm.

Mara turned, surprised at the princess's boldness.

"What?" she asked impatiently.

"We're just going to leave them here?" Rylan asked her incredulously.

"We can't take them with us and leave everyone else. And we can't bring them all. The knights would follow easily," Mara replied, thinking about everyone back at The Cave.

"So we leave them here to fend for themselves? That doesn't seem right," Rylan said defiantly.

"You heard Sari, they're already doing that. What seems right is winning this war…saving everyone!" Mara almost yelled.

"If I may," Sari interrupted before Rylan could respond even louder. Both of them turned to look at the stout blacksmith.

"We don't need defendin'. I have weapons hidden in a cellar under the forge. We can take care of ourselves, just as we did when the king came callin'. Yer job is to end this conflict. You can't do that here. Ma'am, I admire yer passion to help us, but Mara is right. Yer needed elsewhere, and we can't be takin' everyone from here. When the time's right, we will be ready to help ya," Sari said confidently.

Mara nodded in agreement and looked at Rylan.

"I know how to pick my battles," Rylan said, shrugging.

"I know being here puts you in danger, but is there any chance we could rest for a bit before riding back?" Mara asked Sari, suddenly aware of how tired she felt.

"Of course," Sari said without hesitation. "We can hide the two of you for a night."

Rylan and Mara went to collect their horses, and hid them in the woods behind the forge so as not to draw any more attention from the knights.

Once in the safety of their home, Keylon poured them some tea. "The patrols here only go up and down the main street, and I suspect the men on said patrols are drunk more often than not. Bess is out of ale constantly."

"How have they been treating you?" Rylan asked, concerned.

"Well enough," Sari replied. "Seems like they don' really wanna be here so they cause little trouble."

Rylan relaxed a little, but Mara could tell she was still on edge. She gave Rylan a confused look, but the princess dismissed her subtly.

"How is Kei?" Keylon asked Mara.

"Oh, he's fine! He was integral in helping get me out of the castle." Mara proceeded to fill them in on everything that had happened since she left Saros. She told them about how Kei had been 'captured' by a rebel spy and sent to her with a note from Zhira about breaking out, and then helped her do so, how they had fought against Gjanion and fled to the rebellion's secret base, and how they had lost Zhira in the fight.

Keylon teared up at the news of Zhira and hugged Mara. "Oh…Mara I'm so sorry."

"Thanks," Mara hugged her back.

"Kei's doing well, he's working with the rebellion's blacksmith now," said Rylan, lightening the mood. Mara gave her an appreciative look.

"That's wonderful! Where is he now? Why didn't he come back with you?" Keylon asked, worried about her son's absence.

"We didn't think we'd see anyone. Our task was simple: in and out of the cabin with the books. Rylan and I are the fastest riders, so we went," Mara explained.

"Rylan?" Sari asked, perking up at the name and narrowing his eyes at the princess.

"What?" Rylan replied, suddenly nervous.

"Yer…" Sari began but was unable to continue his thought.

"Sari, what's the matter?" Keylon asked her husband.

"She's…she's the king's daughter, the princess! I overheard some knights talkin' about you…some serious guts you have there, lass, leavin' yer father." Sari looked at Rylan more intensely.

Mara was unsure of what to do. She hadn't realized that they would know her by name. Before she could defend her friend, Rylan spoke up.

"You are correct, I am the daughter of King Gjanion, but I promise you I am no princess." The edge in her voice was intimidating. "Mara helped me realize what side I was on and find the courage to stand up to him. I am a rebel now, same as anyone else."

"I applaud your strength, little lady," Sari replied. "It takes serious conviction to stand up to what is right even when it means losin' what you love."

"I do not love the man my father is," Rylan stated, turned towards the small fire Keylon had made in the hearth.

Keylon gave Rylan a sympathetic look. "But he is your father…your family. You left behind a world you knew for one you didn't, all in the name of what you believe to be right. Not many people have that strength, but those that do find happiness and peace. When I left the capital, it was mired in corruption and I could see that your father's style would only make things worse. I knew I wanted no part of it. I had no plan and no belongings, but I trusted myself and set off to find a better life. I wound up here and met Sari, and instantly knew where my true happiness lied."

Mara stared at Keylon. She had never talked about her past in the capital. Mara was eager to hear more, but read the room and realized now was not the time to pry.

"That means a lot, thank you Keylon." Rylan smiled.

"You are going to be something special. You will find your happiness, I promise." Keylon returned the smile.

"It's gettin' pretty late, why don' you two bunk in Kei's old room? I'll wake ya when I start the forge. It'll still be plenty dark then," Sari offered.

"Thank you both so much," Mara said as she showed Rylan where Kei's room was.

"Been here before, huh?" Rylan gave Mara a knowing smile.

"Don't get any ideas," Mara joked back.

Rylan took off her tunic, choosing to sleep in her undershirt and pants while Mara left everything she was wearing on. Autumn was coming to an end and the air was dry and cold. With some awkward shuffling of blankets, the two women made themselves as comfortable as possible in a bed meant for one, and Rylan quickly fell asleep facing the wall. Mara laid with her back to Rylan's and leaned against her friend. She had a hard time getting to sleep, acutely aware of the closeness between them, but as it hadn't stopped Rylan from drifting off quickly, Mara soon followed the former princess and found a dreamless sleep awaiting her.

The next morning, while the stars still adorned the velvet sky and the sun's orange glow barely traced the horizon, Mara and Rylan mounted their steeds in the woods.

"Thank you, again," Rylan said to Sari.

"'Tis my pleasure, miss. 'Twas an honor to meet such an inspirin' leader," he replied.

"I'm no leader," Rylan corrected him.

"Not yet," he said as he walked back inside to start his forge.

Mara snapped her reins and took off into the woods. Rylan lingered a moment, caught off guard by what Sari had said, then urged Neela to follow Mara into the trees.

Chapter Four
A Change of Plans

Tren was the first to awaken in the army's makeshift camp. While the night prior had been full of singing and ale, he and three others had quietly removed themselves from the festivities to prepare for this morning's mission. Tren woke his companions and reported to Mai's tent while they dressed. As he suspected, Mai was wide awake, poring over maps of the area.

"Morning," Tren yawned. "Did you even sleep?"

"No. Here," Mai handed him a rolled up piece of parchment. "It's a condensed map of the area. Ride ahead and scout out all you can. Report back before the sun goes down."

"Yes ma'am. Hopefully I will find something useful," Tren said, holding up the map. "I'll see you this evening."

"Tren?" Mai called as he reached the purple and white striped flap.

"Yes, ma'am?" he replied.

"Don't get caught."

Tren nodded and exited the tent to find the rest of his small team waiting for him. They were dressed in their mottled orange and red tunics with gray boots and gloves, designed to blend in with the colorful fall surroundings.

"Stay quiet, stay together, and note *anything* you see out of the ordinary. We are to be back here before sundown, so stay sharp," he instructed as they mounted their horses.

The knights that made up his team were the best riders he knew. Two were experienced knights, Captain Pike and Dame Darren. Pike was a tall young man that was one promotion away from becoming a commander himself. A loyal knight, he had been one of the youngest to take the oath, demonstrating superb skills in all facets of knighthood. Dame Darren was, by any measure, one of the most experienced knights in the ranks. She had been in the king's ranks for fifteen years before the war started and had been integral in winning some of the first battles. Her ferocity had begun to fade as the color in her hair did, and now she mostly provided counsel to the younger knights.

The third knight on their team was not yet a knight. Dame Darren's squire Kyra, a small, lean, and fierce fighter, was one of the army's most capable riders. Tren was reminded of Rylan when he had first witnessed Kyra training, both in her abilities on a horse and with her skill with a staff. Kyra wielded a unique and unusual metal-studded staff, which seemed too heavy to be worth the added damage, but she wielded it with ease, so Tren had said nothing.

The four of them raced off into the woods towards the spot Mai had marked on his map—the place she had observed from not two weeks ago. When they arrived, the sun had risen above the trees and shone through the multicolored canopy, creating a mosaic ceiling in the leaves reminiscent of beautiful stained glass. They distanced themselves from their horses and Tren crouched down in the brush with Pike and Darren flanking him on either side. Kyra watched their backs as they looked for any sign of rebel activity.

Tren led them through the underbrush, following what looked like game trails. He picked up on a few footprints that could only be human, and began tracing out the paths as best he could on the map Mai had given him. The four of them spent the morning wandering between the trees and marking the map until they came to a clearing next to the side of a small cliff. The area seemed ordinary and unassuming, but Tren noticed that the grass closer to the cliff face was flattened.

He was unsure of what to make of this until he heard the sound of hooves crunching dry leaves in the distance. They crouched down lower and watched as none other than Rylan and Mara themselves rode past them towards a seemingly blank and useless cliff side— until it was suddenly neither. The rock face fell away uniformly as they approached, revealing a large entrance that could comfortably fit five horses side by side. As Rylan and Mara rode in, the wall retracted as fast as it fell, disguising itself once more.

Tren instructed Pike to find a way to open the door from the outside. Darren and Kyra watched with Tren as Pike snuck around the edge of the clearing and began running his hands along where he thought the door should be. Risking being seen, he worked his way across the entire surface before sneaking back to where his companions were hiding.

"If there is a way to open it from the outside, it's well hidden." Pike shrugged.

"No matter, we have what we need. There is no chance that this isn't their main route of escape. I think General Mai will be pleased. We'll smoke them out and they'll run right into us, right here." Tren marked the location of the door on his map, then led his team back to their horses.

~~~

"Welcome back," Mai said as Tren stepped into her tent. "Find anything?"

Tren pulled out the map and rolled it out on the general's table.

"A door?" Mai noticed Tren's marking as her eyes traced the map.
~~~

"Yes ma'am, a door. A large door. Built right into the side of the hill. That will likely be their main escape route. We should position as many troops as we can there."

"Agreed. Send a small team, no more than is absolutely necessary, and position them in view of the door. Let's get an idea of how much it's used and what it's used for. If they start to feel our pressure they may try to get supplies out that way early," she commanded.

Tren nodded and left to coordinate the team. Mai walked out after him and began to give orders to her captains as they finished packing up camp. Small groups broke off in both directions to surround the area that she believed would encompass the rebellion's hideout. The paths Tren had traced intersected at several points, which Mai could only assume were at least close to hidden exits. She would bring the remaining knights to an obvious location and set up camp, making it look like they were oblivious to the rebellion's presence.

A few hours went by and Mai's team set up in a clearing near the entrance where she had observed Gant and the others. Pointed white tents with purple flags went up in rows while horses were stabled at makeshift posts. As the sun set, fires sprung up in the spaces between tents and knights settled in to cook tigerdeer they had hunted earlier that day. Some of them carved the antlers into handles for their daggers and others worked the black and brown striped pelts into warmer gear for the coming winter months.

Mai sat alone at a fire just outside her tent, looking over a map of the surrounding area the king's cartographer had provided her. She had promised to do her best to mark the cave network as it was discovered. As she thumbed through preliminary reports from the closest groups, a young squire approached her camp.

"Excuse me, General Mai?" The girl couldn't have been more than seventeen. With her skinny frame and her blonde hair pulled back in a ponytail, she reminded Mai of Rylan. Mai suddenly felt a sadness creep up on her like a shadow in the sunset. Mai had trained Rylan in self-defense from a young age, but the princess had turned out to be a natural. As they trained together, Mai had formed a bond with the motherless princess. Now here she was, trapping Rylan in a cave. Not prepared to face her feelings for Rylan, she pushed them down as quickly as they had bubbled up and addressed the girl.

"How can I help you?" Mai asked impatiently.

"I wanted to ask…if you needed a squire," the girl asked, clearly mustering all of the confidence she could.

Mai was surprised by the question. "Are you not satisfied with your charge? Is something wrong?"

Mai had high standards for her knights, but unlike her predecessor General Long, she tolerated a bit more personality and individuality in her ranks. Where Long would silence anyone who spoke up, she tried to listen. Where Long had his knights on a rigorous schedule, Mai made sure that so long as the job got done to her satisfaction, the knight could exercise more freedom in their down time. One thing she did not tolerate in the slightest was disrespect to others in their unit, no matter the rank.

"No ma'am. Dame Darren is a fine teacher and knight. I just…I want more than she has to offer." The girl winced at her own words, clearly worried she had gone too far.

Mai looked at the girl more seriously. She was dressed in standard squire attire—tough leather armor dyed a dark purple to match King Gjanion's royal colors—and she carried a quarterstaff that had sharp metal studs covering the upper and lower thirds of the pole. The girl held herself confidently and Mai appreciated the girl's honesty.

"It's true that Darren is one of our older knights, approaching the end of her long tenure as a knight of the Royal Guard. She is wise, but she is not the fighter she once was. Still, I have no need for a squire and I don't have time to look after you," Mai said dismissively, returning to her map.

The girl did not leave. She remained where she was and stood a little taller.

"I want to learn from you. I want to be you. I'll work hard and won't ever get in your way. Dame Darren is a fine teacher, but she is no general," the girl's voice did not waver this time.

Mai took a deep breath and looked up again from the map. "What is your name?"

"Kyra, ma'am," she replied, still standing at perfect attention.

"Come sit, Kyra," Mai nodded towards a log to her right.

The girl eagerly sat next to the general, placing her staff on the ground between them. Mai was unsure what to say. She liked the girl well enough, but had no desire to groom her replacement. She had only just become general. Succession was not at the top of her priority list.

"I admire your drive, Kyra. I wish all of our knights were like you. The truth is many of them only became knights to save their own skins. General Long offered many a life of service over a life in prison, regardless of skill, to help bolster our numbers. They're content to follow orders and to have a purpose over sitting in a damp cell under the castle forever."

"I know. I didn't choose this life either, I was conscripted after I was found stealing some bread to feed myself in the capital," Kyra admitted. "But I'm here and want to make the most of it. I know I can be something great."

Kyra's attempt to climb the ladder was admirable. Mai saw a desperate girl trying to make the most of a poor hand dealt to her, but the fact remained that she did not want a squire. Not only because she had little time to train someone, but because her feelings towards this war were becoming more and more complicated by the day.

"I will not take you on as a squire, but I will offer this advice: never stop. I got to where I am because I treated every step like it could be my last. I am always alert, always learning, always training, and always ready to do whatever I had to in order to get to where I wanted to go. You want to be general of this army one day? You have to be ready to kill for it."

Mai finished speaking and looked the girl dead in the eye, waiting for her reaction. It didn't come. Mai was impressed, either this girl was colder than she looked, or she was not so easily discouraged. Mai decided to keep an eye on her. Kyra grabbed her staff and rose from her seated position.

"Thank you for your guidance, General Mai. I hope to impress you at every turn."

She bowed her head slightly and left, swallowed slowly by the darkness that lay just beyond the firelight. Once she was out of sight, Mai returned her gaze to her map.

The girl even uses a staff like Rylan.

As the rest of the knights turned in, Mai folded the map up and packed it and a short note in a small leather tube which she tied to the leg of the nighthawk. *Gjanion was right,* she thought as she watched the bird's silver speckled feathers disappear against the clear night sky. *Much better than pigeons.*

The following morning, there was a fresh layer of frost on the ground. The grass and dead leaves crunched underfoot as Mai went to meet with the captain on the night shift, who had compiled reports overnight from the groups surrounding the rebellion's hideout. A few of the reports noted the presence of rebels, the discovery of two new entrances, and one reported back part of an overheard conversation regarding a hidden forge. Mai took particular interest in this report, and asked the captain which group had delivered it.

"It was this group here." He pointed to a chart that had their teams laid out in relation to their own camp.

"Thank you." Mai turned to Captain Pike, who had emerged from his tent and meandered over to see the reports himself. "Come with me."

The two of them walked over to the makeshift stables, mounted their horses, and took off into the woods. They bypassed the closest few teams of knights stationed around the hideout and soon arrived at the camp where the knights who had reported the possible hidden forge were stationed. There were four of them; one was on watch while the other three slept. At the sight of her coming through the brush, the knight went to go wake his companions.

"No need," Mai said quietly as she came into the small clearing.

She had dismounted just out of sight so as not to attract attention to their camp with her horse. The knight paused, then stood at attention.

"At ease, at ease," Mai dismissively waved her left arm, which sported her riding grip: a small double-sided hook.

"What can I do for you, General Mai?" the knight asked, still surprised to see her at his camp.

"I am interested in the report your team delivered overnight regarding an underground forge. How is that possible?" she asked him.

"We overheard two rebels talking about a sword their blacksmith had made one of them. They must have some sort of ventilation system for a forge, or they'd be smoking themselves out. We've kept an eye out for smoke, but so far there's been none."

"We have not been here long. Perhaps they haven't used it in our time here," Mai suggested. "Keep an eye out for smoke of any kind."

"You mean like that?" Pike pointed to the horizon where, sure enough, smoke rose from the tree line.

"Wake another man to take watch, and come with me," Mai directed the knight.

~~~

"Think the army knows we are here?" Forbin asked Radion as they walked together down the main path. Despite his age, Radion was intent on getting exercise every day, cave or no cave. He walked most days with Forbin, and when Forbin wasn't available, Gladys usually accompanied him.
~~~

"No. If they did, they wouldn't have been so careless. We heard and saw them coming from a day out," the old king observed.

"What if that's part of their plan? Make us think we're secret and safe?" Forbin questioned.

"Then it's a stupid plan. They haven't attacked anyone coming or going and nobody has seen any knights near the entrances. That new general of theirs must not be very bright," Radion chuckled.

"I wouldn't underestimate Mai," Gant said, walking up behind them.

"Oh?" Forbin turned to Gant.

"You'd be hard pressed to find someone to match her drive. Anything she does, she does purposefully."

Radion noticed the worried look on the alchemist's face. "Should we call the council, son? Decide to make a break for it and give up our considerable advantage?" Radion gestured broadly to the cave that surrounded them. "Tell me, how would they know where we are?"

Despite the king's strong line of questioning, for which Gant had no answers, he still felt something was amiss. Mai wouldn't just happen to plant her army atop their hideout. Somehow he knew that she knew they were here.

"Radion, you need to trust me. I just know. Something's not right about this. Mai would not just *happen* to plant her army on top of our hideout. Besides, what are the odds of that? A whole army just setting up camp above our secret hideout?" Gant argued back.

"The odds do seem low, yet we have been successfully hiding here for over a decade. I don't see a reason to panic. Not yet," Radion said, reassuring him before continuing on his walk.

~~~

From her spot leaning against the counter of the forge that faced out into the cave, Mara watched as her father walked away from the old king, looking exasperated. He waved to her before disappearing into his hut, which stood beside Radion's on the main drag. Mara went back to chatting with Kei and Jerra as the two of them moved a large piece of heated metal from the forge onto an anvil. While Kei held it in place, Jerra hammered away at one of the edges, rounding it. The forge in The Cave was smaller than Sari's back in Saros, but it was far more organized. The main flame sat centered on the back wall with its chimney carved into the rock above.

"How many horses does the rebellion have?" Mara asked as she thumbed through one of the books she had retrieved in Saros. It contained notes on constellations and the paths of stars, but nothing that obviously helped identify The Bright One as a planet like her father had supposedly observed.

"Not that many—probably about a dozen. They don't do well underground, so we have to get them out
~~~

fairly consistently to ride and roam," Jerra replied as she took another swing with her hammer.

"Doesn't that draw attention? The door is rather large," Kei observed.

"Sure, it could bring about some issues, but it's also our largest escape route," Jerra replied.

Jerra and Kei lifted the heavy metal piece back into the fire to reheat the edge Jerra was working. The smoke coming from the furnace was a thick river running up into a hole in the ceiling.

"Where does that go?" Mara asked.

"The forge's chimney goes up through the hill. Its exit is hidden by a fireplace directly above—part of a lookout spot we have that is disguised as a hunting cabin," Jerra said, picking up her hammer.

"It's brilliant," said Kei.

"Yeah, really clever. Being able to make weapons and repair armor down here has been quite a boon for the rebellion," Jerra said, swinging her hammer.

"I can imagine," Mara said, though something about the smoke suddenly seemed wrong. It had stopped flowing up through the hole and had started pooling on the ceiling. "Does the chimney ever get clogged?"

"No, it handles everything I can throw at it. I've had it running for days at a time," Jerra explained.

Mara gave Kei a worried look, and he understood. *Something's wrong.*

~~~

Mai threw the door of the cabin open to reveal two men sitting across from each other in front of a roaring fire. *Last time I checked, hunters did not use swords,* she thought as she examined the men she had burst in on.

"Who are you?" The first one asked menacingly.

"So hostile!" Mai said, before darting forward and pulling back her cape, revealing her bladed left arm. The man barely had time to gasp before the point of her arm-blade was sticking out of his back.

The second man rose from his chair and drew his sword, but Pike made short work of him in such a small space. The captain wiped his blade, sheathed it, and stood at attention. The other knight that had accompanied them stood outside, watching for additional rebels.

"What now, ma'am?" he asked.

"Put the fire out, then stuff the grating with their bodies. Our troops are in place, now let's smoke out the rebellion. Literally."

~~~

"I'll catch up with you two later," Mara said, dismissing herself.

Mara walked around to a small space between the forge and the next dome-shaped structure. She sat down and crossed her legs, taking up a meditative pose. The air hung still around Mara as she slowed her breathing, calmed her mind, and waited. After a moment, she found what she was looking for.

Her mind's eye opened on a room in a small shack. From her perspective, Mara could see two startled men sitting in front of a roaring fire. She heard a familiar voice that wasn't hers speaking to them.

"So hostile!" Mara heard Mai say. She watched with horror, from what could only be Mai's perspective, as the two men were quickly struck down. The knights that had accompanied Mai put the fire out and began stuffing the grate to block the flow of the smoke.

Mara opened her eyes, reorienting herself in her current surroundings, and stood up.

"KEI!" She yelled as she ran back around the forge.

Kei looked up, panicked. "What? What is it?"

"Turn off the forge. Douse the fire. They've clogged the vent!" Mara exclaimed.

Jerra and Kei worked fast, using their emergency supply of water to quickly douse the flames in the forge.

"What do we do now?" Jerra asked, wide-eyed and clearly worried.

Mara looked at the both of them, their scared faces looking to her for direction. *I'm not the leader, Radion is,* she thought.

"Let's gather everyone and explain the situation. I think it's time to leave."

~~~

"You really think we're ready?" Tren asked. "We've only been here a day."

"I do. It's time. This rebellion ends today," Mai replied coldly. "As for you all," Mai said, turning to address the captains she had gathered, "ready your troops. Find the best vantage point for archers, conceal knights close to the entrances, and show no mercy to anyone who comes through the exits."

The captains affirmed her commands and left to organize their men.

"I'm sensing hesitation on your part?" Tren questioned carefully as he and Mai walked to their horses.

"There is no hesitation," Mai lied. "This war needs to end. We have the chance to do so today."

"With all due respect, I'm not buying it. Something's wrong. What's going on?" Tren asked.

Mai grabbed him by the collar of his armor and dragged him into her tent. She dismissed the steward that was packing up her things, and once she was sure they were alone, she turned and faced Tren.

"Those people down in those caves are fighting to save themselves…from us. They're not all bad. One even saved my life."
~~~

"Are you saying that you're feeling sympathetic towards them?" Tren asked, clearly astonished by what she had said.

"No, no. Of course not. They are the enemy and they need to be disposed of," Mai said with resolve.

"There's the ferocious General Mai that I know," Tren said approvingly. "Come on. Let's go end a war."

Chapter Five
Escape

Rylan swung her staff relentlessly at Gladys, who had agreed to help keep up her training regimen when they had arrived at the cave. The rebel commander wielded the same silver sword that Zhira had used in the throne room the night Rylan had abandoned her father. Sweat dripped down her forehead as she twirled the long, dense, wooden rod around her body and met the slice Gladys had directed at her. The sword left a sizable notch in the staff as Rylan spun away and pushed a stray hair out of her face.

"Are you trying to look pretty?" Gladys taunted her.

"I certainly have time to," Rylan said with a smirk before charging the commander.

Rylan had insisted that Gladys use a real weapon. Nobody knew just how good Rylan was with her staff, but she was only this good because Mai had not held back. Mai had insisted that she use real weapons for many reasons, foremost of which was to be ready for the real thing. Dull wooden training swords weren't as motivating as sharpened steel ones. *Train how you would fight!* Mai words echoed in her head as she dueled with Gladys in the empty cavern.

Rylan managed to get close enough to Gladys to hit her in the chest with a well-placed shoulder, knocking the commander out of the area they had marked on the ground. Satisfied with her victory, Rylan held her hand out and helped Gladys to her feet.

Gladys sheathed the sword. "You really are something else."

"Thanks. I had a lot of practice."

"Whoever taught you must've been quite the fighter," said Gladys.

"I hope you never find out just how good." Rylan said, somberly.

"Why…oh, right," said Gladys, realizing who must have trained the princess all those years in the castle.

Rylan nodded. "Anyway, thanks for being my sparring partner. I'm surprised Radion let you use the sword."

"This thing?" Gladys patted the ruby-emblazoned hilt at her side. "Radion has said for a while now that as many of us as possible should get familiar with it, in case any of us have to use it."

"Can you show me how it works?" Rylan asked.

"Sure, stand over there." Gladys motioned to one side of the ferrosol-lit cavern.

Rylan took her spot a safe distance from Gladys and watched as she unsheathed the silver sword once again. The blade gleamed in the light of the stones that jutted from the walls and ceiling, and Gladys held it in front of her with both hands.

"This sword is imbued with magic. Anyone who wields it can tap into its power. Watch." Gladys gave the sword a few swings. Where she slashed the air, streaks of light appeared, then darted forward suddenly until they hit the far wall. When she stabbed the sword in front of her point-first, an invisible shockwave shot from the tip and caused a crack in the rock on the far wall.

"Wow," Rylan said, impressed. "Can I try?"

"Sure. Just be careful," Gladys said before handing the sword to the princess and standing behind her.

Rylan took a swing with the sword but nothing happened. She tried again, then stabbed as Gladys had, but there were no arcs of light and the far wall remained unscathed.

"What am I doing wrong?" Rylan asked.

"It takes some getting used to. Be patient and *feel* the sword."

Rylan nodded and took a deep breath, trying again. She swung the sword in a more fluid motion and sure enough an arc of light appeared and dashed forward, hitting the rock wall opposite her. Rylan grinned. *This feels good.* She gave the sword a few more swings, then finished her movements with a stab, sending a shockwave at the wall. The rock cracked completely, blowing a hole into the next cavern over, where many of the huts that the rebels slept in were.

"Oops!" Rylan exclaimed, dropping the sword in surprise.

"Wow," Gladys said, picking up the relic and placing it back in its sheath. "Nobody's ever done that before."

"I thought you said it was supposed to do that?"

"It is, but not to that degree. What did you do?" Gladys eyed Rylan curiously.

"I have no idea," Rylan replied, looking through the new hole in the wall.

~~~

As she waited for Radion to gather a meeting to enact an escape plan, Mara sat alone in her hut with the satchel of leather books she and Rylan had retrieved from Saros. She had already flipped through several that contained the records of many failed attempts at making potions. Unsure of when she would get another chance to read them, she picked up a small tattered book and a smile crossed her face as she read through several pages detailing failed attempts at her fathers' signature recipe for the potion they used to help the farmers of Saros with their crops. The notes in this particular book were
~~~

old and not nearly as comprehensive as some of the others she had read.

They had developed the potion for the crops before she had come into their lives. After reading through some of the books, it was apparent to Mara that by the time she was a toddler, their knowledge of the many ingredients they used had grown. The newer the notes, the less mistakes they had made. She admired their commitment to learning and mastering their craft, and understood why not everyone was an alchemist.

Mara got lost in the pages of her father's handwriting, happy to have something so intimately close to him. His own hand had inked these words onto the page. His own thoughts, untarnished by the veil of memory or the incompleteness of a story told to her by Gant. This was the purest way that remained to experience him—in his own words. She cherished the opportunity, knowing full well that a fight was imminent, whether the rebellion would stand their ground or flee for another chance.

Eventually Gant came to fetch her for the meeting, and she shoved the small tattered book back into the bag. She emerged from her hut and followed him to the council chamber. The Cave had become hazy—despite Kei and Jerra putting out the fire almost instantly—and the crisp shine of the ferrosols that lined the walls and ceiling had been replaced with a fuzzy, yellowish glow.

"You and dad really put some work into becoming alchemists," Mara reflected on their notes.

Gant smiled. "We sure did. While we had a natural affinity for creating unique mixtures. The understanding of the ingredients and their properties was a product of tedious study. Your grandmother was less than pleased with our constant explosions and terrible smells, hence why she moved into the shop full time."

"I expect it wasn't a tough decision for her to relocate away from two adolescent boys literally playing with fire," Mara joked.

Gant chuckled. "No, it wasn't. I think your grandmother would have stayed, though, if Zhira hadn't been so stubborn. He was dead set on building the tower, on watching the stars, and on working on potions. He cared little about how in the way he was around the house. That infuriated Mom. I remember talking with her one night soon after she had moved to the shop permanently, and she worried that Zhira was too cold and scientific. His people skills were poor, and he cared little to improve them. In a small town, that makes life difficult."

"I don't remember Dad ever being that way," Mara said as they went single file down a narrow pathway.

"That's because the day he found you changed him profoundly. I'll never know exactly what did it, but you coming along was the greatest thing to ever happen to him. Not alchemy, not the discovery of The Bright One. Finding you in the woods that day seemed to unlock a version of himself that had been lying in wait."

"I didn't know that," Mara said, feeling a pang of sadness.

"I was actually skeptical at first about raising a child together. I didn't think we were ready, and I didn't want to burden your grandmother with the task either. But Zhira was adamant that we could do it."

"You didn't want to keep me?" Mara teased. "I'm glad Dad convinced you."

"It didn't take much. You were a cute baby, it was hard to say no to those big blue eyes."

"I'm sure the magic played no part in that decision, either." Mara winked.

"It certainly didn't hurt," Gant said, putting his arm around her. "But magic or no magic, you are and always will be my daughter."

~~~

In the council chamber, Rylan and Radion were the first to arrive. They sat at the far end of the large stone table, which was carved out of the bedrock and stood alone in the center of the small room. As they waited for the rest of the group to arrive and begin discussing options now that they knew they were under attack, Rylan played with the end of her hair nervously.

"You seem troubled," Radion observed.

"It's just...I know a lot of the knights out there. General Mai was sort of a mother to me after my real mother's death," Rylan said quietly. "Well...not really a
~~~

mother so much as a woman who looked out for me." Mai had never been loving the way Rylan suspected mothers were, but she had facilitated her education in practical things like self-defense.

"You're afraid of what you may have to do to people you've known, people you cared for, and who have cared for you. You're afraid of facing them, aren't you?" Radion asked.

Rylan nodded. "I've already faced Mai once, when we confronted my father. I…I can't do that again."

"I understand that this may be a difficult transition for you, but I hope you know that what you did was courageous."

"People keep saying that, but I don't feel courageous."

"Leaving behind the life you knew and standing up for yourself and what you think is right is not an easy thing to do. Ask anyone and they'll tell you that given a difficult choice they'll always choose what's right, but few actually do it when the time comes," Radion reassured her.

Rylan smiled. "Thank you. This hasn't been easy. I betrayed my father and while I know he is a horrible man, he wasn't a horrible father. I still feel guilty for leaving."

"You are a kind soul, and being able to see the good in others is a gift. People have been written off for far less than what your father has done. To still find part of him redeemable is admirable," Radion said kindly.

"Nobody is purely bad or good. We have all done things we regret," Rylan said, wiping her eyes.

"Indeed we have," Radion said, looking away from Rylan.

Did I say something wrong? Rylan wondered as the old king suddenly went quiet.

"We all are capable of kindness and compassion, as well," Rylan added after a moment.

"Yes, we are," Radion said quietly, then, straightening up and meeting her eyes once again, added, "You would make a fine leader."

"I'm not sure I want that."

"All the more reason you would be good at it."

"*You* are a great leader. You knew when to give up the crown, you organized a rebellion…you lead with confidence and grace, and it's obvious that everyone here likes you," Rylan observed.

Radion's eyes darkened, but this time he did not turn away. "Being liked doesn't make you a great leader," he explained. "Having in mind the best interests of the people who follow you and acting on those interests…that's what counts."

"My father certainly does not. He only cares to be in control."

Radion nodded. "A leader won't get everything right, but if he treats his position as one of service to his people, rarely will he go wrong. I will always work for the people I lead."

"My father is only serving himself."

"Your father was already on the path to war when your mother was killed. After that night, there was no turning back. He never healed, and his anger festered like an infected wound."

"What was he supposed to do? Nothing? My mother, his wife, was murdered in cold blood! I'm not trying to defend the last twelve years, but I understand his fury," Rylan said in defense of her father.

"As do I. Losing a loved one, especially someone as kind and innocent as your mother, is tragic. But here we are, about to run for our own lives. Was all of this, every life lost, every village burned, worth the revenge for your mother? You clearly don't think so, or you wouldn't be here. A leader needs to be level-headed, even in crisis. Your father struck the flint and steel over the kindling of war the day he publicly executed Captain Genda."

"Did you know her? Genda, I mean," Rylan asked.

"Not directly, but she was the spark that set this whole kingdom ablaze and the reason I came back to organize the rebellion." Radion's face grew more serious. "Rylan, if we do not come out victorious, I fear Kyros will meet its end."

Rylan nodded. "I think either way Kyros as we know it must change."

Radion said nothing as Forbin walked in, followed by Mara, Kei, and Jerra who all took seats around the table.

"Dad, Gladys, and the others are right behind us," Mara said as she took a seat next to Rylan.

A moment later, Commander Hearth, Gant, Gladys, Biranel, and a few others entered and encircled the table. Once they were all settled in, and Mara had managed to pull a few extra mounds out of the ground to act as stools for people to sit on, the discussion turned to the matter at hand.

"General Mai is ruthless. If she knows about the cabin, it is likely she's been watching us for some time now. She knew we were here," Gant said to the group.

"We need to assume the worst. There is no doubt that she has The Cave surrounded. I talked to a few of our gatherers and the only thing we know for sure is that there are a lot of them," Biranel said.

"We always thought that living here would provide us a concealed exit, but we can't be sure which ones are safe," Forbin chimed in.

"I was foolish not to prepare for this when we saw her armies coming," Radion said, conceding that he had underestimated the new leader of the king's army.

"Mai's gotten the better of us. So what? We're fighters, let's fight," Gant replied, standing up as he spoke.

"You got a plan for how to do that? In case you forgot, we're trapped underground," Gladys pointed out dejectedly.

"In order to have us surrounded, Mai's forces will need to be spread relatively thin," Rylan said.

"But *we* don't have to be," Mara said, picking up on Rylan's idea.

"What are you suggesting, girls?" Hearth asked, his gut pressing up against the stone table.

"We all leave through one exit," Rylan offered the idea to the room, proud of herself.

"If the general is worried about us trying to sneak out, let's hit her with the opposite," Mara explained. "Take most of the knights waiting for us at all the other exits out of the equation."

"Send everyone out through the stable door and break the line. Mai won't be able to gather her forces in time to stop us," Kei said from where he was leaning against the wall behind Mara's seat.

"It's a good plan, but if we are assuming the worst, we have to expect that Mai knows the door is there. That will be their heaviest force," Hearth retorted.

"It's our best chance to get everyone out quickly," said Radion.

"How do we break through? We'll be up against royal knights—highly trained and armed to the teeth," Gladys observed.

"We have magic," Mara said, twirling her dagger between her fingers. "Not to mention we have a couple of fairly accomplished alchemists in our midst."

"We will do whatever we can," Gant said in solidarity. Radion nodded in agreement.

"Preparations must begin immediately," Radion said, turning to Forbin, Biranel, and Hearth, "and we need to get supplies out of here."

"Not to mention arming everyone," Kei said. "If we are sending people out into the woods alone, where plenty of knights are supposedly hiding, they need defense."

"Where are we all going to meet?" Rylan asked the group.

"We send everyone to Varyn, the port city east of here," Gladys offered.

"That's two weeks' ride, and not everyone has a horse!" Rylan countered.

"It's the best chance we have. At the end of the kingdom…that's where we will have to make our last stand," Radion said somewhat quietly.

"Our what?" Mara asked him, confused.

"Our last stand. In case you haven't noticed, Gjanion is beating us. We're trapped in a cave, we have lost three quarters of the kingdom over a decade, and we're about to be on the run again. We have one last chance to put out this fire and we need the resources of a city like Varyn to make it happen. Varyn is the last major settlement on our side. They've denounced Gjanion entirely. Without them we don't stand a chance, no matter how much magic we have," Radion argued.

"Okay, so back to the matter at hand. Eventually Mai will realize what's happening, so we need to be efficient," Hearth directed.

Gladys turned to Forbin and Biranel. "Load as many supplies as you can at the stable and be ready to go."

The two of them nodded and raced off, followed by a few helpers.

"Kei, you and Jerra start handing out armor and weapons, then load what you can into a cart as well. I will ride out with you. I am a bit too old to ride on my own anymore," Radion said. Rylan watched the old king stand from the table and walk out towards the forge. Kei gave Mara a quick kiss and followed him.

"Dad, you and I will provide protection as the carts make their break for the woods. Rylan, you stay with us. We're going to need some help bringing up the rear, you can use potions, and you're the best rider we have," Mara explained.

"Mara, I—

"Okay, let's get to it," Hearth cut her off. "I'll meet you all at the stables. I'll begin preparations there."

The rest of the rebellion filed out of the meeting room, but Rylan grabbed Mara's arm and held her back.

"What're you doing?" Mara asked. "We need to go."

"I've denounced potions. I'm not an alchemist. I won't be like my father," Rylan said firmly.

"Fine," Mara said, annoyed. "We're running for our lives, but sure, go ahead and toss an advantage by the wayside right now. Makes sense."

"Mara, please," Rylan said, sounding hurt. "My father has ruined so many lives with his alchemy. I don't want to follow in those footsteps."

"My father hasn't," Mara rebutted. "Do what you want, but we need all the help we can get."

"I can help, just not in that way."

"Whatever," Mara said and stormed off, leaving Rylan standing in the light of the ferrosols alone.

~~~

The Cave quickly became a bustling hive of energy as rebels darted every which way compiling supplies, loading carts, and arming themselves. Kei and Jerra had their hands full distributing maces, longswords, axes, shields, and various pieces of armor. Rylan was impressed at how much weaponry and armor the rebellion had amassed in their time underground. Every rebel had sharpened, well-crafted weapons and most of their armor was either strong leather or metal.

"Make sure to leave a space for the commander," Biranel explained as Rylan pushed a crate of cabbages towards the front of a cart tied to the horse Biranel would be riding.

"Hearth's riding in the cart?" Rylan asked.

"Of course he is, we don't have a horse big enough for him!" Biranel chuckled as she lifted another crate up to the former princess.
~~~

At the other end of the stable, Radion was helping Hearth toss sacks of miscellaneous supplies onto another cart.

"You sure you should be doing this, sir?" Hearth asked.

"I will pull my weight the same as you, commander," Radion replied as he tossed a smaller sack onto the pile.

"Nobody's weight is the same as mine!" Hearth gave a hearty laugh as he slapped his stomach.

Mara walked up with Kei, each of them carrying a small yet heavy crate of steel ingots and set them in the cart that Radion was packing. Rylan walked over to help them load the crates, taking Kei's from him so he could go back to the forge to grab his things. As Rylan shoved the crate onto the cart, she overheard Mara talking with Gant.

"Are you okay?" Gant asked his daughter.

"I think so. I'm ready to fight, and I know not everyone is going to make it. I just wish I didn't have to take other peoples' lives in the process." Mara stared at the ground as she spoke.

"If you don't kill them, they'll kill you," Gant replied.

"I know they want to, but I won't give them the chance," Mara said.

"There are a lot of people suffering because of the king's knights. You're doing a service by removing them from the equation."

"What if the knights are only acting that way to protect themselves? What if the king is the only reason they are the way that they are?" Mara asked him.

Rylan stepped over. "Sorry, I overheard…a lot of the knights out there are in the army because they'd rather be soldiers than prisoners. They chose the lesser of two evils—dying for their king as opposed to dying in a cell."

"So they're just people," Mara said, furrowing her brow.

"Bad people," Rylan clarified. "Everyone out there either signed up to be a knight, or was arrested and given the option in lieu of a cold, damp, lonely death below the castle."

"How kind of your father to provide such an opportunity," Mara said sarcastically.

Rylan just shrugged. "Are you ready to go?"

"Yeah, you decide to take every advantage you can get for this fight?" Mara asked.

"I'm not using potions," Rylan said stubbornly. "I am not my father. Besides, I've never liked them, but he forced them upon me. Now that I have the choice, I'm not using them."

"Why would you not—"

"Mara, let it go," Gant interrupted.

"But she—"

"Can make her own choices," he interrupted again, with a tone that sounded to Rylan like Gant was talking to twelve-year-old Mara.

Before Mara could respond, someone yelled from the main cavern below them.

"Time to go!" Kei's voice preceded his arrival in the stable. He ran up the pathway carrying an axe and a satchel slung over his shoulder. He hopped onto the back of the cart with forge supplies pulled by Jerra's horse.

"Be safe. I'll see you soon," Mara said to him before taking up her position just inside the stable door.

Forbin mounted one of the dark brown horses, ready to take point and draw the first wave of attacks before the carts made their escape. Commander Hearth positioned himself in the cart next to Kei's while Gladys helped Radion into a cart pulled by her horse.

Mara turned towards the exit. The tension was palpable and the silence was deafening. Rylan could hear her own heartbeat in her ears along with the slight jingling of reins from the anxious horses. A minute later, Hearth swung his sword and the door fell open. In their view were no less than fifty knights, led by Commander Tren. Hearth had been right, Mai was ready for them.

~~~

As Forbin began his charge, Mara pointed her dagger directly at the rows of armor-clad men and closed her eyes to focus. In front of the knights, vines sprouted out of the ground and began wrapping tendrils around their feet and ankles. The purple amethyst glowed bright as the vines extended faster than the
~~~

knights could cut them away. While the attackers were distracted, Forbin began the exodus.

Mara opened her eyes and watched as Forbin rode at full tilt towards the knights with a few other mounted rebels close behind. They managed to knock a few tangled knights over en route to the woods before the supply carts started their escape. The first, driven by Jerra, carried Kei and the smithing supplies safely to the woods without incident. Gladys and Radion's cart was close behind, and disappeared into the trees. Mara breathed a sigh of relief. *Kei is safe.*

Biranel snapped her reins and her horse pulled a cart that supported Hearth and food supplies out of the cave next, but some of the knights had gotten free. An arrow flew through the air and caught Biranel in the shoulder, knocking her off her horse. The light brown mare, startled by the sudden attack, turned sharply away from the knights and overturned the cart it was harnessed to. The ropes snapped and the horse ran panicked into the woods.

Biranel hit the ground and did not move. Hearth scrambled out of the overturned cart and drew his large broadsword. Mara continued to slow the knights with vines while Hearth made his way over to Biranel. He knelt down and put a hand to her neck, checking for a pulse. When he bowed his head, she knew the worst had happened. Biranel was gone. With no time to grieve, Hearth turned to face the few knights closest to him that had cut themselves free of Mara's greenery.

He looked terrifying.

The commander was overweight, but something about a man his size wielding his broadsword made him look daunting and menacing. The knights that rushed him were no match for the sweeping arcs of his blade.

Rylan spun her metal spear and ran to his aid while Gant ignited his hands in flames and began the second phase of his and Mara's plan. Mara stopped growing the vines and began drying them out. They quickly shriveled and turned brown, becoming brittle around the knights' legs and arms. Gant began rapidly hurling fireballs at the knights, catching the now dried vines on fire. Half of the knights were still caught when the vines ignited, and the cries that followed burned themselves into Mara's mind forever. The agony and pain was pronounced as knights clawed at their super-heated armor.

Mara tried her best to ignore the gruesome scene she orchestrated, and began tossing fire alongside her father's. Rebels ran and rode out of the cave as fast as they could. Some carried sacks of supplies while others ran with swords and axes drawn to protect themselves. Streaks of blue and orange rained from the mouth of the cave to cover them as Tren, a fresh burn shining on his face, cut himself free and escaped the onslaught along with some of his soldiers. Mara kept hurling fire, directing some towards Tren, though it did not deter the commander. Her father drew his sword, applied a thick paste to its blade from a leather pouch on his belt, and waited. The blade disappeared and he swung at the nearest knight just in time.

~~~

Rylan caught up to Hearth, who, despite his size and lack of fitness, was having no trouble wielding his large two-handed sword. His blade was so massive and strong that it broke the swords of the first two knights who attempted to take him down. They were so surprised by this development that they were not prepared for their former commander's second swing, which did to them what he had done to their swords. Rylan's stomach turned over at the sight of the sudden gore, but she held her composure and began swinging her spear at the next armored attacker.

The assailant sported a staff with metal studs on both ends, and wielded it like a master. Rylan was overwhelmed to fight against someone who matched her capabilities with a staff. The attacker's face was obscured by their helmet, but their lean frame and leather armor allowed them to move quickly. Rylan knew by the armor that this person was no knight; only squires wore leather armor. Despite their youth, the squire's strikes came so rapidly that Rylan found herself continuously taking steps back and to the side to try and gain an extra second between blows. The squire caught Rylan in the side and swung up, hitting her arm at a point where her armor had a small gap. Rylan's left arm went numb and she began to panic.

And then her training took over.

Mai had trained her for years, insisting on using real weapons to be as ready as possible for real fights.
~~~

As a result, Rylan was able to do with one arm what most people needed two for. Rylan released the spear and spun it around the knight while spinning herself the opposite way. She grabbed the end of her spear and whipped it around, lowering it, and catching the squire in the back of the knees, sending them to the ground. The knight's leather helmet came off as she collapsed, revealing a very young woman's face to Rylan.

Rylan held the spear above the girl but hesitated at the sight of her. Kyra's blonde hair highlighted the similarities Rylan saw between herself and this girl she held at spearpoint beneath her. Kyra took advantage of the hesitation, kicking Rylan in the leg. As the princess reeled, Kyra grabbed her staff and fled.

"Who was that girl?" Hearth called out to Rylan.

"I don't know but I hope I never see her again," she replied, staring off into the woods where the girl had disappeared to.

Behind her, Rylan heard the clanging of swords and saw Gant swinging his seemingly bladeless sword at Tren, who had pulled both of his swords on the alchemist.

"Oh no he doesn't!" Hearth yelled as he charged towards the fray. Rylan gave chase behind him but was stopped by more knights.

Hearth ran to Gant's side and helped in his fight against Tren.

Tren landed a kick squarely in Gant's chest, sending him sprawling. The commander turned and focused on his former companion.

"Traitor!" he yelled at Hearth as he began a flurry of attacks that the fat man was very clearly not prepared for. Hearth parried the first few swings, but Tren's speed and dexterity gave him the upper hand. In a few quick moves, Tren had cut Hearth in several places. On his next jab, he landed the point of his sword in a gap in Hearth's armor, sinking deep into his shoulder. Hearth's eyes went wide as he tried helplessly to push Tren away. Tren swung his other sword around and drove it underneath Hearth's chest plate.

Wordlessly, Hearth sank to his knees and then fell over, seemingly in slow motion, blood rushing from the fresh wounds and painting the ground around him red.

"No!" Rylan yelled, punching a helmetless knight square in the jaw. Despite being nearly twice her size, he crumpled to the ground completely unconscious. Rylan ran towards the fallen commander.

"Rylan!" Mara, mounted on her black stallion, intercepted the princess's path. Neela was in tow behind her.

"We need to go. Our goal was to escape. Everyone is gone, let's move!" She untied Neela's reigns and handed them to the princess.

Rylan stared at where Hearth had fallen. She had known the commander for most of her life—he had always been a smiling, friendly face to her. *Run now, grieve later.* Her heart ached as she grabbed the reins from Mara. Taking advantage of Hearth's distraction, Gant came out of the cave's entrance on the back of a grey mare and joined them. Rylan hopped up into Neela's saddle and the three of them took off into the woods. Mara heard the sound of knights on horseback behind them and began to slow, letting Gant and Rylan ride ahead of her.

"What are you doing?!" Gant yelled at her.

"Trust me!" she yelled back.

Mara stood on her saddle, turned around, and pointed her dagger in the direction of the pursuing knights, tracing a large circle. Flames exploded from the dagger's tip and ignited the trees, bushes, and other shrubbery between them. She heard the whinnies of the knights' horses as they were startled by the sudden fire.

Figuring this would buy them enough time to get away, Mara spun around and willed her horse to catch up with the others.

~~~

Tren watched, still standing where he had slain Hearth, as the trees became engulfed in blue flames and his mounted knights came back from their pursuit of the wizard. He sighed and sheathed his swords.
~~~

Chapter Six
Last Chance

"Now," General Mai commanded her knights.

They were positioned at every exit of the subterranean rebel base that they knew of and were wearing flexible leather armor in lieu of their usual metallic protection. Their plan was to maneuver as quickly as possible down the entrances and block the exits, causing mass panic and destroying resources once they were inside, all the while killing rebels and forcing the rest out towards Tren's squadron.

As Mai gave her command, a knight blew a horn signaling to the rest of the teams to begin the invasion from their respective locations. The knights began to squeeze through the gaps, blocking every escape route. They made their way down with speed and one by one emerged into the main cavern. An eerie silence was all that greeted them in the hazy and abandoned cavern.

General Mai came through one of the larger openings, brandishing her bladed left arm and a longsword in the other. The blade glinted in the light of the ferrosols.

"What is the meaning of this?!" she asked, confused by the lack of rebels present.

"We are searching the other caverns now, but it appears that the caves have been deserted, ma'am," Captain Pike spoke up.

"How is that POSSIBLE?" Mai raged.

From the far side of the main cave, one of the knights cried out. "General, I think you need to see this!"

Mai walked past the confused knights in front of the abandoned forge and followed the knight who had called to her. He led her through a room full of small dome huts that looked like stone versions of her knights' tents. Mai and the knight walked through quickly and went up a sloped walkway that opened up into another large room that appeared to be missing a wall. What Mai saw enraged her.

Tren stood beside the corpse of their former fellow commander and in front of a scene that could only be described as a disaster. More than half of Tren's knights lay unmoving on the ground with either large slash wounds or scorched armor that left them barely recognizable. A foul stench of burning hung in the air as Mai approached her leading commander, fury building inside of her.

"What. Happened." Mai did not ask so much as demand the information from Tren.

"We were overwhelmed. The wizard's abilities are not something we are equipped to deal with, and I'm fairly certain they sent the entire rebellion our way. We were outnumbered." Tren gestured to his fallen squadron.

"And him?" Mai nodded towards Hearth.

"Took a few knights down, more out of surprise than skill. I made short work of him. He knew our strategies, but he can't help anymore. No more traitors, no more spies. It's just power against power now."

"They got away, didn't they?" Mai asked, not addressing Tren's last answer.

"Unfortunately," said Tren, a little quieter.

Mai stared past him at nothing in particular while her mind raced. They could pursue the fugitive rebels now or return to the castle with bad news and lose ground. *The king will want an update,* she thought. *I have to pick my next move carefully and correctly.* As this was her first major charge as general, the pressure was on. And she felt it. With no Mara, no Rylan, and no sword, this was a report she was not keen on writing. Mai was finally in the position she had dreamed of and already things were going awry. She was about to direct Tren to pursue Mara and the rest of them when something inside her made her pause.

She was happy they got away.

Mai tried to shake the feeling, but it wouldn't abide this time. How could she side with the rebels in any way? Why did she care that they were okay? They were the enemy. They were in the way of her king's goals. If she purposefully gave them any advantage, Gjanion would have her title, if not her head.

"Excuse me, general?" a familiar voice interrupted her train of thought.

Mai turned and saw Kyra standing just a little beyond where she and Tren were having their conversation.

"Kyra, I am glad to see you are okay," Mai observed as she beckoned the squire forward.

"As am I," she replied.

"You're the one who was dueling with the princess, right?" Tren asked her.

"Yes, Commander. Though I was outmatched—the princess is extremely skilled with a spear." Kyra's head fell slightly.

"No need to be ashamed, kid. You're what, seventeen? Rylan has years of training on you. You fought admirably," Tren replied with a kind smile. "Dame Darren is your charge, yes?"

"Yes, sir," Kyra replied, standing up a little straighter.

"Not anymore. I'll have a word with her—I'd like you to be my personal squire. Your potential is wasted on a knight who will likely retire the next time she sees the castle." Tren's voice conveyed more authority as he turned to Mai with a look that asked her to back him up.

Mai nodded in approval, happy to see this girl's hard work paying off for her. Kyra did her best to look professional, but she could not stop a large smile from crossing her face.

"Commander, take your new squire and follow the carts. I will take a team myself and follow the riders," Mai said, returning to the matters at hand.

"Yes, ma'am." Tren bowed slightly and walked away conversing with Kyra.

Mai's anger resurfaced as she stood alone with the reality of the situation. The rebels escaped, her plan failed, and worst of all Mara was gone. Gjanion would not be pleased.

~~~

Rylan, Mara, and Gant rode until the sun set, hoping to put plenty of distance between them and the knights. Shortly after escaping the battle, the three of them turned north. It had been Gant's idea; he figured that Mai and her army assumed they were headed east to Varyn—which they were—and would follow east-bound tracks. Anyone headed north could look like they were running away, and be less of a target to hunt down. Once they felt they were safe enough, the three of them stopped and made camp for the evening. The stars were obscured by clouds and the air was still, but there was no threat of rain. Where the firelight ended, the blackness around them seemed thick.

"Now Hearth too…and Biranel…so much loss," Gant said as he stared into the flames.
~~~

"They won't be forgotten, we will keep fighting. For them and all of the others who have given their lives to the cause," said Mara, resolved. She took a drink from her flask.

"That reminds me!" Rylan bounced on her stump as she remembered her encounter with Zhira. "Mara, my dream!"

"Oh, right!" Mara turned to face the princess and closed her eyes.

"What's happening?" Gant asked, confused.

"I'm trying to retrieve a memory from her. Hang on," Mara said before concentrating harder.

Rylan closed her eyes too, unsure of what to do while her friend penetrated her mind.

Mara's mind flooded with Rylan's memories. She watched the most recent scenes from their day of escape flash by in reverse until eventually the memories started blurring. As she dove further back into Rylan's memories, the details became fuzzier until suddenly everything went black. Mara's mind was faced with pure nothingness. Rylan's mind was dark and silent.

"There's nothing. Where that dream should be is black," Mara said, opening her eyes.

Rylan gave a confused look. "I can think about it right now, recall it. Does that help?"

"I don't think that matters," Mara said. She had tried this before with Kei while sitting in her jail cell in the castle, but the results had been fruitless.

"What's so special about this dream? Why do you want to see it?" Gant asked his daughter.

"Because Rylan saw dad," Mara said, a serious look on her face.

"You *what?!*" Gant asked Rylan incredulously.

"I saw him. It felt just like my vision I had with Dazel showing me the eclipse. Zhira was in pain, but he was alive," Rylan recalled.

"You think Dazel showed him to you?" Gant quizzed her.

"I think so. I heard her voice again this time too. She's trying to communicate something to me, but I don't know how to communicate with her." Rylan's face contorted in frustration as she worked through her thoughts.

"Didn't you have your first vision with her when you prayed?" Mara asked her.

"Yes, but that was one time out of thousands! I pray to her every night. There doesn't seem to be a connection there," she replied dejectedly.

"I'm sure we can figure it out," Gant reassured her.

A slight rustling came from the bushes behind Mara. The noise caught her attention and she stood up immediately, facing the woods with her hands lit in blue flames. Gant and Rylan turned towards the source of the noise, staying seated but wound like springs and ready to act. Rylan put a hand on her spear and Gant gripped his sword's hilt.

From the bushes, a tall figure emerged wearing a dark green tunic and black pants. Her left arm sported a metal double-sided hook that glinted in the firelight.

"General," Mara sneered.

Gant and Rylan stood up and faced Mai.

"What are you doing here? You're stupid if you think you could sneak up on us," Gant remarked.

"Trust me, if I wanted to sneak up on you, I would have done so. I am not here to fight," she held up her hand and hook in surrender.

"Then what do you want?" Rylan asked her angrily.

"To offer you a chance to escape and keep heading north." Mai's tone caught all three of them off guard. She sounded almost concerned.

"Escape?" Mara asked, confused.

"Yes, escape. I followed you myself to make sure nobody else found you. My entire life, I have avoided connections with people. I've always made sure I am never in debt to anyone. Everything I have in my life I have gotten by my own hand. That is, until I met you." Mai turned and looked at Gant. "You saved my life. You helped me survive…and I can't shake it. I thought letting you out of the dungeons back at the castle would be enough for me to feel even, but apparently I was wrong. I don't want you or any of your family to suffer any more. I understand you aren't all bad people—this war was brought to your doorstep and you had no choice." Mai glanced at Mara.

"So what, you're going to give up chasing the rebellion now?" Mara asked her.

"Don't be stupid. Your pathetic operation is on the brink of destruction. The king is close to victory and he won't tolerate anything less than total annihilation of your resistance. I'm giving you all a chance to escape it, to save yourselves. Go north. Go east across the sea. I don't care. I just don't want to have to kill you." Mai's eyes looked almost desperate.

Gant, however, did not flinch. "You'll have to kill us to kill the rebellion. What Gjanion is doing is horrible. The lives he has ruined are countless. You expect us to just roll over and let you take this kingdom so that we can save our own hides? This rebellion survives because we are all ready to die for each other. Too many of our friends and family have died for us to just walk away and let you win." His words cut like knives.

"You can't win!" Mai yelled suddenly at him. "We have bested you twice and now you're running through the woods, scattered. Let me help you!" The desperation in Mai's voice surprised Rylan.

"I saved you because it was the right thing to do, not to gain favor. I don't need you to save me, but if that's what you really want, then help us defeat the king. You can turn your whole army against him. Turn the tides and save not just us, but the whole kingdom." Gant stared at her with conviction.

"If you want to die, that's your choice. When the time comes, don't beg me for mercy. I gave you your chance." Mai turned and walked back into the bushes.

Gant said nothing as she disappeared into the black; all three of them relaxed once she was out of sight.

"Do you think she meant it?" Mara asked her father.

"Yes. But I don't think that matters now," he replied.

~~~

Mai returned to her camp, where three knights sat around their own fire. Captain Pike was among them.

"Find anything?" he asked the general.

"No," she replied shortly. She had sent Pike and the others searching in the opposite direction to give herself the opportunity to confront Gant alone. Frustrated by how that had turned out, she stomped over to an empty seat around the fire.

"General, this nighthawk came for you." The knight sitting across from her motioned to the black and silver bird sitting on one a horse's saddle.

General Mai's shoulders dropped as she strode over to the patiently waiting messenger bird. She untied the small scroll from its leg, broke the king's seal, and unrolled the parchment. It was a simple message asking
~~~

for a report on the siege. Mai crumpled the note and threw it into the fire angrily, startling the other knights.

"Is something wrong, ma'am?" Pike asked.

"Everything's perfect," Mai replied sarcastically.

She went into her bag and found her parchment and quill. She scratched a note to the king and tied it back onto the nighthawk. It screeched once and disappeared into the trees.

"What was it?" One of the other knights asked her.

"The king wanted an update on our siege," she said dryly.

"What did you tell him?" Pike inquired cautiously.

"The truth. That we flushed them out, but that some got away and we are tracking them down," she replied without looking up from the fire.

"I'm guessing you don't expect his response to be very positive," Pike remarked.

"No, I don't think it will be," Mai said, somewhat dejectedly.

~~~

Gjanion unrolled the note. He would have screamed had it not been for his son, Karbalion, fast asleep in the bassinet beside him. It was late, and the king had directed his guard to wake him only if a note
~~~

was received by nighthawk. Waking to this news was not what he had hoped for.

Gjanion quietly slipped out of the room where his wife and son continued to sleep and paced the hall, fuming.

"Everything okay, sire?" one of the knights on guard duty asked him.

"Would I be pacing if it was?" he snarled.

Gjanion's frustration built as he walked back and forth. He should have been there. The only reason the rebels survived this attack was because of magic. Because of Mara.

That damn wizard, Gjanion thought. *If it wasn't for her, this war would be over.*

Mai was a good general, but it was clear more drastic measures needed to be taken. Since Long's death, their progress had slowed. Sure, they had identified the rebel base and destroyed it, but the wizard and her team of insurgents remained at large.

The king walked with purpose to his study and wrote out instructions on a small piece of parchment. When he finished, he sealed it with his royal sigil and handed it off to the messenger who had woken him.

"Ready my envoy, we ride at dawn."

Chapter Seven
The Healer

The next three days of riding were uneventful. Each morning, Mara, Rylan, and Gant awoke and rode mostly in silence until the sun was high, then took a break to water the horses briefly before continuing on their journey. Once the sun was behind the trees, Gant would set up camp in a secluded place while Rylan hunted for dinner if they hadn't caught something during the day. As they rode on each day, Mara found herself increasingly frustrated with Rylan.

Potions can only help, she thought. *Why would she not take the advantage? We could have died. So what if her father uses potions?*

Her thoughts festered as they rode east towards the city of Varyn by way of a more northern route— away from Mai's army but also the rest of the rebels headed that way. Despite her annoyance with Rylan, Mara soon got bored of their daily routine quickly and, on their fourth day of riding, was happy to see a small town up ahead, sitting atop a hill. Mara rode with Gant and Rylan on either side of her as their horses climbed towards the village.

"This town can't be bigger than Saros," Gant observed as they approached.

"I can't imagine many people want to live so far away from civilization," Rylan replied.

"The isolation has its perks," Mara remarked, thinking back to before Mai's first visit to Saros.

It seemed so long ago to her now, the quiet life she had with her fathers back home, helping her grandmother at the shop, even the Festival of Dazel every other summer. That all came crashing down when she had confronted Mai outside of Bess's inn. Mara's mind wandered through memories of recent events. Confronting Mai and saving Reg, the assault on Saros where her grandmother had died, the ambush in the woods where she had managed to save Forbin's life, the fight in the throne room where her father had died, and the siege at The Cave and losing Commander Hearth. So much fighting. So much death. Mara felt as though she had lived a full life in the span of a few months.

The sun dipped behind one of the large hills adjacent to the village and Mara shivered at the sudden change in temperature. Winter was fast approaching and the air had gone from the crisp refreshment of fall breezes to the biting pain of winter winds. Rylan pulled her cloak tighter around herself.

"I wonder if they have an inn. They can't get many visitors," Gant said as he rubbed his hands together.

The three of them slowed their horses to walking pace as they entered the town. It reminded Mara of Saros. There was a main street with the biggest buildings on each side, except that no building was greater than one story high, and nothing was made of stone. All of the shops and homes were wooden structures with either thatch or log roofs. The windows were nothing more than glassless holes in the wall with shutters to cover them. The street itself was only packed down dirt with some hay strewn about to help the people and horses keep their footing when it got wet.

A few people were out and about, none of which paid them any mind. The three of them identified the inn and a moment later, their horses were tied up on the post as they carried their bags into the small building made of logs with a thick thatch roof.

The inside of the inn was nothing like the outside. Animal furs covered the walls and a large lunawolf pelt graced the floor, its white coat reflecting the candlelight and brightening the room. The main hall was simply a large room with two tables, a few chairs, and two barrels of ale up against one of the walls. A young man emerged from one of the doors at the back of the room and walked over to greet them.

"Greetings! Unfortunately, we only have two rooms available. We rarely see visitors, and when we do, it tends to be just a single passerby," the man informed them through his long brown beard.

"That'll be no trouble. Girls, you can share a room right?" Gant asked as he pulled out some coins.

"Not like we have a choice," Mara said, letting her irritation with Rylan leak out a bit more than she intended.

The rooms were decorated similarly to the main hall—pelts and furs covered most surfaces to keep the cold night air out. Gant fell asleep immediately upon contact with his bed; Mara could hear his snoring through the wall. She and Rylan stood in the center of the room and took stock of the situation. There was a single bed sitting in one corner that was clearly meant for one person, a nightstand, oil lamp, and small chest for belongings. Mara realized that having traveled for several days, neither of them had changed clothes nor bathed.

"We should probably at least change if we're going to share a bed," Mara suggested.

Instead of moving to do so, Rylan just stood in the center of the room with her arms crossed. "You have something you want to talk about? Is there a problem?"

"The answers to those questions are not the same," Mara said, pulling a change of clothes from her bag.

"You're still mad at me for not using alchemy during our escape, aren't you?" Rylan asked, correctly assuming what Mara was upset about.

"I just don't understand how you could disregard such a distinct advantage. You could have made yourself stronger, or faster, or used flames, or—"

"Did I need to though?" Rylan cut her off. "We're here, aren't we? I made it out alive."

"Biranel didn't. Hearth didn't."

"And would I have been able to change that? Were you or your father able to stop either of them from dying?" Rylan asked bluntly.

"That's different, we were—"

"Busy with other soldiers? So was I. I couldn't have saved Hearth. Neither could your father, and he was there with him fighting Commander Tren!"

Mara had no response. Rylan was right. The way that events had played out back at The Cave were unlikely to have been altered if Rylan had utilized alchemy. Mara turned away from Rylan and pretended to look for something in her bag. *Why does this bother me so much?*

"I know you want to protect everyone. I admire that, actually," Rylan said kindly. "But stop putting that pressure on yourself. I can handle myself without alchemy. I chose that for myself. It's not like I'm expecting you to protect me with your magic or anything."

Something clicked inside Mara. That was the impetus of her frustration. Rylan had perfectly captured what she was feeling. Being the last wizard, she had a distinct advantage that people looked to in order to turn the tides of the war, and to defeat Gjanion. So far that had not happened, and Mara felt the pressure.

"When you decided to go on without alchemy, it made my job harder. People expect me to be the secret to winning against your father. So far, I've failed. People have died. We're on the run. When you chose to forego potions, I felt the pressure even more. I can't do this alone. I am not the savior people think I can be. My magic is strong, but I cannot take on an entire army and your father."

Rylan nodded in understanding. "Nobody said you had to do it alone." Then without warning, Rylan walked over and hugged Mara.

Mara stood there and let Rylan embrace her. She had been feeling better after her father and the princess had gotten through to her back in The Cave, but standing here, she realized that there were still many complicated emotions still swirling about unattended inside of her. Along with her grief for losing more of their friends and fellow rebels, she felt a mounting pressure to ensure they did not lose again. Her magic had not yet been the difference the rebellion hoped it would be, and with their backs against the wall, fleeing to kingdom's end, Mara was unsure it could be.

"I'm worried we won't win," Mara said once Rylan let her go.

"Worry about that when it happens," Rylan said, her face growing dark.

"What do you mean?"

"The way I see it, we either win or…or it isn't our problem anymore."

Mara understood what Rylan meant, and nodded in agreement. If they didn't defeat her father, they wouldn't live to see the aftermath.

"We should probably get some sleep," Mara said, her feelings towards the princess quelled.

"Good idea."

The mood was somber. Without another word, Rylan sat down on the bed and set to taking off her boots and cloak. Mara turned the opposite direction and changed slowly, suddenly feeling drained. When the two of them had redressed, they turned around and Rylan burst out laughing. In her tiredness, Mara had put her pants on backwards. There was nothing to do but laugh, and it felt good. She quickly corrected the orientation of her pants, all the while laughing along with the princess.

The release from the laughter was a welcome one. In no time at all, Mara's stress began to evaporate and her and Rylan's despair towards the upcoming battle was pushed aside. They flopped on the bed beside one another and stared up at the ceiling, letting aftershocks of laughter roll over them. Eventually, the two of them again situated themselves as comfortably as possible for sharing a bed meant for one, similarly to the night they had spent in Saros. They laid back to back, leaning against each other.

"Are you comfortable?" Rylan asked Mara.

"It could be worse," Mara replied, thinking about her dungeon cell at the castle.

"Fair point," Rylan giggled, catching on. "If I ever get the chance, I'll inform my father the dungeon needs better beds."

Mara smiled and closed her eyes. More comfortable than she had been in days, sleep found her quickly.

~~~

Rylan…

The princess shot up. Her surroundings were unfamiliar. The room she had fallen asleep in was gone. No pelts on the walls. No bed. No Mara. She once again found herself standing in front of the structure that resembled a crescent moon on its side. A beautiful, smooth voice came from the open doors.

I have seen your heart.

Rylan stepped forward into the building. Unlike last time, there was much more to see. The building's light colored stone seemed to glow, giving off a soft and consistent light. The entrance hall had a high ceiling, which confused Rylan as the center of the building did not seem that tall from the outside. There was a hallway to either side that each ended in a staircase leading up and out of sight while a third hallway directly in front of her led, as she recalled from her last vision, to where Zhira had been laying on the floor in pain. She walked that way again, eager to see if he was alright. When she came to the door, she found it locked.

"Where is he?" Rylan tried to ask, but no sound came from her throat. She began to panic and ran back to the entrance hall and up the stairs to her right, coming to another door she could not open. Frustrated
~~~

and upset, she ran back down the stairs and up the other set which led her into a room that looked identical to her father's study. Confused, Rylan stood there staring at the shelves of ingredients and potions. Suddenly, one of the cabinets exploded, which made her jump. The cabinet beside it exploded next, sending its contents flying about the room, though none of it hit her. The rest of the shelving followed suit until the room was in a state of complete disarray. Rylan stood in the doorway, baffled by what she had just witnessed.

You are not your father. Your path is your own.

Rylan blinked and when her eyes opened, Dazel stood in the middle of the room. Rylan took in the goddess, her radiant beauty exactly as she remembered it from the throne room: golden skin and silver hair that flowed as if underwater.

Where is Zhira? Rylan thought, which manifested as her voice. Her eyes got wider.

You have learned. Beings do not have a voice here, our thoughts are what carry. Dazel replied calmly before answering Rylan's question. *Zhira is alive. He is extremely weak, but being here has saved him.*

Where is 'here'? Rylan asked the goddess of magic. It was odd to communicate without moving her mouth. *This is going to take some getting used to. Whoops, I didn't mean…how do I…*

The magic of this place projects thoughts. You will become accustomed to it soon. Regarding your question, you know this place as The Bright One.

You mean…we are on another planet? Rylan asked in bewilderment.

For the first time Rylan had seen, Dazel's face showed emotion. She was smiling. *Yes, child. Zhira was correct. The Bright One is another planet. My planet. My home.*

How did I get to another planet? Rylan thought to the goddess.

You did not, your body is still on your planet, but your mind is here by my projection. Dazel explained.

You're bringing me here? Why? Rylan's curiosity was bubbling over.

Because your path is a special one. You are pure of heart, and that is rare.

But I still do not understand why I am here. What are you trying to show me?

I understand you have many questions, and they will be answered in time. For now I must bid farewell. The sun rises on you. We will meet again. Remember, your path is your own.

Rylan tried to think of something else to say to the goddess, but before she could, the building melted away and her surroundings faded to black.

Rylan opened her eyes and upon seeing the room around her, sighed in frustration.

"'The sun rises on you'…what does that mean?" Rylan asked herself aloud as sunlight peeked through small gaps where tigerdeer pelts covered a window. "Oh, she meant literally."

Rylan sat up and shook Mara.

"Wake up, wake up!" Rylan yelled as Mara rolled over, clearly annoyed that she had been woken.

"I liked falling asleep better," Mara grumbled.

"This is important. I had another vision, but this time I know why!" Rylan was practically bouncing on the bed.

"Let's get my father and you can explain it to us over breakfast," Mara suggested.

The two of them got changed, and Mara left to retrieve Gant while Rylan packed her bag.

~~~

"Dad, breakfast!" Mara called to him.

"Okay…" Mara heard his groggy voice through the fur-covered door. "Mara!" he yelled suddenly, sounding terrified. "MARA!"

Mara burst in and nearly threw up at what she saw. From the knee down, her father's right leg was swollen to twice its normal size, covered in multiple shades of green, purple, and blue.

"What in Eres' name is happening?!" Mara exclaimed.

"I don't know!" Gant replied, panicked.

"Why aren't you wearing pants?!" Mara asked.

"It was hot under the…can we not focus on that right now?!" Gant nearly screamed.
~~~

The innkeeper appeared in the doorway behind Mara, drawn by the commotion.

"Oh dear, you've been bitten by a necrospider," he observed, shocking Mara with his calm demeanor.

"What's a…never mind. How do we fix him?!" Mara asked, extremely distressed.

Rylan ran up behind the innkeeper and vomited instantly at the sight of Gant's leg.

"We will take him to the healer," the innkeeper said, ignoring Rylan's visceral reaction. "Let's get him up."

Together, Mara and the innkeeper made to carry Gant, when Rylan yelled at Mara.

"Are you stupid?!" she asked, pointing to Mara's hip.

"Oh! Right!" Mara exclaimed as she whipped out her dagger and pointed it at her father.

Gant began to levitate off the bed.

"What in Dazel's name…" The innkeeper stumbled back as Mara backed out of the room with her floating father. The amethyst in the hilt glowed faintly.

"Can you kindly and *immediately* show us to the healer?!" Mara's voice rose with every word until she was screaming.

The man nodded and pushed open the door leading out into the street. The sun had risen, but the town was quiet. He led them across the street to a small hut with no windows and a wooden door painted red. Rylan rapped furiously on the door until it opened and a man in a brown cloak stepped out to greet them. Judging by his appearance, Mara figured he was older than her father, but not by much. He was bald with a short dark beard and thick eyebrows; Mara noticed he was rather tall, his head barely clearing the doorframe.

"Good morning, what can I…" his voice trailed off at the sight of Gant, who was no longer floating. He was supported by Mara and was groaning in pain.

"Bring him in, bring him in!" The man hurried Mara, Gant, and Rylan inside and shut the door behind them. "Lay him there," he pointed to an empty cot to their right.

The hut was a single, candle lit room with two beds on each side and a long table at the back strewn with a cornucopia of medical ingredients and supplies ranging from roots and berries to thread and needles.

"What's happening to him?" Mara asked impatiently.

"He has been bitten by a necrospider, yes?" the man asked as he busied himself at the long table, gathering ingredients together.

"Yes, but…" Mara began to reply, but the healer cut her off.

"One moment!" he said, and he opened a door Mara had not seen before and disappeared into a back room. Gant moaned louder as Mara and Rylan watched the infection spread to his thigh.

The healer returned with a bottle of dark blue liquid and added a few ingredients to it from the table. The liquid turned a bright purple and seemed to glow mildly as the healer swirled it around. He walked over to Gant's bed and sat him up.

"Drink this," he said calmly, handing the bottle to Gant who downed it in one gulp.

"Oooooooh dear goddess," Gant said, clutching at his stomach.

"There will be some discomfort—a small price to pay for life!" the healer said as he held his hands out over Gant.

Mara and Rylan watched as the colors in Gant's leg changed. The blues and purples overtook the greens near his shin and got brighter and brighter until they began to seep out of his pores. Rylan turned away to vomit again, but Mara was mesmerized by what this man was doing to her father. The healer made his fingers dance slightly and what Mara assumed was the necrospider's venom seeped from her father's leg until there was not a trace of any dark colors left in Gant's leg. The venom now hovered in front of the healer in a small grape-sized ball.

"The little monster got you good. It's not often you see this much venom in one person," the healer observed as he directed the venom into the empty bottle that Gant had drank from earlier.

"What…what did you just do?" Gant asked as he lifted himself from the bed, sweating from his experience.

"I gave you an agent that bonds with the venom, which enables me to extract it," the healer explained.

"How did you extract it?" Rylan asked.

"Simple alchemy, of course! I know I can control the fluid he drank, and I know it bonds to venom instantly. So I know I can pull it out of him."

"You're an alchemist?" Mara asked.

"Yes ma'am. Tanen the healer, at your service!" Tanen replied with a slight bow.

"I have so many questions…" Gant stared at Tanen.

"How about we go grab some breakfast first?" Rylan suggested as her stomach rumbled, recently emptied.

"Grand idea, let's walk over to Deri's. She's the baker, and her muffins are marvelous!" Tanen suggested enthusiastically. His demeanor reminded Mara of Litik back at home in Saros.

"Can you walk, dad?" Mara asked Gant, still concerned.

Gant stood up slowly and added weight on his leg until he stood normally, and smiled. The four of them left Tanen's hut and followed the sweet smells that filled the air. They were so strong, Mara swore she could see the aroma floating around them. Rylan's mouth watered and she quickened her pace, reaching the bakery before the rest of them.

Rylan selected a massive muffin full of blueberries without any hesitation. Gant and Tanen both grabbed small cakes resembling rocks that Mara hoped tasted better than they looked. She grabbed a handful of small knotted bread laced with garlic for herself.

"I can't stand the smell of those," Tanen said as she placed the handful on a small platter.

"Really? I've always loved the smell of garlic." Mara sat down with her knots and popped one in her mouth.

"Not me," Tanen replied as he sat across from her, the furthest seat from the pungent bread.

"I've never done any alchemy like that before," Gant remarked as he sat down at the small table bathed in yellow morning sunlight.

"That's because you don't know my methods! Not many do, and even fewer can stomach them," Tanen said before taking a large bite of his breakfast.

"What do you mean? Don't you just make potions?" Rylan asked, her mouth full.

"I do, but my ingredients of choice are…unorthodox." Tanen paused, looking at all three of them. Mara got the feeling he was judging them and their ability to handle the next bit of information he planned to divulge. "I use more than just plants and roots to concoct my potions. For the things I do, I need blood."

Rylan choked on her muffin and Gant's eyes got wide. Mara looked at Tanen more intently.

"Let me explain," he said quickly, reacting to their sudden changes in expression.

"Please." Mara did not blink.

"I used to only use flora in my mixtures, but one day after I had returned from hunting, I accidentally spilled some pheasant blood into one of my bowls. The blend of roots I had made reacted and began to glow. Naturally I was curious and began testing the effects of the blood on different potions, until I realized that it was an extremely potent and viable option for making stronger and more useful potions.

"Every time I hunted, I made sure to save some of the blood to use in my testing. I never killed for the sake of my alchemy, I only used what I already had. We are people of the land here, and I would never disrespect nature in that way," Tanen explained.

Gant relaxed a little and Rylan managed to clear her throat.

"So you have discovered a way to make more intense potions by using blood?" Rylan clarified.

"Basically, yes. Alchemy is a fantastic skill, allowing one to enhance the potential of the body and even imitate magic, to an extent. What I do simply amplifies those same traits. My potions more vigorously imitate magic and actually allow the body to perform beyond its physical limits," Tanen confirmed before finishing his rock-inspired cake.

"Blood Alchemy," Mara said, eyeing Tanen warily.

"I guess you could call it that, yes," Tanen responded, unnerved by Mara's gaze.

"Mara, relax. There is nothing wrong with what this man is doing. The animals are dead, being hunted anyway for food and clothing." Gant's words pulled Mara out of her focus on Tanen; she sat back, marginally more relaxed.

"Does it work with any animal?" Rylan asked.

"So far that I have found, yes. The effects do vary by animal, but I have only been at this for a few years, so I have limited experience. My daughter and I began the research together about four years ago."

"Where is your daughter?" Mara asked him.

"Unfortunately," Tanen's voice dropped slightly, "she ran off three years ago. Didn't want to live in our little town any more. After her mother died, her desire to be here waned. She wanted something bigger. She told me she was headed to the capital, to start a new life in a place she could 'actually grow' or something like that. She was only fourteen."

"What was her name?" Rylan asked, her concern for people overtaking her curiosity about blood alchemy.

"Kyra. She was a brilliant…uh…blood alchemist." Tanen looked at Mara as he said it. "But her ambitions were elsewhere, so she packed up one night and left. I haven't heard from her since." The alchemist hung his head.

"I'm sorry, Tanen. I can't imagine what it must be like to have your daughter abandon you," Gant consoled him. Mara gave her father a look, indicating that what he had just said was in poor taste given their present company. "Oh, sorry Rylan, I didn't mean—"

"It's okay," she replied kindly.

Mara watched Rylan's eyes glaze over. She could only imagine that the former princess was thinking about what abandoning her father had done to him. Mara wondered if Gjanion would even be upset that Rylan had left. *He probably was,* she thought, *but only since he wanted her to take care of his legacy when he died.* Gjanion did not care about her, not from what Mara knew of their relationship. Mara focused back on the conversation between Tanen and her father.

"We don't get travelers often, we're not exactly on the beaten path. Where are you three headed?" Tanen asked Gant, snapping Rylan back to the conversation.

"We're headed to Varyn. We are…looking for the rebellion," Mara lied. She still did not trust this man completely.

"Ah, well I wish you all luck. That King Gjanion is a nasty piece of work. So power hungry and delusional, I hope someone finds a way to kill him," Tanen mused.

"Killing him won't solve anything," Rylan said, surprisingly defiant.

"Oh? Do we have a sympathizer in our midst?" Tanen asked.

"No! No, I just…simply removing him isn't enough. Whoever steps up after him to lead must be better than he was. A better precedent needs to be set." Rylan recovered well, Mara was impressed.

"Why even have a king? Do you think anyone in that position can do a good enough job?" Tanen challenged her.

Rylan sat on the question for a moment. She hoped that in a position of power, she would work towards the common good, but that was her father's justification as well. "Power is not the problem, but how it is used. Maybe they need to share the load or be kept in check, but I don't think it's impossible to do well in that role," Rylan finally answered.

"I see…you'd make a fine leader, young lady. You have a good head on your shoulders." Tanen praised Rylan, who blushed slightly.

"Our new leader should be someone strong and with a mind for peace," Gant said to Rylan. "You are both of those things."

Replacing King Gjanion hit Mara like a ton of bricks. She had not thought about what would happen if the rebellion succeeded. *Rylan would make a good leader,* Mara thought. *She's so poised, so good with people, and so determined to protect others.*

A sudden wave of nervousness washed over Mara. *I hope people don't expect me to assume control.* She sat back and finished her garlic bread, deep in thought about the future of Kyros.

Chapter Eight
The Death Mist

Kei listened to the bugs and watched the stars overhead. Gladys snored in her sleeping bag next to the glowing red embers from their fire, Jerra was sound asleep to his right, and Radion sat awake alongside him. They were leaving the forests of the central kingdom behind and entering into the salt flats that preceded the eastern coast of Kyros. With sparser shrubbery and wildlife, hunting was becoming more difficult. Their camp was set up with almost no cover, save for a pair of short, leafless trees that stood guard nearby.

"Can't sleep, boy?" Radion asked him. It was the old king's turn to be on watch, having taken over for Kei an hour ago.

"No. Too much on my mind," Kei said, staring off at the dark horizon to the north.

"You seem worried," Radion observed.

"I am. I'm worried about Mara. Is she okay? Is she even alive? We've lost so many people. I'm worried about Rylan, Forbin, Gant, and the others too, of course. We are literally running for our lives hoping that we can pull off one last stand in Varyn," Kei said with very little hope in his voice.

"You worry too much," Radion replied, looking up at the sky.

"How can you say that? There is so much to think about, to worry about—the rebellion winning, saving our friends and family, preparing those who can't fight along with those who can…" Kei trailed off as he noticed Radion's wrinkled face staring at him. His white beard glowed red in the light of the embers.

"Look up," Radion said, nodding his head towards the night sky.

Kei obliged, trying to keep an eye on the old king at the same time.

"Each of those stars is either home to a number of worlds, or is a world themselves. Countless places that are completely unaware of us, and do not care if we live or die. I tried for many years to control Kyros, to make it the best that I could. Despite my best efforts, my grandson mucked it all up anyway," Radion said as they stargazed.

"What are you saying?" Kei asked him, eyes still on the multitude of stars that peppered the night sky.

"I am saying that whatever is meant to happen will happen. We are such an insignificant part of the universe…of our own planet even!" Radion laughed heartily. "We cannot control the world. In fact, there is little use in worrying about those things we cannot control. We can only be prepared for whatever life has to throw at us and make the most of it."

He and Kei stared at the sky for a little while longer. Kei felt both scared and comforted by the old king's words. In the grand scheme of things, this conflict was nothing despite feeling like the only thing. Nevertheless, Kei still couldn't help worrying about Mara. However insignificant they were compared to the stars, Mara would always be important to him. Kei's eyes wandered from star to star, his peripheral vision noticing different worlds and points of light as he went along. A new fascination budded in him fed by all the possibilities that could exist in the infinite blackness above him.

Eventually the embers died off and the cold almost-winter winds took hold. Kei tore his eyes away from the sky and got up to retrieve another layer from the cart to keep the bitter winds at bay. As he rummaged through his bag for a coat, his vision crossed the horizon and he noticed something strange.

"Radion?" He got the old man's attention and pointed to the horizon, which had blurred from black to grey, and expanded as he and Radion looked on.

"What is that? My eyes aren't what they used to be. All I see is a grey blur," Radion observed to the best of his ability.

"That's what I see too, which worries me," Kei replied, reaching for his axe.

"Everyone up!" Radion announced in his kingly and commanding voice as he drew his sword.

In an instant, Jerra and Gladys were awake and alert, looking around for further instruction.

"What is it?" Jerra asked Kei.

"That." Kei pointed at what he could now identify as fog rolling in on them from the north.

"Fog at night? That seems unusual…" Gladys remarked.

"It's probably nothing, we're out near the salt flats, there is not a lot to divert weather out here," Radion replied.

"Still, I don't like it. It doesn't seem natural," said Kei, gripping his axe.

Radion re-lit their fire to provide additional warmth as well as light while the air around them began to blur steadily into a dense mist. The stars above them slowly disappeared and soon they couldn't even see the two dead-looking trees standing twenty feet from them.

"Stay close to the fire, we need to be able to see each other," Kei said, more commandingly than he intended, but everyone listened.

Their senses were heightened as the sounds of the bugs and the wind went away. Nothing penetrated the dense mist around them. The only sounds to be heard were the crackling of the fire. The four of them stood with their weapons drawn as they waited out the sudden change in weather. Kei's stomach turned. *I have a bad feeling about this.*

A shriek pierced the mist and made the hairs on the back of Kei's neck stand on end. He looked around but couldn't figure out which way the horrible sound was coming from. The mist was thick and stifling. Kei glanced to his left and noticed that Gladys looked disoriented, not being able to see anything other than their fire. Another shriek came, louder than the first. To Kei's right, Jerra started to shake.

Radion downed two potions and stood up straighter, gripping the relic sword tightly. For the first time, Kei saw him as the king who had overthrown wizards. There was an air about the old man that seemed invincible. A small wave of comfort washed over him right before he was thrown to the ground by something that ran into him from behind. He quickly turned over and swung his axe blindly, hitting nothing. He stopped, looked around, and saw no target.

"What was that?" he asked the group.

Nobody had an answer.

The four of them stood with their backs to the fire, facing outwards and prepared for whatever threat stalked them in the mist. Something ran past Gladys, looking like nothing more than a hazy shadow. Another movement caught their eye as a larger black figure swept through the mist just past the edge of the firelight. Soon they were watching shadows cross back and forth just beyond where they could see. Nobody moved as the creatures started shrieking. The shadows circling them and the accompanying high pitched noises were disorienting, making Kei dizzy.

Suddenly, Gladys fell down, knocked over by one of the creatures who had swooped in closer. She got back up quickly and swung her sword. Radion's right hand ignited in flame, his left handling the sword. Jerra was not much of a fighter, but had forged most of the weapons the rebellion had used, including the sword and mace she was currently wielding. Kei figured she could hold her own.

Another creature dove at them from the mist and this time, Kei was ready. He swung his axe and it struck home, slicing the monster clean in half. It landed at his feet, allowing him to get a good look at what was pursuing them. The creature was roughly their size, and built like a human. It walked on two legs and had two arms with hands that ended in elongated fingers. The creature had a slimy grey body, black beady eyes, and a mouth with three rows of needle-like teeth.

"What the hell is that?" Jerra asked, very obviously frightened by it.

"They're called ghouls, and if one gets its spindly fingers on you, do yourself a favor and chop off your own head. It'll be less painful," Radion replied.

"What do you mean?" Gladys asked the old king.

"They're horrible creatures that will eat you alive. Stay near the fire and fight like your life depends on it," he said, eyes on the mist in front of him. Kei wondered how Radion knew this, but decided now was not the time to ask.

"It does depend on it!" Gladys replied as she swung at another ghoul coming at her from the grey.

The ghouls' attacks grew more confident as they started taking shots more consistently at the four of them. At first, the disgusting grey monsters simply dashed close and tried to grab at the humans, but an increasing number of ghouls flooded in until they were as dense as the mist from whence they had come.

Radion threw fireball after fireball, hitting the ghouls in the head and dropping them almost instantly. Using the sword, he felled several ghouls at a time with the magical arcs of light that flew from the blade. Kei's axe traced arc after arc in front of him, slicing off limbs and heads and cutting ghouls in half. Jerra held her own, clobbering each ghoul that came too close with the mace or stabbing them through the face with her sword and dropping them.

Gladys wielded her sword with grace and fluidity, bringing it up through one ghoul and down through the next. Each motion leading into her next attack, dropping a ghoul with every swing. Her style was efficient in contrast to Jerra's more wild and brutal approach. The bodies began to pile up in front of them, and the attack slowed.

"I think we've gotten the better of them!" Jerra exclaimed.

But Kei watched as the most impossible thing he had ever witnessed occurred. The bodies of the dead ghouls started dissolving, eventually evaporating into the mist around them, which seemed to get denser as the ghouls' bodies disappeared.

"Well that was unexpected," Radion commented.

"They don't seem to be going away!" Kei called their attention back to the swirling shadows in the mist. The remaining ghouls were aggravated; their movements seemed less coordinated as they circled the four rebels.

Suddenly, the grey monsters started springing from the mist at full speed. Kei, Radion, Gladys, and Jerra fought with renewed energy and desperation as the attacks came swiftly. Kei hacked ghoul after ghoul apart, his mind focused solely on keeping himself alive until he heard a cry from behind him. He could not spare a glance backwards as he continued to defend himself from the onslaught.

"Gladys, are you all right?!" he called out.

The only response was more desperate cries as he, Jerra, and Radion continued to fight off the swarm of ghouls. Kei began to tear up as Gladys' pleas for help grew more panicked and then began to fade. He felt helpless and empty as he protected himself and the others that still stood from the foul monsters. Kei knew that the moment he turned around to help Gladys, he was a dead man too. It was hopeless. The cries faded until it was clear Gladys was gone. Kei began to cry as he hacked and mauled the oncoming ghouls. After what felt like an hour, the attacks finally started to slow and eventually the ghouls retreated back into the mist. Their shadows slowly disappeared as the mist began to recede.

Kei dropped his axe in exhaustion, feeling as if he had been fighting for hours. He turned around. Only a skid mark remained indicating where the ghouls had dragged Gladys away. Jerra and Radion noticed as well, and Jerra began to cry. The mist thinned out until the stars above them returned and the landscape around them came back into focus.

They sat in silence for the remainder of the night, unable to find anything to say, but too shaken to sleep. When the sun's rays began to color the horizon orange to the east, they began packing up their camp, though Kei found it difficult to motivate himself. Another soldier had fallen, and the sun would not rise for her. Kei fell into a seated position where he had been standing and bowed his head. Anger, sadness, and frustration all swirled inside of him. Radion hobbled over and sat beside him.

"Gladys was a good soldier. She will be missed," he rasped, clearly exhausted from the attack.

Jerra came to sit next to him and said nothing. Eventually, her sobs broke out into cries, which echoed out onto the flats. Nobody said anything as exhaustion took over. After a few minutes, Kei got up and finished cleaning up what remained of their camp. Jerra began to help as well while Radion made his way to the cart. The assault by the ghouls had clearly drained him, Kei noticed, as the old king moved considerably slower than usual.

"Radion are you okay?" Kei asked as he rolled up his sleeping bag.

"Fine, fine. Don't worry about me. I just don't have the stamina I once did," he replied.

"Good thing. It'll make this that much easier," a voice came from behind them.

Kei spun around to see Commander Tren and five knights standing just beyond their camp. In his exhaustion, Kei hadn't been paying attention to anything but preparing to leave. Jerra and Radion must have missed their arrival too.

"Run!" Kei yelled as he dropped what he was carrying and bolted for the horse that Gladys had been riding.

They never had a chance. Tren and his knights were fresh and moved quickly, intercepting their path. Kei looked helplessly at the commander and his team of five fully armored soldiers. He knew their luck had run out.

"Commander, these two are innocent. They were conscripted by me against their will to produce weapons and armor for the rebellion. Let them go and I shall come with you without a fuss," Radion lied smoothly, not looking at Kei or Jerra.

"A fuss? Old man, you don't scare me. I should have all three of you killed here and now. Three less rebels in our way!" Tren scoffed.

"Go ahead and try then." There was something in Radion's voice that sent shivers down Kei's spine. The old king looked surprisingly menacing.

"Kill them," Tren commanded, stepping back to allow his knights to do their task.

Kei gripped his axe tight and swung at the nearest assailant; a young girl whose blonde curls stuck out from under her helmet. She was dressed in dark purple leather armor and wielded a staff that was covered with metal studs on either end. With a flurry of attacking swings, she took little time in overpowering Kei and knocked him off balance. Kei fell and rolled onto the balls of his feet. His muscles argued with his movements, still tired from the encounter with the ghouls.

Adrenaline and survival instincts driving his actions, Kei took a retaliatory swing at Kyra who sidestepped his axe with ease and punished him with a swift blow to the back of his uncovered legs. Kei cried out in pain and turned, blindly swinging his axe in an uppercut at his attacker. Kyra parried the axe and continued spinning her staff, hitting Kei in the arm with the other end. He howled as the metal studs connected with the bony part of his elbow, drawing blood. Kei realized that he was outmatched.

Kyra's attacks were swift and the fight was brief; she overwhelmed Kei until he was on one knee, breathing hard and bleeding in several places. Kyra spun around him and took a full two-handed swing to his back, which resulted in a loud cracking noise. Kei slumped to the ground, tears streaming from his face as he lay face down, still holding his axe.

I'm going to be next.

~~~
~~~

Radion's alchemical abilities were on full display. He had taken a strength potion and moved with the speed of someone fifty years younger, surprising everyone around him. With the ruby sword in his left hand, he parried every attack that came his way. With his right, he guided the knights' swords away from him with some invisible force.

Tren backed away and watched as the old man moved with a grace well beyond his years. Radion pushed his right hand down and sunk the knights' feet into the salty ground, immobilizing them before knocking them all out. Tren looked from his fallen soldiers to the old man who stood before him.

"Who are you?" Tren asked.

"I am Radion, leader of the rebellion," he said.

"Radion? Like the old king?" Tren began to sweat despite the cold.

"Not 'like', young man." Without looking, Radion thrust his hand towards Kyra, who stood over Kei with her knife drawn. She was sent tumbling by some unseen burst of energy.

"You can't be him. Gjanion is Radion reincarnate, he is a god!" Tren exclaimed, taking a more aggressive stance with his swords.

"I believe you are mistaken, seeing as how I am still very much alive."

"Prove it," Tren commanded.

"Prove I am alive?" Radion chuckled and took a deep breath. "See? Dead people can't do that."

"No, prove you're Radion."

Kyra got up and rushed to Tren's side, ready to defend her commander.

"I assume you know what this is?" Radion held up the relic sword.

Tren nodded. "That belongs to the king. His grandfather—"

"*I* found this sword, the crown, and the staff prior to overthrowing the wizards some sixty odd years ago. I know what these relics are, I know what they do, and I know Gjanion is not getting his greedy hands on this one," Radion said confidently.

"That does not prove you are who you say you are," Tren said firmly.

"Fine, here." Radion pulled a small vial of pink liquid from beneath his tunic, swallowed its contents, and closed his eyes.

Tren's mind was instantly flooded with scenes and memories that were not his. He watched a much younger Radion storm the castle with a force that would dwarf the king's army. Radion showed Tren how he left the throne to his son and disappeared, faking his own death. Tren watched as Radion conversed with Geralith about adding Hearth as one of the commanders in Gjanion's army. This man was who he said he was, Tren was certain. Only the true Radion would know of these events so intimately.

"So Gjanion…" Tren began to speak, reeling from what had just happened in his mind.

"Is not who he says he is. He is not Knorr. My son, Gjanion's father, was the true god reincarnate. Lord Geralith purposefully misled Gjanion at my direction,"

"I…you're coming with me," Tren said shakily, unsure of how to proceed.

"No thank you. Jerra, ready the cart," Radion said as he sheathed the sword.

"No thank you?" Tren asked, incredulously.

"You are welcome to try and take me hostage, but as you have just seen, I do not believe that is in your best interests." Radion gestured to the four unconscious knights.

~~~

While Tren conversed with Radion, Kyra subtly took her dagger and pricked her finger. She removed a small vial from an unseen pocket on the inside of her armor and let her blood drip into its contents before swirling them around and drinking them. She pulled her leather helmet back down over her head as Tren threatened to take Radion hostage.

"You are welcome to try and take me hostage, but as you have just seen, I do not believe that is in your best interests." Radion gestured to the four unconscious knights.
~~~

"I'll take a stab at it," Kyra said menacingly.

"Oh, child," Radion chuckled and flicked his hand, but nothing happened.

Tren and Radion stared at the girl, both equally surprised.

"My father taught me a few things before I fled home," she said before charging the old king.

Radion redrew his sword and parried blow after blow. Kyra was moving faster than Radion could handle, but Radion was smarter. He baited her until she was in a fully offensive position, taking swings with her full strength. Sidestepping one particularly heavy swing, Radion swept at Kyra's leg and attempted to knock her to the ground. Kyra took the fall and rolled back onto the balls of her feet, a few feet away. That was all Radion needed.

"Jerra!" Radion called out, running faster than Kyra thought was possible for a man so ancient.

She watched him jump into the cart that the woman, Jerra, had apparently loaded their friend she had injured into while she and Radion had dueled. Kyra gave chase but her prey was moving too quickly. As they rolled out of range, she heard Radion call out, "Give my best to my grandson, I am sure he will be pleased to know I am alive!"

Kyra gave a frustrated sigh and walked back to Tren.

"What the hell just happened?" Tren asked her.

"I tried to capture a king. Thanks for the help," Kyra snapped.

"Are you an alchemist?" Tren asked, ignoring her quip.

"Yes," Kyra admitted. There was no use in lying, Tren had seen what happened. "I used a potion my dad taught me to make me significantly stronger. That old king could never have knocked me over with his alchemy," she said with confidence.

"Why didn't you tell me?"

"King Gjanion banned alchemy. If he finds out, I'll likely be killed."

Kyra watched as Tren considered this development. She knew that the rebellion had the likes of Mara, along with what appeared to be more alchemists than they knew of. Kyra hoped that Tren would see her alchemy as a way to help even the odds.

"Your secret is safe with me," he said to her after a moment.

"Really?" Kyra looked at him, stunned.

"Really. Just be careful when and where you use it," Tren advised.

Kyra smiled as they went to dig out their companions.

Chapter Nine
Connections

"Rylan, you were going to tell me something this morning? You woke me all excited," Mara said, reminding the princess as the two of them loaded up their horses back at the inn.

"OH! Oh goddess, of course! Your dad will want to hear this too," Rylan exclaimed.

"Hear what?" Gant walked over.

"My vision…or whatever we're calling them. I had another one, and this time I actually talked to Dazel!" Rylan was practically yelling.

"You what?!" Mara asked incredulously. She had been trying for years to connect to peoples' minds and was just recently having success, fueled by the events of the last few weeks. Frustration bubbled up inside her at how easy it was for Rylan to make such a special connection.

"I don't think I did anything really, it seems to be Dazel's doing. Anyways, Zhira was right. The Bright One is a planet. It is Dazel's home," Rylan explained.

"That's incredible…" Gant said, wide eyed.

"I know, and she brought Zhira there. He's alive! Dazel said he survived, but she didn't explain how."

"So dad is alive on another planet?" Mara tried to wrap her head around what Rylan was saying.

"What else did Dazel tell you?" Gant asked, trying to get any more information about his brother as he could. Knowing he was alive had clearly lit a new fire inside him.

"Not much, unfortunately. The only other thing she said was to not follow the ways of my father—that my path was my own." Rylan looked encouraged.

"That's supportive," Mara mused, still a bit frustrated by her friend's easy connection with a goddess. *I am the wizard, not her.* Mara was taken back by her own thoughts. She and Rylan had become fast friends; she should be happy for and supportive of Rylan, not jealous and frustrated. Mara tried to calm herself. They had a connection to a goddess, albeit one they didn't understand. *This connection could prove useful. This is bigger than me.*

"Do you know how this connection works?" Gant asked.

"All she said was my body remained where it was, but my mind was there by her projection," Rylan explained to them.

"If we understand this connection better, it could be really useful. I wonder why they saved Dad and nobody else," said Mara, realizing the frustration she was feeling was actually directed towards the goddess.

"I just wonder if we can get Zhira back," Gant began to speculate.

"Next time it happens, I'll ask," Rylan suggested, though her voice did not project confidence.

"I bet there is something in his books. I haven't looked in all of them yet," Mara said.

"You think Zhira took notes on magic planets?" Gant asked.

"He took notes on The Bright One, and you both thought it was a sign from Dazel, so…yes?" Mara said, already pulling out a small brown book of his notes.

"That's fair," conceded Gant.

"Wait, Mara," Rylan said, making her pause.

"What?" She replied impatiently; there had been no time to continue reading her father's notes since they were flushed out of The Cave.

"Let's continue this on the road, we need to get moving," Rylan said, noticing how high the sun had gotten since their ordeal this morning. "We can start looking through some of his notes once we are on the way to Varyn."

Rylan was right. They had spent a lot of time here and needed to get moving towards Varyn. Mara nodded in agreement and placed the book back in the bag. Rylan gathered food from the farmers that were out selling their goods while Mara and Gant finished saddling the horses and loading their bags. The three of them left with Gant's leg still sporting a nasty green bruise from the necrospider bite. They thanked Tanen and bid him farewell before riding off down the far side of the hill.

Once they settled into a good pace, Mara reached into her bag and pulled out the same brown book. She handed it to her father and grabbed another leather-bound one. Rylan acted as a sentry on Neela's back, keeping them on course and keeping watch for any other travelers.

"Find anything useful?" Mara asked after a while.

"No…wait, yes! Here," Gant said, pointing to a page he had been scanning.

"What does it say?" Mara asked from atop her horse.

"The Bright One appears to diminish in luminosity not so much with the phases of the moon but the passing of the seasons. It retains its brightness better whether the moon is full or new, unlike the many other stars in the sky. I suspect it may be a fair bit closer to us than those stars that get washed out by the moon's glow."

"That would support it being a planet, but what does that have to do with my powers?" Mara asked when her father had finished reading.

"I don't know, let me keep browsing," he said as he turned the page to find a sketch of the position of The Bright One at the time, high in the summer sky.

"Dad, what about this?" Mara got his attention before reading a passage from the dark leather book she held open, balanced on her saddle's pommel. "The Bright One's path cycles every two years. It returns to its brightest in summer every other year."

"Yeah, we know that, that's when the Festival of Dazel occurs back home. The Bright One is brightest that summer, then dimmest the following, and at a much lower point in the sky. The cycle repeats over two years as far as we have observed," Gant replied.

"So what does that have to do with my magic?" Mara asked.

~~~

Zhira opened his eyes slowly; the light was painful. His head hurt and he felt as though he had been kicked in the chest by a horse. As he sat up, he found that he could barely lift his head before his whole body screamed in resistance. He laid his head back down and closed his eyes.

When he opened them again a few moments later, he turned his head slowly and took in his surroundings. The room was bare, with light colored stone walls and a ceiling to match. Zhira realized there were no windows. The walls were glowing.
~~~

I have been watching you for some time. A voice emanated from the walls.

"Who are you?" Zhira tried to ask, but no sound came from his throat.

Think, do not speak. The voice directed him.

Who are you? Zhira heard his voice loud and clear though his mouth did not move.

I am Eres. My sister brought you to me so that you may live.

Your sister…what happened to me? Zhira thought, confused. Little pieces of the battle in the throne room began to come back to him.

King Gjanion tried to end your life. Your daughter did what she could, but in her distress she could not focus. My sister took you here, where we could save you, said Eres.

The memories suddenly flooded Zhira's mind like a dam breaking. He remembered fighting alongside Mara, trying everything to disarm the king of his relics. Zhira's mind raced as the battle was fought again in his mind, until he remembered the king coming towards him with his sword drawn. With no time to react, Zhira's chest had taken the sword from the king. Everything after that was a blur.

Where am I? Zhira looked around at the empty room.

The Bright One, Eres replied.

I was right? It is a planet? Zhira asked, shocked. He looked around at the walls, unable to address the goddess directly.

Eres seemed to notice this. Zhira blinked and there she was, floating slightly above the ground in the center of the room. Eres looked identical to Dazel except for her coloring. Her skin was golden and her hair was silver and flowed around her as if in weightlessness.

Yes, this is our planet, our home. This was once a world full of magic and life, but Knorr was greedy and desired worship for his efforts in making it what it was. The people of this planet wanted his powers and they warred for his approval. All life here was destroyed and together Dazel and I banished him to your planet without any magical ability, doomed to an endless cycle of rebirth. We had hoped in time he would forget who he was, but it appears our efforts were not enough, the goddess of life explained to him.

The broken planet story is real… Zhira thought, which he did not intend to manifest out loud.

Yes, the fable has a core of truth, Eres confirmed.

Zhira pondered this development for a moment before eventually and intentionally changing the subject.

So Gjanion is not who he thinks he is, Zhira thought, intending to confirm what he knew from Radion.

Correct. Gjanion believes himself to be Knorr, but Radion still lives, said Eres.

So if Radion is Knorr, then what happens when he dies? Does Gjanion become Knorr? Zhira asked.

You assume that Radion is Knorr, but this is untrue, Eres replied.

WHAT?! Zhira asked, stunned.

It is not Radion who is Knorr reincarnated. Gjanion's newborn son—the one called Karbalion—is the true reincarnation.

Zhira was reeling. He had assumed that Radion being alive meant that Gjanion could not have been reborn as Knorr, but he was wrong. The cycle was off by a generation. Gjanion's father was Knorr, and he had never been aware. Zhira wondered if Radion knew this and had hidden it from his own son on purpose.

If Gjanion can be defeated before his son can learn of the family history, perhaps Knorr will be forgotten for good, Dazel suggested.

Why don't you just do it yourselves? You're goddesses, Zhira challenged her, managing to sit up and stare her down.

Because then the cycle would begin anew. People would fight for our favor and pray to us as war gods to dispose of their enemies. No, it must be your daughter and your friends. You all must end this conflict. The true leader is among you. Peace will be brought by those who seek it truly.

Who is the true leader? How do we defeat Gjanion? Zhira got worked up and his body protested. He winced in pain and laid back down.

In time. For now, rest. You must heal, Eres instructed, her physical form evaporating into nothing before him.

With a groan Zhira laid back down, significant pain reminding him that he was still recovering from a stab wound directly to the chest. His body ached and begged him to sleep but his mind would not allow it. He needed to get back to Mara and Gant and the rebellion. How were they supposed to end the reign of a king, god or not? They had faced Gjanion head on and failed, and he had nearly died.

~~~

King Gjanion sat in full armor atop his massive horse, save for a helmet. His long black hair looked almost cape-like flowing down over the magnificent purple steel that made up his armor. Each plate of his armor was trimmed with gold while his boots and gloves were a darker purple than the rest of the metal. He sat very straight and carried the silver staff in his left hand while guiding his horse with the reins in his right. Behind him was a small caravan of knights in silver armor sporting Gjanion's crest, a purple moon and lightning bolt, boldly on their chest plates.

Riding right behind the king and in front of the caravan were an elite group of knights that made up Gjanion's personal guard. These select knights, of which there were five, answered only to the king himself, along with General Mai and Commander Tren. Their battle armor was black with the king's crest emblazoned in white on their chests. The hilts of their weapons as well as their gloves were a deep purple color to match their helmets.

Gjanion watched as three of General Mai's knights, led by Captain Pike, rode out to greet them. Pike rode ahead of his men and turned his horse around
~~~

to keep pace next to the king. The other two knights fell in behind them.

"Your Majesty, it is an honor and a privilege to escort you to—"

"Save your pleasantries, Captain," Gjanion interrupted.

"Yes, sire," Pike said, shifting his gaze from the king awkwardly. "Shall I ride ahead and announce your presence?"

"If they are not aware of my presence by now, they should no longer be a part of this army." Gjanion still did not look at Pike, his gaze fixed at the camp ahead.

Pike rode silently beside the king until they entered the camp of purple and white tents. As they rode towards Mai's tent, knights knelt and bowed and made gestures to acknowledge the king. Gjanion did not acknowledge a single one.

Outside of the General's tent, Gjanion dismounted and handed the reins to one of Pike's men.

"See that he is watered and fed," Gjanion commanded before pulling the flap of the tent back and entering.

General Mai's tent was modest, larger than her knights' only to accommodate the table she used to look at maps and plan out attacks and patrols. It housed a bed with a small table beside it, and a couple of chests that contained her armor, battle plans, maps, and other items Mai relied on to lead her troops. Besides that, the tent was fairly empty. The purple and white striping created awkward lighting inside, which Gjanion's eyes took a moment to adjust to.

The king found his general bent over the table, studying a map with Commander Tren. Tren was still in his dark blue armor, which was covered in dust. He had clearly just returned from somewhere and was reporting back to the general before retiring for the afternoon.

"General," Gjanion made himself known when neither Mai nor Tren looked up when he entered the tent.

Mai looked up at the king with a face that did its best to look surprised, though Gjanion suspected it was not. Tren, however, was very clearly not expecting the king's arrival and stood up straight as an arrow instantly.

"Your Majesty, it is an honor to welcome you to our camp." Tren bowed his head.

"I'm sure," Gjanion said, waving a hand dismissively at the commander.

"I figured you'd come," Mai said, a tiredness in her voice.

"I don't blame you for the failure at the rebels' base, general. You were up against a powerful wizard," Gjanion said mildly despite his disappointment.

"Not to mention her alchemist father. We tried to catch them by surprise, but—"

"I don't want to hear EXCUSES!" Gjanion suddenly bellowed as he ditched the calm facade.

"Sir, if I may…" Commander Tren tried to speak up.

"You may not. In fact, you may leave. *Now.*" The sharp look lit a fire under Tren and the commander exited the tent as fast as he could. Angrily, Gjanion turned back to Mai. "It is clear to me that you are not ready for this responsibility. I will be leading the army to Varyn myself."

"Sir! That's not—"

"Not what? Fair? Are you going to whine like a child? General, I trusted you to snuff this out and you assured me your plan would not fail. Not only did you manage to let most of the rebels escape, but the wizard and her friends are still at large. While I do not blame you directly for this, it is clear that you need help, and we cannot allow them to escape again. Mara is the one person in this kingdom that can possibly undo all I have worked for these last twelve years. Her mere *existence* is a threat! If more people catch wind that there is another wizard, my legitimacy will be undermined. The people of Kyros will begin to ask questions and my rule will come crumbling down. You were supposed to end this conflict, and instead we are on a wild goose chase to find her! Do you have *any* idea where she is?" Gjanion finished his rant and stared angrily at Mai.

"No, we do not. I had my men search, but the tracks went stale in the woods."

"General Mai, I do not wish to hear more excuses. I want results."

"Then you should bring Commander Tren back in here, because he was just informing me of another alchemist. A powerful one." Mai stood a little straighter.

"Another alchemist? I thought her fathers were the only ones?" Gjanion's anger was replaced with confusion.

"As did I," Mai said as she walked around the king.

Mai poked her head out of the tent.

"Get in here," Mai said to Tren, who apparently was standing just outside.

"Mai tells me you encountered another alchemist," said Gjanion as they situated themselves around the table.

Tren looked nervously at Mai. "Speak, you oaf," Mai directed him.

"I…I met your grandfather," Tren said extremely quietly.

"Commander, I have very little patience. I would prefer if you saved the jokes," Gjanion said, crossing his arms.

"It's no joke, Your Majesty. I managed to follow one of the rebellion's carts and came upon a small team of them," Tren explained sheepishly. "We tried to capture them, but the old man that was with them got the better of us. He claimed to be your grandfather, Radion, and then went on to prove it."

"He proved it? How?" Gjanion asked, his eyes darkening.

"He…shared his memories with me. Things only Radion could have seen and known."

"If Radion is the only one who could have…" suddenly the king burst into laughter. "The rebellion really is getting desperate. That is rich, commander!"

"Sir, I don't understand. He showed me his memories. I can't explain why, but I am certain it is him," Tren said, defending himself.

"The wizard girl must have been nearby and manipulated your mind. That is clever, I will give them that!" Gjanion dismissed Tren's story.

"Sir, I don't think—"

"Commander, if my grandfather was alive, how could I be here? I am his reincarnation. In order for me to be alive, Radion must be dead. If he lives, that would mean I am no god, and if I was no god, could I do this?" Gjanion asked before firing a bolt of lightning from the top of his staff and out the tent's door. The bolt collided with a tree in a deafening *crack*.

"I…suppose not." Tren felt foolish and decided to leave the issue alone.

Gjanion turned to Mai. "General, this army rides at dawn. We will make haste after the rebels. There is no time to spare"

"Yes sir," Mai said as Gjanion left the tent.

Tren turned and began pleading his case. "Mai I'm telling you, it was—"

"I believe you," Mai said, unsure of why she said it. Something in her gut told her that Tren's story was right. Surprisingly, and for the first time in recent memory, Mai felt hopeful.

Chapter Ten
Darkness

"So you're saying my magic gets stronger and weaker based on where a star is in the sky?" Mara asked her father.

"Well, if your dad's notes are to be believed, it's not a star, but a planet. The Bright One does follow a unique pattern across the sky, so that makes sense at least," Gant replied.

"Okay, so what does that have to do with my powers?"

"Well…" Gant mused, "If The Bright One is a planet, then its distance from our own varies since its orbit is different from ours. It must be a magical source, or an amplifier or something."

"That's cool!" Rylan exclaimed.

Mara sat with this for some time. She did feel stronger at night, and when the moon was new the stars shone brighter. *Is my magic really related to a single point of light in the night sky?* They rode on through the morning in silence. As they rode into a valley, the air got significantly colder. The sun was still low in the sky, and their surroundings hadn't yet woken from the chilly night.

"The faster we ride the colder this is going to be," Rylan shivered and pulled her cloak tighter around her.

"We'll take it slow until the sun gets a bit higher," Gant agreed, riding just ahead of her and Mara.

They slowly rode on. Zhira's books had been put away as their sole focus became staying warm and staying alive. Winter had truly begun to engulf the landscape in its chilling embrace. The air was still and cold. No leaves were left on the trees. No wildlife made itself heard, save for some ravens searching for scraps. The landscape was grey, their breaths condensed in front of them and their horses, catching the rays of the sun as it began to peek over the hilltops and provide a little warmth.

Once the sky had gone from a miserable grey to a cheerier blue and the sun soared above them, they picked up the pace. A few animals stirred in the temporary sunlight to forage or hunt for food. Tigerdeer with their thick seasonal fur bounded between the trees, searching for any form of nourishment. Their pointed teeth allowed them to hunt for smaller game when the flora did not provide what they needed. Birds zoomed from tree to tree in search of any remaining berries or nuts that may still have been holding on for dear life. Mara watched a squirrel successfully run from a large brown hawk and bury the nut it was carrying before the hawk caught up with it again.

As they continued to ride, the sun dipped back below the hills around them and the world once again plunged into a cold, still state. The three of them wasted no time in setting up camp and getting a strong fire going, but as evening crept in and the stars came out, it was apparent they were ill-prepared for the bitterness of the long night ahead of them.

"W-w-we should probably g-get thicker gear," Rylan said, shivering.

"Dad, d-d-don't you have a p-potion to m-m-make us warmer?" Mara asked, her teeth chattering.

"I don't have a lot t-t-to work with out here." Gant shook as he motioned to the mostly barren landscape around them.

"Can't y-y-y-you make us feel warmer with m-magic?" Rylan asked Mara.

"Not unless you w-want me to start a fire inside y-you," she said, irritated at not being able to use her powers to help.

"It's t-tempting," Gant said, trying to crack a joke and keep their spirits up.

The three of them shivered through the night and stayed as close to the fire as they could without burning the few furs they did have, though Mara would have welcomed the sudden burst of warmth. When morning came and the sun crested the hills, they packed up and set off. Exhausted from shaking all night, Mara was eager to find any sort of town from which to obtain better supplies.

As the day warmed with the sun, Mara began to feel that their luck was running thin. She flipped through her old personal journal that she had retrieved when she and Rylan had gone back to Saros for her father's notes. Mara hoped that there was something in all of her experimentation that could help them fight this cold, but the longer she browsed, the more it added to her frustration. There was nothing. Feeling doomed to the cold, she angrily closed the book and stuffed it back into her saddle bag as they trotted along. She stared off at nothing in particular, feeling a sense of hopelessness that was only encouraged by the grey, barren, and bitter landscape they rode through.

"Look!" Rylan exclaimed, catching both Mara and Gant off guard.

Gant whipped his head around and Mara's heart skipped a beat. They had rounded a bend in the road and not far in front of them stood a small village. No more than two dozen stick-and-mud huts stood in a somewhat circular fashion with the road running right through the middle.

Gant kicked his horse onward. Mara and Rylan followed, catching up with him as they reached the first ring of huts. The three of them stopped their horses and dismounted, walking their steeds by the reins into the center of town. A few people meandered about, and as the alchemist, wizard, and princess approached, they hurried off to their homes. Rylan tried getting the attention of an elderly woman who didn't seem as afraid of the newcomers, and to their surprise the lady walked over to them aided by a cane.

"What can I do for you, riders?" The old woman looked like a sun-dried raisin. Her skin was dark and wrinkled, and her hair was nothing more than a few white wisps on the top of her head. She had a very stooped posture reminiscent of Radion's own hunch. Despite all of that, Mara noticed that the woman had the liveliest eyes she had ever seen: golden brown, wide, and taking in every detail they saw.

"We are in need of some warmer supplies than we currently have. I fear we were ill-prepared for our journey," Rylan spoke with the grace of a princess.

"We can certainly assist you with that," the old lady replied warmly.

"You would have our gratitude!" Rylan bowed politely. Mara liked this side of Rylan; she had a way with people.

"I would have your weapons," the woman replied in a sudden change of tone as she eyed their horses and the gear they carried

"I'm sorry, I don't understand," Rylan said, confused.

"We are happy to give you the supplies you need. In exchange, I ask that you stay until the new moon, which happens to be tomorrow night," the woman explained, staring at Rylan intensely.

"What need do you have of our weapons?" Gant asked from behind Rylan.

"Our village is plagued by a monster that has come every new moon for the last few years. We are not a village of fighters and would appreciate your help in ridding us of the nightmare that befalls us." The woman begged with her eyes, which broke Rylan.

"Of course we will help you," Rylan said reassuringly.

"Rylan, can we talk for a moment?" Mara finally spoke.

"Sure. Excuse me," the princess dismissed herself politely.

"We need to get to Varyn as fast as possible. For all we know, Mai is chasing us down as we speak," Gant said, referring to the general's words that first night over their fire.

"I know, but we need these supplies and these people need help. We can't take what we need and turn our backs on them. We can provide them relief from this creature," Rylan stood her ground, stubborn as ever.

"I admire your passion, I really do, but I think my dad is right," Mara said, trying to convince her friend.

"No. You're both wrong. I'm staying to help these people. I won't turn my back on people who need us. We did it in Saros—we can't let this be our story." Rylan looked close to tears.

"Saros didn't need us. Sari explicitly told us to leave. They—"

"No. They do need us," Rylan said, cutting Mara off. "Everyone does. I will not take what I need from these people without giving something in return. I am not my father."

"Is that what this is about?" Mara asked. "Not being like Gjanion?"

Rylan nodded. "He uses people for his own gain. He doesn't actually care about the kingdom. I don't want to be like that. Ever. I want to actually help the people of this kingdom.

"What's one night?" Gant shrugged. "Rylan is right. If we can help these people, then we should."

Rylan smiled and looked at Mara hopefully.

"All right, we'll help," Mara said, smiling a little at Rylan's enthusiasm and care for people.

"Wonderful!" Rylan clapped her hands together and returned to the lady.

"So what does this monster do?" Mara asked the old lady as she walked up beside Rylan.

"When the night is darkest, during the new moon, it appears. Silent and evil, it combs our town and selects its victim. We never hear it, we rarely see it, and when morning comes, one of our own is gone for good, stolen right out of their beds," the old woman explained, tearing up slightly.

"So it abducts people?" Gant asked.

"Yes. That's why there are so few of us left. We were once more than twice this size, but people are afraid. Afraid to bring children into this nightmare, afraid to live here, afraid of strangers. But this is our home, we cannot just leave."

"I understand," Mara said, Rylan's resolve rubbing off on her. She was angry these people had to live this way, scared in their own homes.

"We will do everything we can to help you," Rylan said softly, taking the woman's hand.

"You are kind, young one," the old woman smiled.

~~~

Gjanion sat in his tent alone. Radion could not be alive, of that Gjanion was sure. He looked down at his goblet and noticed that the win he had poured himself was nearly gone.

How has this happened?

He got up to replenish the mysteriously vanishing wine and as he walked by the entrance to his tent, he paused and looked out. A smattering of fires covered the grass as soldiers hunkered down for a meal and some banter. The light was amplified by the metal armor most still wore, ready for a fight at a moment's notice. Feeling confident, Gjanion smirked to himself and continued on towards the wine. This old man Tren had come across was an imposter and a liar. Gjanion knew he was a god reborn, he could feel it in every fiber of his being. He was surer of this than anything in his life. He was born to rule, and he would not doubt his
~~~

birthright on account of the lies of some senile old rebel.

"You called for me sir?" Commander Tren stood at the entrance of the king's large, purple tent.

"Yes. Come and sit." Gjanion beckoned the commander to a compact wooden chair beside his own. "You have been bested by magic, I wanted to ensure that you are unharmed and your mind has not strayed from the mission."

"Of course not, sir. I want to apologize, you were right. I was fooled by Mara and her magic and I admit that I was too proud to see it," Tren admitted remorsefully as the king handed him a goblet.

"It is of little consequence. Most are not prepared for the overwhelming power of magic. I myself have trouble controlling it at times. To be influenced by it is an inescapable fact," Gjanion said, draining his goblet in one gulp. There was no need for Tren to know the secret. Mai knew that he was no wizard, but Gjanion believed it was important for his right hand woman to know, just as Long had.

Tren politely took a sip of his wine and set it on the table. "So what do we do now? We don't know the rebellion's plan."

"We will go after them and hunt them down with the full force of this army and my powers. Nothing stands in the way of a god, it is my destiny to rule this kingdom, and rule it I shall." Gjanion got up to refill his wine again and stumbled slightly. He grabbed the back of Tren's chair for support.

"I have no doubt that you will prevail sir. The rebellion must be crushed into nothingness, but…" Tren paused, "what will become of your daughter?"

Gjanion returned to his seat, goblet again full of wine, and stared off towards the canvas wall. "My daughter…"

"Sir, I am no father, nor do I ever intend to be one, but I cannot imagine the pain you must be feeling at her betrayal. She was your only family for so long," Tren said, sympathetically.

Gjanion stood up, yelled, and threw his goblet across the tent, spilling wine everywhere. "She was all I had left!" Gjanion stormed around the tent angrily. "That damned wizard got into my castle and manipulated my own daughter to turn against me! Now I'm marching to who-knows-where, looking for a scattered rebellion because I'm the only one that can hold my own against…*her*! After twelve years, all that stands between me and my kingdom is some girl…some girl who has managed to steal my daughter, outsmart Mai, convince you that I am no god, and disappear!"

"We are still winning. We have the rebellion on the run. You said it yourself, they are scattered. We're pushing them to the edge," Tren said cautiously.

"That's what scares me, commander. A panicked animal backed into a corner will lash out with all of the ferocity it can muster. I fear we have yet to see the full capabilities of the rebellion or Mara's magic." The king began pacing, thinking of ways to up his advantage. "We need more power...I need more power. I cannot lose to her."

The two of them sat in silence for a moment, Gjanion continuing to help the wine disappear.

"The sword."

"Sir?" Tren did not understand.

"The sword! The sword! I need the sword! I have the staff and crown, but without the complete set, I am not what I could be. My grandfather harnessed the power of the relics together. I need to get that sword."

Tren grimaced. "That may be easier said than done. The sword is currently in possession of the rebel who claims to be Radion."

"Damn rebels."

~~~

Kei opened his eyes and stared up at the passing clouds. The cart rattled beneath him as Jerra pulled him and the remainder of their supplies towards Varyn. Kei tried to sit up but the pain was too much.

"Save your strength," Jerra said in a calm tone that worried Kei.

"Why? What happened? What's wrong?" he asked groggily.

"Your fight with that girl left you...hurt," Jerra replied, choosing her last word with care.
~~~

"What happened to me?" Kei asked as he pushed through the pain and attempted sitting up again.

"Easy, Kei. Don't overdo it out the gate!" Jerra called back from the horse.

"What are you…" as he sat all the way up, a sharp pain shot up through his spine and he fell back down as he cried out.

"Kei!" Jerra stopped the horse and climbed into the cart. She shifted some of the bags behind him so he could lay flat.

"What did she do to me?" Kei asked with tears in his eyes.

"I'm not sure yet. I'm no healer, but I fear there may be something wrong with your back," Jerra said, concerned.

"My back…" Kei lifted his head and looked down at his feet. His face bunched up in frustration and Radion looked confused.

"What's wrong?" he asked.

"I can't move my feet!" Kei exclaimed, anger building in his voice.

"Let's hope it's only temporary, love. We'll get you to Varyn as fast as we can and find you a healer!" Jerra said, getting back on the horse and picking up the pace slightly from before.

Kei laid his head back down. He was angry. He needed his legs, he needed to fight, and yet he had been bested by some girl with a stick. Kei tried to close his eyes and relax, but images of ghouls and the horrific sounds of Gladys being taken in the mist filled his mind and brought a fresh bout of tears. Beginning to feel the true weight of what they were up against, he wondered where Mara was. Did Rylan and Gant make it out too? Gladys was gone and they hadn't met up with Forbin after the escape from The Cave, as was planned. Kei felt hopeless. They were losing, and if they lost there would be nobody to stand up to the king and his armies.

Chapter Eleven
Power

When Zhira awoke again, he was unsure of how long he had slept. The room was lit exactly the same. His attempt to get up went better than the last time, managing to stand up and get out of the bed, but having to steady himself on the bed's frame when he got lightheaded. Zhira stood for a moment until his equilibrium came back to him.

He was dressed in a simple cream colored tunic and brown pants, and when he pulled back the folds, he saw a large pink gash across the left side of his chest.

Must've been some magic. Zhira thought to himself, hearing his voice. He made a mental note to be more careful of the thoughts he projected; this place did not seem to amplify all thoughts, just the ones at the very forefront of his mind.

Zhira walked towards the solitary door in the wall across from the bed, and stepped out into the hallway. The walls here were also made of the same glowing stone and were bare—no decorations or embellishments of any kind. Zhira hobbled slowly down the empty corridor, which opened up into a room with a high ceiling. In the wall across from him were a set of large doors, while to his left and right were hallways that both led to staircases. Zhira decided he needed a change of scenery and opened one of the doors in front of him. He stepped outside, not knowing what to expect from a planet that was not his own.

The first thing he noticed was that the grass was blue. It rippled like the surface of a lake in the light breeze. The second thing he noticed was pitch black sky adorned with more stars than he ever could see back home. They looked less like the pinholes in a canvas he was used to and more like swirling clouds of millions of tiny fireflies frozen in time. He looked up in wonder, his eyes tracing new patterns in the multitude of previously unseen stars. Some even had different colors, which he had never noticed before.

The sky above him played host to more than just stars; set low in the sky was a bright yellow moon and a smaller white one. The yellow moon was similar in size to the one he was familiar with back home, but the white one was less than half the size of its big sister and was oddly shaped. Zhira was startled to notice that he could see the smaller white moon moving.

That is Hertica, and her sister Iones, Eres said, startling Zhira with her sudden and silent appearance.

Why is that one moving and the other not? Zhira asked, still looking at the sky and not the goddess.

Because it is closer. Hertica was our only moon for a long time, then one day Iones came hurtling from the great beyond, jealous of her sister. It took most of Knorr, Dazel, and I's power combined to stop her from destroying our home. Now Iones dances around us, content to be closer than her sister is, the golden, silver-haired goddess explained.

Amazing… Zhira watched as Iones disappeared below the horizon, leaving her sister alone in the night.

He stood and gazed up at the incredible night sky for some time, attention captured by the sheer volume of celestial glow. Eres said nothing, floating patiently by his side as if ready to assist him in some task. After a while, Zhira seemed to remember where he was and turned his attention back to the goddess.

How do I get home? Zhira asked Eres.

We can return you at any time, Eres said, matter-of-factly.

What?! Zhira's heart nearly leapt from his chest.

We brought you here and we can bring you back just as easily. There remains, however, a single problem. If we returned you, the word would spread. Your people would think we could bring others back from the dead.

You can't, right? Zhira asked, longing to see his mother again.

No. We may be goddesses to you, but here we are simply magical beings not unlike your daughter. We are closer to a magical source and therefore have abilities not seen elsewhere, but we cannot bring back that which is gone. Eres floated beside Zhira as he began walking again through the blue grass.

What do you mean by 'magical source'?

This planet is a source of magic. Its core is pure crystal, and was once home to many incredible, brilliant, and magical creatures. Now it is home to only my sister and me, Eres explained.

The broken planet… Zhira thought aloud.

We have destroyed everything once, and will do so again if need be, Dazel said in reference to the tale as she appeared next to her sister.

Zhira stopped walking and took in the sight of both goddesses together. He had worshipped these two beings for most of his life, even celebrating one with a festival. Zhira realized he had so many questions for them both—about their planet, about being goddesses, about magic, and about his family back home. He felt the questions boiling over inside him but he restrained himself. He was tired, still healing, and needed their help. The last thing he wanted to do was overwhelm himself or them.

It is an honor to be in your presence, goddesses. Especially you, Dazel. Thank you for saving my life. I hope you have enjoyed our festival. Zhira tried to be reverent, but some of his boyish excitement bled through.

The festival is pure and beautiful, and Sari is quite the blacksmith, Dazel said in reference to the statue he had built for the festival twenty years ago.

What did you mean when you said you would destroy what you have created…again? Zhira nervously asked, though he felt he knew the answer.

Close your eyes, Eres said, and touched his forehead.

Zhira's mind exploded. He saw the invasion of The Cave. Mara and Gant helping others escape, Tren killing Hearth, ghouls taking Gladys, some girl he didn't know beating Kei before Radion saved him, and Gant almost dying in his sleep from a poisonous necrospider before being rescued by some healer in a town he didn't recognize. The rebellion was scattered, shattered, and on the run. Zhira felt a sense of despair as he watched his family and friends lose and flee.

Gjanion is winning. If he controls all of Kyros, his lust for power will grow beyond the borders of the kingdom. He may not be Knorr, but it does not matter now. The damage is done. Gjanion will not rest until he achieves the status he thinks he deserves, all because of what we did, Dazel said.

You're goddesses…or magical beings…or whatever! Heal me now and let me go help them, Zhira pleaded desperately.

We are unsure if we can send you back, Eres spoke, *your return would only add to the powers he and many others will strive for.*

Why did you save me? Zhira challenged them, forgetting for a second that he was talking to the goddesses he had worshipped for so long.

It was a moment of weakness, Dazel admitted, surprising Zhira. *I should not have interfered.*

The look on Eres' face made it clear to Zhira that the sisters had discussed at length the consequences of Dazel's actions. *Well you can't undo it,* Zhira said, unsure if that was actually a power they might have. *You may as well make the most of it.*

What do you suggest? Dazel looked at him hopefully.

Nobody knows I'm dead besides those that were in the throne room that night, and according to your visions, Gjanion thinks it was just some trick Gant or Mara pulled to aid their escape. Nobody has to know you're involved. Please send me back. Let me help. The secret will be kept and you two will be free and clear forever.

Secrets are what got your friends into the mess that they are in, Eres said defiantly.

Then what's one more? Zhira challenged, desperate to return to his family.

Dazel saw distress in Zhira's eyes. *Eres, would it be so right of us to hold this man hostage because I made an error?*

Do not put this on me as well. You are the one who intervened again, Eres scoffed.

You would withhold an asset from those trying to do right by the kingdom and its people? Zhira asked Eres bluntly. *Based on what you have shown me, they're going to need all the help they can get.*

Neither sister spoke as they weighed the possible consequences of Zhira's plan. Zhira couldn't be sure, but it seemed like they were communicating through some means that Zhira was unaware of. After a moment, Eres looked back at Zhira. *We will send you back.*

~~~

The moon was nothing more than a black disc in the starry night sky. The Bright One glowed prominently below it, surrounded by thousands of unknown worlds much farther off in the universe. Mara gazed up as she stood next to Rylan and Gant in the center of the small barely-town.

"Do you think they're watching us?" Rylan asked, talking about the goddesses.

"I hope so, we could really use their help," Mara replied.

Mara was worried about slowing their progress, but without any supplies to protect them from the biting winter winds, they were doomed if they continued towards Varyn. Now they stood together, the residents of the tiny village holed up in their homes awake and ready to call to them should they be attacked by the monster in the shadows. She gripped her dagger and looked around, trying to catch a glimpse of any movement beyond the huts.

"Hey Rylan?" Mara got the princess's attention.

"What's up?"

"Thank you for being right," Mara said as she pulled the wool cap tighter over her ears. "I'm glad your stubbornness and passion for people won out. Out on the flats, we would be icicles by now."

"You're welcome," Rylan replied, her cheeks red from the cold.
~~~

"Back in Saros, you were right too, you know," Mara continued.

Rylan sighed. "I know, but there was nothing we could do there. I wanted to help, but we would have endangered too many lives. People keep saying I have what it takes to be a great leader, but how can I lead if I can't even improve the lives of a few people?"

"Isn't that what we are doing now?"

"Sure, but it's…different. How are we to overthrow my father if we can't liberate one town? This is just an errand. Besides, what if I end up like him?"

"What we are doing here is still helping people," Gant chimed in. "That's what sets you and your father apart. You care about people. He does not. That's why you'd be better than him. You're pure-hearted and you acknowledge your father's mistakes."

"What about you?" Rylan turned to Mara. "You're the reason we are still in this fight!"

"If I took over, it would just look like a power struggle," Mara pointed out.

"That's true, we don't want that."

"No, and besides, we're going from town to town and you're making your mark on these people. Even if you can't help them in the moment, they know you care. That's worth something. Just think about it, okay?"

"All right." Rylan smiled softly.

"There doesn't seem to be much by way of a monster around here," Mara observed, changing the subject.

"Maybe we should split up and hide. The…whatever it is…might not make an appearance if it feels threatened," Rylan said, and Gant nodded in agreement.

"Find a spot to conceal yourself, but stay in view of each other. I don't want this thing sneaking up on one of us without the others knowing." Mara scanned the fairly empty square for any sign of a concealed location. She decided to duck down behind a couple of barrels beside one of the vacant huts. Gant took up a similar position directly across from her, while Rylan hid herself in the shadow of a building's overhanging roof.

The night was windless and quiet and the stars looked on in anticipation. The stillness made Mara uneasy but it also allowed for her and the others to pick out any noises that signaled the approaching nightmare. It was the coldest night they had experienced yet, but the villagers had held up their end of the bargain ahead of time, providing them with warm fur vests, lined leather boots, and some gloves and hats to keep them warm.

The hours went by and Rylan shifted from kneeling to sitting, groaning as her knees stretched out. Gant was sitting on one of the barrels, not trying very hard to conceal himself and playing with the tassels of his hat. Mara was nodding off as she leaned up against the wall of the abandoned building when she thought she heard the swishing of a cloak dragging through the fallen frosted leaves surrounding the few trees outside the village. She listened closer for footsteps and sure enough, very faintly, Mara made out the sound of something walking closer.

Rylan noticed too and got back up into a more ready position. Gant hopped off his barrel and hid behind it. The creature must not have noticed them, as it walked right through the center of the square towards one of the huts. Mara tried to get a better look, but the only thing she saw was a figure in a long, black, hooded cloak with boots to match.

She didn't wait. She pointed her dagger at the humanoid monster and shot a fireball directly at it. The sudden flash of light alerted the being to the incoming danger and it moved like a phantom out of the path of the flaming ball. It ducked under the fire, which hit the side of a hut and petered out. The monster turned towards Mara and extended a very human-looking hand. Suddenly, Mara was rising off the ground, weightless. Not expecting this, she began to panic and her eyes flashed blue briefly before the amethyst in her dagger took over and glowed a bright purple. The tip of the dagger exploded with lightning which barely missed the creature's head. Mara did not get a good look at the face as her lightning flashed, but she got the impression that it was human.

Rylan launched from her hidden position and swept the tall figure's legs with her staff. The creature fell backward, but grabbed Rylan by her fur vest and took her down with it. Mara fell back to the ground and caught herself, landing on the balls of her feet. She used the momentum to spring towards the attacker.

Gant stood up from behind his barrel and lifted his hands, fingers pointed down. The small drifts of snow nestled in the shadowy corners around the huts came to life and swirled around the feet of the fallen cloaked assailant. Its feet frozen in place, the cloaked being lit a fire in its left hand and worked quickly, melting its way out. Mara was nearly upon it, and was about to thrust the dagger into its back when the monster turned sharply and landed an elbow squarely in her stomach, knocking all of the wind out of her and sending her crumpling. Without hesitation, the creature swung back around and sent two large blasts of fire hurtling towards Gant. He managed to deflect the first, but the second found its mark, sending him flying back towards one of the huts, singing the fur on his clothing.

Mara managed to sit up and watched as Rylan fearlessly threw herself at the cloaked figure. She swung her staff, which was caught easily by the attacker's outstretched hand. Suddenly off her guard, Rylan threw a hand up quickly and, to Mara's immense surprise, her eyes began to flash with golden light. Snow came flying from behind her, throwing the monster's hood back and freezing him in place.

"Thanks," Rylan said, turning to Mara.

"That…wasn't me." Mara stared at her with huge eyes.

"What do you…" Rylan trailed off. Mara saw the weight of what just happened hit her friend like a ton of bricks.

"Your eyes glowed," Mara said softly, then far more excitedly, "Your *eyes glowed!*"

"They what?" Rylan did not know what to think.

Gant got up from where he had been thrown against a nearby hut. "Tanen?"

Rylan turned and got a look at the creature's frozen face for the first time and gasped.

"Tanen?!" Rylan exclaimed as Mara slowly got to her feet and melted the snow and ice around the healer.

"You three…what are you doing here?" Tanen asked, as he lit a flame of his own and melted off the rest of the ice that had encased him.

"Protecting this town from a monster that comes in the night and steals them…" Mara said, realization slowly dawning on her. Gant and Rylan made the connection too.

"Oh my goddess, you steal people for your blood alchemy?!" Mara asked accusingly. She had never fully trusted him. Feeling validated, her hands ignited with blue flames.

"You have to understand, I have tapped into something amazing. The blood of animals is good, but human blood is the most potent!" Tanen exclaimed, defending himself. "I can do amazing things—like heal your father's leg instantly—because of these discoveries!"

"These people are right, you are a monster!" Rylan exclaimed, holding her staff menacingly.

"No, please, listen to me! The blood must be fresh for the mixtures to work properly. I didn't have a choice. I have to take them alive and siphon what I need, otherwise my people would suffer," he said.

"You say that like it should sound logical to us," Gant said, glaring at Tanen. "You keep individuals as prisoners and slowly drain them of their blood so that you can heal your own people?" Gant asked, shocked by Tanen's egregious actions.

"Well when you put it that way…" Tanen replied.

"And how would you put it? Choose wisely," Mara threatened him as her flames grew, giving the village square a bluish hue.

"Our village does not have many resources, and the war has cut off what supplies we used to get from travelers. We are a poor town and make do with what we have. When I discovered blood alchemy, I never meant to be an evil person. I was only trying to help my people. You think this was my first choice? We don't have medicines, we don't even have an herbalist. I am all they have. Tell me you wouldn't do anything to help the people you loved, especially if it meant saving their lives." Tanen glared at the three of them.

Mara hesitated. She felt an odd sympathy fighting with her disgust at this revelation. Before she could say anything, however, Rylan spoke up.

"I would do anything for my family, but I wouldn't torture and terrorize innocent people. There are other ways to help those you love besides enslaving and ultimately killing someone else's loved ones." Rylan challenged him.

"Like what? What was I supposed to do? Pray to the goddesses to heal everyone? Do a half-assed job with the meager resources we have? This helps people…*my* people. Why shouldn't I take what I need to heal them? It's not my fault these people can't defend themselves!" Tanen shot back.

"It is the responsibility of those who have power to protect those who don't from those who would abuse their power. If you want to help your people, be my guest, but you will NOT make these people live in fear any longer and you certainly won't be taking any more of them for your disgusting practices!" Rylan yelled at the healer. The bitter winter wind suddenly began to pick up around them.

"You are a healer of wounds in your town, but a dealer of pain in this one. That does not make you a hero," Gant added his voice to Rylan's.

"You all are so naive!" Tanen exclaimed. "For the last twelve years, those with power have abused it to get their way! To control every life they come across. The king and his men end lives they deem unworthy and enslave the rest. This kingdom is becoming a prison for all who live in it. I am doing my part to survive, and if these people help me and my people do that, then so be it!"

"Naive?" Mara finally spoke up, and the tone in her voice had all three sets of eyes on her instantly. "You think we are naive? I watched my grandmother die at the hand of the king. My father was skewered through the chest with a sword while we challenged the king in his own throne room. We've seen countless rebels slain by the king's knights, and we've killed many of his soldiers ourselves. We are all that stands between total control by the king and freedom from him, so don't you DARE lecture us on the merits of power. Us three and those that are left of the rebellion are regrouping to face the king one last time. We are using *our* power to try and save everyone, including these people, your people, and you!"

Silence. Mara's face was red, even in the blue light of her fire. Mara stared at Tanen, aware that Rylan and Gant's eyes were locked on her. She did not waver.

"I will make this plain—leave these people alone and come with us to take down the king, or die right here, right now," Mara threatened Tanen.

"Mara, what are you doing?" Gant asked. "This man is dangerous! We don't know him."

Still staring at Tanen, Mara replied to her father, "I know that without his blood, this man is nothing. I know that if he's with us, he isn't hurting these innocent people. I know that the rebellion needs all the help it can get. I know that if he makes one false move, I'll burn him from the inside out."

Tanen had retreated into his cloak until he no longer had a neck. When Mara finished talking, he looked up at her. "Who *are* you?"

"I am..." Mara faltered. She was going to say 'I am the last wizard' but after what had just happened a few moments ago, she was unsure if that was true. *Had Rylan really performed magic?* Mara was unsure of what she saw, but there was not another explanation to be had. It would also explain Rylan's visions of Dazel.

"I am someone willing to risk everything," Mara finally said. "The king has lied to everyone. He is nothing more than a well-versed alchemist. He uses fear to win his battles, instilling a sense of hopelessness in his enemies—they're defeated before his armies even show up. Give up doing the same to these people, and I promise I won't kill you." Mara did not blink as she challenged Tanen.

"If you really think you can take down the king, I'll help you," Tanen said, looking cautiously at Mara. "I want this war to be over just as much as anyone else. It has ruined my town. Bringing about an end to it would be the best thing I could do for my town."

"I don't know if we can take down Gjanion, but I do know that if we can't, nobody can. I'm glad to hear you'll join us," Mara said dryly, putting out her fires and walking away to inform the old lady that the threat was gone.

Chapter Twelve
The Tale of the Goddesses

You must promise us not to tell anyone how you returned, Eres said to Zhira.

We want your kind to forget us. Help us become nonexistent and remove our influence from your world, not make it worse than it already is, Dazel added.

I will do my best, but don't you think that is a little extreme? Some people rely on you for a sense of hope that someone is watching over them. Gant and I sure did! Seeing this planet behave so uniquely in the sky was a significant sign to us that we were doing something right by ourselves, Zhira explained.

I appreciate your kind words, Zhira, but we are not goddesses, we are simply all that is left of a great tragedy, Eres spoke, her face unchanging.

What do you mean? Zhira was confused.

You know we banished Knorr, but do you know why? Eres asked.

He sought too much power, he caused others to go to war. He wanted recognition for what he had done and... Zhira's thoughts trailed off. He saw it—the parallel between Knorr's story and their own. The pieces began to fall into place in his head as Dazel began to explain.

Knorr is our brother. He, like us, was superbly gifted with magic. We lived in an era of great prosperity and peace, due in part to our brother and his magic. Before we discovered and honed our powers, our world was on the verge of collapse. Our planet was not inclined to support life in a way that was sustainable. Our people pushed it to the brink, utilizing and consuming all of its resources. Knorr helped grow our world into a rich, beautiful land full of life and magic at a time where it seemed that magic alone would never be enough to survive. Creative, inventive, and courageous, our brother devised new methods of using magic and applied them to the best of his ability. The lush landscape you see before you is a product of our brother's skills. He saved environments by regrowing local flora, saved many of our people from the brink of starvation by changing our atmosphere to amplify the effects of the sun and improve harvests, and eliminated crime almost overnight with his incredible powers and positive changes to the lifestyles of many.

But as is too often the case with success, greed follows like a shadow. Many of your kind often claim that power corrupts. I find this to be untrue. I believe that power attracts the corruptible, and Knorr was no exception. Knorr became obsessed with being recognized for all he had done. He claimed that had he not stepped in, our planet would have gone past the point of saving, and everyone would have perished. As repayment for his deeds, he asked to be made the ruler of our planet. While they were grateful, some of our people were wary of putting a single person in charge of our entire world. Others thought that the honor was just, and

Knorr was entitled to ask whatever he wished of the people who owed him their lives.

The back and forth eventually turned violent, and Knorr decided to give those on his side an advantage. Everywhere he could, he made sure that those who opposed him suffered. He began to reverse the things he had done to improve the lives of our people, claiming that if they were not grateful, then they had no right to what he could give. This made those who supported him fight harder to keep his graces, and caused those who opposed him to suffer. Knorr wanted one unified planet that bowed to him and his power.

Sounds familiar, said Zhira, thinking about what was currently happening back home.

Dazel continued, *Eres and I knew that if we did not step in, he would never be stopped. Only we, his sisters who share his blood, had the ability to put an end to the conflict. The war raged on for what you would consider decades, and many succumbed to the reaping of death. Knorr never realized that the continuous fighting would eventually leave him with no people to rule. Eres and I figured if we removed Knorr, we could save those that remained.*

Zhira sat in the blue grass and absentmindedly ran the blades through his fingers while he listened intently. Eres took up the story.

Using our combined power, Dazel and I stripped him of his. It took every bit of strength we had, but we succeeded. Knorr was nearly powerless. The only thing that remained of the powers he once had was the ability to reincarnate. We could not remove his nature from him, so we sent him to live out his days on your planet. Our hopes were simple: as the cycle continued, he would lose all proof of who he was and eventually forget forever, lost to the ravages of time.

And that didn't happen, Zhira said, referencing the current state of his home planet.

No, something occurred that, in our haste to banish him, we had not expected, Eres replied.

Knorr had the forethought to document his life which subsequently led to the archival of many generations of his reincarnation, Dazel said, grimly. *The knowledge survived, albeit haphazardly, and now Gjanion wrongly believes that he is Knorr. This is not the first time the knowledge of Knorr has threatened your world, but it is by far the most dangerous and that is all that truly matters. The knowledge you humans have of us as 'gods' taints you. You strive for something beyond your grasp and now it threatens to destroy your world as it destroyed ours. We did not destroy our home, Knorr did. By the time we tried to save it, it was too late. Those few that remained were imbued with so much hate and desire that they fought each other until this planet was devoid of life, consumed by the fires of war and greed. We are all that is left of a great tragedy. In order for your world to avoid the same fate and be better than we were, your kind must be rid of us. Forever.*

You have an opportunity to act this time! Zhira exclaimed. *You were too late to save your home here, but it's not too late to save ours. Gjanion is a terrible and delusional man who needs to be stopped. Who better to help ensure that happens than you two? We can't forget you, we need you.*

Eres shook her head. *If you remove the lust for our powers, remove the temptation, then there will be no more war for Gjanion, and those who come after, to fight.*

With all due respect, we are well past that, Zhira said, getting angry with the goddesses. *Gjanion is already knocking on the door of total domination of Kyros. He's already fought the war. Now he's just trying to clean up what's left. We have one chance to break his grip. We need to stop* this *war. You said that if anyone knows that you intervened it will change nothing. If it changes nothing, then intervene!*

You are a clever man, alchemist, Eres observed, her face breaking out into a smile.

And a pure soul, Dazel added.

So you'll help?

Eres and Dazel looked at one another, then nodded simultaneously. Zhira wanted to jump for joy, but held his composure in the presence of the two beings he had prayed to since he could speak. The three of them started back towards the crescent moon shaped building to prepare Zhira for his journey home.

~~~

Sari struck sparks into the kindling repeatedly until his forge began to glow a soft orange. He blew gently on the flames, enticing them to dance along the wood. They quickly spread to the coals below, and the giant clay oven began to radiate heat. The burly blacksmith grabbed a dented sword with a purple handle, one of the knights' blades, and stuck it in the forge to heat it properly so that it would not dent again. He was conflicted about making the knights' weapons
~~~

any better, but he could not help himself. Sari took too much pride in his work.

The sooner he got done with the tasks set to him by his very unwelcome customers, the sooner they would leave him to his own work. For the first few hours of the day, he repaired several pieces of royal armor and weapons. The sun rose and stayed low in the winter sky. A heavy snow had covered the street the previous night, and Sari could not help but think back to when Mara would plow the street in a matter of minutes, pushing the snow off of the road and into the alleys so the town could go about their day. He smiled as he remembered eight year old Mara standing in the cleared street, quite proud of herself.

Hoping she and Kei were still alright, he pulled out a project of his own and set to work. After a while, Keylon came down with a plate of cheese and dried meat for lunch and sat with him in the warmth of the forge.

"I'm sure they're taking great care of each other," Keylon reassured Sari as he conveyed his thoughts.

"We should be helpin' 'em. We should be out there," Sari said as he tore through a piece of jerky.

"Our people need us here. Could you imagine Rezzik trying to handle this occupation alone?" Keylon asked with a tone that implied she knew the answer.

Sari grunted in acknowledgement. Their eccentric governor and friend was no match for the likes of a royal garrison. If the knights wanted something, they took it for themselves. At first, Rezzik had tried to convince the people of Saros to be kind and courteous to their new guests. He had hoped that their hospitality would soften the soldiers over time, and lead to a more relaxed coexistence.

Unfortunately, when the people of Saros gave an inch, the soldiers took a mile. It had been Sari who convinced Rezzik to organize a more clever way to disrupt the militant presence. The two had called upon the tradespeople of the town individually so as not to arouse suspicion and directed them to slow down everything they did, and do it worse. The longer it took to mend helmets, sew clothes, and manufacture gloves and boots, the harder the lives of the soldiers would be. Meanwhile the farmers, who were in the middle of harvesting, stored away more food than usual—in unmarked containers hidden away from the town—to make their crops appear less bountiful. While the knights were sitting around grumbling about the state of things, Keylon scheduled secret deliveries of the excess foods to different residents of Saros to keep them well fed.

There was inherent protection of those involved in their plan: it wasn't an open rebellion. To the knights, it appeared as though everyone in town was either slow or bad at what they did. As the knights didn't have any other options, they had to be content with the purposely shoddy and slow craftsmanship that came from the limited number of craftspeople in town.

"I've made and stored enough weapons, why not gear up and go find our son?" Sari asked stubbornly.

It pained Sari to not be fighting alongside the rebellion, instead staying cooped up under the watchful eye of the knights day in and day out. He was practically bursting at the seams to take action, but he knew that their best chance was to continue their underground disruption.

"We can't endanger our people, not until the time is right. For all we know, the rebellion has a plan. If we take uninformed action, we could disrupt that plan," Keylon said, trying to calm Sari down.

"I know it don' make much sense, but I have this…this feelin'. We gotta fight back, take our home back," Sari argued as he scarfed down some cheese.

"We'll know when the time is right. For now let's keep our heads down and continue causing trouble," Keylon kissed him on his soot-covered forehead.

Sari nodded and the two of them finished the lunch Keylon had made.

~~~

Dazel, can I ask you something? Zhira asked as they walked out of her and her sister's crescent-shaped home.

What is it?

The sword that Gjanion stabbed me with, when he wielded it, seemed to increase his powers. He isn't a wizard, so…
~~~

So how did it work? Dazel finished Zhira's question for him. He nodded. *That sword is one of three relics that were created long before your kingdom existed. In the old times there were three kings, all wizards, who sought to protect their lands from invaders. They banded together and used an ancient magic that has long since been forgotten to bind gems to certain objects, imbuing them with magic. The wielder would be granted great power, regardless of whether they were a wizard or not, ensuring that magic could be used to defend their people long after the kings passed on.*

So these weapons give the holder, who can be anyone, magic power? Zhira clarified.

Dazel nodded. *Each relic maintains a specific kind of magic. The sword allows you to throw arcs of pure energy as you slash. The staff provides lightning to discharge at will, and the crown acts as an enhancer to any alchemy done by the user. If all three are in one user's possession, they provide a shielding aura around them, protecting them.*

How do you know all this? Zhira asked, looking back up at Dazel.

That is unimportant. Are you ready to return? Dazel asked Zhira as they stood in the waving blue grass.

I am. I'm ready to help save my people, my friends, and my family, Zhira replied with confidence

Sister, wait. Eres reached out and pulled Dazel's arm back as she reached for Zhira.

What is it, Eres? Dazel looked confused, which to Zhira was an odd look upon a goddess's face.

*Perhaps it is time for us to leave this world behind. This world; an empty shell of its former self, which has caused us so

much pain and isolation, has nothing more to offer us. Eres suggested.

Dazel stood motionless and thought about Eres' words. *You mean for us to go with the alchemist.*

I do, Eres confirmed. *We are as much a part of this as he is.*

You know what that will do to us, Dazel replied.

Wait, what will it do to you? Zhira suddenly began to worry.

We have the powers that we do because of our proximity to this planet. If we leave, our powers will dwindle. It is likely we will be far less magical than your daughter before long.

But you came and saved me, Zhira reminded her. *And you were fine!*

In a short amount of time, the effect is negligible. If we are to stay and assist, we will not have the magical capability to return here. We will have to live out our days on your planet. Among you.

You would really do that?

Eres nodded. *There is nothing left for us here. It is time for us to leave.*

Chapter Thirteen
The Flats

The sun rose as Mara and Rylan rode out of the small town, followed by Gant and Tanen. Now wearing gear far more appropriate for the weather, they were able to make much better time. Despite the previous night's revelations, Mara and Rylan had gone to bed shortly after their encounter with Tanen. Mara had not yet spoken to Rylan about her seemingly sudden ability to do magic, but she figured that the longer she waited, the more awkward it was going to get.

"I'm sorry," Rylan said to her as they trotted along.

Mara looked at the princess, shocked. "What for?"

"You were the last wizard, and I've taken that from you. I'm sorry," Rylan said, genuine regret in her voice.

"You're joking right? Do you know how exciting this is? There is another wizard! You have magic too! It's what you always wanted, right?" Mara could not believe Rylan actually felt bad given the circumstances. *She has spent her entire life wanting to be a wizard, and now that she is, the first thing she's doing is apologizing.* Mara was confused.

"This is *your* thing, though. I feel like I'm intruding," said Rylan.

"Goddess…that's nonsense! Stop apologizing. Between the two of us, we will be able to discover so much more!" *Why is she not more excited about this?*

"I suppose it is rather exciting, isn't it? But…I am not sure that I need it."

"What do you mean?" Mara asked, baffled by her friend's response. *Hadn't she wanted this her whole life?*

"I just…I don't need it to be the leader I know I can be. And I certainly don't want people to think that if I take the throne, that I took it by force."

"Your powers don't define you, your actions do. Look at your father. He is a very accomplished alchemist, but that's not what makes him terrible. He hardly even used his powers in his conquest—he gets others to do his bidding. Gjanion just uses his powers as a threat so that nobody challenges him. Just because you have magic doesn't mean that peoples' opinions of you will change. Mine won't," Mara said encouragingly.

"You're right, but I still worry. I looked forward to this for as long as I can remember. Now that I have it, I'm just…scared."

"Well that's why you have me around! Remember back when I was in my cell, and we were trying to better understand magic together? Where'd that hope go? That excitement I saw in your eyes every time you talked about it?"

Rylan smiled softly. "I guess I had become resigned to who I was, rather than hold out hope for something that probably wouldn't happen. It's just such a shock to finally have these powers I wanted. I almost can't believe it."

"Well believe it or not, you are a wizard now. You'll be able to do all the things I can…probably!" Mara said, trying to get Rylan excited. "Your powers could be entirely different. I have no idea."

Rylan's smile got bigger. "I could be the one to make the fires when we camp…"

"Too small, think bigger!"

"I can grow a beautiful field of flowers around the castle during springtime, make the hills a tapestry of color…"

"Better! Keep going."

"I could ensure that our harvest is always bountiful and that our people never go hungry in winter!"

"That's more like it!" Mara said, mirroring Rylan's growing excitement.

"You're right. How I use my powers is far more important. Thanks, Mara," Rylan said, now sporting a smile that brought Mara right back to their days in the dungeon. So innocent. So much zeal.

"What're friends for?" Mara replied.

"And my eyes glowed, you said?" Rylan asked.

"Yes. They glowed yellowish gold, the same as your normal eye color."

"So wizards don't *have* to have blue eyes," Rylan observed.

"I guess not," Mara mused. "Though I have met other people with golden eyes who aren't wizards, as far as I know. Blue is likely still a trait specific to wizards, but it's not the lone identifier."

"So what does this mean? Have I always been a wizard? Why is this happening? Was my mother a wizard?" Rylan sounded lost. "How did I not know? How did my father not know?"

"Maybe your mother was unaware of her abilities," Mara suggested.

"Maybe…" Rylan trailed off.

"So what do we know?" Mara asked. "Wizards can be men or women, but only women can pass down magic to their offspring."

"So a male wizard still needs to be with a female wizard to make little wizard babies," Rylan clarified.

"Right. We also know that blue eyes are a sure-fire sign of a wizard. They can have other colors—yours are golden—but blue means wizard."

"And," Rylan added, "if your father's notes are right, then the strength of the magic you and I can do is impacted by The Bright One. The closer it is, the stronger we are."

"That's so weird," Mara said, laughing as she spoke. "How does a planet influence magic?"

"No clue," Rylan said with a shrug. "But what I want to know is why are my powers manifesting now? Why was I not able to do it previously?"

"I have no idea," Mara admitted. "What has changed recently that might have unlocked them?"

"What hasn't changed lately? Abandoning my father, joining the rebellion, surviving attacks on our lives…even travelling a lot!"

"Speaking of which, what's our plan when we get to Varyn?"

"I don't know. We were supposed to meet up with the others after the escape and arrive together…but that clearly didn't work out," Rylan replied.

"I guess we just hope they get there safely." Mara's worry for Kei grew.

"Can't you access peoples' memories? Maybe try and find anyone nearby? We could be closer than we think," Rylan suggested.

"I can try, but don't hope for much. Kyros is a big place, and even though we're all going the same way, we took very different paths. Hold my reins." Mara handed her the leather straps to make sure she didn't veer off course.

Mara closed her eyes and focused, drowning out the world around her until there was nothing. Her mind was totally at peace, completely open to anyone's thoughts. She ignored Gant, Tanen, and Rylan's memories and reached further out. The bleakness that met her was disappointing, until she felt a searing pain and saw nothing but a flash of white light. She opened her eyes suddenly and yelled. Gant came riding up.

"What's wrong?" he asked.

"It's Kei. He's close by, and he's hurt," Mara replied, tears forming in her eyes.

She urged her horse into a full sprint and the others followed. The brief but intense vision she had gotten from his mind had been one of grief, pain, and hopelessness.

I've lost too many people. I can't lose you too.

She urged her horse to ride faster, and the other three kept pace. While Gant and Tanen seemed to be struggling to keep their horses going at full tilt, Mara noticed that the task seemed effortless for Rylan and Neela.

I wonder if that has something to do with her magic, Mara thought as they tore across the flats.

Eventually, they had to stop for the sake of the horses. While their mounts drank and rested, the four of them rubbed the coldest parts of their bodies. Mara could not feel her nose, Rylan was rubbing her toes, and Gant and Tanen were attending to some very blue ears and cheeks.

"Neela is a spectacular horse," Mara observed as she put her gloves back on.

"I know, we've always had a connection. I've always felt most comfortable on her back. Sometimes I think she can understand me," Rylan mused. "Maybe it's magic. Maybe it has been there all along."

"Wouldn't that be something!" Tanen said as he walked over. Mara had started a small fire to help warm them up before the next sprint.

"Indeed," Mara said coldly. She still did not trust the man.

Tanen seemed to read her mind. "Mara, I know you don't like me but I made my choice. I left my people behind. I'm here, I'm willing to stand up to Gjanion. I don't know what else I can do to prove to you that I am not a threat to you or your friends."

"Are you willing to die?" Mara asked him bluntly.

"Yes," he replied without hesitation.

"What if you come up against your own daughter? You said she went to the capital, maybe she joined the king's side. Would you kill her?" Mara challenged him.

"What is the point of this exercise? Do you want me to say I'd kill my own daughter in cold blood? Would that satisfy your worries about me?" Tanen was getting impatient.

"Mara, enough. He is here, and he is helping. We can take him if he becomes a problem." Rylan said.

"True, an alchemist against *two* alchemists and a wizard is pretty lopsided," Mara said, forgetting for a moment that Rylan was, in fact, a wizard.

"Actually…just the one alchemist," Rylan said, reminding Mara.

"Oh, right. Sorry, two wizards and an alchemist."

"Well technically, Rylan is both," Gant clarified. "She's had years of practice with potions."

"That does not matter anymore," said Rylan, somewhat somberly.

"What do you mean?" Tanen asked, his feud with Mara evaporating as interest in what Rylan was saying swept over him.

"I renounced alchemy when I abandoned my father, the king," Rylan revealed to Tanen. "That is his way of life. I decided it was not going to be mine as well."

Mara watched Tanen's expression soften. "I had no idea," Tanen said in shock. "I know it isn't the same, but Kyra left because she could not reconcile what I was doing with what she thought was right. I have always been proud of her for that, even if we didn't see eye to eye. What you've done is far braver, and I commend you for choosing the path *you* believe to be right."

Mara side-eyed Tanen as he spoke. Something about the way he had said that gave her pause. "So you think Gjanion could be right?"

"Only in his own mind. I don't agree with him, but I understand why he thinks he is right."

"Anyone can justify their actions with their own perspective," Gant chimed in. "But how your actions impact others is what really matters."

"I still can't believe you'd give up such an advantage, especially now," said Mara.

"I don't want to be like my father in *any* way. I can help win this war without any of the tools he uses."

"Good thing magic isn't one of them," Mara said, giving Rylan a wink. "Now, I don't mean to cut this off, but we need to keep moving. We need to find Kei."

The four of them quickly mounted their steeds and resumed their gallop towards Varyn. Mara didn't know where Kei was, but hoped they would run into him before they reached the city. The bare trees became fewer as they rode into the flats that preceded Varyn. The white salty ground they rode over reflected the sunlight from the clear blue sky. The brightness hurt their eyes, but eventually they adjusted, squinting heavily against wind and sun as they rode.

"How are we going to find anyone out here?" Gant yelled to his daughter as their horses raced alongside each other.

"No idea, hopefully we get lucky!" Mara shouted back.

They rode on until the sun thought about touching the horizon. Rylan, slightly ahead of the other three, slowed Neela to a halt and surveyed the landscape. Her eyes were met with the nothingness of the flat, white, salty ground. As the others rode up beside her, Rylan dismounted and let Neela wander to forage for any small and hardy shrubbery poking through the cold, cracked ground. Mara stayed in her saddle and continued to look around, hoping for any sign of Kei or any of the other rebels that had gotten away.

Gant had begun to set up tents when Mara cried out. "Look!"

Tanen, Rylan, and Gant looked up in the direction Mara was pointing and saw a small indistinguishable shape against the orange sky.

"That's got to be them!" Gant exclaimed, stuffing the tents haphazardly back into their saddle bag.

Mara didn't wait. She kicked her heels and her black stallion took off like an arrow let loose from a longbow.

~~~

A large crescent moon sat just above the horizon and illuminated the eastern sky while the west was still clinging to its last bit of orange sunlight. Mai stared out over the fires that dotted the surrounding landscape. The army was made up of hundreds of knights, dozens of squires, a few battlefield doctors, and a handful of farm hands to tend to the animals that helped pull carts full of supplies. She sat with Tren, Kyra, and Pike around a fire and listened to Kyra,
~~~

whom Tren had invited to sit with them. Mai was typically against squires mingling casually with the knights in off-hours. She felt that the separation helped push the squires, give them something to want to be a part of. Tonight, Tren had insisted Kyra join them, telling Mai that he had a good reason, though he would not tell her what that reason was. As Kyra spoke, Mai began to understand.

"My father is an alchemist, but more of a healer really. Our village is small, so people rely on him like most other towns rely on their herbalist or apothecary. One day he accidentally spilled blood into a mixture and realized it worked really well to help amplify the effects of the potion he was making," Kyra explained to them.

"So your father uses animal blood in alchemy?" Mai asked, intrigued. She had only seen Gant make a potion once, when they went after General Long, but she doubted he ever used blood in his concoctions. It didn't strike her as something he would consider.

"More than that. He uses human blood too," Kyra said, her eyes reflecting the fire.

"What?" Pike looked nauseous.

"My father discovered that blood makes potions more potent, but human blood was the strongest by far. He started by experimenting with his own—pricking his finger or something small like that. But once he learned that human blood was the strongest catalyst for his mixtures, he wanted more. He was doing incredible things with his alchemy, and the village was better off for it. In order to keep experimenting, he needed a source other than himself. I don't know where he got them, but he found…'participants' for his work." Kyra's inflection made it clear to Mai that these participants were not volunteers.

"So your father takes human blood and makes potions and other concoctions to help the people that live in your village?" Tren clarified, looking uneasy.

"Yes, and it's why I left. He tried his best to hide his methods from me, but about a year into his experiments, I eventually discovered his back room and the prisoner he kept here. It was a horrible sight, and I was disgusted by what he was doing. I freed the man— though I doubt he lasted long—and made my way to the capital to start my own life. I never thought I'd be a knight…er, squire…but it's better than living on the street," Kyra finished explaining to her superiors.

"Do you think you can replicate some of your father's work to help us even the playing field against the rebellion's alchemists?" Mai asked her directly, wasting no time.

"I do, but, cards on the table, I don't know how to use blood that well. I left pretty soon after he started those experiments. As Commander Tren saw, I've dabbled with using my own, and in very small quantities."

"There is another problem," Tren piped up. "I don't know how we would hide that from the rest of the army or the king."

"I agree," Mai said, backing him up. "The king can't know yet. This stays between us. Captain Pike, congratulations. I am promoting you to Commander. From now on you will report directly to me."

"Thank you ma'am, I will make you proud." Pike gave a respectful nod from where he sat.

"Tren, as Kyra is your squire, you will be her direct support. If she needs supplies beyond usual rations, make it happen. Find her a safe, isolated place to work."

The two men nodded, and Pike asked, "What if we're found out?"

"Let's hope that doesn't happen, Commander," Mai said, watching his reaction carefully. *Can I trust him? He was not on board with our plans last we spoke. Why the change?*

At that moment, one of the king's elite knights came up hurriedly to their fire. He was dressed in his black battle armor, holding his helmet in one hand and his sword in the other. Against the blackening sky, his head appeared to be floating where he stood.

"What is it?" Mai said, noticing his anxious look.

The man simply pointed to where the horizon should have been. Instead, there was a large grey blur that appeared to be growing.

"Suit up!" Mai yelled, unsure of what was about to happen. She had a sinking feeling in the pit of her stomach.

Knights were woken and the army of men and women began dressing quickly into suits of armor and grabbing their weapons. The stable hands corralled the horses and steers that pulled the carts and drove them to the middle of the camp.

"I want two secure lines!" Mai barked as she ran into her tent to grab her sword, and to change her left arm's attachment to its long, deadly blade. When she emerged again, knights were already lining up with large shields and metal spears facing the oncoming mist. The second line formed up behind them wielding swords, axes, scythes, and hammers. The remaining knights served as an emergency backup force. Should the line break, their task was to rush the gap and contain the leak.

"Ma'am, what are we facing?" one of the king's guards asked her.

"I've never seen them before, but this bears all the signs of…" a shriek in the night interrupted Mai. The guard gave her a worried look as she directed a few knights at her end of the line to curve back and semi-enclose the camp.

The mist began to blur out the sky above. The moon had disappeared. Mai looked up and watched as the last of the brightest stars disappeared behind the grey foggy curtain. Tren stood at the other end of the line, both swords drawn. Kyra stood next to him gripping her staff. The king remained in his tent, which was fortified by wooden boards and guarded by his five elite knights dressed in their menacing black armor.

Mai looked down the line as the fog got thicker. She lost sight of her men halfway down. A screech came from deep in the mist. The sound was blood-curdling, but if any of her knights were unnerved, they didn't show it. A shadow flashed past—a black blob against the grey curtain. One of her knights took a stab into the thick fog with his spear and hit nothing, but when he tried to pull his spear back, it did not budge. Instead, he was suddenly and violently pulled into the abyss so fast that he didn't even have time to cry out.

Mai watched as the knights sealed up the line obediently. They waited in the silence of the mist, anticipation building and nerves tightly wound. Nobody spoke. The only sounds came from the metallic clinking of armor as knights shifted their stances and readjusted shields. The fires they had left in a hurry crackled behind them.

Out of the mist, the black shadows came in droves. The ghouls rushed the knights and crashed into their shields. Knights began stabbing back and connected repeatedly with their slimy flesh. Mai was shocked by what they were up against, but quickly joined her soldiers in beating back the threat.

The line held as the ghouls' bodies piled up in front of them. More ghouls climbed over the mounds and tried to grab at the knights' shields and spears. When a few ghouls began breaking through the first line of soldiers, disposing of their shields and pushing past the terrified men, the second line would fight them off with their swords and hammers, securing the breaches. Seeing this, Mai adjusted their strategy to stay ahead of the onslaught.

"Form around the king! Fall back and circle up!" She called out.

In a fluid motion, the knights worked together to hold the line and move back, encircling the king's tent. As they did so, Gjanion stepped out of his tent, resplendent in his purple battle armor. His sudden appearance surprised Mai, but she said nothing as he walked clear of his tent and let loose a remarkable display of lightning and fire. The emerald in the head of his staff gleamed bright green as bolts of white-hot lightning exploded in all directions and connected with multiple ghouls at a time. Tren watched as the chain reaction that coursed through their bodies was so intense that they were fried where they stood, skin turning from a slimy grey to a smoldering black.

Gjanion didn't stop there. His other hand directed a torrent of fire over the heads of the knights that was not unlike waves crashing on a beach. The flames engulfed the ghouls lucky enough to have avoided the lightning, and in little more than a minute, the threat had been neutralized. Knights drove the remaining stragglers back as the bodies of the fallen ghouls dissolved and became part of the mist.

Tren came running full speed at the king and thrust his swords at him. Before Gjanion realized what was happening, each of Tren's blades whizzed past him and sunk deep into the chest of a ghoul Gjanion had not seen behind him. Wide-eyed, Gjanion turned to see the monster slump over and dissolve into nonexistence.

"Sir! What are you doing? We need to keep you safe!" Tren exclaimed as he sheathed his weapons.

"We need this army. We can't lose good men and women now. I'm simply protecting my people," Gjanion replied.

"That was incredible, sir." Mai walked up with the newly minted Commander Pike. "Tren, please see that the captains count their men." Tren nodded and walked away with Kyra in tow.

Mai was shaken, but she didn't show it. To her, it was obvious that Gjanion had prevented a much larger disaster. Their swords and shields were no match for the likes of creatures like that.   "You have never interfered like that before," Mai said to him as knights began to disband and return to their tents. "Why now?"

"Because I need this army," Gjanion answered bluntly. "We cannot afford to lose a single soldier now."

"We had the situation under con—"

"No! Mara has been one step ahead of me this entire time. She was IN MY THRONE ROOM and managed to escape! She was trapped in a CAVE, and yet she rode free! Mara is the only true threat to my reign, and I WILL SEE HER DEAD."

"So all of this is about Mara? It's all for just one girl?"

"She's not just some girl. You know that! She's all that stands in my way. Without her the rebellion is nothing!"

"So you would have your whole army die to take down a single girl?" Mai asked, astonished.

"Soldiers die. That's war, General."

"I know that, but I also know these knights of yours look to you and believe in you. You can't just dismiss their lives like that. Especially in pursuit of one person."

"I am the king and they are my army. Varyn is a stronghold, and we will need every knight in our ranks to take it, let alone face Mara. Individual lives are of small importance. Securing this kingdom under my rule is what is most critical," Gjanion said with conviction. "Tonight would have been a waste of lives. I cannot take Mara alone—the fight in the throne room proved that. I am not a one man army."

"You were tonight," said Mai, looking over the scorched landscape that now surrounded the camp.

"I will do all I can to win, general," Gjanion said with a depraved look in his eye. "Whatever the cost.

"If they all die in your quest to defeat Mara, who will enforce your reign?" Mai asked, hoping he would understand.

"When Mara loses, the hope of resistance dies with her. Nothing will stand in my way ever again. Nothing. I won't need an army. Nobody will even think of betraying me!"

The realization hit Mai like lightning. Gjanion was becoming desperate and unhinged because Rylan had betrayed him after meeting Mara. Once the two had become acquainted, something in Rylan had changed, and she had defied her own father, joining Mara and the rebellion. Mai saw clearly the pain and desperation that Gjanion tried to hide.

Without a word, Gjanion turned and, with the fires reflecting in his purple armor, retired to his tent, leaving Mai to walk back to hers. As she did, she looked around at the men and women who made up their forces. This was her army, the one she had worked so hard to lead. These were her soldiers.

Mai's heart sank, and by the time she returned to her tent, her jaw was set in frustration. Gjanion would throw all of this away to get to Mara. He was going to destroy this army and possibly even Kyros itself—everything Mai had devoted her life to—just to satisfy this one obsession. Mai's anger flared as she thought about his plan. Varyn was a well-fortified city, and the flats would offer them no protection from its defenses. Gjanion's plan was blindingly bad, but he didn't care. He only wanted Mara. Mai closed her eyes, surprised at herself for harboring so much anger towards her king. But slowly, reality came into focus. Gjanion had no plan, he only wanted Mara dead.

Meanwhile, Gant, Mara, Rylan, and what remained of the rebellion were doing all that they could to save the kingdom. They claimed to want to keep it safe, and Mai finally began to understand what they meant. Gjanion had no actual regard for the kingdom. His vanity and obsession would bring it to ruin. If she really cared about this army, this kingdom, and the people they had sworn to protect, she had to save them. She had to save them from Gjanion.

Chapter Fourteen
Alone

Forbin woke up as the sun poked through a hole in the tent and shone directly in his face. He pushed himself up and rubbed the tiredness from his eyes. The night had been rough. Alone, he had nobody to share being on watch with, so he had to take his chances when he slept. He was tired of being cold, too. The only time Forbin made a fire was to cook, and he kept it small to avoid drawing any attention. The rest of the time he lived in darkness and survived each night with a bit of luck.

As he rolled up his tent, he looked around. He'd lost count of the days since the escape from The Cave, but he imagined he must be close to the city by now. He hadn't seen a tree in three days. The salt flats were boring, empty, and white. *What I wouldn't give for a conversation with another human…or something to drink other than water.*

After the events that had played out at The Cave, Forbin had ridden off into the woods with a few other rebels. Their job was to protect the rebellion's horses and see them safely to Varyn; there were roughly a dozen of them, and were some of the few assets they had left. The woods had been infested with teams of knights and the small team of riders he had been with was quickly broken apart. Without looking back, he rode as fast as he could away from The Cave. There was nothing he could do for the others. All he could manage was making sure he got away with his horse and supplies. He'd seen fires roar to life in the trees, heard the screams of terrified rebels, and the metallic *clang* of sword against sword as they tried to escape.

Once he was sure he was free of the conflict, he settled his horse into a trot and continued through the woods. Forbin noticed how beautiful the sun's rays made the late-fall colors look. The canopy took on the appearance of a mosaic stained glass window. Reds, yellows, and oranges all mixed together to form a stunning display as he stopped to set up camp for the evening. It was hard to tell how much ground he had covered, but he felt sure that nobody would find him. Depleted from the day's events, he quickly fell asleep in his tent, not even bothering to make himself dinner.

The next few days had been far less exciting. Forbin settled into a routine: get up, ride, break around noon to eat and rest his horse, ride again, stop to hunt, ride until sunset, make camp. As he rode towards Varyn, the trees became scarcer and hunting became more challenging. Once Forbin was well into the salt flats, he relied solely on his rations.

Now, on what he thought was likely his thirteenth day after the escape, he packed his horse and rode east. The morning light was blocked by storm clouds, and soon a cold rain began to fall. Forbin grumbled as he pulled his cloak up over himself. He hated winter rains, preferring instead that it fall as a beautiful white blanket that fell on the world. This insufferable grey sheet that came down instead soaked him and chilled him to his core.

Miserable and wet, he rode on until he spotted something that made him feel warm inside. On the horizon, blurred by the falling rain, were the gates to Varyn. Forbin urged his horse to speed up as he approached his destination. Exhaustion was replaced with elation and his misery gave way to happiness. He thanked the goddesses for the beautiful tall gates and the city behind them.

Forbin approached the gargantuan metal doors that were taller than anything he'd seen in his life, aside from the king's castle. Stationed at the top were several guards armed with bows and arrows. As he got closer, he noticed a smaller door carved into the much larger gates. He rode up to it and, seeing no other option, knocked.

The door opened and out stepped a knight dressed in standard silver armor. He sported a blue cape with white trim and a white sunrise stitched into it.

"How may I help you, sir?" the knight asked Forbin.

"Greetings," Forbin said as he dismounted. He gave the knight a slight bow. "My name is Forbin, I am a commander in the rebellion and I am here to seek refuge and an audience with your leadership."

"You have no allegiances to the king?" the knight inquired.

"Of course not!" Forbin exclaimed. "I'm a rebel, I'm working to end the reign of that monster."

"What is your purpose for your audience with our leadership?" The knight continued to ask Forbin questions.

Forbin was impatient to get out of the rain. "Judging by your questions, I'm going to assume that I am the first of the many rebels making their way to this city. I'm here to request asylum for myself and them and ask for help in defeating Gjanion once and for all. Our backs are against the wall and we have nowhere else to turn," Forbin pleaded with the knight.

The knight surveyed Forbin and his horse as if looking for any reason not to let him in. After a moment, he replied. "Very well, you may enter our city. I will send word to our queen that you wish to see her."

"Your queen?" Forbin asked as the knight led him and his horse through the small door he had come from.

"Yes. In the wake of Gjanion's campaign against freedom in Kyros, Varyn has declared itself an independent city. King Gjanion does not rule us, we rule ourselves," the knight explained. "As such, we elected our own leader. She and her advisors now oversee Varyn and the People of The First Light."

"People of the what now?" Forbin asked as he walked behind the knight through the thick wall's tunnel.

"People of The First Light. The sun rises on us and our beautiful city before any others," the knight said, somewhat shortly.

"Well that's…literal." Forbin observed.

They exited the tunnel and stepped out into a large courtyard. *A beautiful city indeed*, Forbin thought as he took in the large, sprawling mass that was Varyn. Twice the size of the capital, Forbin could tell that it was home to thousands of people. Buildings were made of marble and other light colored stone and stood at least three stories tall. Forbin looked around and saw no carts for vendors of goods. Each seller either had a shop or their own permanent stall attached to what Forbin assumed was also their building. The street that led into the city from the main gates was wide and bustling with activity. People dressed in brilliant colored robes and togas moved from shop to shop exchanging goods and talking merrily.

So this is what peace looks like, Forbin thought.

These people were not worried about supplies nor did they fear for their lives each day as Forbin had for so long. He saw genuine happiness, glee, and whimsicality in these people's faces. They were more worried about a good story or trading apples for cheese. They did not consider how many people each loaf of bread could sustain. They did not worry about drawing attention, about who went where and when. Forbin felt sorry for these people. He knew what his presence would mean to them, how their lives would change as soon as the rest of his friends arrived, and the king behind them. This city was a haven, an oasis, and he was going to be personally responsible for its ruination.

The knight led him over a bridge that spanned a small, natural canal and down a side street that was equally as large and as beautiful as the one he had just been on. The streets were all paved with what appeared to be shells mixed into some sort of hardened paste. It was beautiful and smooth. With his horse in tow, Forbin followed the knight down two more streets until they came to a large, grey building four stories tall. The windows had no glass in them but had beautiful light blue shutters that looked thick enough to keep out any weather.

"You'll be staying here," the knight gestured to the building.

"Thank you, sir. I look forward to meeting with your leaders," Forbin replied, suddenly realizing how tired he was.

"I shall call upon you tomorrow with word from the queen." The knight turned and walked back from whence they had come.

Forbin tied his horse to the post outside the building and pushed open the door.

"Good day, young man. How can I help you?" asked an older lady with grey streaks in her black hair, wearing a bright blue toga tied with a white rope.

"Oh, hello. I was told by the knight that escorted me here that this was where I would be staying," Forbin replied, realizing he had no money on him.

"Of course dear, this is where most refugees stay until they can find something more permanent."

"I don't have any money…" Forbin began but the lady shook her head and smiled.

"You're in Varyn! The queen makes sure that anyone seeking asylum is taken care of until they get on their feet."

"Really?" Forbin asked, bewildered. It sounded too good to be true.

"Yes, dear, really. It does not do well to not help newcomers get on their feet. We find that putting in the time to help people now pays off in the future. Is it not better to start with something than have to work from nothing? Those who choose to stay repay their debts by being supportive and caring members of our city. Now, let me show you to your room. Never mind your horse, our stable hand will take care of him," she said as Forbin started to move towards the door.

Forbin turned back and followed the short, skinny woman up the stairs to the top floor of the building. She handed him a small brass key. "This will be your home for now. Please make yourself comfortable."

Forbin thanked the lady and entered the room. It was nothing extraordinary, but it was far better accommodations than the stone dome he had lived in back in The Cave. The door opened to a simple square room with a table and four chairs set in front of a brick fireplace. A door on the left led to the bedroom, where a bed with green blankets and two feather pillows was situated on the far wall. In each of the two rooms there were windows overlooking the street. The building was positioned near the top of the street, so Forbin had a decent view of most of the activity going on below. What he hadn't expected to see was the ocean.

Forbin had never seen so much water in his life. He had known Varyn was a port city but he hadn't been prepared for how vast and incredible the ocean was. The street that the building was on sloped down towards the docks, granting his top floor room a view of the great expanse that was the sea. The blue water shimmered in the sun beyond where the grey rain clouds ended, while boats slowly made their way in and out of the harbor. Forbin looked out and couldn't tell where the sky and sea met. It was simply blue.

He put his bag on the table and sat down on the bed. Within minutes, tiredness swept over him and he was fast asleep.

~~~

When Forbin awoke again, he wasn't sure if he had slept for an hour or a day. His confusion was
~~~

answered by a knock at his door. He opened it to find the knight who had escorted him here.

"Good morning, sir," the knight said.

So I did sleep through the night, Forbin thought. He gestured for the knight to come into the room.

"Thank you for the invitation but this will be brief. The queen will see you. Today." The knight stood stiff and straight, helmet under one arm as he delivered the message.

"Oh, that's great!" Forbin exclaimed. "Where exactly do I go?"

"I am to escort you as soon as you are prepared."

"Oh, okay. Could you give me a moment?" Forbin asked the knight, realizing he hadn't changed his clothes from the previous day, nor had he bathed in weeks.

"Take the time you need, I shall wait here," the knight replied stoically.

"Thank you. Are you sure you don't want to wait inside? Seems a bit awkward to just stand out in the hall."

"I'm fine," the knight said.

"All right," Forbin said, closing the door. *Strange man,* he thought.

He got himself together quickly, rinsing in the small wash bin in the bedroom and putting on a fresh dark red tunic and brown pants. When he returned, he found the knight waiting patiently outside his door as promised.

"Ready, sir…?" The knight asked, realizing he didn't know Forbin's name.

"Forbin."

"Sir Forbin." The knight gestured for him to follow.

"Just Forbin is fine. I'm no knight!" Forbin chuckled. The knight nodded respectfully, though he looked uncomfortable with the informality.

They walked out onto the street and back towards the main gate. When they got to the road that led to the big metal doors, they turned towards the center of Varyn. They walked for some time, passing shops selling everything from horseshoes to fruit cakes to cabbages to leather satchels in colors Forbin had never seen. They turned onto another street that had less shops and more dark-colored buildings.

"The color of the building is indicative of its purpose. Shops and stores are white, homes and dwellings are of a greyish color, and buildings that host services such as the blacksmiths or cobblers are darker still," the knight explained without prompting. "Our queen's estate is this way."

The knight led Forbin down another narrower street that opened up into a giant cobblestone courtyard. Overlooking the vast square was a modestly sized but certainly regal building that stood two stories tall and extended halfway around the square. In front were knights dressed similarly to Forbin's companion.

Their armor was shining silver and they all either wore capes that matched the knight's or had shields emblazoned with the white rising sun against a royal blue background.

"Welcome to Her Majesty's estate, The Pearl House of Varyn. This is where all of our leaders work and meet to run the city." The knight gestured to the building in front of them. It lived up to its namesake. The building was almost blindingly white, even in the gloomy morning light. It had no embellishments save for the two white columns ornately carved to look like squidhorses that framed the grey double doors. Their long snouts pointed up at the ceiling while their tentacles wrapped around each other to form the base of the column. The rest of the building was solid white with shutters to match. Forbin found the building imposing but not threatening.

He followed the knight up the steps that led down from the doors to the square, and entered behind him. The entry hall was modest, with a painting of the sea on the wall across from the doors, and a set of equally sized blue double doors off to the left. To the right were some grey chairs for those waiting for an audience with whomever they'd come to see.

"The queen will be with you momentarily," the knight said before disappearing through the doors to the left.

Forbin took a seat in one of the chairs along the wall to his right. It was a nice building and a nice city. He liked it here. The painting of the sea caught his eye and he stared at it for a moment. As he looked, he noticed more and more details. There were ships peppered amongst the small waves. A whale with a single horn swam below. To one side, framing the picture, was a woman on the bow of a ship staring over the whole scene. Forbin stood up and walked closer to the painting. It was surprisingly detailed and impressively done. He was so mesmerized by the image that he almost missed the doors opening to his left.

"The queen is ready for you," said a different knight than the one who had escorted him here. He wore blue armor with the same white sunrise on the capes and shields of other knights emblazoned on his chest.

Forbin straightened his tunic and walked through the doors, which closed behind him.

Chapter Fifteen
Reunion

Two knights marched by as Litik closed up his store for the evening. The days had gotten significantly shorter as the air chilled and the leaves had fallen one by one from their branches, littering the ground with their brittle, brown corpses. The sky was already showing stars as the sun made its nightly retreat behind the trees, the only reminder of its light being the faint orange glow of the clouds to the west. Litik placed the key in his pocket and walked around the back of the building to another door. He unlocked it with a different key and entered, shutting and locking it behind him before ascending the short set of stairs.

His home was modest in size but eccentric in furnishings. Being the only one who lived there, Litik didn't need much space, especially as he spent most of his time in his shop. There was one window centered on the far wall that overlooked the street, which offered little light. To compensate, Litik had spared no expense in acquiring the most ornate and peculiar candelabras to help light each room. On the table in the center of the room stood a piece made of polished silver that held five curved candles, all at different heights. The stand next to his overly stuffed blue armchair played host to a unique piece made of a tigerdeer antler whose prongs had been hollowed out to hold candles. Hanging from the ceiling was a chandelier he had asked Sari to make. Made of lighter metals so it would not fall and crush him, it took up more space than necessary and held twenty total candles split between two tiers.

None of it matched, but Litik didn't care. He liked them, and that's all that mattered. Once he had finished lighting all of his candles, he entered his bedroom through the curtain that separated it from the living space and changed into a comfier night shirt made of orange-dyed cotton. He reemerged and started heating a kettle of water for some tea before picking up the book he had been waiting all day to keep reading. The blue armchair enveloped him as he sat down and returned to the fantastical futuristic world he was so obsessed with. A few moments later, the kettle began to whistle and Litik, being so engrossed in the novel and the chair, almost didn't hear it. With some effort, he escaped the chair and poured the steaming water over the ground leaves that had been waiting patiently in his wooden mug.

He turned back around, hot tea in hand, and was ready to dive back into the novel. What he wasn't ready for were the three strangers suddenly standing in his living room.

~~~

"KEI!" Mara screamed as she, Rylan, Gant, and Tanen came upon the single cart trundling along the bleak and barren landscape. The sun had set as Mara and the others raced towards the speck they had seen on the horizon, but Radion had lit a flame in the back of the cart to keep them warm while they continued moving towards Varyn, making them easy to follow. As they reached the cart, Mara dismounted her horse mid-stride and hurled herself onto the back.

"Careful!" Radion exclaimed as the cart lurched under the sudden addition.

"What happened to you?" Mara asked Kei, ignoring the old king.

"I got into a fight…you should see the other girl," Kei grinned weakly.

"We had a run in with Commander Tren and a knight who is quite impressive with a staff as well as potions," Radion explained.

"Potions? You mean the army is using alchemy now?" Gant asked, a look of surprise and concern on his face.

"No. Judging by the commander's reaction, I'm guessing he didn't know this girl was an alchemist. She only pulled it out when I stepped up to challenge her. She beat Kei with her staff." Radion leaned back against the cart's front edge.
~~~

"Can this wait? Can we focus on Kei please?!" Mara asked, angrily.

"Sorry," Gant and Radion said in unison.

Mara looked down at Kei. He was clearly in a lot of pain, though he did his best to mask it in her presence. His legs were limp and Mara could see on his tunic where blood had dried around the wound on his back. *I could have lost him. I needed to be there. I got lucky this time.* Mara pushed these thoughts out of her mind and focused on Kei's injury. Suddenly, she rounded on Tanen.

"Heal him," she said, commandingly.

"Sorry?" Tanen looked confused.

"Show us how you used your skills to help your people. *We* are your people now. Give me a reason, a *real* reason, to trust you." Mara did not blink.

"Let me see," Tanen said as he bent down to examine the extent of Kei's injury.

Tanen touched his legs in several places and asked if Kei could feel any of it. Kei shook his head in response. The blood alchemist began examining Kei's hips and back, and when he found where Kyra's staff had connected with his spine, Kei let out a blood curdling scream of pain.

"Can you fix him?" Mara asked, still trying to come off as menacing, despite her overwhelming worry.

"I don't know if I can fully repair the damage, but I think I can help," Tanen replied.

Using a mortar and pestle he found in a bag, he crushed a pink berry into a mixture of leaves and it began to glow a soft purple as he pricked his own finger and added a few drops of his blood. Tanen continued crushing the mixture until it was a smooth paste and then asked Gant and Mara to help flip Kei over, exposing his back. Tanen smeared the paste until his entire lower back glowed purple. Gant watched with wide eyes as dark purple lines began to develop in the paste.

"What's happening?" Kei asked, unable to see. Gant looked at Tanen with the same question plastered on his face.

"The dark purple lines you're seeing are a mirror of Kei's bones inside his body. The light purple is his muscles, and the white are nerves. It allows me to see inside him without cutting him open," Tanen explained.

"That's…amazing," Gant observed.

"Thanks, but it's only part of the process," Tanen said, frowning as he looked at the complex weave of purple lines on Kei's back. "That bone there is broken and I'm guessing that it's pushing on this nerve here hard enough to disable any use of his legs."

"Can you fix it?" Rylan asked, worried.

"I don't have the necessary ingredients to make something strong enough to heal a bone, let alone pull it back into place," Tanen said regretfully.

"I can," Mara said suddenly. "I can fix it."

"You…what?" Gant asked in disbelief.

"I can fix him. Dad fell down the stairs once and broke his leg. I fixed it on impulse. I couldn't see what I was doing inside him, I just acted on what felt right in the moment. Having a map will make it even easier," Mara said confidently before pulling out her dagger, figuring she should do anything she could to help concentrate her powers.

"Mara, are you sure?" Kei said weakly.

"I'll have you better in a minute. It may hurt a bit," Mara replied, focusing on the pattern of lines on his back.

She was locked in on the broken bone. She could feel where it was, and where it wanted to be. Mara's eyes flashed blue before the amethyst began to emit a steady bright purple light. Kei screamed in pain as the bone moved along his insides. Mara ignored his cries and guided the bone back to where it was supposed to be. The white line that marked the pinched nerve moved with the bone until they were both lined up again in a much more natural looking position.

Mara breathed a sigh of relief. Now all she had to do was fuse the bone. Needing more raw power, she put her dagger down and placed her hand on his back. Kei screamed again, and Mara's eyes shone blue as she poured pure magical energy into the bone and fused it back into one piece. When she was done, she sat back, exhausted from the concentrated effort. When she had healed her father's leg, the adrenaline had given her more energy than she could have wanted. This time she had needed to muster all of the strength she could to pull it off.

"That was incredible!" Jerra exclaimed.

"Truly remarkable," Tanen added, genuinely impressed.

"Kei?" Mara ignored them and bent down next to his face. "How do you feel?"

Kei groaned and rolled over on his own. He pushed himself up into a sitting position with significant effort and sat looking at everyone crowded around him.

"Like an animal in a cage. Could you all back up a bit?" he asked politely.

They all took a step back and gave Kei some breathing room. Mara looked down at his feet and waited to see if her efforts had paid off. Kei turned one foot and then the other, and everyone cheered as if he had just won them the war.

"Thank the goddesses," Mara said, finally relaxed.

"No, thank you," Kei smiled and pulled her in for a kiss.

"Whoever did this certainly did a number on you," Tanen said.

"Didn't you say the girl who beat him used a staff?" Rylan asked Radion.

"I did, yes."

"Was the girl blonde? Did her staff have metal studs in it?" Rylan asked.

"Those are specific questions…but the answer is yes, to both," Kei answered.

"I encountered her during the escape. She's a menace with that staff," Rylan said, lifting the side of her tunic and revealing a dot-patterned bruise that looked like it might never fully heal.

"There is something else. The girl did something to a potion I had never seen, nor even considered, until just a moment ago when this man here did it. She added her own blood," Radion said.

"She what?" Tanen asked, stunned by the news.

"Who, may I ask, are you?" Radion asked, wary of the newcomer.

"This is Tanen, he's an alchemist like us," Gant said, introducing the newest addition to the rebellion. "Tanen, this is Radion, the old king of Kyros and leader of the rebellion."

"It's an honor, my liege." Tanen bowed.

Radion sighed. "There is no crown upon my head. I am no king."

"Sorry…sir," Tanen said tentatively. "You said this girl added blood to her potion?"

"I did."

"I've never known another alchemist to use such a technique…other than myself," Tanen explained. "Now it seems my daughter, Kyra, has taken up the skill, despite her previously staunch disapproval of it."

"How do you know it's her?" Rylan asked.

"There are not many people in this kingdom willing to use alchemy at all let alone openly in front of the king's knights. My daughter is talented, but she is also bold. She showed herself and her forbidden skills to a commander in the king's army. It's her," Tanen smiled, though Mara noticed a sadness in his face as well.

"This is becoming quite the family affair," Radion said.

"Indeed," Tanen agreed.

"How did you become acquainted with our friends here?" Jerra asked Tanen, sitting backwards on the horse that had been pulling the cart.

Together, Tanen and Gant explained how they had met, sparing no detail. Gant recounted his run-in with the necrospider, and Tanen explained what happened in the village and why he had been studying blood alchemy. When they finished, Radion looked at the new member of their team intently.

"You are quite the interesting character, Tanen. Your willingness to survive by any means is exactly what this rebellion needs right now. I applaud you for making hard decisions for the benefit of those you care about," said the old king.

Mara couldn't believe his words. "You're joking, right? This man was preying on innocent lives, torturing people for his own gain. He ran a town into ruin with fear and power. How is that any different from what Gjanion is doing to us right now? Tanen's actions were selfish and cruel!"

"Was it for his own gain? Did he directly benefit from those actions? Did you ever ask him how those decisions affected him?" Radion asked her point blank.

Mara was staggered by Radion's response. *How could he ask such things? The audacity!* She opened her mouth to retaliate, but something stopped her. Deep down, part of her knew that what the old king was saying had some merit. Tanen wasn't power-hungry, he was just trying to care for and protect the people he cared about. So far as she knew, he had never used his powers to expand his influence. He was a healer, he was trying to help. It was far from the most moral solution, but it was the one he was presented with.

"Is he right? Was the choice to prey on weaker beings hard for you?" Mara asked, somewhat sarcastically.

"More than anyone will ever know," Tanen replied, hanging his head.

The instant and genuine remorse surprised Mara.

"Let us try," Radion said comfortingly.

"When I came upon the town in the valley, I saw an opportunity. I won't deny that the thought of what I could do, what I could *really* do with this power was enticing. But I knew that I had a responsibility to my village and my daughter. I had the ability to protect them, to care for them in a way nobody else could." Tanen began to tear up and his voice cracked slightly. "If I abused that power, they would never trust me. I cared more about my people than gaining rapport. I sought a solution and this one was presented to me. I don't regret my decision, though the cries of the people I stole away haunt me. I did what I had to do, even if my daughter didn't agree."

All eyes were on Tanen, whose own eyes were full of tears. Mara realized that there had been far deeper motives connected to this man's decision than simple desire for power.

"I'm glad you're here with us," Jerra said first, placing a hand on his shoulder. Tanen smiled.

"Me too, maybe you could teach me a few things!" Gant exclaimed. Mara shot him a look. "Not with human blood, of course," he clarified.

"Do I have your trust now, Mara? Have I said and done enough for you to believe me? I helped heal the boy, I've poured my heart out, what more can I do to show you that I am not your enemy?" Tanen asked her.

Mara looked around at the rest of the group, and her eyes eventually locked with Kei's. She could tell what he was thinking, and with a slight nod, he encouraged her to let go of her reservations.

"Don't make me regret this."

~~~

"How did you get in here? Who are you?" Litik shook as he wielded his mug of tea in front of him like a weapon.
~~~

"Litik relax," Zhira said, lowering the hood of his blue cloak.

"Zhira?" Litik lowered his tea.

"In the flesh!"

"How did you get in here?" Litik asked again.

"That would be the work of my friends here," Zhira said, motioning to Dazel and Eres, who were standing behind him.

Having traveled to a different world than their own, Eres and Dazel had opted to change their appearances so as not to stand out as much. Reminiscent of their original forms, Eres now had stark white hair and a dark complexion while her sister had dark blonde hair and fairer skin. Both goddesses stood taller than either Litik or Zhira and looked very out of place in the small living room.

"Welcome to my humble abode, ladies. I am Litik," he began to introduce himself but Dazel stopped him.

"The tanner, we know." Her voice was exactly as Zhira had heard it in his head, but he realized that they were now speaking aloud.

"You know?" Litik asked, clearly confused.

"Litik, allow me to introduce…" Zhira began to introduce the goddesses, but Eres beat him to it.

"I am Eres and this is my sister, Dazel," Eres said matter-of-factly.

"You…you're…" Litik stammered, then turned to Zhira. "They're…"

"Goddesses, yes," Zhira confirmed.

"In my home!" Litik got down on his knees and bowed. "It is an honor to meet you both, I am truly humbled to be in your presence."

"Please get up," Dazel said. "We may be goddesses to you, but here we are nothing more than magical beings from another world."

"Oh, well when you put it that way…" Litik said sarcastically. He gave Zhira a look of disbelief.

"The goddesses have agreed to assist in the rebellion against King Gjanion," Zhira explained.

Litik was beside himself. "How did you manage to meet them, let alone convince them to come to our little town and help us?"

They sat down and Zhira recounted what happened, from the fight in the throne room and Dazel's rescue to being revived on The Bright One and convincing the two goddesses to help end the conflict in their kingdom. Dazel explained why they felt compelled to help, including the history of Knorr's banishment. There was a pause as Litik, who was literally on the edge of his seat, took all of this information in.

"So what now? How do we help from here?" he asked Zhira after a moment.

It was Eres who answered. "We get you all out of here."

"Without drawing too much attention to us," Dazel said, reminding her sister.

"Why not? You're goddesses! If the king and his knights learn that you're on our side, they'll run screaming! They won't stand a chance," Litik said confidently.

"It is not that straightforward," Eres said, quelling Litik's excitement.

"Simply 'being goddesses' will not end this conflict. We feel responsible for the current state of your kingdom and are willing to help, but people must not know who we are," Dazel explained.

"What do you mean?" Litik asked, looking from the two women to Zhira.

"The reason this war is happening is because Gjanion believes he is a god. He is obsessed with power and control. He strives to be something that he isn't. That draw, that desire for more is what we want to avoid. If the goddesses magically intervene, more and more people will seek to use that power," said Zhira.

"We wish to reduce our influence in this world, not increase it. We must not be the ones to win this war, or others will seek our powers and our graces to grant them freedoms from their own foes. Wars will be fought for our favor, which, now that we are here, is an ability that will eventually leave us," Eres clarified.

"What do you mean?" Litik asked.

"The longer my sister and I stay here," Dazel explained, "the weaker our powers become. Being far from home means we are not as close to a source of magic as we once were. Our powers will wane."

"Will you lose them entirely?" Zhira asked.

"That remains unclear," Eres replied.

"So does that mean you aren't going to fight with us?" Litik asked.

"We never said we were not going to fight, master Litik," Dazel said with a sly grin.

Chapter Sixteen
Campfire

The throne room in The Pearl House was not at all what Forbin had expected. As the doors closed behind him, Forbin looked around expecting to find a big chair, a raised platform, or even some ornate decorations. What he found instead was a simple room that had been painted with two colors: white and grey. The floor was a checkered pattern of tiles, and there were four thin, white pillars that held up the ceiling. Along the far wall was a grey table with five identical chairs behind it, all of which were empty. Painted on the wall above the table was the same sunrise found on the knights' capes and armor. The only splash of color in the room came from the knights dressed in royal blue armor, one standing to either side of the table.

Forbin walked forward and stood at the center of the room. There was nothing interesting to look at, nor was there a place for him to sit. He was not kept waiting long, however, as a door he had not previously noticed opened to his right. A tall woman with bright orange hair pulled back in a tight bun walked out and took a seat in the center chair. She was almost as tall sitting down as Forbin was standing up. Her face gave away no hint of emotion, but her green eyes stood out against the white and grey details of the room.

"Come forward," the woman commanded in an accent Forbin did not recognize.

Forbin obliged and stepped closer to the table.

"That's far enough," one of the knights said, without turning his head. The room echoed so much that Forbin was unsure which knight had said the words.

"Declare yourself," the woman said firmly.

"Oh, sorry, right. I am Forbin. I have come seeking asylum from the war for myself and my friends." His voice was shaky.

"Confidence goes a long way when asking for something," the woman said, an amused look on her face.

Forbin stood up straighter and spoke more strongly. "I am Forbin, and I—"

"I heard you the first time," the woman said, grinning. Forbin realized he was being messed with. "Sorry, it just gets so boring around here, I have to entertain myself somehow. My name is Enli, and I am the queen of Varyn." Queen Enli stood from her chair and bowed towards Forbin.

Forbin bowed in return. "The pleasure is mine, Queen Enli."

"So you say that you are seeking asylum for you and your friends? Where might your friends be?" the queen asked as she sat back down and folded her hands under her chin.

"Hopefully on their way. See, I am part of the rebellion," he explained.

"You are?" Queen Enli's face got much more serious. "Why is the rebellion at my gates?"

"We're losing," Forbin answered honestly. "There aren't many of us left, and Gjanion has pushed us to the edge. We have nowhere else to turn. He's taken over the rest of Kyros and will not stop until he is sure there is nobody left to oppose him."

"I see…" The queen sat in thought for a moment. Forbin shifted anxiously. "How many of you are left?"

"I can't be sure, I haven't seen anyone since we were driven from our hideout. Optimistically, probably two dozen or so," Forbin replied dejectedly. He was suddenly very aware of the tiredness in his voice.

"Forbin, you and your friends in the rebellion have been doing a noble thing. I regret that you are losing your fight, but you are safe within the walls of Varyn. We will take it from here," said Enli.

Forbin's eyes lit up. He had expected more of a push back from the queen. "It is no small gesture to pledge help in this fight."

"Let me be clear—I do not pledge help. I am telling you that we will handle the tyrant king when he appears on our doorstep. You need not worry any longer with this fight."

"With all due respect, Queen Enli, you don't know what you're up against. We have been fighting this war for over a decade, and—"

"And how has that gone for you and your…rebellion?" Enli asked pointedly. "We have an entire force dedicated to the safety of Varyn. We have knights, a massive wall, impenetrable doors, and a flourishing, self-sustaining economy. We can push back an assault. We can endure a siege. We are more than capable of handling the threat you bring our way."

"Yes, but—"

"You say you bring a mere twenty people to join this fight. What kind of queen would I be if I just turned over the control of this problem to an unknown group of people who don't know Varyn's resources and haven't been winning in the first place?

"You make a compelling argument, Your Majesty, but the knowledge we have of the enemy could prove useful to you. King Gjanion is not just some tyrant. He is the most powerful alchemist anyone has ever seen and his army alone has forced Kyros to its knees. Trust me, you are going to need our help," Forbin argued.

"And why is that? Why should I allow strangers to help lead us?"

"Because we have Radion, the old king of Kyros, leading us. Gjanion's daughter, who saw his evil and left the castle to join our cause, also fights with us now. And, most importantly, we have the only person in the kingdom who stands a chance at defeating Gjanion—we have the last wizard."

Queen Enli leaned forward at this news. "You mean to tell me that Gjanion's own flesh and blood leads the rebellion against him with a wizard? Nobody has seen a wizard in decades. Why should I believe you?"

Forbin grinned. "You don't have to. You can meet them when they arrive."

Enli sat back again. "I did not get to be queen without knowing when people were lying to me. You seem an honest man, Forbin, and I am inclined to believe you. If what you say is true, then I would be a fool not to accept the help of those so experienced in dealing with Gjanion."

Forbin bowed deeply. "I cannot begin to express my gratitude. Thank you for—"

"I do ask one thing in return," Queen Enli interrupted him. "You will all become People of The First Light—citizens of Varyn and the new kingdom to come," Enli declared.

"I…I don't understand," Forbin said, taking an involuntary step back at the queen's sudden intensity. "Varyn is supposed to be a free city."

"It is." The redheaded queen stood from her chair and walked around to Forbin's side of the table. "This city, my city, is free from King Gjanion's rule. He and his family—yes Radion included—have had generations to run Kyros. Look where it has gotten us."

Enli made a sweeping gesture as though they could see the whole kingdom from the confines of the white and grey room.

"People were happy before Gjanion took over. Things were good. He is an anomaly," Forbin retorted. Forbin was Radion's man. It was Radion who would take the throne and transition the kingdom back to an era of peace. It was what they had been working towards for over a decade. He would not let this woman interfere with their plan.

Queen Enli walked towards him slowly. "Were things good? Did everyone live happily ever after, Forbin? King Radion committed genocide against the wizards, wiping them all out to reclaim the throne, which he saw as his family's birthright. His son hunted down the last unicorns of Kyros and further divided the kingdom's people by amassing wealth under the crown. Now Gjanion is marching through the kingdom, holding peoples' right to live hostage in exchange for complete obedience."

"Why does that mean someone should try and take it from him? Isn't that just perpetuating the cycle of power grabbing?" he asked her bluntly.

"No. For too long the rule of this kingdom has been in the hands of power hungry men who see it as their right. I do not see ruling Kyros as my right, I see it as something I have earned. It is an opportunity, a privilege. My people have chosen me to lead Varyn. They have given me that opportunity. I have proven I can handle the task, just look around. Varyn is a thriving city even during wartime. Kyros will be the same under my rule."

Forbin sighed. He knew the rebellion would never win the fight to come without the resources Varyn had available, but becoming part of another regime that intended to take over under the guise of 'proving itself' wasn't something he was interested in, nor did he think the others would accept it.

~~~

Mai sat alone at the fire she had built. While her tent was certainly big enough to house a fire, she never lit one inside. She didn't feel it was worth the risk and it allowed her to keep an eye on her troops. It also made her more available to any of her charges should they have need of her, be it a grievance against another knight, advice, or just a simple question. Mai wanted her knights to trust her, and part of that meant supporting them. She had always resented General Long for being so distant and holed up, always having the knights go through her, Tren, or Hearth before coming to him. She felt her way was better.

The evening was quiet. Knights and squires sat around fires with little to talk about. They had been away from home for over two weeks and all of the fresh stories had run out. Mai had seen this happen every time they left the castle during the war. The troops would be buzzing with the excitement of another tour, swapping bets and stories over flagons of wine. As the days
~~~

dragged on, the initial excitement faded and was replaced by the lull of reality. Most of the time they were either marching, setting up that day's camp, or sleeping. The actual action took up very little time in their lives away from home.

She watched the flames dance over the logs they burned, reminding her of Gjanion's torrent of fire that had repelled the ghouls. The flames got lower and lower until they were nothing but glowing coals as Mai sat there, thinking about the events of the previous night. The clear sky was littered with more stars than she had ever seen. She watched a star shoot across the void with a brief and brilliant display of orange. As she gazed upwards, Tren approached and sat beside her.

"You okay?" he asked.

"What? Oh, yes," she replied, eyes still on the sky, hoping to catch another star showing off its speed and light.

"Pardon my saying so, general, but you have never struck me as a contemplative person. So finding you in a very…well…contemplative state makes me think that you might not be," Tren explained hesitantly.

Mai sighed. *If I can't trust Tren, then who can I trust?*

"I talked with Gjanion after the assault in the mist," Mai began. "I…don't think that his motivations are what they were when we started this war."

"What do you mean?"

"He's obsessed with Mara. He would see each and every one of us dead if it meant taking her down. Gjanion doesn't realize that he has already achieved what he wants. Kyros is his. He is its king. But he worries that Mara can undo all of that, and is focusing all of his efforts on taking her down."

"I thought we were marching to take Varyn?"

"I believe that we will," Mai explained. "But Gjanion will not stop there if Mara is not captured or killed. He'll burn Kyros to the ground looking for her."

"What are you saying?" Tren asked.

"I'm saying that Gjanion may be a bigger threat to the kingdom than Mara or the rebellion. Think about it—Mara, Rylan, and the rest of the rebels claim to be trying to help and protect people. Gjanion is the one bringing about pain and suffering. He's ordered villages burned, executed traitors, even killed rebels in cold blood. The rebellion doesn't do that. They protect themselves…from us. They're not the enemy…we are."

Tren sat quietly for a moment, which made Mai nervous. Had she gone too far? Did Tren sympathize with Gjanion more than her? Was he about to turn her in for treason?

"You're absolutely right," Tren said finally.

Mai relaxed. "I'm glad you see it, too."

"So what now? We can't just attack him, he'll kill us both."

"I don't think we're meant to defeat him, Tren."

"So then…what do we do?"

"Go get Kyra and Pike, we need to talk," Mai commanded.

Without a word, Tren went to fetch his squire and the newly minted commander. When he returned, Mai had stoked the flames of her campfire and it was flaring once again. The newcomers sat down across from Tren and Mai and listened as Mai told them what Gjanion had said about Mara.

"So the king protected us to ensure that we have our full army when we confront the wizard, what's wrong with that?" Pike asked. "Taking her out wins this war."

"It means he doesn't care about us. Not you, not me, not a single knight in our ranks. He only cares that we are here to fight for him and to give him the best chance he has at bringing Mara down," Mai said angrily. "He won't stop at Varyn if Mara lives."

"He shouldn't. If she lives, there is still hope," Pike retorted.

Tren snorted. "I didn't realize you were so naive, Pike."

"That's not helping," Mai snapped at Tren.

"Sorry," Tren said, retreating slightly into his armor.

"Why are we discussing this?" Kyra asked.

"Because I think Gjanion is a larger threat to the kingdom than he claims the rebellion is. Our king has fought a twelve year war on the basis of uniting our kingdom and keeping his subjects safe. He's certainly united it, by sheer power if nothing else, but the people of Kyros may be more in danger from him than any other outside force," Mai explained.

"You're telling me that you, the general of this entire army," he waved his arm in the direction of the other campsites to emphasize his point, "are thinking of just walking away?" Pike asked.

"No, Commander Pike, I am not walking away from this fight. I am just concerned that our king may not have the best interests of Kyros at heart. I want to live to see the kingdom united and peace restored after the years of work we have put in. Gjanion does not care about that."

"But that's the risk we all take. We pledge our lives to the crown, the king, and our kingdom so that we can help ensure it has a better future. We understand that we may not return from any particular battle, or live to see the fruits of our labor. We're sowing seeds for trees whose shade we will never sit under. That's how this goes," Pike said confidently.

"Well that's stupid," Kyra replied, nearly laughing. Pike looked at her incredulously.

"Kyra!" Tren gasped.

"No, seriously." Kyra turned to Pike. "If you signed up to 'better the kingdom' as you call it, then good for you, commander. But most of these knights chose being in this army over being hung, a life of poverty, or a life in the dungeons being fed scraps in a dank cell. I'm here because I couldn't make it on my own like I thought. When I was caught trying to feed myself, I was given a choice and I chose to live this life instead of the one waiting for me beneath the castle.

Most of your knights chose to be knights in order to live. They certainly did not sign up to die."

Mai, Tren, and Pike stared at Kyra. Mai secretly loved watching Kyra challenge Pike's argument, but her face remained stoic. Tren shifted nervously as he looked from Kyra to Pike and back, awaiting the commander's response. Pike sat motionless, processing Kyra's words.

"I think your squire needs to be reminded of her position, Commander Tren," Pike spoke through gritted teeth.

"Is she so wrong?" Tren asked, surprising Mai.

Pike turned to Mai. "Well?"

"Well what?" Mai asked him.

"Never mind," Pike said, defeated.

Feeling bolstered, Kyra continued. "The general said it right—King Gjanion doesn't care about any of us, and that includes you. He needs you to fulfill his mission, and nothing more. If you die, it's just another body to him. His only goal is to bring Mara down. You want to be remembered? You want to die for something real? End this war."

"I will end this war by destroying what remains of the rebellion and bringing Varyn under our control. I would never betray our king!" Pike exclaimed.

"But when the time comes, if it benefits him, he *will* betray you," Kyra said with a quiet strength that sent chills down Mai's spine.

"I am not sure you are right," Pike said, pondering her words. "Gjanion is the king. It is not his job to care about each individual person's life, but the overall well-being of the kingdom. If his way is what he thinks is right, who are we to question him?"

Mai was about to respond, but Tren beat her to it. "Why is Gjanion king, if not for the fact that the crown was handed to him? Who is to say there is not someone else better to lead us?"

Rylan. The thought came to Mai immediately, and without warning. Surprised by this thought, she was quick to dismiss it, but it would not go away. *She's strong. She saw what was right when I couldn't. She stood up to him, she can do the hard things.*

"What exactly are we discussing, general?" Pike asked, breaking her train of thought. "What's the point of all of this? Do you actually think you can overthrow him? Did you not see what he did to the ghouls?"

Poor Pike, Mai thought, *driven by the fear Gjanion rules by. Nobody dares to challenge him because nobody thinks they can win.*

"We are discussing our place in this war, commander, and whether or not we will finish this war for Gjanion," she replied bluntly.

"What's the alternative? Mai, if we upend this now, what is the point of everything we have done over the years? Where does that leave us? How would we even go about changing course?" Pike asked.

"I don't know," Mai said, answering all of his questions at once as she stared into the dying flames.

Chapter Seventeen
Varyn

The cart rumbled along the cracked, white ground, creaking with every turn of its wheels. Bitter wind whipped violently and threw loose salt directly into the eyes of anyone who dared to open them. Gant had originally suggested slowing down the pace to lessen the sting of the wind and salt, but Rylan had argued that it wouldn't make much of a difference. The wind would still blow and it would still hurt; better to just keep pace and end the torture faster.

To help pass the time, Mara had begun teaching Rylan some basic magic. Riding side-by-side, Mara showed Rylan how to control a flame in her hand. Mara's blue flame flickered and danced in the wind, but held steady. Rylan's orange fire was smaller and more erratic, appearing and disappearing as she tried to form one the same size as Mara's.

"Why can't I get this? You make it look so easy!" Rylan said, clearly frustrated.

"I've had years of practice. It isn't easy," Mara replied. She knew the disparity between their powers would likely frustrate Rylan, so she was as patient as possible while teaching the princess.

"It could be the potions," Radion said from his spot in the cart.

"What do you mean?" Rylan asked.

"Well, when I overthrew the wizards, we had spies slip potions that we concocted to cause all sorts of problems into their drinks. Over time, we learned that the potions themselves were dampening the wizards' powers. Maybe all of the potions your father had you using were preventing your powers from manifesting," he explained.

"So that's how you defeated the wizards?" Mara asked. "You actually took their powers away!"

Radion nodded. "Without that discovery, there would have been no chance of victory."

"This makes sense." Rylan again tried to spark a flame in her hand. It flickered briefly, then petered out. "I swore off potions after we left the castle. It's been a few weeks, so maybe my body is slowly returning to normal. I can't remember a time where I didn't use..." Rylan said, trailing off in thought.

"Maybe you just need time to gain your full abilities," Radion said as Rylan tried to form a flame again. It was stronger than the last, giving off a small amount of heat before the wind kicked up and snuffed it out.

"I suppose," Mara said. She could sense Rylan's frustration and felt it herself. She knew so little about who she was. Now that she had Rylan, the two of them could spend years figuring out all the secrets of their powers. That part excited her. What did not excite her was the fact that they were likely the last two wizards alive. They were going to be responsible for either the continuation or the death of magic entirely. If she and Rylan did not have kids, specifically girls since they were the ones who passed on the magic gene, magic was doomed.

Thinking of her children, Mara glanced down at Kei, who was still sleeping and recovering from last night's events. She was beyond relieved that, using her magic and Tanen's assistance, she had been able to heal him. Kei not being by her side in a fight wasn't something she could stomach. Everyone had their talents, but Kei was her rock. He'd watched her train from the beginning, made her special armor that had helped discover the magic-channeling properties of gemstones, fought alongside her in Saros, chased after her when she'd gone to the castle and helped rescue her, made her amethyst dagger, and had even been there to see her grandmother off when she couldn't.

Kei was always there, always helping, never questioning. She needed him, and the thought of losing him made her angry. This war had taken so much from her: her grandmother, her father, her life, her home, and now almost Kei. Mara vowed to herself that as soon as she could end this war, she would. She wiped the wind-induced tears from her eyes and turned back around. What she saw stunned her.

Varyn was a fortress. Mara had been held captive at the castle, had seen it's regal shape and foreboding size in person as she had been escorted inside the gates, but nowhere had there been doors this big, or a wall this thick. Something inside Mara relaxed as she saw just how well defended this city was. She felt as though she was looking upon the physical manifestation of the word 'safety'. Their caravan rode up to a smaller door set in the gargantuan gates that loomed above them. Mara and Rylan rode up and were greeted by nobody.

Rylan looked up and frowned. "I am certain that the wall had guards. They had to have seen us approaching."

Mara felt similarly, but was far less patient. She banged on the door and heard the metallic echo of the hallway behind it. Nobody answered.

"What gives?" Mara asked, annoyed.

"Maybe they're in between shifts?" Rylan suggested.

"This salt is unbearable!" Tanen exclaimed from behind them as the wind whipped against the towering stone wall and metal doors.

"If they would just let us in!" Still sitting atop her stallion, Mara started banging on the door with both fists.

Eventually Mara heard several metallic *clicks* in rapid succession and the door opened just enough for

Mara to make out the silhouette of a man's face. She could see that the door was still very much locked; the chains holding it looking strained against the wind.

"Let us in!" Mara screamed.

"I can't! Not during a salt storm!" the man yelled over the howling wind. "If I open this door, it will funnel the wind into the city and cause much damage! I am afraid you will have to wait until the storm subsides!"

Mara fumed, then realized she could do something about it. "Be ready with the door! Jerra, pull forward!" Mara yelled, not bothering to explain her plan over the wind.

Jerra did as she was told and pulled the cart to just outside the door. Mara hoped the man behind the door did as she asked. She whipped her dagger out and pointed away from the wall in the direction of the wind. All of a sudden, the wind stopped.

"Open it! NOW!" Rylan screamed at the man tending the door. Mara was glad the princess had caught on to her plan quickly.

Clearly confused, but very much aware of the situation, the door guard undid the final locks and allowed the refugees to enter. They filed in until Mara was the only one left.

"Mara! Let's go!" Rylan called out to her.

Mara released the wind and urged her horse into a full sprint. She passed through the archway and the man slammed the door behind her just as the wind slammed against the wall once again. He bolted all of the locks and turned to take stock of his new guests.

"What was that?" The man looked bewildered. He stood no taller than Radion and his round stomach and bald head made him look like an upright cantaloupe.

"Hi," Mara breathed heavily as she introduced herself. "My name…is Mara…and I'm a wizard."

"A what? Young lady, I am not sure what just happened but the wizards were killed off years ago by King Radion. Now the only wizard that remains is King Gjanion."

"I did not, in fact, kill off the wizards. Many survived after I took the throne until Gjanion hunted them down." Radion explained, introducing himself in the process.

The man didn't know what to say. He straightened his blue tunic that bore a white sunrise on the chest, and began what sounded like a very well-rehearsed introduction.

"Regardless of who you are, you are now within the walls of Varyn, the free city of the People of the First Light. We no longer recognize King Gjanion as our ruler and—"

"I'm sorry to interrupt," Gant said unapologetically. "But we have been out there for weeks with no baths, hunting for our food, and trekking across that barren, desolate, unforgiving land you've decided to put between you and the rest of the world."

"Oh yes, the salt flats act as a natural deterrent from—"

"We would love nothing more than to sleep in a bed, clean ourselves, and enjoy a hot meal that we didn't have to chase through a forest first," Gant continued, interrupting the man again.

"Oh, certainly. Right this way!" The man waddled past them towards the far end of the tunnel. Before they exited, he turned around, seeming to have remembered something. "I must ask you, before you enter our city, what your intentions are."

"Not much of a question," Jerra observed.

"We are the fragments of a rebellion that has been working for the last twelve years to stop King Gjanion," Radion said bluntly.

"Ah, I see. Well you are not the first from the rebellion to claim refuge! We were told you would arrive soon. Come, I will show you where you will be staying. Now that you are here, we will arrange your audience with Queen Enli posthaste." The man turned back around and led them out of the wall.

"Did he say we aren't the first to arrive?" Kei chimed in from the back of the cart.

"He did indeed, I wonder who else made it," Radion mused.

The small caravan exited out the other side of the wall and into a small courtyard that was laid with stone and ground up shells. Mara's eyes hurt as they adjusted to the sudden brightness of the buildings and pathways around her. The salt flats had been stark and reflective, but inside the city it also rose up around them. She rubbed her eyes and took in the white and grey buildings, the paved roads that ran between, and the vastness of the city that stretched away from them and down towards the sea. Mara had never seen or even been near the ocean before, but the change in the way the air felt indicated to her that it was close.

"This is not what I expected," Gant remarked as they followed the rotund man down one of the shell-paved roads.

"I don't think any of us expected this," Rylan agreed, guiding Neela around a group of purple toga-clad pedestrians that paid her no mind.

"Their outfits are…odd," Jerra commented as she rode past more people wearing togas and sashes of various colors and shades.

"Our people wanted to do away with anything that resembled the kingdom we left behind," their guide explained. "We changed our culture as much as we could to be unique. Many of our brightest minds thought far beyond the expected norms of a culture and came up with this beautiful, beautiful city!"

The squat man seemed very proud of Varyn, and Mara could see why. She had felt that something was off about the city as soon as she entered, but listening to the guide talk, she realized what it was. Everywhere she looked, people were happy—nobody begging for help from a food vendor, nobody sleeping in alleys between the buildings, nobody fighting over a price. Varyn was pristine, paradisiacal, and free of the usual squalor and ruin that filled the gaps of a place like the capital.

"You mentioned that you call yourselves the People of the First Light," Radion spoke from the back of the cart. "What exactly does that mean?"

"Every night is dark, but the sun always rises and a new day begins. We wanted to be a place of hope, a new beginning for those who could not find a place in the old order of things in Kyros," the guide explained as they turned a corner and came to a grey building with several stories. It overlooked most of the street and Mara was certain that from the top floor, she could finally see the ocean.

"Good day to you all," a skinny woman in a blue toga came out to greet them. Behind her were several young boys and girls dressed in light blue. Without a word, they began unloading the back of the cart and helping the riders off of their horses. "We are honored to be the home of the rebellion. Please come inside. My children will take care of your things and your horses," the woman explained.

Mara made sure to grab the bag with her father's books in them before helping Kei out of the cart. Jerra stayed outside to help the kids with some of the heavier smithing equipment while Mara supported Kei and helped him inside behind Tanen and Rylan. Despite his quick healing, Kei was still in pain from Mara's operation and needed some help walking.

Once inside, the woman showed them to the top floor and gave them all keys to their rooms. As they made their way down the hallway and the woman explained that they need not pay to stay in her establishment, a door to the left opened and Forbin stepped out, dressed in a green tunic and brown pants.

"Radion! Rylan! Goddess above, you're all okay!" Forbin hugged the old king as if he was a long lost brother. Radion's face indicated he was clearly not fond of the act, but let it continue.

"Forbin, it is a great relief to see you alive and well," said Radion.

"When did you get here?" Rylan asked, hugging the man.

"A few days ago. You all are really going to like it here," Forbin visibly shook with the excitement of seeing his friends again.

"Why don't we all get cleaned up and reconvene to catch up?" Gant suggested.

"Good idea, I'll meet you all on the roof!" Forbin practically bounded towards the other end of the hall and opened a door revealing a set of stairs that led up to the roof.

Once they were all clean, Mara, Rylan, Gant, Tanen, Kei, and Radion joined Forbin on the roof. Mara looked out and saw the vast grey-blue ocean stretching out to meet the sky on the horizon. Riding along the salt flats had seemed endless, but the sea just seemed to be truly so. She could not imagine how deep it was, or how far it went. What were the far off kingdoms like? Were there more wizards out there? Did they know about

Gjanion's conquest? Her mind obsessed over these questions until Gant introduced Tanen.

"Forbin, this is Tanen. He's from a small village up in the hills north of The Cave and he's an alchemist, like Radion and myself."

"Pleasure to meet you, sir." Forbin stood and shook Tanen's hand.

"Likewise," Tanen said, not unkindly.

"How did you get here? Who did you travel with?" Rylan asked Forbin as he sat back down.

"I came alone. I got separated from the rest of the riders as soon as we hit the woods. There were ambushes behind every shrub and tree. I was lucky to make it out alive. After that, I stuck to my mission and made it here," Forbin explained.

"You must be one tough fighter, Forbin," Tanen remarked. "Trekking across the salt flats on your own is dangerous business."

"Sure, but I was determined. I never thought I couldn't do it. I'm a survivor. I've never lived somewhere for very long, nor had any family that I can recall. The rebellion is my family. Has been for a while. Besides, we need every man we can get. I had to make it to Varyn." Forbin spoke with such confidence that Mara believed there was no alternative. Forbin was always going to make it.

"You're a loyal and dependable man, Forbin," said Rylan with a smile.

"Thank you, princess, that means a lot."

Mara noticed that Forbin looked down as he spoke.

"Have you spoken with the queen yet?" Radion asked.

"I have," Forbin answered, grabbing everyone's full attention. "Queen Enli wants to help, they despise Gjanion as much as we do. So much so, in fact, that they've separated from Kyros and are starting their own kingdom with Varyn as its capital." Forbin spoke at length about his conversation with Queen Enli and how she was selected by her people to take charge and rule. When he was done, the group sat silently in thought until Rylan spoke up.

"That's no better than what my father is doing. She just wants control the same as him."

"I disagree. Queen Enli was selected by her people, and talks of serving them, not ruling them. That being said, I still think that Radion is more equipped to handle a transition should we win this war. I think, to help get Enli on our side and not her own, Mara should be the one to talk to her," Forbin turned to Mara.

"Me? Why?" Mara asked with genuine confusion.

"Because you're a wizard!" Forbin exclaimed rather loudly.

"How will that help anything? Do you want me to just hit her with some lightning if she doesn't agree? Should I freeze her in place and only let her go if she backs down? I won't use my magic to bully anyone into doing what I or any of us want them to," Mara said stubbornly.

"Maybe there is another option," Kei suggested. "What if we all go? We all have our reasons for being here. Maybe if we bombard her with alternative motives, one will stick."

"You're suggesting we guilt her into helping?" Gant clarified.

"Not *guilt* per se, just…encourage her to consider other reasons to fight. She'll never say it out loud, but she wants the power. She may talk of 'serving her people' like Forbin said, but we need to show her there is more to this fight than just who is in charge."

"I like it," Mara said, smiling at Kei.

"Me too," Rylan chimed in.

"I think this plan is naive, but until we come up with something better, I think it's our best chance to convince her to help us without having to bend the knee," Radion agreed.

"Okay, so how do we meet with her?" Tanen asked, looking at Forbin.

"I'll ask my friend, he's a knight who has been showing me around. He got me an audience with her the first time, I am sure he can do it again."

"Does your friend have a name?" Gant asked.

"Oh, yeah…it's…uh…come to think of it I don't know what it is!" Forbin's face scrunched up in confusion.

"Some friend," Rylan joked.

Chapter Eighteen
Liberation

Dazel observed the newcomers with curiosity. At Litik's invitation, their friends Sari, Keylon, Rezzik, and Bess filed into the small living room that she, her sister, and Zhira had appeared in the night before. While Litik made tea, the people of Saros sat down and listened intently as Zhira recounted the events of the last few weeks—from the fight in the throne room and his almost-death all the way to last night, where they had appeared in Litik's living room.

"That's a hell of a story," Keylon said, eyes wide with wonder. "A whole different planet..."

"Our home is beautiful, yes, but it is now also dead. We were the last beings on what you call The Bright One and we felt our time there had come to an end," Eres said somberly.

"What did you call it?" Rezzik asked in reference to their home planet.

"We never had a need for a name. Other planets and celestial bodies were named, but to us our planet was just Home," Dazel answered.

"So how are we gonna go help the rebellion in Varyn?" Sari changed the subject.

"We need to get out of here first," Zhira said, pointing out the obvious. "I think tonight we should make our break for it. Have horses saddled and bags packed and—"

"We will never reach the fight in time if we travel by normal methods," Dazel interrupted him.

Zhira looked at her, confused. "Is there another way to get there?"

"There is," Eres chimed in. "We can take you there."

The residents of Saros that sat in Litik's living room all turned to look at the white-haired goddess. Seeing their confusion, Eres continued, "Having left The Bright One, we are further from our source of power. We cannot do all that we used to, and the longer we are away, the more our abilities will fade. It would be wise to take advantage of our abilities while we still have them. Dazel and I can transport you all to Varyn as soon as you are ready."

Dazel did not approve. "Sister, might I have a word in the next room?" She stood up before she had finished asking, not giving Eres a chance to answer.

The two of them walked into Litik's bedroom. "What are you doing?" Eres asked, frustrated.

"Stopping you from making a mistake!" Dazel replied, equally annoyed.

"What mistake? We are here to help, we should help however we can while we can."

"We promised not to use our abilities to this magnitude," Dazel glared at her sister.

"We promised to help them win this war. They cannot win if they are not there to fight!" Eres stood her ground. "Why did you interrupt Zhira anyways, if not to help them reach Varyn faster?"

"I only meant to speed up the process, perhaps enhance the horses somehow. It was not my intent to teleport them there," Dazel said, exasperated.

There was a pause as neither sister knew who would cave. They stared at each other for a moment, but Dazel realized that Eres was right; there was no way they would get to Varyn in time to help unless they did something drastic.

"Fine," Dazel relented. "We will help them get to Varyn, but we must not draw attention to ourselves beyond this."

"I agree," Eres nodded. "Did you tell the girl?"

"What?" Dazel asked, confused.

"Rylan. Did you tell her we are here, and we are coming?"

"No, do you think I should?"

"They'll find out soon enough," Eres said dismissively.

Dazel suddenly noticed a weird silence in the next room, and sighed. "You have been listening to every word?" she asked loudly to the rest of the group.

After a moment, Zhira replied with a sheepish "yes."

Dazel grinned and returned to the living room with her sister. "I suppose two 'goddesses' arguing would be an interesting affair to the likes of you humans."

"Couldn't help it! You both are far too interesting to not keep an eye, or in this case, ear on!" said Litik with, Dazel noticed, an obvious bit of charm.

Eres smiled in thanks, then sat back down next to Zhira. "We can transport you to the city whenever you all are ready."

"How long will it take?" Sari asked.

"When you disappear here, you will appear there. The trip will be instant," Dazel explained.

"Well then what are we waiting for? Let's get out of here!" Rezzik exclaimed, practically jumping from his seat.

"Hang on, I think there is something we need to do first," Keylon said, taking the wind out of Rezzik's sails. "We can't leave our friends here unprotected. We are the leaders of this town."

"What do you suggest?" Zhira asked as all of them turned their attention to her.

"I believe it's time for liberation," Keylon grinned mischievously.

~~~

Rylan sat on the roof with her tea, watching the sun crest over the shimmering waves of the ocean. A smile crept over her face as she took in the stunning view. She had never seen anything like it—so serene yet so powerful. Rylan could sense the push and pull of the waves as they rolled into the city's harbor and along the adjacent beaches.

She closed her eyes and felt the growing warmth of the sun on her face. A calm she had never felt before washed over her like one of the many waves washing over the sand. The city had just begun to wake up; the sounds of vendors opening their store windows, setting up their awnings, and talking to one another wafted up from the street like a low hum accompanying the sound of the waves crashing far below and the sea birds calling from high above.

Rylan opened her eyes and watched a boat with three tall masts sail out of the harbor and unfurl its massive white sails. The fabric caught the wind and billowed out, looking like clouds coasting along the surface of the ocean. Rylan wondered where it was headed. Several smaller boats darted around the shallows just beyond the harbor pulling up nets of fish, crabs, and other sea life that Rylan had only ever seen cooked on a plate.

Rylan noticed that despite it being close to winter, she wasn't cold. The many white buildings and
~~~

roads reflected much of the sun's light, and the heat rose to where she sat on the roof. The biting winds she had grown accustomed to on their rides had been replaced with a warmer sea breeze.

This peacefulness will not last, Rylan thought sadly. Her father was days away at most, bringing with him a war that was coming to its finale, like a piece of music crescendoing to its epic conclusion. She could feel that too. Like the tide in the harbor, Rylan's feelings towards her father rose and fell with time.

I had always wanted magic, and he kept me from it, Rylan thought. *He fed me potions and took away what I wanted.*

She was unsure if he had done it purposefully or not, but she was angry regardless. Countering this feeling of anger, however, was one of sadness.

I have what I wanted, and now I have to face him. Up until a few days ago, Mara had been the last wizard. Now there are two of us. Am I the reason we will win this time? Will Mara and I be enough? Rylan watched as the sun climbed higher over the water, considering her fate. *Am I bound to this? Must I fight him? What happens if we win? What will it take to win?*

She took a sip of her tea and stood to go wake Mara. She couldn't sit alone with her own thoughts any longer. She needed her friend. As she reached the door leading back into the building, it opened and nearly hit her in the face. Rylan leapt out of the way, saving her tea, as Radion emerged onto the roof.

"Good morning, princess," Radion nodded.

"Just as you are no longer a king, I am no longer a princess," Rylan said, reminding him for what felt like the tenth time.

"Your father is still the king, is he not?" Radion replied, not accepting the denouncement of her title.

Rylan frowned as she walked past him and down the stairs. She knocked on Mara's door and waited for a response. When none came, she knocked again. A moment later, Kei answered the door wearing only his pants. Rylan could see that the bruising on his back had spread around his right side as well.

"Oh, sorry, I thought this was Mara's room."

Kei's face went slightly pink. "It is."

It took Rylan's mind an embarrassingly long time to connect the dots, but when she did, she got bright red. "Oh…oh! I'm sorry…sorry…I hope I didn't…I mean…" Rylan stumbled, unable to form a sentence.

Kei laughed. "It's alright, Mara is still asleep. I was just stretching out my back. It's still really sore from—"

"It's okay, I don't need to know," Rylan interrupted him.

"I was going to say it's still really sore from my injury," Kei pushed the door open wide and invited Rylan in, laughing again.

Rylan forced a small chuckle and followed Kei in. He sat down on the floor and extended his legs in front of him, then reached for his toes.

"I can come back later. I'll just go…" Rylan began to say, but Mara emerged from her bedroom wearing a blue tunic and grey pants.

"Good morning. Sleep well?" Mara asked as she poured some water from a pitcher.

"First real bed in weeks, how could I not?" she replied, sitting down in one of the chairs.

"This place is weird," Mara said, putting the pitcher down and coming over to sit beside Rylan.

"How do you mean?" Rylan asked.

"Well, for starters, it seems like the war has never even touched this place. They're not worried about spies or informants, their city has a robust economy despite over a decade of war ravaging the kingdom, and it just seems so…clean. It can't be this good, can it?"

Rylan pondered what Mara said. "For starters, that massive salt flat we had to cross to get here was not an easy trek. I can't imagine that people are coming and going so frequently. If you're here, you're here. This isolation also means that Varyn must have been extremely self-sufficient anyway."

"Okay, fine," Mara conceded, "but what about spies? Surely your father sent people to infiltrate the hard-to-conquer places like this?"

"Oh sure, but in a city trapped between an ocean and the salt flats, spies aren't coming and going constantly. There isn't exactly a way to sneak in and out, at least not that I saw. Besides, what is an informant going to report back? That Varyn is stable, has their economy figured out, and that the people around here seem genuinely kind and helpful?"

"Well…yes, actually," Kei chimed in. "Doesn't that give your father a lot of options for disruption?"

"Normally, yes. But it seems to me that Varyn runs as well as it does because it has no other option. If people here abandoned that helpful and embracing mentality, then the whole place would collapse."

"Right, that's kind of my point," Kei said as he stretched out on the floor.

"But in this case, that's nearly impossible to break. Success breeds success. If the people here know that their survival depends on buying into a way of life, it would take something extreme to break it. Subtle espionage wouldn't cut it."

"It still seems odd to me," Mara said warily.

"I think we should accept this place for what it is. It's a shining example of what Kyros can be, and I—or whoever is in charge when this is all over—should take inspiration from this place when rebuilding our kingdom."

"First we have to finally take down Gjanion…" Mara reminded them.

"Do you think we can do it this time?" Kei asked.

"We have to," Mara said seriously. "But we'll have a bit more help this time. Between Varyn's forces and adding another wizard to the mix, it's our best chance."

"That's all well and good, but what happens next? How do we transition after we—hopefully—win?" Rylan asked.

"Wasn't the rebellion's plan to return Radion to the throne to secure the transition, then pick a new leader?"

"So we're going to help Radion reclaim the throne, this time with the *help* of wizards?" Rylan asked. "There's some irony there."

Kei laughed. "Poetic."

"Unless someone else wants to take up the mantle," Mara said, looking at Rylan.

"What a daunting task. Not only disposing of my father but replacing him? Fixing the mess he made?"

"You won't be doing it alone," said Mara.

"Yeah, of course you'll have us," Kei agreed.

"And how exactly would you be helpful, Mister 'I got beat up by a girl with a stick'?" Mara joked, causing all three of them to laugh.

"What's wrong with a girl with a stick? Put your magic away and I could best you with one hand!" Rylan proclaimed.

"I'll keep the magic *and* my pride, thanks."

"I could be the royal blacksmith," Kei said proudly. "I'd make the finest weapons the kingdom's ever seen!"

"Good thing it'll be a time of peace. We'll need *so* many weapons," Rylan jested.

"Can't hurt to be prepared!"

~~~

Sari closed down his forge and was finishing putting his tools away when two knights walked over to the counter that faced the street.

"Can I help ye?" Sari asked without turning around.

"Do you know anything about the disappearance of the statue?" asked one of the knights in an obviously bored tone.

"The statue is missin'?" Sari asked, whipping around at the news.

"According to your governor, the statue was taken sometime between our noon patrol and now," the other knight explained monotonously.

"I built that statue with me bare hands!" Sari roared in anger. "How could ye let it be taken in broad daylight? 'Tis a giant metal statue!"

The knights straightened up and took the issue a bit more seriously in the presence of the angry blacksmith.

"Sir, I promise we will do everything we can to help find the statue. It can't have gone far," the first knight said with more vigor in his voice.

"You are damn right it can't've! Shall we go look for it?" Sari asked, vaulting his counter and closing the window behind him with a *slam*.
~~~

"Lead the way," the second knight gestured for Sari to begin walking towards the square.

"The problems these people deem important," the first knight whispered to his companion, rolling his eyes.

The knights chuckled as they followed Sari to the square, where the statue stood gleaming in the light of the torches the knights carried. The knights stared in confusion, certain that it had not been there before.

"What's the meanin' of this, then?" Sari pointed at the metallic rendition of Dazel. "You think it's funny to lie and anger people?"

"I don't understand…it wasn't there…" the first knight stammered as the statue's silver skin reflected the torchlight brilliantly. Its golden hair shimmered like stars falling in a wave.

"I would like to speak with your captain. NOW!" Sari said, yelling as loud as he could.

The commotion was drawing people to their windows and knights out of the barracks beside Rezzik's house. Before they could leave to fetch him, the captain strode into the town square, his purple cape flowing behind his bulky figure.

"What's all the fuss about, boys?" His bald head shone in the torchlight.

"These two came 'round to my forge tellin' me some nonsense about the statue bein' stolen! As you can see, it's right there. Do your men have nothin' better to do than cause problems?" Sari was yelling at the captain.

"Sari, please calm down, the statue is clearly still there, safe and sound. No need to cause a scene," the captain said, trying to defuse the situation.

"A scene? That statue wasn't there an hour ago!" Rezzik came out of his oversized house in a huff. "I reported it stolen, and it just happens to reappear just as they bring Sari around? Your men are here to protect us, captain, not mess with our things and our peaceful existence."

"Rezzik, I'm sorry, but the statue is there!" The captain pointed at the silver and gold statue. "I don't see the problem."

"That's because you're a fool." Keylon said from behind him before clubbing him over the head with the hilt of her sword.

Dazel moved from the center of the square, where she had been posing as the statue, and rushed the two knights Sari had brought along. Before they could even draw their swords, she had covered the distance between them. Grabbing them by their throats, she lifted them up and threw them against the closest tree. With a resounding *crunch*, they fell to the ground, unmoving. The knights that had been standing around watching suddenly sprung to action. Litik appeared from an alley and tossed Sari his axe.

Some of the knights were not dressed in full armor, and they fought much more defensively as a result. Eres dashed from her hiding place behind the Rezzik's house and quickly disposed of the two nearest knights. The whole affair was over as quickly as it had started, as the knights had been caught by complete surprise and were overwhelmed by the speed and ferocity of the two goddesses. Dazel and Eres dashed from knight to knight utilizing magic none of the residents of Saros had ever seen. Pure energy came from their hands as the sisters vaulted over and around their adversaries, knocking them down and relieving them of their consciousness.

A younger squire tried to sneak up on Sari with a knife as the blacksmith went blade to blade with a tall, beefy woman wielding a greatsword, but Zhira appeared from the same alley Litik had been waiting in and put the young man in a headlock.

"That's not a very honorable way to fight," Zhira said before clamping down and forcing the squire to the ground. Eventually he passed out, and Zhira ignited his hand in flames to join the fight, only to be greeted by the smattering of knights lying about the square unconscious. The goddesses had done most of the work without even breaking a sweat. Dazel returned to her more human form, her silver skin dulling to a pale tone that glowed in the firelight.

"What now? They won't be out for long," Litik observed.

Zhira turned to the people that had been watching from their homes. "We are going to end this fight. Tie these men up and reclaim our home!"

The door to the inn opened and out walked Bess, arms laden with rope. The other villagers emerged as well and began rounding up the unconscious knights.

"Thank you for not killing them," Keylon addressed the goddesses. "Most of them are here only because it was the least worst option. They obey the king because he gave them a life worth living."

"You are an honorable soul, Keylon. It is good of you to have requested this," Dazel nodded respectfully. Sari was proud of his wife. She could hold her own with the best knight, but she was kind and pure to her core. Sari knew she would never kill if she could help it.

"Are you all ready to go?" Eres asked. Litik, Rezzik, Sari, Keylon, and Zhira all nodded, clutching bags of supplies as well as their weapons.

"We will arrive at the entrance to the city, so as not to attract any unwanted attention. They will let us in, we will be their guests. None will be wise to how we got there," Dazel explained.

"Let's go," Sari said impatiently.

Dazel and Eres each raised a hand and pressed their palms together. A soft red glow emanated from their hands and grew steadily until they were all bathed in a blinding red light. It continued to grow until it was so bright that Sari couldn't see who was standing next to him. He felt a strange sensation in his arms and legs, as though they were filled with a million tiny honey bees buzzing about. Eventually, dizziness set in; he could no longer tell which way was up and which was down.

As soon as it had started, the experience was over. The seven of them were now standing in front of a massive set of metal doors. Sari looked around and saw nothing but a barren white landscape stretching as far as he could see in every other direction. The stars above them were veiled by clouds as the whole world seemed to have been drained of color and texture. It felt as though whoever had designed their world had left this part unfinished.

"What are we waiting for?" Litik walked towards the metal doors and knocked.

Chapter Nineteen
A Change of Heart

Mai wasn't sure when she first saw the wall, it was suddenly just there—a small strip on the horizon. Even from a distance, Varyn looked strong and fortified. Now that the city was actually in their sights, Mai felt like she was being torn in two. She wanted this war to be over, but she was not sure she wanted Gjanion to be the one to win it. In the back of her mind, she hoped that Pike would not inform the king of what they had discussed around the fire, but Gjanion had given no sign that he was wise to her mutinous ideas.

They still had another two days of marching ahead of them, but the atmosphere in camp had changed. Everyone knew that they were closing in on the final fight. Gjanion had instructed that camp be set up early, as the final approach would be done swiftly to allow Varyn as little time as possible to prepare their defenses. He had also claimed that he wanted his forces to be prepared and rested for the battle that lay ahead.

"Mai, we need to talk," Pike said as he poked his head through the flap of her tent.

Mai sighed. "What is it, Commander?"

"I've been thinking more about what we discussed around the fire the other night," Pike said rather sheepishly.

"And?" Mai asked, impatiently.

"I'm in." Pike stood up straighter.

This caught Mai off guard, but she didn't show it. "In for what?" *I am going to hear him say it. I have to know he is committed.*

"Gjanion doesn't care about us—or Kyros—so why should we follow blindly? Let's take him out." Pike shuffled his feet as he grew more excited.

"Great idea, let's try and take out a man who could torch us all with a flick of his wrist," Tren said, entering the tent behind Pike. "You saw what he did to the ghouls. Do you really think he wouldn't waste every single one of us without a thought?"

"Look," Mai interjected. "We can't defeat him, but we can make sure he doesn't win."

"How?" Pike and Tren both asked.

"How has Kyra managed? Have you two been able to build up a decent supply of potions?" Mai asked, to the confusion of both men.

"Yes, but—" Tren began to reply, but Mai held up her hand.

"Go get her."

Tren nodded and exited the tent. Mai said nothing until he returned, leaving Pike to stand awkwardly near the entrance. Once all four of them had convened, Mai began to lay out her plan.

"We need to convince the knights to leave, and we need to be able to defend them while they do."

"That won't be easy, General. We don't exactly have a ton of supplies left for the return journey. The king's plan relied on us pillaging supplies from Varyn and leaving a large garrison there as well," Pike explained.

Mai had not considered this, and furrowed her brow in frustration at this wrinkle. Tren was about to offer a suggestion when Kyra spoke.

"Then we make our move once we are in the city. Make him fight for it on his own. Convince as many as possible to join the rebellion with us when we get there. We just have to bide our time a little longer."

Mai stared at Kyra. Would Gant and the rest really take them in? The rebellion would likely reject them out of fear of being destroyed from within. Mai understood that her and her team had no record by which the rebellion could trust them. It was a major gamble, but she didn't see another option. Mai finally accepted that the people of Saros had changed her. She could only hope that they would accept her.

"Okay," Mai agreed. "We will make our move in Varyn. We will not fight this war with him. If Gjanion wants to defeat Mara and claim this kingdom so badly, he'll have to do it himself."

~~~

"I find that fire is the most versatile magic I can do," Mara explained as she weaved a blue flame through her fingers. "Getting a good handle on it is important. One misstep and you could burn a whole building down."

Rylan cradled her yellow flame carefully, as if supporting an infant's head. Mara could see that Rylan was extremely hesitant to try anything too real, but if she never experienced what it felt like, she would never be able to control it.

"I'm not sure I'm ready," Rylan said.

"The army is days away. It doesn't matter if you think you're ready. You need to be," Mara replied.

"Okay, fine. So I just…" Rylan stretched out her fingers and the flame sputtered before breaking apart into two wavering streaks. Mara had procured some candles for Rylan to practice with, and two of the wicks sprung to life, catching Rylan's weak flames.

"This is much harder. I knew how to do this with potions, but it's entirely different now," Rylan said, frustrated.

"Patience and practice," Mara said, echoing her father's lessons from when she was a child. "You already know how to do it, you're just drawing energy from a new place. Hopefully it won't take too long to figure out."
~~~

"I just feel so weak," Rylan replied as Mara extinguished the candles with a wave of her hand. "I thought magic would feel strong."

"You used potions regularly for nearly fifteen years. Your body is only just now discovering its abilities. Of course you're going to feel weak. Keep practicing!"

"You're right. Besides, I doubt I can do any real damage if I mess anything up," Rylan said, cracking a smile.

Mara appreciated her friend's good nature about her situation. *It must be hard to feel so limited,* she thought.

"Try again," Mara said, nodding towards the candles.

Rylan concentrated, creating a new flame and extending her fingers once more. This time the fire shot straight at Mara in a large burst. Mara quickly caught before it collided with her, and in her control, the flames began to turn blue.

"That's pretty cool," Rylan observed.

"Guess there will be no secrets about whose fire is whose," Mara replied, studying the blast of Rylan's flame as she diminished it to a flickering ball hovering in her right hand. She snuffed it out.

"Again."

Before Rylan could ignite another flame, Gant came flying up the steps and doubled over, clearly out of breath, as soon as he reached the top.

"Dad? What's wrong?" Mara asked as he heaved from his sprint up the stairs.

"Someone's here. Come downstairs," Gant looked up, a childlike grin plastered across his face.

~~~

"General Mai, thank you for joining me," Gjanion said as Mai pushed the flap of his tent aside and entered the king's lavish tent.

"Of course." Mai stood at stiff attention, her real hand clasping her fake one behind her back. Her dark grey armor absorbed the light of the brazier lit off to the side, making her look like a void in the otherwise well-lit tent.

"Tomorrow we begin our final approach on Varyn. I figured we should go over the strategy."

"Wise choice, Your Highness," Mai replied, conveying no emotion whatsoever. Her years of staying purposely distant and cold were great practice for keeping herself in check now. This was a critical juncture. Mai would get all of the information she needed from the king and he would be none the wiser that she was planning to betray him. As she stepped closer to the battle plans laid out on the table between herself and Gjanion, she heard the flap fold behind her and turned to see Pike and Tren walk in.

"I have asked the commanders to join us as well, this attack is going to be extremely coordinated and
~~~

swift. We still do not have the sword relic, so we will need to rely on everything else going perfectly to give us enough of an advantage to mitigate Mara's influence. Understanding and communication are key," Gjanion prefaced the discussion.

All three of them nodded. Each commander took an available side of the table—Tren to Mai's left and Pike to her right—and the four of them sat down together in one coordinated movement.

"I have divided the forces evenly amongst our two leading men here," Gjanion spread his arms wide and motioned to Tren and Pike. "Commander Pike will see to the cavalry unit that will charge through the gate once it is open. Tren will lead the ground forces that follow and sweep up any stragglers, clear any ambushes that may try to assault our ground troops, and spread themselves through the areas of the city that the horses cannot reach as easily."

Mai was confused. "Where does that leave me, sir?" She was suddenly hot under her armor. *Does he really consider me to be a failure after the siege of the rebel base? Is he shelving me so he doesn't have to worry about me? I am far from incompetent.* Her mind strayed from betraying Gjanion as it was consumed by this insult to her abilities.

Gjanion seemed to read her mind. "That leaves you with me. I need you by my side. I will be using a great amount of strength to bring down Varyn's doors, so I will need protection while I gather myself for phase two."

"Phase two?" Tren asked.

"Once our forces have entered the city, there will be no avoiding the battle that follows. The people of Varyn will do whatever they can to expel us and, aided by the rebellion, they may stand a decent chance. Your job is to not lose the city, my job is to take it," Gjanion explained.

"How do you plan on doing that?" Pike asked him.

"By utilizing the relics I still have in my possession." He rubbed the top of the staff that leaned against his chair. "And by using as much alchemy as I can manage. You all will protect me as I move through the city searching for the wizard and her friends. They'll be spread thin trying to protect a whole city. Taking them by surprise, and breaking apart their forces, they will be no match."

Mai snapped out of her defensive trance. She was impressed by this plan and worried about how well it could work. She had to be certain she could get the majority of the army to drop their swords or turn them on Gjanion, or she was sure he was going to win this war before the sun set.

"I will protect you," Mai said with the straightest face she'd ever worn.

"I am sure that you will," Gjanion nodded.

Mai wasn't fast enough. In a single motion, Pike drew a long dagger and thrust it between the plates of Mai's armor, stabbing her between the ribs. Tren watched in horror as Pike stood to drive the dagger deeper into the general's side.

"Wh…why…" Mai sputtered at Pike as she began to bleed from under the dark metal.

"You will not stand in my way, general," Gjanion answered. "I will NOT be denied the victory I have sought for twelve years. You will protect me by being removed from the picture. Your *ashes* will watch as I take the city and the kingdom." The king's hands burst into flames.

Before he could strike her down, the flames went out. Confused, Gjanion reignited the orange fires and cradled them more carefully, but they disappeared once again. Tren turned around to see Kyra standing in the doorway of the tent.

"Commander! MOVE!" Kyra screamed before throwing her hands in front of her.

Tren dropped to the floor just in time to avoid the gust of wind that came flying from the direction of his squire. The table in the middle of the room flew at Gjanion and knocked him over, pinning him to the ground. Pike lost his balance and fell to the side, leaving Mai unattended in her chair. Tren moved quickly, grabbing Mai under her arms and dragging her out of the tent before either Gjanion or Pike could get up and retaliate.

"I got it," Kyra said, pointing one hand at Mai. She rose up off the ground and floated wherever Kyra's hand directed her. Tren drew both of his swords and protected the two women as they fled to the stables.

"We need to get out of here and we need to do it fast," Tren yelled as they sprinted across the camp, leaving a wake of commotion and confusion in their wake.

"I have an idea," Kyra said, pulling out a vial of reddish liquid from under her tunic.

They approached the makeshift stable and Tren yelled so fiercely at the stable hands that they ran away without question. He untied two horses who were already saddled and led them away from the camp.

Kyra put Mai down on the ground for a moment and unstoppered the vial. She held it down to Mai's side and let a few drops of blood flow into the mixture before resealing it and giving it a good shake. Tren stared at her incredulously.

"What? She's already bleeding! Do you want to get out of here or not?" Kyra dismissed the commander's judgmental look. She poured the potions into the horses' mouths and made sure they ingested it. They immediately got antsy and started hoofing the ground impatiently. "Get on!" Kyra yelled at Tren as she mounted the shorter of the two horses. She pointed at Mai again and lifted her up onto the saddle with her.

Tren swung himself up onto the other and followed Kyra towards Varyn faster than any horse had ever run.

Chapter Twenty
Unified

Mara flew down the stairs at a dangerous pace and landed with a *thud* at the bottom. Her heart was racing and she was out of breath, but she didn't stop. She rushed across the room and barreled into her father, hugging him and knocking him over simultaneously.

Mara began to cry. "I never thought I would see you again."

"I am glad you were wrong," Zhira said, tearing up as well.

As the two of them got up off of the floor, Kei and Rylan descended the stairs. Kei gasped and ran over to where his mother and father were standing and embraced them. The two families, reunited at last, remained in each others' arms for some time. Rylan stood off to the side, happy for her friends, but tears came to her eyes as she realized that she would never get to have this moment. Her mother and brother were truly dead and her father would never accept her again.

There was the matter of her half-sibling, which she assumed was born by now given how pregnant her step-mother had been, but Rylan was not holding out hope.

Rylan caught the eye of one of the tall women standing behind the emotional families. Her features looked familiar, but Rylan couldn't recall where she would have seen her. *The woman certainly has the elegance of a noblewoman, maybe she is from the capital*, Rylan thought. Her brain churned for a moment and then lightning struck.

"Dazel?!" Rylan exclaimed, distracting Mara and Kei from their reunions.

Everyone's attention was suddenly on the two women standing just inside the doorway. Dazel nodded, her fair skin and flowing blonde hair standing out against her black and grey cloak.

"In the flesh," the goddess said with a voice as calming as a quiet stream.

"Holy goddess…" Gant said.

"Yes?" Dazel and Eres both responded.

"Oh, no, I just…I mean…"

"Sari, Litik, Keylon, Rez, it is so good to see you all," Mara said, breaking from the awe-struck group and hugging each of the newcomers in turn.

"Good to see you too," Keylon smiled warmly, her hand on Sari's shoulder.

"So what's the plan?" Litik asked impatiently.

"What plan?" Kei replied.

"The plan to take down Gjanion! Where is the rebellion? The queen's forces?" Litik looked around as if expecting them to suddenly appear out of thin air.

Gant's voice dropped to a more serious tone. "I'm afraid it's a bit more complicated than that."

~~~

Tren and Kyra watched as the doctor tied off the stitches, closing the wound in Mai's side. She had given the general a sedative and then set to work repairing the damage the dagger had done internally.

"You are lucky to have been so close to the city. Much longer, and she would have lost too much blood," the doctor said honestly, her age showing in the dark lines on her face.

"Thank you for saving her. What do we owe you?" Tren asked, worried they would not be able to pay.

"There is no cost. My services are supported by Varyn. Nobody living within these walls should worry about being taken care of, especially in life or death scenarios, simply because they cannot pay," she explained.

Kyra was stunned by this. *How did these people live?* Back home her father traded his service in exchange for goods from others. Together they formed a community based on give and take. It took Kyra a moment, but she realized that this was the same give and take, just in a
~~~

different form. Instead of directly exchanging goods and services, there were people like this woman that fixed people and Kyra was sure there were others that fed, clothed, and housed many more. In turn, those that received what they needed were able to contribute in other ways, as opposed to worrying about themselves. The trust that this city was built on impressed her.

"Thank you," Tren said, offering his sincere thanks, and the doctor left the room.

"Where are we going to stay? What are we going to do? We are fugitives now. Gjanion will have our heads on sight. We can't convince the knights to leave him if we aren't there." Kyra spewed worries left and right, but she could tell that they simply went in one of Tren's ears and out the other.

~~~

First my arm and now this, Mai thought.

Time and again, she had been betrayed by those who claimed to be doing what was in the best interests of the people they protected and ruled. How could that include killing anyone? Death is never in anyone's best interests, nor is being a killer. Mai hoped that Tren also realized just how wrong it was to be on Gjanion's side for so long. Waves of guilt crashed over her as he thought of all the misdeeds and horrible actions she had performed in the name of unity. Kyros' people were not united, they were fearfully obedient.
~~~

"I know there is much to do. We do need a plan and a place to stay. Why don't you saddle up our horses so we can look for something," Mai heard Tren say to Kyra.

Without a word, Kyra left. Once her footsteps could no longer be heard, Mai opened her eyes slightly, wincing at the brightness of the stark white room.

"I thought she would never shut up." Mai's voice was raspy.

Tren laughed. "She means well."

"How am I, doctor?" Mai asked with as much sarcasm as she could muster.

"Unfortunately, you'll live," Tren smiled.

"Two for two," Mai gave a shaky thumbs up.

"Kyra and I are going to find a place where we can lay low and come up with a plan. Stay here and rest. We'll be back for you," Tren explained before walking out after Kyra.

Mai put her head back, frustrated. She sat in the room alone, the silence and the blankness quickly driving her crazy. Impatient, she decided she would not wait until Tren found a place for them. There was no point in waiting, she knew what she had to do next, and she was sure that showing up alone gave her a better chance.

Using all of her strength, got out of the bed and stumbled out into the hallway. In a crate beside the door was her armor and her riding hook for her left arm. The rest, including her blade, had been left at the king's camp. She dragged the crate into her room, dressed herself and attached her two-pronged hook, and returned to the hallway. It was empty, save for a doctor walking away from her down the hall to her right. Mai went left and walked down the hallway, her hand against the wall to support her. When she came to the door, she shoved it open and took in Varyn and all of its white and grey buildings. People dressed in colorful robes walked in every direction, and Mai quickly realized that her armor was a dead giveaway to who she was.

Cursing, she removed the metal that had kept her safe for so long, and left it in a pile in the cleanest alley she had ever laid eyes on. In nothing but her brown pants and grey tunic, she felt exposed—a turtle without its shell. As she cast aside her armor, Mai felt exposed in more ways than one. For so long, she had been closed off to the world. She never sought help, never showed weakness, and never gave anyone leverage over her. Mai reminded herself that this city was the one place that Gjanion's forces were not, and she felt a little better. Still, to be safe, she kept her head down and went to look for the one person that she was mostly sure wouldn't kill her on sight.

<center>~~~</center>

Everyone sat on the roof and watched the sun reach towards the horizon, making the salt flats look like an orange sea of molten metal. The reflection was so brilliant that the guards manning the walls had special visors to protect their eyes from being damaged. Zhira reunited with Forbin and Radion, who were both glad to see him alive, and introduced them and Jerra to Sari, Keylon, Litik, and Rezzik. Eres and Dazel stood off to the side as Gant recounted all that had happened since he had last seen Zhira, while Sari and Rezzik explained how things were in Saros as well as their revolt and escape. They left out how they arrived at Varyn, but nobody questioned it.

After a while, Jerra announced that she had located an unused building around the corner and was busy revitalizing it for her needs as a new forge. Sari and Kei both seemed interested, and Mara rolled her eyes as the two followed her down the stairs to assist with the construction efforts.

"So we are all that is left of the rebellion?" Litik clarified as he leaned back in his seat next to his brother.

"As far as we know," Radion replied.

"If Queen Enli decides to go to war on her own, she will either lose, which means Gjanion completes his conquest, or she will win and a new conquest will start anew. Another Gjanion with a different coat of paint," Forbin explained. "She believes she has a mandate to rule, given to her by her people. She has proven that she can run a city, but Radion has run a country before—quite successfully, I might add."

"So we need to make sure that we are at the head of the fight against Gjanion?" Keylon asked.

Zhira nodded. "If we want this to go our way, we need to control the outcome. Otherwise Enli ends up on top, and we have no idea how that will go."

"And what exactly is our way?" Mara asked seriously.

"We want Kyros to actually be free. It doesn't need a ruler like Gjanion or Enli. It needs to make its own decisions. It needs to govern itself," Forbin answered. "Radion is a temporary option. A veteran of the throne to help with the transition."

"No leader?" Rylan questioned. "Nobody to oversee the kingdom and make sure that everyone behaves and levy punishments if they don't? I like where your head is, Forbin, but I don't know if that is feasible. If we leave the kingdom leaderless, it may be all too easy for someone to come along and do exactly what my father is doing."

Mara sat and listened to idea after idea of what the actual outcome of this conflict should be. Everyone was in agreement that Radion would assume control if they were victorious, to ensure a smooth transition. The question that still needed answering was: what next? Rylan argued that there should be someone in charge to make sure people behaved. Without a threat of punishment, some people would just do as they pleased with no regard for those around them. Feeling slightly called out in Rylan's interpretation, Tanen countered with a suggestion that a team of people work together to help run the kingdom, using a representative from each of the territories.

As the arguments flew left and right, Mara noticed that the only two people who had not offered an opinion were Dazel and Eres. Mara got up from her seat and made her way over to them as the conversation heated up.

"Do you care to weigh in?" Mara asked the sisters.

"We do not. This is not our place. We promised to help bring the kingdom back from the brink of Gjanion's total domination, as we are partly to blame for the current state of things. How you all choose to live after this, however, is up to you," Eres explained.

"You mean you're not staying? You're returning to your home? The one you described as desolate and empty?" Mara knew what she was doing, but she had no idea if appealing to a goddess' emotions would work.

Eres looked at Dazel and shrugged. "It is unlikely we will be able to return home. Our powers wane with each passing day. We will not have the strength to return to what you call The Bright One. Our plans for after the war are undecided. Once we have fulfilled our duty here, we will address what comes next."

Mara rolled her eyes. "I used to pray to you, to worship you. Rylan used to pray to you every night that she would get what she wanted. You may not be goddesses in your world, but you are here. You are revered. Anything you say and do holds more weight. Use that!"

"What you are saying is precisely why we are abstaining from the conversation," Dazel said. "You have deified us to the point that most people will blindly follow what we say as if it is the absolute truth. We wish for humans to think for themselves, not accept without question anything we have to say. People have prayed to us for generations, and we have done nothing to show that we are still listening since we banished Knorr. We want humanity to be rid of this…habit. You all must decide on your own."

Mara sat with this for a moment. They were right, what they could do to this entire situation with just a few words was far too impactful to actually be useful. She realized they were smart to stay out of it, but it made her question something else.

"Do you think I should stay out of this fight?" Mara asked bluntly.

"You are worried about your powers glorifying you to those without them, yes? Worried that people will look to you for answers and to solve their problems should you prevail," Dazel observed.

Mara nodded. "I don't want to lead, I don't want to be in charge, and I don't want people seeking me out to abolish their enemies or magically fix something that can't normally be. I don't want to be like you."

Eres wore a look of compassion. "You are smart to think of these things, but it is selfish. You do not have a choice. You must help. If you do not, and Gjanion wins, you will be vilified far worse. In cases like this where you have the chance to do good, choosing to do nothing will do harm. If you can help, help."

Mara understood completely, and thanked the goddesses for their wisdom. Behind her, the argument had subsided and her friends and family were laughing together about something she had not heard. She smiled softly and rejoined the group.

The sun had long set and the bitter winter chill swirled around them, urging them to seek the comfort of their beds. The group dispersed and went their separate ways. Mara gave Keylon the key to Kei's room and Litik and Rezzik bunked with Forbin. Mara was unsure where the goddesses went, but after looking for a few minutes, she gave up and retired to her own room and quickly fell asleep beside Kei.

~~~

"I still can't believe you're alive," Gant said to his brother as they gathered bags from the entrance hall. "You are the last person I expected to be here!"

Before Zhira could respond, the front door of the inn suddenly swung open to reveal a woman dressed in grey and brown. She fell forward and Gant caught her before she hit the floor.

"Are you sure?" Zhira asked, beyond shocked at who had just come through the door.

"Hi Gant," Mai greeted him with a look of exhaustion and a voice to match.
~~~

Chapter Twenty One
A New Path

The building was quiet. Rylan closed her door as silently as possible and crept towards the stairs leading to the roof. Floorboards creaked underfoot as she walked down the hallway and up into the cold night air. The sky was clear, but the full moon and its reflection on the ocean's surface outshone most of the stars. She wrapped a thick fur cloak around herself, sat cross-legged on one of the chairs, and stared out over the calm mirrored surface of the sea.

"Can't sleep?" Dazel asked from somewhere behind Rylan, causing her to jump and fall off the chair.

"Not really," Rylan admitted as she picked herself and her cloak up off the floor and resituated herself.

Dazel came and sat next to her. "What's troubling you?"

"My entire life, I wanted to be a wizard. Now I am one, or…I've always been one, and…" Rylan trailed off, afraid to say what she was thinking.

Dazel seemed to understand. "It's not all you expected it to be."

"It's *hard*. I thought it would feel natural. Mara makes it look so effortless."

"Mara has had her entire life to practice, learn, and feel the magic that she possesses. You discovered your powers barely a week ago, and you have been unable to feel the magic until recently. Your body is not prepared to do what Mara's can. Do not despair, time will change this, I think," Dazel said.

Rylan heard the uncertainty in the woman's voice. It was odd to hear someone she used to pray to not sound confident in their words. It was humanizing. Rylan was just beginning to think of the beings she had once known as goddesses as something more familiar, more normal. Hearing Dazel's hesitancy pulled the veil back further. Despite this, Rylan had questions, and she hoped Dazel had answers.

"Why did my mother marry him?" Rylan asked somberly. "If I am a wizard, she had to have been as well. Only women can pass on magic. Wouldn't she hate him for his persecution of her own kind?"

"Your mother's motivations are unknown to me. Your father was not always a tyrant, and perhaps your mother was unaware of what she truly was. Perhaps she knew and wanted power, or to see the throne restored to the wizards after Radion took it from them. Perhaps not. I only know that she never told your father what she was. For all I know, it could be that her hope was for you to be the one to bring magic back to the crown."

"So my father didn't know, and my mother might not have either."

"Correct. Your father does not have any reason to suspect that you are a wizard. He did not actively work against you—the potions were coincidental, in case you suspect otherwise."

"It's not personal," Rylan agreed. "How could it be? I was a child. I was no threat."

The two sat in silence, the light of the full moon washing over them. A single boat sailed over the calm, mirrored surface of the water, leaving long lines to roll away in its wake, crossing the moon's reflection and rippling its craters briefly before moving on.

Rylan turned to Dazel. "Could you help me recover? Help me get past the effects of the alchemy?"

"No," Dazel answered bluntly. "I can heal, I can cleanse, but what the potions have done to you is different. Beings with magical abilities have magic flowing through them like a current. It is not a physical flow like blood or water, but a more spiritual one. Your body's ability to channel that flow has been diminished by the potions you used. That is not something I or anyone else has the power to change. I cannot reach into your spirit to heal it."

As Rylan listened to Dazel's explanation, a wave of anger washed over her unexpectedly. "What use are these powers if I can't use them? I don't have *time* to heal! My father will be here any day now. I need to be able to help! Right now, I know I'm a wizard. What good is knowing if I can hardly light a candle?"

"Knowledge is never not useful," Dazel responded calmly. "You are a wizard. It is unclear how long the effects of potions will take to reverse themselves, but more importantly you can pass on the ability and the knowledge. Your children can be wizards, as can Mara's, and only you two can teach them, so far as we know."

Rylan realized what the goddess was telling her. It was not her duty to wield the powers like Mara, but to pass them on and help restore the ways of magic. Her father had raised her to be the bearer of his secret so that she may teach his next life all he had learned. Her new destiny was not so different. She would learn all she could from Dazel and Eres, and help her and Mara's children learn who they were and how to use their gifts, no matter how much magic she ever got to use herself.

"I understand," Rylan replied, her confidence rising like the tide.

~~~

"It's almost noon, Gant," Zhira said impatiently.

"I know. She'll wake when she is ready. It looked like she had been through hell," Gant replied.
~~~

"What is she doing here? How did she get into the city? Are there other knights here too?" Zhira started spewing off questions. Gant understood his brother's trepidation at Mai's sudden arrival, but he remained calm.

"She found us. I don't know how, but she's resourceful. I'm sure she had a good reason."

"Why are you helping her?" Zhira turned his questioning on his brother.

"Some people just need help. She obviously didn't come here to kill me or anyone else, or she would not have announced herself." Gant thought back to the last time he had seen the general. She had offered them an escape, but after he, Mara, and Rylan refused, she wrote them off, telling them to expect no mercy next time.

"I don't trust her," Zhira stated defiantly.

"I never said I trusted her, but it's like Rylan said—if we treat the enemy like they treat us, then we are no better than them. I won't deny her help if she needs it and I certainly won't kill her," Gant responded stubbornly.

"I appreciate that," Mai said from the doorway to the bedroom. She looked weak and tired leaning on the door frame.

"Sleep well?" Gant asked her.

"Well enough," she replied as she joined the two brothers at the small table in the center of the room.

"What are you doing here?" Zhira glowered at Mai.

"Running," Mai replied candidly.

Zhira and Gant both raised their eyebrows in surprise. Gant was sure she would have some story involving her own skills, making herself seem strong and infallible. As she explained what happened, however, Gant's face went from surprise to pure shock.

"Gjanion doesn't care about us, he only needs us to complete his goal, and to take down your daughter. He's obsessed. If Varyn falls but Mara escapes, he'll burn down Kyros looking for her. The army is nothing but a show of force, and he'd see every single knight dead if it meant taking Mara down and 'securing' Kyros. I began to voice my thoughts on the matter and was caught off guard." Mai lifted her tunic to show the stitched gash in her side.

"Who attacked you?" Zhira asked.

"The newest commander. His name is Pike and he is loyal beyond logic to Gjanion. I thought he was on our side, but clearly I was mistaken," Mai admitted.

"When you say 'our', who do you mean?" Gant asked, suddenly aware that Mai was talking about more than just herself.

"Tren came with me, along with his squire Kyra. They saved my life after Pike stabbed me."

"Kyra…" Gant trailed off in thought. *Why do I know that name?* He didn't know a Kyra, but he suddenly remembered who did. "Tanen!"

"What?" Mai asked.

"Is Kyra an alchemist, perchance?" Gant asked excitedly.

"Yes, but how did you—"

"Kyra is Tanen's daughter. He's here with us!" Gant nearly jumped out of his chair.

"Quite the family affair this is turning into," Mai observed.

"So what now? We just bring you on board? You're going to help us fight Gjanion, just like that?" Zhira snapped his fingers to emphasize his point.

"More or less," she said bluntly.

"Why should we trust you? How do I know you won't stab one of us in the back at the first chance you get?" Zhira was getting worked up.

"You're alive now, aren't you?" Mai asked in response, acknowledging that she had a whole night to kill them and she had not.

Gant shrugged, looking at his brother. "She has a point."

"So that's it then? She's in?" Zhira asked incredulously.

"It's not for us to decide. This decision is for everyone to make. I'll gather everyone, you stay here and rest," Gant said to Mai.

~~~
~~~

As Gant approached the new forge that Jerra, Sari, and Kei had been working on furiously for the last few days, he noticed that people he did not recognize were already patronizing the front counter.

"Up and running already?" Gant asked Sari as he hopped up casually onto the counter and leaned against one of the walls.

"Aye, 'tis been quite a bit o' work, but we got it done." Sari swung his short, hairy arm around as if to show off the new forge.

"We've been taking orders to help finance the forge itself," Jerra said, nodding towards the few people at the far end of the counter talking to Kei.

"Glad to see it's going so well," Gant replied.

"Wasn't hard," Jerra replied as she and Sari heaved a large anvil into place near the main furnace. "Apparently there isn't much by way of blacksmiths in Varyn, so when people saw us setting up shop, they were interested. Not much need outside of horseshoes and various building supplies around here. Weapons aren't much of a necessity in a city as fortified as this place, but we will make do!"

"Makes sense. Hey, any chance I could steal you three for a meeting?" Gant withheld the crucial information so as not to alert any unwanted ears to who they were. Mai appearing in the city had made him more wary of who could be watching and listening.

"Sure. We ain't technically open yet anyways," Sari replied.

"What's it about?" Kei asked as he walked over to add a fresh stack of orders to their pile.

Gant glanced around. Feeling that there were too many non-rebel ears around, he played it safe. "Just some…updates to the plan."

"We'll be there in a few," Jerra grunted as she pushed another anvil across the floor.

Gant made his way back to their temporary home and reconvened with Mai, asking her to stay out of sight until he had everyone together. On the roof, most of the rebellion had already gathered. Jerra, Sari, and Kei came from the forge and took their seats, followed by Mara, Rylan, and Litik, who were the last to arrive.

"All right, Gant, what's going on?" Jerra asked.

"Today we need to make a very important decision. There had been an unforeseen…"

"Skip the pleasantries, son. What's this about?" Radion interrupted him.

"Fine, here." Gant walked over to the staircase door and threw it open. Behind it stood Mai.

There were many gasps and surprised faces. Rezzik and Keylon stood up suddenly, taking defensive stances. Dazel and Eres stood stoic and indifferent behind Mara, who narrowed her eyes at the sight of the general. Litik was the only one to speak.

"How did *you* get in here?"

"Long story," Mai replied dryly.

Mara glared at her. "We have time."

Mai sighed and recounted what happened back at the army's camp and showed them all the wound in her side. Nobody spoke as she explained, but at the sound of his daughter's name, Tanen perked up.

"Wait, Kyra is here? Where?" he asked excitedly.

"I don't know. She and Tanen went to find a place to stay but I left the hospital to seek you all out. More specifically, I sought out Gant since I was fairly certain he wouldn't kill me on sight."

"So you want to join us? Just like that?" Mara asked suspiciously.

"You sound just like your father." Mai gestured at Zhira.

"The apple didn't fall far from the tree," Zhira replied.

"That apple did not come from your tree," Mai pointed out, garnering a surprised snort from Litik and a laugh from Kei that he quickly stifled when Mara shot him a disapproving look.

"You expect us to take you in, after all you've done?" Mara asked Mai.

"What exactly have I done? You're all still here, I freed your father after he saved my life, I gave you the chance to escape that night at the campfire…how have I personally done anything to get on your bad side except *be* on the bad side?"

Mara stood up angrily. "You tried to kill Reg, and would have if I hadn't interfered. You fought Rylan and my father in the throne room, who are alive because they are good fighters, not because you spared them.

You brought the whole army down on The Cave, where your knights slaughtered rebels. Don't try to paint yourself as something you're not. You are a cold, murderous woman who only looks after herself!"

Mara was breathing heavily as the two of them stared each other down. Nobody dared speak as the air between them sizzled with tension. Gant could see the rage in his daughter's eyes, and the desperation in Mai's.

"Look," Gant spoke up, breaking the silence. "We don't have to like each other, but we have a common enemy. This is our last chance to defeat Gjanion, and we need all the help we can get."

Mara turned her glare on him but didn't say anything. He stared back in a way only a father could. With nothing but his eyes, he implored his daughter to trust him.

"You are right, Mara. I've done nothing to earn your trust," Mai said, her tone changing dramatically from one of defiance to one of remorse. "I've been working against the rebellion all these years under the notion that I was helping myself, earning what I could by my own hand. I didn't stop to think about what it was doing to others. I was cold. Gjanion is a convincing man, and I was swept up in the righteousness of his promises. Unite the kingdom! Protect the people! What I didn't realize was that *we* were who the people needed protecting from. We weren't uniting the kingdom, we were subjugating them with fear."

There was a long pause. Gant looked from Mai to his daughter to the rest of the rebellion gathered on the roof. *I wish I knew what they were thinking.* Tension grew as the silence pervaded. Gant begged for someone to speak. *It can't be me. For this to work, she has to convince them herself.*

"I, for one, think that your change of heart is admirable," Keylon said, breaking the silence and surprising everyone. Mai nodded in thanks.

"I agree with Keylon," Litik spoke up.

"Me too," Rezzik joined his brother.

"Aye, me as well," Sari said in support.

Gant watched as Mara looked at them, then back at Mai. *Come on, Mara. Trust her. Trust me.*

Rylan spoke next. "I trust her."

Mara's head whipped around and she gave Rylan a look of disbelief.

"I don't think Mai is stupid," Rylan explained. "She sought us out knowing full well that we may turn on her. She came unarmed and literally bleeding. She left herself vulnerable to us and made her needs known. I've known Mai long enough to understand how hard that is for her to do."

Everyone nodded at that. Even Mara had to admit that Rylan's argument had struck a chord. She opened her mouth to speak, but Forbin beat her out.

"I would like to ask you one simple question, General Mai."

"I will answer honestly, and please do not refer to me by that title. I have renounced my role in the king's army."

Forbin nodded and continued. "Why do you want to fight with us? You're free now. You could disappear, flee, be rid of this fight and rest. Why stay?"

Mara eyed the former general intently. She had been wondering the same thing.

"Because," Mai answered. "Gjanion is power-hungry, and that is a hunger that can never be satisfied. He wants Mara defeated at all costs. He wants Kyros to be completely and totally his. Once he gets those things—*if* he gets those things—do you think he will stop? Do you think he'll be satiated? No. He will travel the world in an attempt to unify it under his sapphire-studded crown. Do you think there will be anywhere to rest if he achieves his goal here?"

Everyone saw the fear in Mai's eyes and understood. This wasn't about the rebellion versus the king, this was about preventing a disease from spreading to the rest of the world. They were the last defense between Gjanion and lands who were unaware of his existence. He would get the jump on other realms and it would be over before it began. Mai knew it, and now the rebellion did too.

"Okay," Mara said finally. "Help us win this fight. But I swear on my grandmother's grave, if you harm anyone here, I will end you."

A breeze came from behind Mara as she spoke, her eyes flashing blue menacingly.

"Save your magic for the fight. You're going to need it." Mai replied, a slight smirk on her face.

Chapter Twenty Two
The Wand

Later that evening, Mara was laying on her bed staring at the ceiling. She was mentally spent from the day's conversation and no thoughts passed through her head. Her mind was as blank as the white plaster above her. Kei walked in and she was suddenly unsure of how long she had been laying there.

"I think you need a break," he said sitting down next to her.

"A break? What's that?" Mara joked, sitting up next to him.

"Why don't we explore the city a bit tonight, just you and me?"

"I'd like that." Mara smiled. "We haven't really had a lot of time together since we arrived at The Cave…or even since I left Saros."

"It'll be fun to get lost in an unfamiliar place with you. Let's get cleaned up!" He jumped up and pulled her up off the bed.

A few minutes later, the two of them walked out into the street. The sun was well behind the wall and most of the city was covered in shadow. Mara tucked her dagger away under her tunic and grabbed Kei's hand. The two of them picked a random direction and strolled off.

"I really have been wound up for so long," Mara said, rolling her shoulders.

"I know," Kei said with a soft smile. "Understandably so, but even you need to let loose once in a while!"

Mara felt the stress leaving her body as she became distracted by all of the unique and non-threatening things Varyn had to offer. They passed vendors and shops that displayed everything from fruits and baked goods to decorative lamps and brilliant artwork. She and Kei stepped into one building whose walls were covered floor to ceiling with different sized paintings. They perused them for some time, admiring the amazingly detailed landscapes and beautiful color combinations.

"I see you are a fan of Hoti Hana's work, yes?" asked a small man with white wispy hair as they looked at a large ocean that was painted so realistically, Mara was sure she could see it moving.

"Oh, no sorry we are new in town and just exploring. Who is Hoti Hana?" Kei asked politely.

"Who is Hoti Hana?!" The little man looked personally offended. "He's only the greatest landscape artist in the world! People travel from all over to seek out his work. His greatest masterpiece sits in the hall of The Pearl House, where our queen lives. Hoti gifted it to her when she was the first elected leader of our great city! The man looked incredibly proud, as if the work was his own.

"I hope to see it someday," Kei said politely. "Thank you for informing us."

He and Mara exited the studio chuckling at the small man's intensity, and continued down the street towards a large building that looked more ornate than the standard white and grey square structures that lined the streets. Intrigued, the two of them approached the rounded, shell-shaped building and as they got closer, realized that it wasn't a building at all. The structure was nothing more than a rounded dome supported by dozens of marble columns, open to the outside in all directions.

Mara and Kei heard music coming from the wall-less building and went inside. Underneath the dome, the ground sloped down to a flat center floor. The slopes were cut at regular right angles to provide long benches for people to sit on.

"It's an amphitheater," Kei observed.

"It's beautiful!" Mara exclaimed, as her eyes came to rest on the main attraction: the source of the music she had heard.

In the middle of the amphitheater were about fifty people all holding various instruments, some of which Mara had never seen. They surrounded a single blonde woman who was holding a short stick and waving it furiously in time with the music. Confused, Mara went down several of the seating rows to observe. Kei followed and the two of them took a seat a few rows up from the bottom.

The woman at the center of the orchestra was tall, wiry, and moved with a purposeful elegance Mara had never encountered anywhere else. It was mesmerizing to watch her sway this way and that, pointing her stick at different groups in the circle of performers around her. As she did, something about the music would change. Louder, softer, faster, slower. The dynamics of the song were grand and it seemed to be directed solely by this one woman.

Mara was wondering how the musicians knew what to do when the blonde lady pointed at them until she realized that the lady was making subtle changes to how she pointed her short, vibrant blue stick at them. When she bounced the stick slightly at the end of her wave, she noticed those who hadn't been playing would play. When she pointed directly at a group, the notes they were playing got suddenly louder and took over the music. As she swept across a group holding what Mara was pretty sure were horns, their notes swelled gradually while the group behind her diminished their sound.

It was incredible to watch this woman direct the sound. It was almost as if she could see the notes in the air, pointing to them and rearranging them as they flew around the dome. Mara couldn't peel her eyes away. Eventually the group finished their piece and the stands, now half-full of people, applauded kindly, but not overenthusiastically. Mara was stunned.

How are these people not jumping from their seats and cheering as loud as they can?

"It must be nice to have something like this to enjoy whenever you want," Kei said as the musicians began to pack up and disperse. "Living here must be a dream! These people don't know how good they have it."

Kei's words hung in the air like the last notes of the piece the orchestra had just played. Mara realized that the reason the people were not cheering raucously is because it was familiar. It was no spectacle to them like it was to her. The two of them stood to leave, but Mara didn't follow Kei up the steps. Instead, she turned and walked down the remaining rows and onto the stage. She looked for the blonde woman and eventually found her talking with two of the horn players.

"Excuse me?" Mara asked, unusually nervous.

"Yes, how may I help you?" The woman asked kindly

Confused, Kei came up behind Mara but did not interrupt her as she spoke. "I was wondering…what were you doing just now? All of that movement and directing with your stick-thing…what was that?"

The woman smiled. "You must be new to Varyn. I understand not much of the rest of the kingdom has this sort of entertainment, at least not yet. What I was doing is called conducting. I guide the musicians through the music and make sure that the sounds you hear are the ones we intend."

Mara's excitement grew. "I noticed that! Certain things you did seemed to correspond with different directions…different sounds." Mara mimicked some of the actions she had seen as she spoke. "When you did this, they slowed down, but when you did this they got louder. I didn't notice at first, but I caught some of the subtleties."

"You are correct—conducting is a fine, subtle art that takes a long time to perfect. The beauty of it is that everyone has their own unique style. You may have noticed that my motions are fairly fluid. Another conductor may move more rigidly yet still produce the exact same music from their group. It's an art, almost like directing the music itself around the space with my wand the same way an artist directs colors with a brush. Put the right strokes together, and you end up with a masterpiece."

Mara suddenly understood why she had been so drawn to the woman's movements. It was not unlike how she directed magic with her dagger.

"A wand? That's what you call it?" Mara clarified, pointing to the thin blue stick in the woman's hands.

"Yes, or a baton. The name is far less important than its purpose. Brightly colored so the musicians can easily follow its movements, it helps me to direct and shape the sounds of my orchestra."

"That's beautiful," Mara replied, already thinking about her dagger more like a wand.

"Thank you, I hope you enjoyed the performance." The woman smiled and nodded, politely indicating that she was finished with this conversation.

"It was marvelous, thank you," Kei said, ushering a still gawking Mara away from the nice woman.

"A wand," Mara said to herself, pulling her dagger out from underneath her tunic.

"It seems a more fitting name. You don't really use it as a dagger, nor do you have much need for the blade," Kei smirked.

"I agree." Mara took Kei's hand. The two of them wandered back out into the courtyard surrounding the dome. The sun had set and the air had gotten cold.

"Thank you," Mara gave Kei's hand a squeeze and put her head on his shoulder.

"For what?"

"For giving me a night off. I loved it."

"Happy to help," Kei replied before kissing her under the light of the rising moon.

~~~

The sun rose and gleamed off the ocean's surface, reflecting directly into Mara's window. Groaning, she rolled over and covered her face with her pillow. Kei was already awake and stretching his back on the floor, continuing to heal from Mara's internal operation.
~~~

"Good morning, sunshine," Kei jested as he twisted and pushed against the floor.

"How are you awake?" Mara mumbled from under the pillow.

"Actually I didn't ever go to bed. After you fell asleep, I snuck out to the forge and made you this." Kei got up and grabbed something from his bag.

Mara sat up, intrigued. "What is it?"

"Our little adventure last night got me thinking. You don't use the dagger like a dagger, you use it like that conductor used her wand. So I thought that you should have something more like that."

Kei revealed a long, slender piece of metal, dyed a deep blue and engraved with a crisscrossing pattern that gave the wand a simple yet elegant texture. The handle was wrapped in black leather, and at the bottom was the amethyst, set in a small frame that had been shaped around the small stone. Mara gave it a few flourishes. It was perfectly weighted—light enough to swing around at will, but heavy enough that it felt durable and strong.

"Kei, this is amazing! Thank you," she said, pulling him towards her and kissing him.

"You're welcome. I figured a wizard like you needed something a bit more specialized than a makeshift dagger."

"That dagger was great. Don't sell yourself short!"

"Regardless, I hope this is better."

"It is. It really is," Mara said as she gave the wand a few more graceful swings, guiding a small arc of flame around the room in an intricate dance.

"Want some breakfast?" Kei asked after a few minutes of watching the blue flame glide around.

Mara nodded, and Kei cut up some unfamiliar melons and put them on a plate with an array of pink and blue berries. They sat together and discussed the events of the previous night, enjoying a quiet breakfast together for what Mara was fairly certain was the first time.

I could get used to this, she thought.

Nights out with him and quiet meals free of dramatic and intense conversations sounded bliss. Her fantasy was short-lived, however, when a colossal explosion shook the whole building. The remaining berries rolled onto the floor while Mara and Kei were thrown from their chairs. They picked themselves up quickly and rushed outside to see what the trouble was. In the middle of the street were Radion, Gant, and Zhira all on their backs. Mara surveyed the scene and saw that they had been thrown from a large black cauldron that was steaming with purple smoke.

"Dad, what the hell are you doing?!" Mara asked, still brandishing her new wand.

Both Zhira and Gant began to explain, and Mara couldn't make out a word they were saying.

"Allow me." Radion hobbled over on his cane. "We were testing the explosive properties of different shells from the creatures this town hauls in on its fishing barges."

"That's…the craziest thing I've ever heard. Why would you even think the shells could be explosive?!" Kei asked.

"It's not the shells themselves we want to explode, it's what we put inside them. We wanted to see how well the shells would hold," Zhira explained.

"We put it in the cauldron to protect ourselves in case of an unwanted blast," Gant gestured to the smoking vat.

"Good thing," Mara replied.

"Is everyone okay?" Kei asked.

Radion waved his hand dismissively. "Yes, yes we are all fine."

"Where is Tanen? I figured he would want to be in on the animal-based alchemy," Mara said, realizing the blood alchemist was nowhere to be seen.

"He went with Mai and Forbin to look for his daughter," Zhira answered.

"I should get over to the forge. Dad and Jerra are probably swamped without me." Kei kissed Mara on the cheek and strode off.

"Good night last night?" Gant asked his daughter as they cleaned up their operation in the middle of the street.

"Great, actually!" Mara said excitedly, regaling her parents and the old king with her best description of the orchestra and the conductor.

"Sounds like a wonderful evening," Zhira said, holding several shards of what looked to Mara like a crab shell that had once been shaped like a pumpkin. "What is that?" he asked, pointing to her new wand.

"Oh, Kei made it for me! It's a new wand," Mara explained.

"It's stunning," Zhira said, examining the new weapon.

"So when are you going to see the queen?" Mara asked Radion as they cleaned up the debris scattered about the street.

"I have been summoned this afternoon. Care to join me?"

"What for?" Mara asked.

"I doubt Queen Enli has seen a wizard before," Radion said.

"I'm not going to intimidate her with my powers. That's no better than Gjanion's strategy."

"Did I ask you to scare her? The war came to your town, same as it will here. You have fought against Gjanion, just as these people are about to do. You joined the rebellion and accepted me, just as I hope they will do. I will try to convince Enli that I am the best option to take over if and when we are victorious, but it is your word that may help tip the scales."

"All right, I'll come." Mara was curious about this queen. Would she be the kind of leader to see reason? Mara thought Rylan was still the best choice to rule Kyros, but she had to admit that Radion was better equipped for the near-term. He'd taken over once, and led the kingdom to a long era of peace. Maybe he could do it again.

~~~

Mara and Radion walked up to The Pearl House and ascended its stairs. In the main hall, Mara saw the painting that Hoti Hana had done for Queen Enli. It was massive, intricate, and stunning. The masterpiece seemed to have a whole world embedded in its frame. Mara stood staring at it and poring over every detail until a knight in blue armor and a white sunrise on his chest plate entered from a door to her left.

"Queen Enli will see you now," he stated before turning back through the door from whence he came.

Radion and Mara followed the knight through the door and into a stark white room with a table. Each of the five chairs was filled, and in the middle sat Queen Enli, her red hair tied up in a bun inside of her crown. The other four chairs were filled by people all wearing different colored togas.

"Your Majesty," Radion greeted the queen, bowing as much as his ancient body would allow. Mara followed suit.

"It is a pleasure to have you here, King Radion." Enli's smooth and regal voice made Mara feel compelled to do whatever this woman said.
~~~

"The pleasure is mine, Queen Enli," Radion replied.

Mara noticed he did not correct the queen on his title like he had with others so many times before. His well-worn line "Do you see a crown on my head?" bounced around in her mind.

"You've come to discuss a joint plan to stop the threat at our doors, yes?" Enli asked.

There was a sudden dismissiveness in the queen's voice that confused Mara. *Isn't she interested in our help?*

"Yes, and I believe time is of the essence. We would appreciate your assistance in dealing with the nuisance that is my grandson." Radion's tone gave nothing away.

"Your man Forbin said something similar when Enli granted him an audience. *You* would like *our* assistance? Preposterous!" exclaimed a man in a green toga sitting immediately to Enli's right.

"My Minister of Defense, Proteus," Queen Enli said, introducing the older, long haired man. He looked like he had spent more of his life on a boat than on land. His dark, sun-tanned skin was leathery and his hair was a tangled greying mess that fell down his back.

"That is my request, Minister Proteus," Radion said, giving no indication that the man's incredulous tone had fazed him.

Proteus leaned forward threateningly. "We are more than capable of defending our city. You've seen the doors, you've seen the walls. Our soldiers are watching the army march across the flats as we speak, and do you see us concerned? No. And yet, you come into our haven and ask *us* to help *you*? You have what, a dozen fighters at your disposal? Without us, you would not be able to achieve your goal. That is why you are here. But without you, our world does not change."

"Do any of you understand what you're up against?" Mara blurted out, earning a look from Radion.

"Who are you?" The queen turned to Mara.

"My name is Mara, and…" she paused. She was about to introduce herself as a wizard, but stopped short, not wanting to use her magic to intimidate them in any way. "…and I'm Radion's right hand woman. His own Minister of Defense, if you will."

Radion raised his eyebrows at her in surprise—a rare look from the old king. Mara ignored it and he played along. "My commander and I would like the full backing of Varyn in exchange for our knowledge of the enemy and the unique skill set we bring to the fight."

"You bring a war to our gates and ask us to risk our entire army for you when you couldn't even win with your own?" Proteus asked them. "Why would we let strangers lead our forces?"

"With respect, Minister, you have declared open rebellion. We did not bring this war to you. It was already coming. You sat back behind your wall while the rest of the kingdom fought and perished at my grandson's hand. Now he marches on your massive doors to finish what he started. We have tried and failed because we did not have the same fortifications as you do here. A coordinated effort utilizing Mara's magic and our intelligence combined with your defenses and man power, it will be a much more even fight," Radion explained.

"Magic?" Enli looked from Radion to Mara.

"She is a wizard, Your Majesty."

Mara didn't even try to hide the glare she shot at Radion. The old king had put her on the spot, and now she had no choice but to admit to being a wizard, despite not wanting to use her magic to intimidate the queen and her advisors.

"I see…" Enli leaned forward.

"We can help each other. This doesn't have to be about who is in charge. We just need to defeat Gjanion before he breaks in and—"

"Actually, Mara, it is about who is in charge," Radion said, interrupting Mara.

"You think you deserve the throne because you have fought him all these years?" Enli asked. "The kingdom of Varyn owes you a debt for what you did years ago, Radion, of that there is no doubt. But your time is past."

"I don't understand," Mara interjected. "Who cares who is in charge right now? We can sort this out later. Right now we need to stop Gjanion's army or else it won't matter who is in charge!"

"No," Queen Enli said firmly.

"No? That's it? That's all you're going to say?" Mara asked, anger beginning to boil inside her.

"I am the queen. The people voted for me to protect them and provide for them. I have done just that. I will not put the fate of *my* people into the hands of a failing rebellion. We will handle this on our own. You may pledge your loyalty to *this* crown and the Kyros I will create. Do so, and I will allow you to join our ranks, but I refuse to give up my position to a has-been king."

Radion sighed. "I admire your passion, Your Majesty. You care deeply for your people, and that alone makes you more fit to rule than my grandson. But I have done this before. I know what must be done in the wake of a victory to ensure it remains peaceful. I will need a successor, and perhaps you could fill that role. Learn what you do not know now so as to lead better later."

"You dare insult our queen's abilities?" Proteus challenged Radion.

"No, Minister. I am simply saying that my experience is valuable now, and her abilities are valuable later, with some new knowledge to buoy them."

"King Radion, I am more than capable of defending my people. I believe you have overstayed your welcome. It is time for you to leave," Queen Enli said with a tone that made it clear that she would not repeat herself. The knights standing to either side of the table took a step forward.

Before Mara could say anything, Radion smirked and dropped his cane. He lit his hands with red hot flames, pointing a hand at each knight. Mara hesitated, then reluctantly followed along, drawing her wand and pointing it directly at Queen Enli. Radion had once again forced her hand. The knights on either side of the table drew their swords.

Curse this crazy old king, Mara thought as she stood beside him.

"Not a step closer," Radion threatened. The tension in the room grew rapidly.

Queen Enli stood. "What is the meaning of this?"

"You tell me, *Your Majesty,*" Radion sneered. "You claim to be capable of defending your people. If that's so, then we shouldn't be a problem."

"You threaten me in my own halls? I would have you jailed!" Enli roared.

"Go ahead," Radion taunted her. "Do you have a defense against us? Could you stop the two of us right now? We could lay waste to all of you and it would take little effort. This is what King Gjanion has at his fingertips, and then some." Radion extinguished his flames. Mara, confused, lowered her wand. "He is a powerful, accomplished alchemist with an entire, well-trained army at his disposal."

The queen stared at both of them. Mara could see in her eyes that she knew the truth: Radion was right. They had no defense against magic or alchemy.

"You would wield this power against us if we denied your request? You are no better than Gjanion, threatening us with your power to get us to do what you want." Enli's face darkened.

"It was not my intent to threaten you, Queen Enli. Only to show you what you are truly up against, and that I am the best man to lead my kingdom."

His kingdom? Mara thought.

"You come into our city and attempt to scare us into following you? Your grandson had quite the role model," Enli fired back. "Your rebellion is on its last legs. You have shown that you are not capable of fighting this war. We will take up the mantle and dispose of the king ourselves."

"You're right," Mara said. "We failed. We came here as a last resort hoping you would help us, but clearly you are too proud to accept that without our leadership you will not succeed."

"So you just plan to sit back and let Gjanion try and take the city? After all the years you spent fighting?" Enli asked Mara.

"No, we will still fight back, but you'll lose far more people without our leadership. How will that look? A queen who refused the assistance of those who can stand against the king? The losses that pile up as a result? I've seen what Gjanion can do. I've gone toe to toe with him twice, and lost people along the way. Trust me, you need us."

"You need us, or you, personally, will lose," Radion said in his kingly voice, echoing Mara's point. "Who will you rule if Gjanion destroys your people? Who will trust you after you denied more resources to fight this fight?"

Enli opened her mouth to respond, but The Pearl House shook suddenly as an explosion rocked the city.

Mara looked at Radion. "That wasn't my dads."

Mara realized what must be happening, and sure enough a deep horn sounded from the direction of the doors, indicating that war was upon them.

Queen Enli's eyes widened as she looked at her ministers and knights, who had been staggered by the blast. She turned back to Mara and Radion and made a decision. "What do we do?"

Chapter Twenty Three
Breach

Tanen, Forbin, and Mai raced back through the city. The strong current of people running in the opposite direction slowed their progress, both with bodies and chaotic clouds of dust that churned up around them. Mai raced out onto the main street and, after a moment of confusion, gasped in horror at what she saw.

Tanen and Forbin came up behind her, equally shocked at the scene. Lying across the road, having crushed several buildings as they fell, were the large metal doors that had been the stoic sentries guarding Varyn like an impenetrable shell. The massive metal had been blown away from the wall as if made of paper. Mai hung her head. *He's already here.*

"How…" Forbin said softly as he surveyed the scene.

"We need to move. Now," Tanen instructed as knights began to march through the large, newly made hole in the wall.

The gleaming river of silver armor that flowed through where the door once stood was all too familiar to Mai. From this side of it, she fully understood. Her army had always been a wave of fear, using sheer force and showings of strength such as this to demoralize their adversaries and subjugate the people of Kyros. Most did not dare to stand up to row after row of fully armored knights brandishing swords, shields, spears and more. Those that did were met with swift and efficient retaliation.

"We need to find Kyra and Tren," Mai shouted above the chaos of the crowd swarming around them.

"No need!" a familiar voice called out.

Mai whipped her head around but couldn't locate the source. Kyra and Tren pushed and shoved their way to the side of the street where Mai, Forbin, and Tanen were standing. Kyra kept pushing through and hugged her father. The two of them embraced for a moment before Forbin interrupted.

"This is a lovely reunion and all, but we need to keep moving. We need to find the others!"

"Others?" Kyra asked, looking at her father.

"I'm with the rebellion, we're here to stop Gjanion," Tanen replied proudly, earning an approving smile from his daughter.

Mai led the group down an alley and deeper into the city, looking for an opening to cross the main street well ahead of Gjanion's forces and reunite with their friends. They dodged between panicked vendors and citizens until there was a clear path across. Once on the other side safely, they ran with the flow of panicked people, making it much easier to get back to the house where the rebellion was staying. They peeled off from the flood of citizens headed for safe houses, bunkers, and other fortified locations throughout the city, and ran down several alleys before reaching the familiar four story building.

"Tanen, take your daughter and Tren and round up everyone still inside. Forbin, come with me to the forge," Mai directed, not bothering to wait for them to listen.

She ran around the corner with Forbin in tow to find Sari, Jerra, and Kei still at the forge.

"Thank goodness!" Jerra exclaimed upon seeing them.

"What the hell happened?" Kei asked.

"Gjanion blew the doors off of the wall. The army has already started marching into the city," Mai replied.

"He what?!" Kei asked in disbelief.

"Where is everyone else?" Sari asked, already grabbing an axe he had recently forged for himself.

"I don't know, we are rounding up everyone we can find," Forbin answered, taking a sword from Jerra.

"Mara and Radion are still at The Pearl House, we need to make our way there," Kei said.

"I know yer…short-handed, so I made you this," Sari handed Mai a nearly identical replacement blade for her left arm. "'Tis not as refined as the one Gant had me make you before, but it'll do."

"Thank you." Mai took the blade and attached it to her stump and gave it a few swings. It felt good to have a useful left arm again.

The five of them ran back to the house to find Tanen, Tren, and Kyra standing with Litik, Rezzik, Keylon, Gant, and Zhira.

"Where are Dazel and Eres?" Kei asked, looking around for the goddesses.

"Here," Dazel said as the sisters appeared seemingly out of nowhere. "We were doing some reconnaissance. It appears Gjanion is marching his knights straight into the heart of the city."

"We know, we saw," said Forbin, sounding genuinely scared.

"Gjanion thinks he can divide the city up if he works from the inside out. He is using the initial shock of destroying the doors to move as deep into the city as he can while people panic. Once Varyn regroups, he will have already created barriers sectioning off the city making it harder for the defenders to work together," said Mai.

"That's pretty smart," Keylon observed.

"It is, but there is something else. Gjanion told me he needed time to recuperate after he blew the doors off. He said it would take so much energy that he would need time before phase two," Mai added.

"What's phase two?" Forbin asked.

"I don't know. I was stabbed before he got to that part."

~~~

"How fast can your forces organize?" Radion asked a still shocked Queen Enli. Mara stood with them on the steps outside of The Pearl House, where they had run to assess the damage. Off in the distance, smoke billowed up from where the doors had once stood.

"They should already be mobilizing. They're always ready enough to respond to any immediate threat, but with the doors already gone, we will be behind."

"I can stall them," Mara said confidently.

"No, you need to find Gjanion," Radion said, turning to her. "This all ends if the knights learn that Gjanion is dead."

Mara nodded, though she had hoped to have more time to figure out how she was going to end this conflict. Consulting the goddesses, Kei, or even Rylan before the fight began would have been helpful, but she was out of time.

"Radion," Mara pulled him aside while Enli conferred with Proteus.

"What do you need?"

"Come with me."
~~~

"I am not the conqueror I once was, and I cannot risk death. Not so close to the end. Kyros needs me when this is all over, otherwise things will devolve into even more chaos. This is your fight, and you know it. Defeat him and win this kingdom back!"

But it's okay if I die? Mara thought, thought she knew that the old king was right. It was time for her to face Gjanion and end the war.

"Good luck," Mara said to Radion before taking off across the courtyard and down a side street.

~~~

Radion watched Mara disappear then turned to the queen, who had just dismissed her ministers to oversee the forthcoming battle. "Everything is set?"

Enli nodded. "Yes, the defense of this city will last until not a single soul remains to fight for it. It will take all of us, but I think we can succeed."

"I agree, though the question remains—who will lead when this is all over?"

"We can discuss that when the battle is won," Enli replied.

"No, I don't think we can," said Radion.

"What do you mean?"

In a deft movement, Radion unsheathed a concealed dagger and drove it under her ribs. Enli barely had time to react before he removed it and stabbed her again. "You may have been given the right to rule, but I
~~~

was born with it. I am the best option this kingdom has to survive when this is over."

"How…dare…you…" Enli sputtered, a defiant look on her face.

"I will always do what I believe is in the best interests of Kyros. Removing you clears the way for me."

Enli tried to say something, but collapsed before she could utter another word. Radion moved her body inside the Pearl House and returned to the steps just in time to see the rebellion burst into the courtyard, led by Zhira wielding the relic sword. Radion looked down to see all that was left of the rebellion standing before him, except for one.

"Where is Rylan?" he asked the group from atop the steps.

"Where is Mara?" Kei asked in response.

"She just left that way." The old king pointed after where Mara had taken off. Without hesitation, Kei shot off after her.

"Kei!" Keylon yelled, running after her son. Sari ran with her.

~~~

Kei weaved through the alleys and streets towards the main gate, where he knew Mara would be going in search of Gjanion.
~~~

350

"Mara!" he cried out repeatedly, hoping to catch her before she caught the king.

A hand wrapped around his mouth. "Shut up, you idiot!" Mara's voice hissed from behind him.

She let go and Kei turned around. "What are you doing charging into battle alone?" he asked as his parents caught up.

"I need to face him. The sooner I find him, the sooner this is over," Mara replied, peeking around a corner with her wand at the ready.

"Okay, how can we help?" Sari asked.

"Stay quiet, for one," Mara said, glaring at Kei. "I don't want him or any knights knowing where I am before I know where he is."

"Can do. What else?" Kei whispered.

"Watch your backs and stick with me. Dispose of any knights we come across, and move towards the gates. With any luck I can get to him before he even enters the city."

~~~

Rylan snuck past the knights guarding the mouth of the street that led into the courtyard. The hood of her grey cloak shaded her face; she couldn't risk any of the knights recognizing her. She moved quickly and quietly, using the shadows of the vendor's awnings as cover and slipping into and out of doors that were left ajar in the initial panic. As she darted about,
~~~

memories of creeping about the castle and seeking out her father in his study while avoiding Lord Geralith seeped back into her mind.

She swept past two unsuspecting knights and climbed the side of a broken building. Crouching at the top, she surveyed the scene. Her father's army had secured the main courtyard and set up a makeshift command table with a crude map of the city. Standing over it was Commander Pike, as well as a few others that she couldn't make out from this distance. She edged around the crumbling roof and looked for an opening. Rylan was sure her father was still outside the walls recovering from what she assumed was an inhuman amount of effort he used to break down the doors.

She jumped and landed with a roll to break her fall, then dashed to another outcrop that provided shadowy cover much closer to where the doors had been. If she made a break for it, she might make it to her father, but there wasn't much cover between her and the gate, and there were a lot of knights guarding the way to him. She had to be fast, and hope that no knights were looking her way.

Now would be a great time for that invisibility paste Mara and I used, Rylan thought.

A memory suddenly flashed to the forefront of her mind. Rylan saw nothing but darkness, and heard the sound of several people in the room with her. Her eyes shut tight, she hoped with all of her might that they would not find her. The invaders crept around the room, and Rylan could make out her name among their whispers.

They won't find me, she thought. *They won't find me.*

When she opened her eyes, the strangers were gone. Not taking any chances, she darted from behind a chest that was far too small to be a good hiding place and wiggled her way behind one of the tapestries that hung from the walls. It was still dark when her father finally burst into the room, his robe splattered with red.

"WHERE IS SHE?" he bellowed.

Rylan opened her eyes. She was once again in the courtyard of Varyn, hiding in the shadow of a destroyed building's remains. Wiping the sweat from her forehead, she noticed something odd. Rylan brought her hand down in front of her face and realized that she couldn't see it. A sudden giddiness surged through her, making her feel like she had been struck by lightning.

"Oh my goddess…"

"Well done," a familiar voice said from behind her, causing her to jump. "You managed to do it again."

"I…I hid from the invaders when they came looking for us. I didn't realize…" Rylan looked down at where her hands should have been.

"You hid yourself in plain sight. Your emotions drove your magic."

"I can turn myself invisible?"

Dazel nodded. "It appears so."

"Did you just make a joke?" Rylan asked, as stunned by this development as the one she could not see.

"I suppose I did. Being here and being more human must be rubbing off on me."

"Dazel, why are you here?"

"I know what you seek to do."

Rylan looked up at the tall, elegant woman. "Are you going to stop me?"

"No, this is your journey. I know you wish to confront your father, but I must ask, what is your goal?"

"I…I'm not sure. Maybe if he sees what I truly am, he'll…I don't know." Rylan realized that she didn't have a true plan. She wanted to change her father, to save him, but she knew how unlikely that was.

"Go and face him. You are his daughter. If he is not too far gone, you may be able to save him," Dazel said, echoing Rylan's thoughts.

"I hope so," Rylan said, looking up at the goddess. She knew Dazel was being kind.

He will never forgive me. There is no ending that includes him. This only ends if he does.

Rylan looked down and saw that she was completely invisible, cloak and all. Cautiously, she crept to the gate, slipped past the multitude of knights, and walked out into the flats unnoticed. Outside of Varyn's massive wall were empty carts, tents in various stages of construction, and a few stable hands tending to the pack animals. An empty war camp. She located her father's tent and walked straight towards it, invisible to everyone around her. When she got to the entrance, she placed her hand on the flap and took a deep breath.

I am ready.

Rylan entered the tent. Her invisibility made it look like the wind had blown the flap open.

"I am sick of these salt flats," her father said to himself. "Desolate, barren, boring…"

Rylan was unsure of how to make herself visible again, but apparently she had already done so. When her father turned around, he gasped, noticing his daughter standing before him.

"How did you get in here?" he asked her.

"I could ask you the same," she retorted, gesturing in the direction of where Varyn's doors once stood.

Gjanion snorted. "Fair enough. Why have you come here? To stab me in the back again?"

"To stop you," Rylan replied, staring him down. "These knights all fight because you tell them to. All you have to do is pull them back."

"And why would I do such a thing?" Gjanion scoffed, sitting in his large, leather chair behind a desk strewn with orders and maps. "Until that wizard is dead, this war will rage on."

"Because I know deep down you're not an evil man," Rylan said, making one last attempt to appeal to the father she hoped was still inside of the man sitting in front of her.

"What if I am? Are you going to kill me?"

"No. I am not like you. I will never be like you. Despite your best efforts, you have failed."

"I hardly think I've failed, Rylan."

"Well you may defeat Mara, but you'll have to kill me to rid Kyros of magic."

That made her father pause, but only for a moment. "Are you telling me you're a wizard?" Prove it. If you're a wizard, you should be able to do magic like your friend! Let's see it, then." Gjanion put his feet up on the table in front of him and leaned back.

Rylan held her hand out to produce a flame, but not even a spark manifested in her palm. *Now is when I struggle? Seriously? So much for 'patience and practice'.* Rylan's face went red, but she quickly collected herself.

"I have nothing to prove to you."

"It makes no difference to me. You claim to be a wizard but you cannot do magic. It wouldn't be the first time you've been unable to deliver on who you are." Gjanion glared at her.

"I learned from the best. You lied to me all those years. You brainwashed me into thinking we were doing something good for this kingdom. You're no wizard, you're a king in title only, and you're not even a god! Yes, Radion is alive," Rylan said as Gjanion began to object. "You're a lying, ruthless alchemist whose lust for power has consumed him! You're a tyrant of a king and a failure of a father." Tears streamed down her cheeks as she hurled word after word at her father.

"Did you come here simply to scold me? Did you really think I'd believe you? Radion cannot live, and I am proof! Do you think a mere king could conquer Kyros the way I have? Could a normal man wield the powers I have at my fingertips?" Gjanion gestured to his crown and staff. "I am a GOD and I will rule this kingdom and many others before your new brother marries and brings me back into the world! He will look after my legacy, the one you decided not to be a part of."

At that moment, Rylan accepted that the father who had cared for her all those years, trained her in using potions, rode with her, and taught her how to be royalty had never been a father at all. He had only been investing in his future—making her reliant on him, training her to keep up his own legacy, not create her own. The man before her was no father.

Something changed in Rylan as she stared at him. She no longer saw him as a king or a father, but someone who needed to be saved. He was lost, consumed by a story; a lie that he used to define himself. Anger turned into sympathy, frustration into understanding, and pain into sadness. Her face must have reflected this, because Gjanion cocked his head in confusion.

Rylan simply said "I'm sorry, dad."

"Sorry? You think after all you threw away, all the effort I put into bringing you up on my own, that *sorry* is good enough?" Gjanion asked her incredulously.

"You misunderstand. I am not apologizing to you, I pity you. I am sorry for your loss, and mine."

"What are you talking about?" Gjanion stood up, anger flaring.

"I'm talking about the life we could have had if you hadn't become so consumed with who you think you are, so consumed with hunting Mara down. You read a book that told you something you wanted to hear and gave you a way to avenge mom's death. All it took was one story, which isn't even true. You were grieving—so ready to accept the first answer you came across...and you became a monster," Rylan finished quietly.

"Monsters were made to be slain, were they not? Then go ahead, cut me down. That's what you're here to do isn't it?"

"No," Rylan said without hesitation. "I will not stoop to your level."

"What a shame," Gjanion said as a bright burst of light came from the emerald staff. The last thing Rylan saw was her father's face, as stoic as a statue.

Chapter Twenty Four
A King's Betrayal

From the courtyard in front of The Pearl House, what remained of the rebellion looked up at Radion as if awaiting instruction.

"What are you all staring at?" the old king asked them.

"What is the plan?" Zhira asked.

"The plan is to win," Radion answered unhelpfully.

"And how do we go about that?" Mai asked impatiently.

"It seems rather simple to me…fight back. Push them out. Retaliate. There is no complicated plan. They're already here taking Varyn. Our job is to make sure they do not accomplish that task."

"Well let's get to it then!" Litik exclaimed.

Zhira turned to Mai. "You know these knights, you know his moves. Can you help us fight this off?"

"We are outnumbered, and the queen's forces were caught off guard. This won't be easy," Mai said.

"You don't say? He asked you to help us, not to do it for us," Forbin chimed in.

"All right, hang on." Mai took a second to formulate a plan. She took stock of who she had in front of her. Zhira and Gant were both competent fighters and accomplished alchemists. Kyra was as well, and Mai assumed Tanen knew enough to keep himself alive. The two brothers, Litik and Rezzik, seemed fairly incompetent but they had heart. They would fight ferociously and unpredictably, which could give them a surprising advantage so long as they had some support. The two goddesses were a mystery, but given their abilities, Mai assumed they could handle themselves just fine. Jerra was small, but she was clearly going to be a handful for anyone that came across her.

"Jerra, right?" Mai asked her. Jerra nodded. "Stay here and guard The Pearl House. Gjanion will likely send a team to find the queen. Make sure they don't."

"Yes ma'am," Jerra said, climbing the steps and standing beside Radion, who Mai noticed looked displeased. She ignored the old king and moved on.

"Tren, you take those two," Mai pointed at Rezzik and Litik, "and the goddesses move west across the city. If we can cut part of the army off from command, they may be easier to deal with. Eres, Dazel, once the five of you manage to separate the army into more manageable groups, your job is to maintain that split. I will take Zhira and Radion north towards the doors and Gjanion."

"What about us?" Kyra asked, standing with Forbin and her father.

"Sweep as much of the city as you can. Help any of Varyn's knights that you come across, as well as their people. You two can turn the tide of any fight with your alchemy, so take Forbin and do so," Mai instructed.

Kyra nodded. Gant turned to Mai with a confused look. In her plans, she had not addressed him. Mai pulled him aside and spoke quietly as everyone else formed into their teams.

"You need to find Mara. Gjanion is unbelievably strong. I know that boy meant well chasing after her and all, but he's not going to be much help. Mara needs someone with your abilities to help take him down. Remember what happened in the throne room? She and your brother couldn't even beat him."

"Then we should both go. I'll take Zhira and find her," Gant said confidently.

"Fine, I'll manage with Radion. Go," Mai said. She watched as Gant walked over to his brother and explained the change. Zhira nodded and they set off in the direction their daughter had gone. "Gant!" Mai called out before they left the courtyard. Gant turned back around, surprised. Mai too, was surprised by her outburst but it was too late to take it back. She walked over to him and held out her hand.

Gant smiled and took her hand, pulling her close for a hug. "Thank you for making the right choice."

"I'm glad you think that sending you off to your death is the right choice," Mai joked.

Gant rejoined his brother and took off down one of the streets that branched away from the courtyard. The rest of the rebellion split into their teams and set off into the city to push out Gjanion's army and prevent him from uniting Kyros in fear.

~~~

Varyn was consumed by fighting. Every street was filled with knights from both sides hacking and slashing at each other. Spears flew, arrows hunted down their prey, swords clashed, and the sounds of war filled the air along with the dust from the ruined streets, crushed buildings, and chaos of the battles taking place. Horses whinnied as knights were struck from their saddles. Citizens who had not been as quick to the safe houses were trapped or struck down. Knights of the queen's army seemed to be on their heels as the silver sea of Gjanion's knights flooded into every street, alley, and nook of the seaside city.

Tren led his team down an alley and popped out behind two knights that used to be in his command. He and Rezzik swiftly dispatched them, and the Varyn knights who had been dueling with them gave thanks and ran off to find more adversaries. Eres and Dazel
~~~

took the lead and went down another street, past a destroyed vegetable stand and a smashed-in glass wares store. Colored shards and trampled cabbage leaves littered the road as Eres and Dazel quickly overpowered a trio of Gjanion's knights, leaving them in a jumbled heap amongst a fallen building's debris.

"Push the knights towards the amphitheater!" Tren yelled at their blue clad allies over the din of war. "It'll separate them!"

The knights understood and went on their way, passing the message along to others. Rezzik turned to charge down the next street when an errant arrow suddenly sunk itself deep into his right shoulder. He howled in pain and Dazel caught him as he fell to the ground.

"Rez!" Litik shouted.

"I'm all right," Rezzik winced as he tugged at the arrow.

"Don't do that!" Tren shouted as he stopped Rezzik from trying to pull out the arrow.
"Our…Gjanion's knights use barbed tips. If you pull it out, it will do far more damage. You have to push it through."

"Goddess above," Rezzik lamented.

"We are no longer above. Hold still," Eres said as she waved her hand over the arrow. It disappeared in a wisp of smoke and the hole in Rezzik's shoulder closed immediately.

He sat up, rolled his shoulder, and smiled. "Thank you."

Eres simply nodded as she helped him up. The five of them resumed their quest through the city, using the goddess's magic to cut a gash through the fighting and split the king's army in two.

~~~

To the north, Tanen and Kyra climbed to the roof of a building that overlooked the main street of the city. Forbin clambered up behind them less gracefully. The three of them had skirted around as many fights as they could and gathered up supplies from ruined stands and abandoned homes. Forbin kept watch as Tanen and Kyra swept the dilapidated buildings for ingredients they needed to unleash their full alchemical fury on the king's knights. Now they sat unnoticed above the fighting and began crushing together a variety of dusty roots and half-squashed berries in a mortar and cracked pestle they had salvaged from an apothecary.

"So you kept up with your alchemy? Even in the capital?" Tanen asked his daughter.

"I didn't intend to originally, but it became a necessity. I don't think I would have survived the streets long enough. Or maybe it would have driven me to extreme measures sooner and I would have been found. Who knows," she replied as she cracked a selaroot in half.

"I am proud of you, you know," Tanen said, smiling at his daughter.
~~~

"You are? Why?" Kyra asked, slightly surprised by her father's words.

"You survived. You protected yourself. You used what was presented to you. It may not have been the best situation, but I'm much happier that you are alive as a squire in the king's army than dead on the streets of the capital."

"You're not mad at me for leaving?" Kyra looked up at Tanen. "Or for joining Gjanion's forces?"

"I was never mad, I was just sorry that what I was doing drove you away. I don't blame you for leaving. You were right, what I was doing was selfish and wrong. I didn't need to harvest the blood of others for our work." Tanen emphasized the point by making a small cut in his finger and letting his own blood drip over the mixture they were making.

Kyra smiled back. "I'm proud of you too. I didn't think you would change."

"I'll admit I took some convincing," Tanen said, thinking back to the night that Mara confronted him. "I want to be a father you're proud of."

"You've succeeded. I never imagined we would be here, using your skills to help the rebellion like this."

"Me neither, but I wouldn't want to be anywhere else. Are you ready?" Tanen asked her as he stood up and held out the dripping bowl of pink juice.

"I wish I had my staff, but otherwise yes," Kyra replied, taking the bowl from him. She took a large gulp and handed it back to him, feeling its effects almost immediately. "Let's go do some damage."

Before they climbed down the building and into the fray, Forbin turned to Tanen. "I noticed that you have some selaroot left. I have a small request, if it can be managed."

A few moments later, Tanen and Kyra were sprinting down an alley with Forbin directly above them, sighting the corners and hidden alleys from several feet up. The feeling of flying was exhilarating, and thinking none of the knights would think to look up, Forbin realized that he could help Tanen and Kyra avoid any surprises and could get the drop on the knights himself.

They rounded a corner and found several Varyn knights going blade to blade with three heavily armored knights that bore the king's lightning bolt and moon on their chests. The king's knights were humongous, and each brandished a two-handed broadsword. Despite their best efforts, the blue-clad knights of Varyn were making no headway against the mountain-sized men. Kyra stepped up behind them and lifted her hands. As one of the king's men swung his sword down towards her, the blade itself stayed levitating above him. Confused, he looked up and saw Forbin take hold of its handle, turn it so it was pointed straight down, and then give it a shove. The blade came down on the knight like a guillotine, cutting through the weak point in the armor around his neck. He crumpled instantly, and the other two knights turned to run, terrified. Tanen cut them off.

The two large men began swinging their broadswords frantically at the alchemist. Tanen dodged the large blades with ease, and moved faster than a man should be able to. With his knife, Tanen slashed at the knees of the knights, who then fell to the ground with cries of pain.

"You all can take it from here, yes?" Forbin asked the Varyn knights from above.

Confused but grateful for the assist, the knights simply nodded. Tanen, Kyra, and Forbin sped off down the next alley to help another group of knights.

~~~

Gant raced towards the main street with his brother directly behind him. They hurdled past several skirmishes going on in the side streets and alleys that connected the larger roads, intent on finding their daughter. The two of them turned down a road that Gant was sure led to the main street, but as they approached the junction, several royal knights blocked their path.

"How unfortunate," Gant said, slowing to a stop.

"Indeed," Zhira said, grinning.

They faced over a dozen knights—some wielding spears, others swords, and two sporting axes, all clad in their standard silver armor.

"Mara can manage for a few minutes on her own, right?" Zhira asked.
~~~

"She'll have to," Gant replied, removing the stopper from a small vial and draining its contents. Zhira did the same, and their hands ignited in flames.

"Mom did always say to be careful with fire," Zhira said to his brother.

"I think it's time we weren't."

The two of them turned into a tornado of flames, throwing arcs and balls of fire at the team of knights. The orange and yellow cascaded down on them like a flood, superheating their armor. A few knights managed to get out of the way, but the majority of them burned where they stood. Gant turned his attention to two knights that had escaped to his left.

"Oh no you don't," he said, as he shot his left arm out, summoning a wall of fire in their path.

The two knights turned and looked in horror at the alchemist, unaware of Zhira, who had drained another flask and pulled the earth up underneath their feet, sending them both flying over the nearest building.

"They won't be getting up from that one," Zhira said with a smirk.

A spear suddenly flew past his head, missing his ear by an uncomfortably small distance.

"Let's finish this, we need to find Mara!" Gant exclaimed.

As he and Zhira turned to clear out the last three knights, another squad came around the corner, continuing to block their path.

"Seriously?" Zhira sighed. "We're never going to get past them."

"Yes we will. Mara needs us," Gant said menacingly as he prepared to throw more fire at their assailants.

~~~

Mai walked with Radion towards the massive doors that lay strewn across the main street. His cane tapped with every other step—a steady rhythm in the chaotic orchestra of war. As they rounded a corner, three knights blocked their path. Two of them drew their swords while the third unhooked a hammer hanging at his side. Radion barely gave the hammer-wielding knight time to move before he was blown back by a sudden blast of air. He sailed past his companions and the two that remained looked at the old man in shock.

"He's not the one you have to worry about," Mai said as she dropped her cloak to reveal her bladed left arm.

"G-g-general?" One of the knights stammered.

"In the flesh," Mai said before charging them with full speed and, with expert precision, targeted the small gaps in their armor that allowed them to bend their legs. She drove her left arm into the right leg of one while her sword struck home in the left leg of the other. The two men fell to the ground instantly. Mai
~~~

calmly and finished the job, silencing each knight's cries of pain.

"You are ruthless," Radion said, sounding impressed.

"I have no choice. They would have killed me for betraying them," Mai replied.

"I admire your willingness to do what must be done."

"I didn't want to kill these knights, but if it's my life or theirs, it's not a hard choice. I will only kill who I must to stay alive. Let's keep moving, old man," Mai said, not wanting to dwell on it.

Radion's cane resumed its rhythmic tapping as he followed the former general. The two of them rounded the corner and, after dispatching a few more knights, came to the courtyard where Commander Pike was issuing orders to captains who were coming and going from the fighting deeper in the city.

"Commander!" Mai shouted, pointing her bladed arm at Pike.

Pike looked up in surprise, then narrowed his eyes at the sight of Mai. He looked more angry than surprised. He said something to the captain standing beside him and the two of them drew their swords.

"Do you want me to take care of him?" Radion asked, cradling a flame in his left hand.

"Save your energy. This won't take long," Mai replied, stepping into the open courtyard. Radion put out the flame and stood back.

"I will make sure you're dead this time," Pike barked.

Mai said nothing, instead choosing to walk slowly and deliberately at the commander. Expecting to feel exposed without her armor, Mai found that she instead felt free. She could move faster and more nimbly, and she would use that to her advantage. She expected Pike to not play fair, but no surprise attack came. It was just him and his captain against her. Mai didn't recognize the woman Pike was challenging her with, but it didn't matter. They'd both be dead soon enough.

Pike took the first swing, which was what Mai had hoped for. She ducked, spun past the commander, and quickly drove left arm at the unsuspecting captain. She deflected Mai's initial jab, but was one blade short. Mai brought her sword around quickly and the captain put her hand up reflexively. The blade struck home but got stuck in the woman's wrist, not quite severing off her hand. The woman screamed, but Mai ignored her. Her sword's blade was stuck in the captain's arm, so she let it go and turned to face Pike with nothing but her arm blade.

"Are you *sure* you don't want help?" Radion asked from the edge of the courtyard.

"Positive!" Mai yelled back.

"Suit yourself," Radion quipped.

Mai trained her attention on Pike's feet. She knew he was a fairly accomplished swordfighter, but the only thing he couldn't hide was his footwork. The position of his feet would give away any attack he brought against her no matter where he was looking or seemed to be aiming. She watched him shuffle towards her, trying his best to disguise his plans, but Mai was smarter.

Pike swung at her head but at the last second, changed direction and drove the point of his sword at her chest. Mai parried with her left arm and thrust her shoulder into him, causing him to stumble back. He tried again, this time attempting to break her base and knock her over, but Mai simply dove over his leg and cut backwards with her blade, leaving a cut along his left cheek. Blood trailed down his face and his eyes got wide. Mai noticed the signs of panic and saw in Pike's eyes the realization that he was on the losing end of this fight. His attacks got desperate, and desperate was easy to follow.

The commander telegraphed his every move, and Mai toyed with him. His slice overshot and she cut his other cheek. His thrust was easily parried and she landed a punch squarely on his jaw. His uppercut left his body exposed and Mai stabbed him straight through the chest, the tip of her blade coming out the other side. She quickly retracted it and prepared for his next attack but it never came. She had speared him through the lung and he was having trouble breathing. Mai almost felt bad for Pike; his loyalty to Gjanion was the reason he was going to die. Pike looked at her, and Mai saw defeat in his eyes. He didn't want to suffer, and she didn't intend to let him. He closed his eyes and Mai swung her blade, relieving him of the agony of a slow death.

"That was impressive," Radion observed, appearing beside her.

"That was hard work and dedication to my craft," Mai corrected him.

"You're right, you are quite the killer. It is not always easy to do the right thing…even if it is against your people."

"They're not my people," said Mai, wiping her blade on her tunic.

"They made you who you are. You feel nothing cutting them down?" he asked, as if he knew the answer.

"It's the price I must pay. I was wrong to help Gjanion, so I will do everything I can to stop him now."

Radion laughed. "Like I have for the last twelve years?"

Mai was thrown off by the old king's reaction. "We're on the verge of victory, Radion. What you have done has led us here."

"What I have done…what *have* I done, exactly? Sent thousands to their deaths in the name of freedom? The very people I wanted to lead back to peace. I've lost my kingdom, my people, and my family in the name of saving them all."

"That is the cost of war," Mai replied. "Sacrifice is necessary for victory."

"I just wish there could have been less of it," Radion mused. "I led the rebellion for twelve years, and it all came to this…this mess of a fight. Despite my best efforts, despite the sacrifice of so many, it became this disastrous war—a war I never wanted. I only wanted the legacy of our family to come to an end. Our story poisons the world. Knorr is an idea, a dangerous, deadly idea that corrupted many before him. I wanted us to be rid of that illness."

"What are you saying?" Mai asked him, confused by his rant.

"I'm saying that I am responsible for this war, because I failed to end the long line of corruption. I came into the knowledge of who we were far too late. I should never have had a son. I had my own son killed, yet even that was not enough," Radion admitted.

Mai's eyes went wide as the truth of the old man's words hit her. "You killed Gjanion's father? Gjanion told me his father died of an illness."

"That's not entirely true," Radion said. "Poison can look an awful lot like sickness."

"Why?" Mai growled, suddenly very angry. "Why did you do this?"

"Because *he* was Knorr. When I found out, I knew I couldn't risk him knowing." Tears came to Radion's eyes. "I had to be sure that the line ended, but by the time I made my move, Gjanion was already born."

Mai was astounded by Radion's actions. "Why didn't you kill Gjanion then, when you killed your son?"

Radion's walls were crumbling. "Because I got greedy. I wanted to rid Kyros of our family's poisonous secret, but I thought perhaps I could guide Gjanion—through Lord Geralith, as I was 'dead'—to be a good king, keeping our family in power. I had worked hard for our family to once again be on the throne, but I knew that was a dangerous place for my son to be."

"So that night, the assault on the castle twelve years ago…why did you try to have Gjanion killed?"

"It wasn't just him," Radion said bluntly.

Suddenly Mai understood. "The assassins were after the whole family."

Radion nodded. "They achieved half of their goal. I thought that by removing Gjanion and his heirs from the picture, the line would die with me."

Mai could not believe what she was hearing. "But Gjanion and Rylan survived. This war is your fault. This whole war…Gjanion's obsession with power…you led him to become what he is. You couldn't stop pulling the strings, even from the shadows!"

"I admit I did not think that Gjanion would become the tyrant that he did. I should have been swifter in my next moves. After he lost his wife and son, I knew I would have to do something else to ensure the family secret was lost. Another assassination attempt was out of the question. My last hope of destroying Knorr forever was to tell Gjanion a lie. With Lord Geralith's help, I made Gjanion believe *he* was Knorr reborn to throw the line of succession off forever. It was a calculated risk, but I knew it could work. In his grief and anger, Gjanion was ready to accept the story, so much so that he would never be convinced otherwise. A war there would be, but never a god."

"You manipulated him, killed his son, and fed him a lie about who he is, sending him into a power-hungry craze. This web of power plays and lies has left you a corrupted and twisted man who just wants to play the hero again. Is this what you wanted? Another chance to save *your* kingdom? Are you so consumed by the need to rule that you were willing to sacrifice your family?" Mai asked, anger boiling over.

"Of course not! I spent my life rebuilding this kingdom, and it is clear to me now that I should never have allowed anyone else to rule it. I let my efforts go to waste. I will reclaim my throne and bring my people back to an era of peace. I never intended to turn my grandson into the tyrant he became, but now his entire line will be wiped out and I will rule until my body turns to dust. I will be the last king, and there will be no more Knorr!"

"His…entire line?"

"Yes, they must all go. Gjanion is a bad seed, and bad seeds grow bad fruit."

"No," Mai said, quietly.

"No?"

"You plunged this kingdom into a world ruled by fear and revenge. You tried to rule from beyond the grave. I feel bad for Gjanion. He is nothing but a victim of your actions. You tried to erase history, to have Gjanion think he was something he isn't. Gjanion became a tyrant and used what *you* taught him to justify his conquest. Now history is fighting back. It doesn't matter if Gjanion really is Knorr. He believes it, and that gave him the motivation. He believes he has the right to rule and be respected, and he's been forcing it upon people for far too long. You have caused enough damage and destroyed enough lives. You may have destroyed Gjanion's, but you will not destroy Rylan's," Mai said menacingly. "She is pure, she cares, and she will be a far better leader than you ever were!"

"I know you care for her. Geralith told me all about how you trained her and looked after her once her mother had passed. But she must go. Our whole family must go. For the good of Kyros."

"You fool," Mai growled.

"Fool? General, you—" Radion began to respond but Mai cut him off.

"You selfish, manipulative, cowardly, despicable old man. You were supposed to be dead long ago. For the good of the kingdom, I think it's time that became a reality."

"So what's your plan, general? Kill me? Your friends have only just come to accept you, how will it look to see me dead by your hand?" Radion asked confidently.

"I killed General Long, and Gjanion promoted me," Mai adopted a more aggressive stance. "I think I can manage."

"Good luck," Radion smiled darkly as he dropped his cane and ignited a flame in his hand.

"She doesn't need luck," said a voice from behind the old king.

Radion turned around quickly and Mai looked up to see Gant and Zhira standing on the edge of the courtyard.

"Gant?" Mai asked, stunned. "I thought you had gone to help Mara?"

"We got sidetracked."

"And now we're here to help you," Zhira said.

"We heard enough. Mai's right, Radion. This is not Gjanion's fault. It's yours," Gant said in a voice that sent chills down Mai's spine.

"Three on one, eh?" Radion observed as Zhira drew the ruby-hilted sword. "Do your worst."

~~~

Outside of the city, Mara led Kei, Sari, and Keylon towards the tent. Piles of half-burned logs dotted the paths between the empty tents that stood waiting for their tenants who were currently fighting in the heart of the city. The sun shone on the ocean out past Varyn, but beyond the wall, it had recently rained. The pooled water on the salt flats had become a perfect mirror of the rolling grey clouds above, mimicking the sky all the way to the horizon.

Sari and Keylon poked their heads in and around the tents as the four of them moved towards the largest of the canvas abodes. Keylon surprised a stable
~~~

hand who was corralling a goat that had escaped from the makeshift pen. His pants turned a darker shade of grey in the front as she put a hand over his mouth before he could scream.

"Make a sound and you won't be able to chase that goat," Keylon threatened. He nodded fervently in understanding and she removed her hand. The boy picked up the goat and hurried away as quietly as he could.

They approached the king's quarters and Mara drew her wand. *This is it.*

Mara gave a signal and the four of them charged into Gjanion's tent. The amethyst glowed as Mara entered first, ready to defend herself from Gjanion. What met her instead was the last thing she expected.

Chapter Twenty Five
The Last King

Mara stared at the lifeless body on the floor in front of her. The princess's blonde hair fell across her face like wavy golden waterfalls. Rylan's eyes were closed as if she was sleeping, but Mara could tell something beyond physical was missing. She bent down and felt for a breath, a pulse, anything to prove to her that Rylan was still alive, but there was nothing. Rylan was gone. Her brain refused to accept reality and desperately tried to come up with another explanation, but Kei, Sari, and Keylon entered the tent behind her and Kei's gasp forced her to confront the truth.

"You…" Mara said quietly under her breath to Gjanion, who stood across the tent from her. The words would not come. Emotions ravaged her like a roiling sea tossing a boat.

"She made her choice, and I made mine," Gjanion said so matter-of-factly that it sounded like he was talking about a simple game of chess.

"You KILLED HER!" Mara screamed.

The sheer power of her magic tore the tent at its seams and blasted its pieces away from them in all directions. The breeze that had been blowing across the open flats ceased, and the world around them went quiet. The thin layer of rain that had fallen on the white salty ground was perfectly still, mirroring the sky above it. Even the clouds above them slowed. Mara's anger was boiling over, and it was being absorbed by her surroundings.

"We should stand back," Mara heard Kei say to his parents. The three of them withdrew, standing at a safe distance and ready to help should she need them.

"You may see me as a monster, but I assure you that I am not. I only wanted to unite the kingdom, and I was so close to my goal…until you appeared. I regret that you survived. It has cost me the lives of many more knights than I had anticipated, but they are expendable compared to the total conquest of Kyros."

"Even your own daughter?" Mara growled.

"I only ever give people a choice: bow to me and join my kingdom, or be removed. Rylan made her choice, and I am a man of my word. The moment she left the castle with you, she chose her fate," Gjanion explained.

"And you have chosen yours," Mara growled before summoning and hurling an enormous ball of fire from her free hand.

Gjanion casually directed it off to his left, where it hit the ground in a blue and white explosion, instantly evaporating the water it smashed into. "You're becoming predictable, Mara. It's only ever fireballs with you."

"You want unpredictable? I'll show you unpredictable."

~~~

Mai ran headlong at Radion, her left arm held out in front of her like a spear. Radion flicked his hand effortlessly and she was sent sprawling across the street with a sudden burst of wind. Gant yelled and lifted his hands, lifting the old king up into the air by forcing up a large slab of earth. Radion frowned and jumped from the slab before it got too high. He landed and sent another gust of wind at Gant, knocking him back. Gant lost focus and the slab of the street he had lifted came crashing down.

Ruby glowing, Zhira swung the sword in front of him in quick arcs sending slices of pure, white energy at the old king. Radion dodged them with the agility of someone half his age then picked his cane up and launched it at Zhira from the side. Zhira turned the blade of sword towards the oncoming projectile and slashed it in half. The two pieces clattered as they fell to the ground.

Mai got up and made eye contact with Gant. They needed to work together, to be coordinated, otherwise Radion severely outmatched them. Gant began lifting small pieces of earth up in front of her that
~~~

ascended into the sky above the old king. Mai took off from the ground and followed the steps Gant made for her until she was directly above Radion. Zhira held his attention with a steady stream of fire that Radion was diverting with as much wind as he could muster. Every so often, Zhira would swing the sword as well, sending more arcs of energy at the king, who would have to avoid them while maintaining his defense of the flames.

Once he noticed Mai above Radion, Zhira let up his attack so that Mai wouldn't burn herself on her descent. Mai jumped from her foot-sized platform and drove her bladed arm down below her, meaning to impale Radion.

She was a second too late. Radion noticed Zhira look up and managed to get out of the way just in time. Mai hit the ground with significant force and instantly blacked out. Everything moved in slow motion as Zhira, realizing what was about to happen, swung the sword to try and hit Radion with another arc of energy. At the same time, Radion reeled his hand back, intending to blast Mai into the nearest building and kill her. Zhira watched as the energy from his latest slash travelled across the courtyard towards Radion, but was surprised by Gant, who had run towards the fallen Mai as soon as she hit the ground. He reached Radion as the old man extended his wrinkly hand, sending him flying over the street and crashing into a building on the other side.

~~~
~~~

Kei had grown up with Mara and watched her discover and hone her powers. He had always been in awe of her commitment to magic—anything she wanted to do, she would eventually accomplish. He had watched her learn to summon lightning at will, send boulders flying across the quarry near Saros, and plow feet of snow off the road with a flourish of her hand. She was a force to be reckoned with, and he understood just how much she was capable of.

Standing beside his parents on the stark, white salt flats that were partially covered in rainwater, Kei watched the most incredible display of magic he had ever seen Mara perform. Not because of the sheer power of her magic, but because of the unique and devastating way she wielded it.

Flames poured out of her wand in one long steady blue ribbon, continuously barraging Gjanion. Mara's movements were reminiscent of how the conductor had guided her orchestra, mimicking the long, swooping motions. There was beauty and grace in the flames as they wove through the air. Gjanion did his best to break and deflect the ceaseless stream of fire, which kept him on the defensive, unable to retaliate. With her other hand, Mara pushed the water at their feet towards the king, creeping up his boots and armor until it came to his knees.

Finding it difficult to move, Gjanion tried to direct the water away with the staff, but every time he thought he had an opening, another swath of cobalt flame came from a different direction, calling his staff away to defend him. Gjanion roared in frustration, but

Mara did not relent. With a flex of her hand, the water froze instantly, becoming crystalline, white ice around the king's legs. Gjanion tried to hack away at the ice with his sword, but it was slow going. The amethyst in Mara's wand glowed the brightest purple Kei had ever seen, helping her control her powers and subdue Gjanion before he could attack. The gemstone glowed brighter still until Kei could barely look in Mara's direction. Purple light emanated from the wand and mixed with Mara's vibrant blue flames, all set against the stark white salt flats. Kei watched as the extreme light engulfed Mara entirely until the amethyst finally gave out, shattering in an incredible and powerful explosion.

~~~

"GANT!" Zhira cried out as his brother's body collided with the building, punched a hole in the stone wall, and disappeared inside. With a fury he had never felt before, Zhira turned and charged at Radion.

The old king tried to wave Zhira away as he had done before with Mai, but the wind was no good. Radion's eyes widened as Zhira came within striking distance and began slashing and hacking maniacally. Zhira had the old king reeling, using every ounce of anger and power combined to strike the ruthless rebel leader down. Radion was an experienced fighter, and after expertly dodging Zhira's relentless assaults, landed a punch, connecting with Zhira's left cheek.
~~~

Zhira staggered back for a moment, allowing Radion time to drink another potion. Radion quickly extended his arm and a piece of the street came loose and flew at Zhira, who was in the middle of uncorking a vial of blue liquid.

Zhira dodged out of the way and drained the vial's contents. "This ends now," he said angrily.

"Have at it then," Radion taunted before punching an enormous fireball towards Zhira.

Zhira pulled his hands up in front of him and the street broke apart, forming a wall for the flame to collide with. When they met, the wall broke into a multitude of pieces that Zhira began launching at Radion. Radion dodged between them and moved closer to Zhira with each step. Streaks of fire and chunks of paved road flew between them and collided in midair until the two men again stood within striking distance of each other.

In a move that surprised Zhira, Radion made a grab for the sword and managed to wrestle it from the alchemist's hand. Zhira recoiled, turned away, and instinctively tried to draw some of the exposed earth from beneath the street up to block the incoming blade, but the strike never came.

Zhira turned back around and saw a slender silver blade sticking out of Radion's chest. The blade retracted and emerged again in a different location before being removed and allowing Radion's body to fall to the ground, revealing Mai. The look on her face terrified Zhira even though he knew she was on his side.

Neither of them said a word as the old king's body slumped to the ground. Once they were sure he was truly dead, the two of them took off towards the building that Gant had gone crashing into.

~~~

How long have I been asleep? Rylan thought to herself as she sat up.

As her eyes adjusted and the scene that lay before her came into focus, pure horror shot through her like lightning. Mara, Kei, Sari, Keylon, and her father all lay unconscious, the thin layer of water that had yet to seep into the salt flats rippling around them slightly in the breeze.

What happened? Why can't I remember anything?

Dread seeped in as she realized they all might be dead. Rylan could feel her heart breaking. She raced over to Mara and put a finger on her neck to feel for a pulse, sighing in relief as she felt the blood still pumping in her friend's veins. She checked on the rest and found them all to be alive, which provided her some comfort. She walked back over to Mara and splashed some water on her face. Mara woke with a start and jumped up, eyes glowing blue. The water around them evaporated.

"Mara, relax," Rylan said, scared of her friend's sudden surge of power.
~~~

"What happened?" Mara asked as the blue flare receded from her eyes. "Rylan!" Mara yelled with relief and wrapped her arms around her friend.

"What's going on?" Kei's voice came from behind the two of them. His face broke into a huge smile at the sight of Rylan. "Glad to see you're alright," he said to her.

"Was I not?" Rylan asked, confused.

Mara opened her mouth to explain but was interrupted by Gjanion, who had regained consciousness and saw his daughter standing across from him.

"That's impossible!" he roared.

"What's impossible?" Rylan asked, distraught.

"Ry, you were…dead," Mara said hesitantly.

"Dead? But how did I…" Rylan's voice trailed off as her eyes fell upon her father, standing alone on the flats that mirrored the sky. The clouds began to roll faster beneath his feet and above his head as Rylan's anger raged inside of her. The last thing she remembered was confronting her father. It all came flooding back. He had killed her.

"I wanted to spare you. I thought deep down there would be something left worth saving…" Rylan said, staring down her father.

"I gave you the choice. You're either with me or you're in my way!" Gjanion replied in defense.

"Oh, I am MUCH more than in your way now," Rylan said as her fingertips began to spark, and her hair began to stand on end.

"Rylan, what are you—" Mara began to ask.

"Stay out of this!" Rylan said, whipping her head around and glaring at Mara with glowing, golden eyes.

"Oh no," Kei said quietly, backing away at the sight of Rylan's eyes.

"Rylan, stop! You don't know what you're doing!" Mara screamed at her as the wind picked up and carried water with it so fast that it stung as it hit her skin.

"I know EXACTLY what I'm doing. I finally get to be the person I always wanted to be!" Rylan laughed, sounding unhinged.

When Mara was a child, her fathers had helped her learn how to control the magic she conjured whenever she became overly emotional. The stronger the emotion, the harder it was to control her abilities. Mara watched as Rylan's emotional dam finally burst, aided by the most abhorrent of betrayals from her father. The clouds above them roiled like the surface of a stormy sea, while the wind picked up so drastically that it was stripping the salt flats.

Mara recognized that Rylan was experiencing a rush of her newfound powers that came with this emotional flood. Her friend was careening towards a point of no return, and Mara had to stop her.

"RYLAN STOP!" Mara roared, knocking her over with a wave of water.

Rylan tumbled over herself and got up on all fours, looking up at Mara in shock. "What the hell was that?!"

"You don't know how to control this, you need to relax!" Mara replied as she froze her friend in place before turning back to Gjanion. "As for you—"

Mara was sent flying back by a bolt of lightning. She tumbled head over heels and knocked over Sari and Kei.

"Save your speech, wizard. This ends now!" Gjanion declared, before sending a barrage of lightning in her direction. Mara pulled up a sheet of water to protect herself and the others before returning fire with a sheer blast of energy from the tip of her wand. The recoil made her stumble, and she realized that she no longer had the amethyst to control her powers. She had to do this on her own.

Or do I?

Mara looked at Rylan, who was figuring out how to unfreeze herself with her newfound powers. If she could get Rylan under control, Gjanion would be no match for the two of them. She deflected a bolt back at Gjanion, which sent him to his knees, and ran over to Rylan to unfreeze her.

"Help me take him down," Mara offered a hand to her friend.

Rylan's face was streaked with tears. Whether it was from the salty wind or her emotional break, Mara was unsure. She suspected the latter.

"You're right, I can't control this. What if I hurt you? Or one of them?" Rylan asked, pointing toward their friends and looking genuinely worried. Mara was glad to see that she had broken through Rylan's crazed state.

"You don't have to control it. If you can distract him, I can take him down," she explained as Gjanion rose to his feet again.

"But how will that look? Another royal takeover with the help of a wizard…"

"How will our bodies look lying lifeless next to each other?" Mara snapped back.

"Okay, okay. Let's do this."

"Just *feel,* don't think," Mara advised the inexperienced wizard. "Your body will guide you."

"I've got this," Rylan replied confidently.

Gjanion looked furious, and the alchemy that ensued matched his rage. Erratic yet powerful, his attacks careened towards the two wizards in rapid succession. Sparking bolts of lightning, spears of ice, and shockwaves of pure energy came at them in a torrent from the king of Kyros. Rylan began tracing a circle in front of her, and the clouds mimicked the motion, swirling down from above her father and funneling water down on him with monsoon-like force. Gjanion looked up, and Mara took advantage of the momentary distraction, launching a ball of blue flame directly at him. He managed to deflect it in time and redirected Rylan's barrage of water her way in retaliation. The wave crashed into Mara, but not before she could manifest a whirlwind around Gjanion that kicked up the salty ground. The fine granules got in his eyes and he cried out as he brought both of his hands to his face, leaving him exposed.

Rylan tried to seize the opportunity and send her father flying across the flats, but she ended up sending herself flying instead and barely managed to catch herself with a cushion of air before crashing into the ground. Gjanion cried out and sent lightning bolts in all directions. Mara managed to avoid them, but watched as several flew towards Kei, Sari, and Keylon.

"Not this time," Mara said to herself as she took a deep breath and reached out towards the bolts.

Kei watched, stunned as the lightning stopped in mid-air. The bolts crackled and fizzled as they were held in place by Mara, whose eyes glowed bright blue.

"Move!" Sari exclaimed. They got out of the path of the bolts and once they were safe, Mara released them.

"Thank you," Kei said, salt coating his tunic.

Mara smiled in reply and turned her attention back to Gjanion. *That was far too close.*

She looked over at Rylan who had managed to figure out how to deflect her father's assailing beams of energy with her own hand. Mara was impressed. While the necessity of the moment seemed to be having a profound effect on her ability to control herself, Rylan was managing to figure things out rather quickly.

Mara's brain worked fast. This fight was going on far too long, and someone was going to get hurt, or worse die. They had to end this. Thinking about what had happened mere moments before when the amethyst exploded, when all of them had been felled by the magic that had poured out from the gemstone, gave Mara an idea.

Perhaps if I channeled that level of magic again…

"Forgive me," Mara said to Rylan, though she knew her friend could not hear.

Mara turned towards Gjanion and began running at him at full speed. Her eyes glowed brighter and brighter until she could no longer control the magic coursing through her. Blue fire sprung from her hands and crept up her arms as she approached a panicked King Gjanion. He tried to slow the sudden blitz, but before he could raise his staff in defense, Mara collided with him at full speed. Her body felt like it was being torn apart piece by piece as she concentrated on her power until the magic erupted from her, creating an explosion that enveloped them both.

Chapter Twenty Six
Daughter

Zhira's heart pounded as he ran into the building, followed closely by Mai.

Please don't be dead, he thought as he crossed the road.

Together, he and Mai dashed inside and began to push away the rubble until they found Gant covered in dust and laying contorted under several large pieces of wall. Zhira dropped to his knees in despair and kept digging, trying to free his brother while Mai stood over him motionless.

"Don't just stand there, help me!" Zhira begged her as he desperately clawed at the mounds of stone surrounding Gant.

His fingers began to bleed as he frantically pushed pieces of stone away from where his brother had landed.

Please don't be dead.

After a couple of desperate minutes, Gant had not moved and Zhira began to run out of steam. He hunched over and began to sob, his whole body shaking.

"Perhaps we can help," a familiar voice said from what remained of the doorway.

Zhira and Mai turned to see Forbin, Tanen, and Kyra standing in the crumbling doorway. Without a word, Tanen knelt down beside Gant and examined him using the same technique he had used to fix Kei's back; a purple latticework of bones and muscles appeared as Tanen ran his hands over Gant's body.

Please don't be…

"I am sorry, Zhira, I cannot bring people back from the dead. Gant is gone," Tanen said, standing up and hanging his head.

Zhira looked up at Tanen with a blank face, managing a nod of appreciation to Tanen for trying his best. He then turned back to his brother's lifeless body, and just sat there.

We will never share a laugh again. You won't be there to watch Mara's family grow. Never again will we brew potions and burn the candle all night doing research. No more drinks and sharing memories of mother.

Gant was gone, and Zhira felt as though a part of himself went with his brother. It was too much. First his mother, and now his brother; Zhira felt empty. Broken. He collapsed into the rubble he had pulled away from his brother's body and began to cry, his whole body shaking with every sob.

~~~

Mai took a step back towards the door. The man who had saved her life, who had given her a chance, who had never hated her, who had convinced the others to accept her, was gone. The feeling of loss was too powerful for her. She could not bear to look at Zhira, nor be in this place a second longer. Never had she cared about someone dying until now. Mai turned on her heel and bolted from the building, unsure of where she was running to, but running all the same. She sprinted across the courtyard and disappeared between two of the buildings.

~~~

The world was blindingly white. Mara squinted as she looked for any sign that her plan had worked. There was nothing—only a white, boundless light surrounded her in all directions. She looked down and realized that her feet were not on the ground. She was floating.

"Where am I?" Mara asked aloud to herself, her voice echoing in the luminous void.

"The Conversion," a familiar voice said behind her.

"Eres." Mara regarded the goddess of life with a respectful nod. "What is The Conversion?"

"It is the place between your past life and the next. The place where you transform from who you were to who you will be next," Eres explained.

"How are you here? Did you die too?"

"No, my magical specialty was the magic surrounding life. The Conversion is part of life's cycle, and with some practice it can be accessed through magic. Your people prayed to me as the goddess of life, and while I am no goddess, I do possess certain unique abilities that helped me steward the souls of loved ones from one life to the next," Eres answered, looking past Mara.

"Mara," said another voice she hadn't expected to hear.

"Dad?" Mara turned to see Gant, dressed in the same clothes she had last seen him in, but far more dusty and torn. "What happened?"

"Radion's motives were not as pure as we had thought. Your father, myself, and General Mai removed him from the equation," said Gant with a soft smile.

Mara suddenly understood why she was seeing her father here. "He killed you."

Gant nodded.

"Gant, it is time," said Eres.

"Time? Time for what?" Mara asked, suddenly panicked.

"Time for me to move on. My next life awaits." Gant gestured to an aetherial vision beside him: a woman holding her husband's hand as she screamed in pain. Somewhere out of view, a voice calmed the woman, telling her to breathe and relax.

"I am proud of you, Mara," Gant said softly. "I am proud to have been your father. I hope we will meet again in another time."

"Wait, no!" Mara cried out, desperate to not lose another family member. "There must be some way to bring him back…to bring us back!"

"I cannot bring people back from the dead, Mara," Eres explained.

"We aren't dead! We haven't transitioned to our next lives yet, you can send us back," Mara said, hoping the loophole would save them.

"Technically, this is untrue. You are dead. Your soul was sent here, you did not choose to be here like me. Now a soul must pass through to the next life. One for one. Never imbalanced."

"But…but…" Mara stammered. She was not ready. Her life was far from over. Panic and fear set in. She had done what she had to in order to defeat Gjanion, but now that she was here, in this place, the reality of her decision set in. Kei, Zhira, Rylan, and the others would all be beyond distraught if she was gone.

Dad. Mara's mind quickly turned to Zhira. *He's going to break. Losing me and Dad and Grandma…he'll never recover.*

"Is there no way to send him back?" Mara asked, pointing to her father. "My father will be devastated beyond anything I can imagine should he lose us both. Gant is his brother, he needs him."

There was a long silence. Mara noticed that The Conversion had a slight hum to it.

"I may be able to send him back," Eres said, breaking the silence, sounding surprisingly somber.

"Really?" Mara asked.

"Yes. Like I said, The Conversion must always be balanced. Your souls are here by fate, and so two souls are required to continue on. But I am here by magic, so I can return the same way. But it does not necessarily have to be me. I can send Gant back through magic, then I can leave the way he was supposed to."

"I could not ask that of you," Gant said to the goddess of life.

Eres smiled softly. "It is a sacrifice I believe fits the responsibility I bear for this situation. You are both here because my sister and I burdened your world with our brother's legacy. I cannot, in good conscience, send you both on from this life."

"Send him back," Mara said. "Let my fathers finally have their own life. I have brought enough pain and death. Without me, the kingdom will be at peace."

Gant smiled. "I admire your sacrifice, Mara, but your father and I have always had our own life, and you were the best part of it. You should go back, they still need you. This fight may be over, but peace is far from certain."

"Dad, you and Dad have both sacrificed your lives. Let me do the same. Please!" Mara began to cry.

"I'm sorry, Mara, but I will not allow you to do this. Zhira still needs you, Rylan still needs you, Kei still needs you, and the kingdom still needs you. Go and be the amazing woman I know you are—help guide our home back from the brink of chaos. Ensure peace and freedom are the future, not power and control," said Gant.

"Dad…" tears rolled down Mara's cheeks. She knew she was not going to win this argument. Her father had that face that showed he knew what was going to happen before it did. It was pointless to continue arguing, but she did not want to let him go.

"I love you, Mara. You are the greatest thing that ever happened to me. You taught me how important patience and compassion can be. Now you must go and teach the rest of the kingdom." Gant turned to Eres. "I am ready to go."

The woman in the vision screamed louder. A voice out of sight told her to give a final push. Mara hugged her father one last time, hoping the moment would last an eternity. She closed her eyes and squeezed him tight, refusing to let go. When she opened her eyes however, he and Eres were gone, and she was laying on the ground next to Rylan, whose long blonde hair had been burned short and scorched black by fire that had exploded from her moments before.

"What happened to you?" Mara asked weakly as she sat up.

"You did," Rylan replied, breaking out into laughter. "I was so stupid!"

"What do…you mean?" Mara said, starting to giggle. Rylan's laughter was contagious, and Mara was emotionally exhausted. There was nothing to do but laugh.

"I saw you running at my father, and I knew what you meant to do. I wanted to help so I started running too…but I had no idea what I was going to do. I realized that and stopped short but I was too close and…" Rylan trailed off, gesturing to her hair and laughing with renewed vigor. "Like, what was I going to do? You were literally on fire!"

Kei walked over to the two of them and knelt down beside Mara. While the two of them were caught in their fit of laughter, Kei pulled out a rag and wet it with what little water was left on the ground. He began wiping a wound on Mara's arm as she came down from her laughing high and realized that despite what Eres had said to her in The Conversion, she hadn't seen Gjanion there.

"Rylan…" Mara began to explain but Rylan put a hand up to silence her.

Rylan had stopped laughing too and was looking over at her father who was now hairless, covered with the singed remains of his robes and armor, and scarred beyond recognition. Rylan stood up and walked over, unsheathing a knife.

"Rylan, what are you doing?" Kei asked as Rylan walked over to what was left of her father.

"I didn't want to kill you," she said softly to Gjanion, who could only groan awfully in reply. "I assume you have something to say, but you've lost that privilege. For once you'll hear me." Rylan paused, tears forming. "You deserve this. No…you *earned* this. You sacrificed everything, including me, for it. I would congratulate you, but your prize doesn't seem worth it. I am sure I'll do better than you did. This is quite the motivator. I don't want to end up like you."

The words were laden with hatred and disdain, but also a hint of sadness. Mara had never heard her friend talk this way; she could feel the hurt that Rylan was feeling. Rylan was broken, and Mara would do everything she could to hold her friend together while she healed from this.

"I am doing this for the good of the kingdom and to end your pain, father. Be free of it all," Rylan said, before plunging the knife straight down into Gjanion's chest, relieving him of his agony and allowing him to slip away forever. She watched as her father, the king, the tyrant who had ruined her life and the lives of so many others, close his eyes and cease to be.

"Why?" Kei asked as Rylan walked back over.

"He was in pain, I ended his suffering," Rylan said, seemingly emotionless.

Mara teared up. "Rylan, I'm so sorry."

Without a word, Rylan collapsed into Mara's arms. The princess shook as she sobbed and bawled into Mara's burnt tunic. Mara wrapped her arms around her, as did Kei, and the three of them sat in the middle of the salt flats, holding and comforting each other as the clouds rolled on overhead.

After a moment, Rylan pulled back and collected herself. "I'm sorry," she sniffled. "Sorry."

"Why are you sorry?" Mara asked, confused.

"It feels selfish to feel this way. Everyone has been through so much, it's not just me."

"We went through it together," said Mara. "And we will heal together."

Rylan smiled. "We will."

"We should probably make sure that the war ends inside the walls," Mara said, standing up.

"You have done enough," Keylon said, walking over with Sari. "Let us go spread the news."

Mara didn't have the energy to fight her. She nodded and thanked them.

"Keylon?" Rylan spoke up. "Please make sure that no harm comes to the knights. If they lay down their weapons, allow them to go free."

"Yes ma'am." Keylon bowed slightly, then added: "You're going to make a fine leader."

Keylon turned and left with Sari to put an end to the fighting in the city.

"The only thing I am interested in is leading the purge of the legend of Knorr. The sooner that is forgotten, the better. My half-brother may be a god reincarnate, but if he never finds out, this legend dies. That is my job. That is how I will protect this kingdom. Nobody will ever again seek the power of a god," Rylan said confidently.

Mara admired her friend's drive. She was right; the sooner Knorr was forgotten, the better off Kyros would be. But these next few months would be critical to their success. The chance that the kingdom devolved into a chaotic power-grab was high in the wake of Gjanion's death.

"Let's go find everyone else," Mara suggested, before suddenly breaking down, remembering that there was one person they were not going to find.

"Mara, what's wrong?" Kei asked her.

"Gant…he…" Mara couldn't say it, but she didn't have to. She knew that Kei understood, even though he would have no idea how she knew. Eventually Mara managed to explain, but it failed to relieve any of the pain. She, like Rylan, was physically and emotionally broken.

~~~

While Kei guided Mara and Rylan back to the inn, Sari and Keylon found the remains of the rebellion. The fighting died off quickly as news spread that Gjanion was dead. After some searching, they located Tren and Rezzik, who were sitting sullenly in an alley not far from the inn. Rezzik looked up at them and Keylon instantly teared up, knowing what he was going to say before he said it.

"Litik didn't make it," Rezzik managed to choke out before crying.
~~~

"What happened?" Sari asked them.

"We got separated from the goddesses for a brief moment, and that's all it took. We turned a corner and a knight had been lying in wait. Litik did not react fast enough. The knight managed to…" Tren trailed off, unable to speak. The former commander turned his head and looked at a covered body that Keylon had not previously noticed. Across the chest of the makeshift shroud was a long gash of dark red. She could infer what happened and did not ask either man to explain further.

"Rez, I'm so sorry," Keylon said through fresh tears.

"It's all right, he'll keep Fiona company now. I'm sure she'll love that," Rezzik managed to joke.

They all managed a small laugh before Sari and Tren lifted Litik's body. Keylon helped Rezzik to his feet and they walked back towards the inn.

~~~

Varyn had gone from a beautiful city painted in a surprisingly diverse array of whites and greys to piles of rubble that all blended together in a morose, grey blur. Kei tended to Mara's wounds but Rylan, despite her hair's sudden change in length, was relatively unscathed. She left to go help look for any stragglers, wandering the streets looking for any sign of Tanen, Kyra, Mai, or Zhira. People started to emerge from underground safe houses and sift through the remains of their stores and homes. Some were luckier than
~~~

others, but the wails and cries that echoed down the broken streets filled Rylan's ears and heart. Varyn had become a city of tears.

The lives of everyone in this city had been up-ended so quickly. They had lost the peace and prosperity they had worked so hard to maintain. Rylan felt for them, and vowed to herself that nobody in Kyros would feel this pain again.

As she crossed one of the central avenues, Rylan saw Mai walk between the remains of two buildings and disappear into an alley.

"Mai!" Rylan cried out as she chased after her.

Mai turned at the sound of Rylan's voice. "Rylan, what are you doing here?"

"Looking for you and the others. It's over," said Rylan.

"Over? You mean your father is…" Mai trailed off, unsure of what to ask.

"Dead." Rylan finished her sentence for her. "I'm sorry…I know you probably didn't want him to die."

"I did not, but then he killed me, so…" Rylan clarified.

"He killed you?"

"Long story."

The two stood in silence for a moment, unsure of what to say next.

"Lots of death today," Mai observed.

"What do you mean?" Rylan asked nervously.

"Radion is dead, too," Mai said, expressionless.

"What?" Rylan asked, surprised.

"Long story."

"Tell me on the way back to the inn," Rylan said as she started to head back towards their friends.

"I'm not going back," Mai said firmly.

"What? Why?" Rylan turned back to the former general.

"All I have known is war and fighting and working to be the best. I have no place in the next chapter of this story. I couldn't even do this part well. I betrayed a king, killed another, and couldn't protect one of the only people I have ever cared about. What makes you think I deserve a role in a peaceful kingdom?" Mai lamented.

"Precisely because of the things you listed. You have seen it all, done it all, and been through it all. We need your experience to help make sure that it doesn't happen again. Give yourself a chance," Rylan replied.

"You are not your father's daughter," Mai observed with a slight smile.

Rylan smiled back. "In every way but blood, we are as different as two people can be. But, intentionally or not, he helped shape me into who I am now. Just as you did, training me all those years and looking out for me after my mother died. I would not have survived these last few weeks without all you had taught me about riding, fighting, and sneaking about. Without you, this story may have ended very differently."

"All right, fine. You win, princess. Back to the inn, then," Mai said with a budding smile.

~~~

Zhira, Tanen, Kyra, and Forbin walked through the front door of the inn and found Kei and Mara resting on one of the couches. At the sight of her father, Mara teared up. Zhira came over and hugged her. Mara felt the weight of Gant's death in Zhira's hug, so she spared him having to break the news to her.

"I got to say goodbye," Mara told him, after explaining what had happened out in the salt flats.

"I am glad one of us did."

"It should have been me, Dad…" she cried into his tunic.

"If I know my brother, he didn't even give you a choice, did he?" Zhira chuckled.

"No. Selfish bastard," Mara laughed through her tears.

"It was the worst day of my life letting Kyra go," Tanen spoke up. "It is my job to always protect her, and the day I let her go, I failed. I am so lucky I raised a resilient, resourceful daughter and we were able to reunite. I understand why Gant chose to go instead of you. If he sent you on, he would not be able to protect you. This way, he knows you're safe in the company of your friends and family."
~~~

"Well said, Tanen," Zhira said, nodding in agreement. "You have been an invaluable asset to our team. Hopefully you'll stick around and we can work together on some alchemy? I would love to learn from you."

"Thank you, but I believe the time has come for me to depart. Our people rely on my abilities to help keep our town healthy and running, and I have been away for some time. It has been an honor to meet you both. Mara, thank you for helping me find the right path. I will return home and resume taking care of our town, and will do so in a sustainable and caring way to all." Tanen bowed towards her respectfully.

"I am glad to hear it." Mara smiled.

"Kyra, are you going too?" Zhira asked.

Kyra shook her head. "I am happy to have reconnected with my father, but life in a small town just isn't for me. I think I am going to head back to the capital and continue pursuing a life there."

"Perhaps I can be of help there," Rylan said, walking in just as Kyra spoke.

"Really?" Kyra asked.

"Sure," Rylan replied with a soft smile. "I believe the castle could use someone to help teach alchemy to those interested in learning. It should be a skill available to anyone, not something to fear."

"That would be amazing! I am a bit young to teach, though. Don't you think?"

"Who cares?" Rylan shrugged. "Someone has to be the first official Royal Alchemist. Besides, it will be nice to have a sparring partner who can give me a run for my money!"

Kyra laughed and she thanked Rylan profusely. "I won't let you down."

"If he returns, could you please thank Commander Tren for me?" Tanen asked the group, changing the subject. "He kept my daughter safe from the king, and I will be forever grateful."

"I shall," Mara agreed.

Zhira thanked Tanen, who hugged his daughter before he left through the front door. Mara wondered if they would ever cross paths again before leaning up against Kei and closing her eyes, exhausted from a war that was finally over.

Chapter Twenty Seven
Goodbyes

The horses weaved through the bare grey trees as they approached Saros. A dense layer of snow covered the ground up to the horses' knees, but Mara and Rylan made the going much easier for their caravan, clearing a path ahead of them. Rylan had caught on quickly to the hand motions inspired by the conductor Mara had seen in the amphitheater in Varyn. Without her wand, Mara was trying her best to control her power on her own. She found that it helped to use more fluid and connected motions, but what was far more helpful was teaching Rylan.

On their ride back home, Mara had taken to helping Rylan understand and control her abilities so as not to accidentally hurt any of them. Constantly thinking about how to guide Rylan helped Mara guide her own power and she found that a little more patience paired with explaining what she knew to her friend helped her understand her own magic much better.

The most interesting development, however, was Rylan's horse, Neela. On their return trip, Rylan had noticed that whatever she thought about telling her horse to do would happen before she could pull on the reins. Neela seemed to be reacting to her very thoughts.

"Is that…possible?" Rylan had asked Mara when they stopped for a break.

"I don't know. We're the only two wizards left. It's possible you have powers I do not. Tanen did say that the blood of different animals had varying levels of potency when added to potions. Maybe some animals are magical like we are."

"Neat," Rylan said, feeding Neela an apple.

The two of them led the caravan along with Kyra, followed by Zhira and Mai who rode side by side discussing what to do with the relics. Kei rode with Tren and his mother while Sari, Rezzik, and Forbin brought up the rear. Jerra had decided to stay in Varyn and continue with the forge she had built in the city.

The return trip home was uneventful, and soon the group came to a split in the road; one path led to Saros while the other went back towards the capital. Mara had known the time would come, but knowing did not make it any easier when it finally came.

"Oh, we're here already?" Keylon asked in surprise.

"It appears so," Tren said, reining in his horse.

"We should make camp for the night, one last time," said Zhira, noting how low the sun was in the sky already.

"Agreed," Mara said quickly, not ready to split their group up.

She and Rylan cleared an area large enough for their tents and horses while Zhira and Tren began unloading equipment with Sari. Mai used her arm-blade to quickly shear off some dead branches for a fire while Kyra and Keylon began prepping some of their rations. Once it was set up, Mara lit the fire with a snap of her fingers, then helped Rylan pull up some mounds of earth to use as seats. They gathered around the campfire as the sun set and the night became illuminated in greys and whites, thanks to the moon and its light being reflected off of the glittering snow piles around them.

Mara looked around at the group. A few months ago, she and her fathers had been living a simple life in a small town tucked away in the woods. Now here she sat, having seen half of the kingdom, and having saved all of it. As her gaze crossed the fire, she felt the absence of those they had lost. Gladys, her father, Biranel, Litik, her grandmother, Commander Hearth, and the countless others who had perished in the wake of their fight. She even felt for Radion, who according to her father and Mai had been more than willing to die for the power he sought.

Power and control was something she never wanted for herself, and she was eager to return home and resume a quiet life away from the world. Mara did not envy Rylan, who had agreed to go back to the capital and help guide the kingdom to an era of peace and freedom. She vowed never to wear a crown, but she knew that with the proper guidance, she could lead the people out of the darkness that her father had beset on them for a dozen years.

"Are you *sure* you don't want to come back to the capital with me?" Rylan asked. "I could use your help."

Mara stared into the fire. "I never wanted this life, but I did what I had to do. I'm not a leader, I'm not like you. I helped save Kyros, but that's where my story ends. Besides, I don't want people thinking that the last wizard took the throne from the royal family," she winked at Rylan.

"I don't care about the optics. You're important. You helped us get here. You should get some credit and some say in how we move forward," said Rylan.

"I appreciate that, but I can assure you that the only thing I want is to return to Saros. It's quiet there. It's my home. It's where I belong."

"All right," Rylan said, sounding displeased.

"What ever happened to Dazel?" Kei asked as he tore into some dried tigerdeer jerky.

Kyra looked up from her soup, confused. "I don't know. Did we leave her in Varyn?"

"Maybe it's for the best," said Zhira. "She didn't want her or Eres to be noticed or associated with removing your father from power. They wanted to avoid another 'Knorr' situation."

"So she's just…gone?" Rylan asked, feeling suddenly emptier. Dazel had been instrumental in breaking Mara out of the castle, keeping Zhira safe, bringing the people of Saros to Varyn to help fight, and providing her hope when all seemed dark.

"It would seem so," Mara said, taking some jerky from Kei.

"Do you think she returned to The Bright One?" Mai asked.

Zhira shook his head. "No, her powers diminished the longer she was here. I doubt she had enough energy to make that return trip."

"Wherever she is, I hope she is safe," said Rylan.

"There is no doubt in my mind that she can take care of herself," Zhira said comfortingly.

They proceeded to eat in relative silence, unsure of what else to say after all that had happened. The two week ride back from Varyn had given them ample time to debrief, but on the eve of splitting up, an unsettled feeling set in like a dense fog. For the last few weeks, they had all been mostly together and reliant on each other. Crisis after crisis, fight after fight, they were a team who kept each other alive and helped each other through the darkest time of their lives.

"I am going to miss you all," Rylan said to the group returning to Saros.

"As will we," Kei said with a smile.

"I am sure we will see each other again!" Forbin exclaimed, looking around hopefully for confirmation.

"Indeed, especially now that we know where you live," said Mai in jest.

Zhira gave a small laugh. "And to think we used to be scared of you."

"You still should be!" Mai grinned as she held up her hook arm.

"Sorry, General, I think that time has passed," Tren said, smirking.

The group poured the rest of their ale and drank long into the night. Mara was fairly quiet as the rest of them swapped stories, sang drinking songs, and eventually retired to their tents until it was just her, Kei, and Rylan remaining.

"I'm going to turn in," Kei said, kissing Mara's forehead.

"I'll be right behind you," Mara lied, knowing full well she would be unable to sleep tonight.

She watched him disappear into their tent and then looked up at the half moon and stars that peppered the sky. Total silence engulfed the woods, the snow muting all noises that would otherwise echo off of the bare trees and cold hard ground. The silence extended between her and Rylan as well.

This is it, Mara thought. *The last night we have before going our separate ways.* She had spent nearly every day and night with the princess since their escape from the capital. Mara hadn't had many friends in her life, but Rylan was by far the best she ever had.

She turned to say as much but Rylan spoke first. "I love you."

Mara looked at her, stunned. "I…"

"No, no not like that!" Rylan laughed. "Like a sister, or a best friend. I just…I didn't have a lot of friends growing up in the castle, especially not ones I got to choose for myself."

Mara began to tear up, the warm droplets freezing as soon as they came in contact with the cold winter air. She wiped her eyes and looked at her friend. "I love you too, Ry. You're amazing, and I am lucky to have a friend like you."

"You're the amazing one, leading a rebellion, sacrificing yourself, teaching me magic…you're the hero."

"You turned your back on your father for what you thought was right, helped me out of my depression in The Cave, were kind to everyone including our enemies, and found the courage to do what needed to be done in the end."

Rylan smiled. "I guess we're both pretty amazing, huh?"

"I guess we are," Mara said, returning the smile.

"There is something I don't understand, though," Rylan said. "If I really was dead, how did I come back?"

Mara pondered this for a moment. What had happened? The amethyst had exploded, sending magic in all directions. Mara had wielded her magic in anger, yet part of her had hoped that Rylan was not dead. *Maybe…*

"I think I brought you back," Mara said, unsure of if it was actually true. "I mean, I was throwing everything I had at your father, but I think that the part of me that hoped you were not dead sort of…willed it to be true. So when the amethyst exploded, the magic amplified it."

"I can't say that makes a lot of sense," Rylan replied after a moment. "Didn't you do the same thing again to my dad?"

"Yes, but that was purely about ending him. All of my energy went towards overpowering and killing him." Mara shuddered. She had never actually said it aloud. It had been the necessary choice, but it still didn't feel good.

"Well, if that's really what happened, then thank you!"

"I don't think we will ever fully know what happened out there."

"The important thing is that we won, and that we are alive. However we got here, we're here. That's what matters."

The two of them sat side by side as the flames of the campfire died out and left only the glowing embers of the wood that birthed them.

"I am going to miss you," Rylan said with a sadness in her voice that struck Mara in her core.

"Me too," Mara managed to say without tearing up.

"I know you don't like the city, but please come visit me? I'm going to go crazy trying to put this kingdom back together."

"I absolutely will, I promise. So long as you do the same."

"Of course."

~~~

The next morning, they packed up camp and said their goodbyes. Rylan, Kyra, Mai, Tren, and Forbin were headed back to the capital while Mara went home with Zhira, Kei, his parents, and Rezzik. As they turned their horses towards the capital, Mai paused. The former general looked back at Zhira with a sadness that had made its home inside her over the return journey. She wanted to say so many things, but could not bring herself to speak.

"He knows," Zhira said to her, understanding what she was feeling.

Mai nodded and turned away. "Let's go," she managed to say to Rylan, who began plowing the snow to carve a path home for them.

Mai turned back one last time and watched Mara, Zhira, and the rest disappear beyond her view, swallowed up by the grey trunks of the trees and the white banks of snow that surrounded them.

~~~

Rylan settled into her old room, which was exactly as she had left it when she fled with Mara. Part of her was saddened by the fact that despite everything, her father had respected her enough to leave her things alone. She flopped down on her bed and took very little to fall into a deep, dreamless sleep.

Rylan. A familiar voice spoke to her.

Rylan woke to find herself in a familiarly black void floating across from Dazel, once again in her goddess form.

Where did you go? Rylan asked her.

Somewhere nobody will ever find me, Dazel replied, clearly uninterested in explaining more.

Why are you here? Rylan was confused, she hadn't had a vision of the goddess in some time.

You called me here. Dazel's voice echoed around her.

I did? I don't remember doing so, Rylan said, confused.

Something still remains unsettled in you, it pushed your subconscious to find me, Dazel explained.

Rylan turned red. She knew what Dazel spoke of, and was unsure if she was ready to ask it. *I'm not ready for this.*

Nobody ever is, Dazel replied. *Do you think Eres and I were ready when we stood up to Knorr? Or Mara was ready when she stood up to Mai? Nobody is ever truly ready to do what needs to be done. The time simply comes when it must be done.*

Rylan's expression hardened. *I do not want anyone to think that I am holding my powers over them, but I understand that my role is to rebuild Kyros. I want Kyros to truly feel free, but*

I am still my father's daughter. The line continues, and now a wizard will be in charge again. If I am to guide them, I want the people to be able to speak without fear. I want them to trust me for me, and not seek to corrupt me and abuse my powers.

You are wise, young one. While you may have control over your abilities, their mere existence would certainly influence others around you. Not only must you control your magic, but you must also control the expectations of others. Give them no reason to fear you, and you will not be feared.

You know, I could use an advisor like you here at the castle, Rylan said hopefully.

Dazel smiled. *If you worry about your magic influencing others, how would it look to have a former goddess by your side?*

That's…a reasonable point.

You can do this, Rylan. Plenty of people believe in you. Kyros may never be perfect, but it will be better off with you leading it.

A sudden *thump thump thump* came front the recesses of the void.

It's time to part, said Dazel. *Good luck, Rylan.*

Will we be able to talk again?

My powers are fading, I do not know how much I will retain. If we can commune again in this way, we will.

The thumping got louder, and the void faded away. Rylan awoke to someone rapping on her bedroom door.

"Rylan? Are you there?" Mai's voice came from the other side of the heavy wooden door.

"Yes, one moment!" she called back.

Rylan smiled and threw on a purple tunic and grey pants and met Mai at her door. She was surprised to see the former general dressed so fancifully. Her green floor-length dress was a departure from her usually rugged military garb, and she wore the emerald from the staff in a necklace around her neck. Rylan noticed that she wore no attachment on her left arm.

"You look stunning," Rylan said, taking in her new advisor.

"Thank you, I hate it." Mai tugged at the dress's sleeve.

"You don't have to wear that, you know."

"People respond first to visual changes. With my reputation, I needed to do something starkly opposite to help them think of me how I want them to," Mai explained.

"Smart," Rylan said, thinking suddenly that her own outfit was horribly understated. "Give me a moment."

Rylan closed the door and rushed over to her wardrobe, where she pulled out a lavender dress and threw it on. She grabbed a pair of silver flats and slipped those on as well before brushing the sleep out of her short, blonde hair. Satisfied with her change, she returned to Mai and the two of them walked down the hall towards the library.

"Are Tren and Forbin coming?" Rylan asked Mai.

"I believe they are already there waiting for us," she replied.

Sure enough, the two men stood at attention in front of the door to the library. Forbin was wearing a dark blue doublet with grey pants while Tren had opted to remain in his armor, as Rylan had asked him to oversee the reorganization of Kyros's military forces.

"Forbin. General." Rylan greeted them with a polite nod.

"Ma'am," they said in unison, returning the nod.

"Let's get this over with," Rylan said, pushing the library door open.

An elderly woman came to greet them almost immediately. "Princess Rylan, I had heard you returned. I am sorry to hear of your loss." The wrinkled, dark-skinned woman's words were clearly rehearsed.

"Yma, you don't need to pretend. Kyros is better off without my father," Rylan said, relieving the librarian of the facade she had practiced.

"Very good, princess. How can I be of service?" Yma asked.

"I need you to find any and all books, scrolls, and notes regarding my family's history," Rylan directed.

"Right away." The old woman shuffled off.

Rylan turned to her cohort. "Same goes for you three. Find anything that has to do with my family, Knorr, or anything else that could lead Karbalion to the truth about who he is."

Mai, Tren, and Forbin nodded and set off without a word to recover anything they could find. An hour later, the four of them convened at a table covered in several piles of old books, dusty scrolls, and loose papers written in many different handwritings. Yma looked at the stacks proudly.

"Here you are, princess, everything about your family that exists in this archive."

"Thank you, now burn it."

"I beg your pardon?!" Yma looked taken aback.

"I want you to destroy all of it. My family did more harm than good to this kingdom and it's time their story came to an end," Rylan spoke with a strength that impressed Mai.

"Princess, I cannot do that. Sure your father was a tyrant, but it is important for the kingdom to learn from his mistakes…to give perspective when the next tyrant comes along. Without history, we cannot learn from it. Without learning from it, we are doomed to repeat it," Yma begged.

"She makes a good point," Forbin chimed in. "We are trying to prevent a recurrence, maybe instead of withholding this information from your brother and the world, we teach it. Spread it as a lesson. The promise of power attracts those who are easily corrupted by it, and those who seek it are doomed to a life of fighting and pain."

"I agree with Forbin," Tren spoke up. "It is important that our fight is not forgotten. The more that people know, the more they can grow and be better than Gjanion or even us."

Rylan considered their points, staring at the stacks of writing containing all there was about her family and its legacy. She turned to Mai. "What do you think?"

"As your newly appointed right hand woman, it is my job to help guide you to the answer, but never tell you what to do. Your choice is your own, and you can lead these people however you choose."

"Well that's unhelpful," Rylan replied immediately. "My father got away with everything he did because people didn't stand up to him and tell him he was doing something wrong. I don't want to be that either. This is not my kingdom to rule, it is the peoples' kingdom to live in."

"Very well, then I agree with Forbin and Tren. Teach it. Use it as a lesson. Let the people know why they have the kingdom that they do," said Mai more decisively.

Rylan smiled. "Alright then."

~~~

Mara and Zhira knelt beside the headstone. They finished filling in the hole where they placed Gant's urn and stood up, admiring the white marble slate that stood to the right of Fiona's. Mara looked to her left and saw Rezzik had finished burying Litik's
~~~

ashes as well and the three of them stepped back. Kei walked up with Sari and Keylon, each of them holding flowers. Behind them, the residents of Saros walked in a line carrying candles and lanterns. They spread out, interspersed between the other headstones in the graveyard.

"Do you want to say anything?" Zhira asked Mara.

"I do," she replied quietly. "My father was the best there was. He was selfless, caring, patient, compassionate, and kind. I know this sounds like the words anyone would use when burying a loved one, but they're true. My father only ever cared about others. He used his alchemy to help this whole town and make sure we were all fed. He taught me how to use my powers when he barely understood them himself. From my earliest memories, he was nothing but patient as I worked through being who I am. He saved so many people, and was willing to die to protect us all. He never judged anyone, and always gave them the space they needed to grow. The world is darker without him…my world is darker without him…but we will carry on his light."

"Well said." Zhira put a hand on her shoulder as tears streamed down his face.

"Thanks, Dad." Mara leaned on him.

"Rez, you want to go?" Keylon asked their governor.

"Sure." Rezzik stepped forward. "I…" he began crying almost immediately. "I only ever had Litik. He was my only family for so many years. He lived his life his way—unapologetically. He was who he was, and his eccentric, whimsical nature was refreshing and entertaining. I will miss my brother forever and will cherish the time we had and the memories he has left me with. I will keep his spirit alive with the stories I will pass down until my last days."

Rezzik stepped back and Keylon put an arm around him as he sobbed. Kei put a hand on his shoulder in support. The entire town stood around them holding their flickering flames. The glow of the orange light was aided by the shimmering snow. The whole scene felt warm, and Mara smiled. She knelt down and placed a single rose at the base of Fiona's headstone, then one at the base of Gant's as well.

~~~

Forbin blew lightly on the paper, making sure the ink would not smudge when he closed the book. He waited until he was sure it was completely matte—no shiny spots remaining—and closed the blue leather cover.

The gold lettering on the front had been done by someone with far more skill than he in the ways of calligraphy, which was just as well. He had been honored to write the book, but worried his handwriting would detract from its importance. Forbin put away his writing materials and left the library, thanking Yma as he exited into the hallway. He walked down the long
~~~

corridor and hung a left, towards Rylan's chambers. As he approached, he suddenly remembered that she wouldn't be there today. He turned around and headed for the former throne room, which had been transformed into a glorified council chamber.

A year had passed since they had returned to guide Kyros to a free existence, and the project was going quite well. The kingdom had taken the news of Gjanion's death well. Many sent correspondence to Rylan acknowledging her loss despite his actions, while many more celebrated the freedom that came from the decree Rylan had sent along with the news of her father's demise. She had informed Kyros that her family would no longer be in charge of the kingdom, that she was choosing, as her first and only act as heir to the throne, to destroy it. Rylan disbanded the monarchy and asked that each major settlement send a representative to the capital, where she would moderate, but not direct or impact, agreements, treaties, and trade negotiations between regions and townships.

The realm had responded well, as there were now almost two dozen chairs at the table in the main council chambers. Rylan had chosen her father's former throne room as the seat of the new order as a reminder of what they had overcome. Save for his banners and the throne itself, the room was unchanged. The gold leafing set in the marble floor danced in the light of the fires that sat in their braziers at the base of each column.

Forbin entered the room, where eight of the twenty or so chairs were taken up at the far end of the table. "Rylan, may I have a word?"

"Certainly. Please excuse me." Rylan stood up from the table and walked around to Forbin. She noticed the book and smiled.

The True & Complete
History of Kyros

The gold lettering reflected the light of the flames and made the words look alive, almost as if they were moving magically about the cover.

"Is it ready?" the former princess asked with unhindered giddiness.

"It is." Forbin smiled.

"Send it to the printer, then. It is time for the history to be known."

"Are you sure this is the version you want to go with? She's going to hate it," Forbin asked.

"That's why it's the right one to tell," Rylan said with a smile.

Forbin took the book to the printer and handed it off, along with a piece of parchment that Rylan had given him to include as the introduction.

"Printed just like this?" a young woman asked as she looked through the blue book.

"Yes please, with that on the first page," Forbin pointed to the parchment.

"Can do!"

"Thank you kindly," Forbin nodded politely before departing.

Forbin hung around, curious as to what Rylan had written. The young woman took the parchment and unfolded it to dictate it to the scribe who would be copying the book. "Start with the following," she began.

"History is often written by the victors, and therefore leaves out details that the losers would have liked to include. This book aims to avoid this mistake, as both perspectives of any conflict are always as important to discuss as the conflict itself. In an attempt to be as unbiased as possible in the presentation of events, the authors of this book have spent the past year searching for testimonies and stories from as many people as possible on all sides. Before you read this book, however, there is one thing that all those interviewed agree on: Mara, the last wizard, saved us all."

Epilogue

"Keri! Get down from there!" Kei yelled.

"You can't make me!" Keri taunted, sticking her hands out from the sides of her head and wiggling them.

"But I can!" Mara said, flying up towards her daughter. Keri gave a squeal of surprise and tried to escape her oncoming mother, but it was pointless. Mara intercepted her, wrapped her in her arms, and brought her back to the ground.

"That's not fair! I can't do that," their son pouted.

"Neither can I, Gant." Kei put a hand on his nine year old son's shoulder.

"You should be excited for your sister! Flying is very difficult magic. It takes a lot of energy," said Mara as she put their daughter, named for Kei's parents, down.

"Which is why a six year old has no problem with it." Kei winked at her.

"But I want to be a wizard!" Gant stomped in frustration.

"You don't need to be a wizard, Gant, you're special just the way you are!" Rylan said from behind them.

"Aunt Rylan! What are you doing here?" Gant asked, completely distracted by her surprise appearance.

Rylan walked up with her eleven year old half-brother, Karbalion, in tow. "It's the night of the festival! You didn't think I'd miss it, did you?"

"Oh yeah! Can I fly with you this year? Pleeeeaaaase?" Gant got down on his knees and looked up with the saddest eyes he could muster.

"That's up to your mother, if she thinks you can handle it…"

"Puh-lease! Keri can fly and she's six! I'm nine, I can do it—probably better than she can!" Gant stuck his tongue out at his sister.

"I'll race you tonight, stupid. You can't beat a wizard!" Keri puffed her chest out confidently.

"Hey now, it's not about being a wizard. That doesn't make you better at anything," Kei said to his daughter.

"Except doing magic!" Keri exclaimed.

"Except doing magic," Kei conceded.

Gant looked dejected.

"You have no control over who you are born as," Mara said to him, "but you have complete control over who you want to become. You may not have magic like your sister, but that makes you no less special."

"Well I'm still gonna race her later and beat her!" Gant smiled and began chasing Keri around the cabin with Karbalion.

"Where is Zhira?" Rylan asked Mara.

"He's out in the square getting everything ready. We were waiting here for you before heading over. Are you ready?" Mara asked her.

"Absolutely. Let's go!" she exclaimed, turning on her heel and heading towards town.

The three of them walked down the main street towards the square, with Karbalion, Gant, and Keri chasing each other in circles around them. Saros had grown in the eleven years since Rylan had set the kingdom on a path to peaceful life. Bess's inn was now four times the size it once was, as visitors came from all over to enjoy the Festival of Dazel, which now occurred annually. Zhira had taken over the herbalist shop and converted it into his own alchemy storefront, selling his concoctions to anyone who needed them for no more than the price of making the potion itself, which was often free.

Rezzik had retired from governing the town and Keylon had been selected as the next governor. She expertly coordinated the expansion of the town, making sure that there was plenty of space for people to build new homes and shops along main street and its sister streets on either side. Sari's forge was fast becoming known as the standard for quality items kingdom-wide, but he refused to forge weapons, figuring that the creation of the weapons themselves could entice some people to use them nefariously. Instead he turned his talents to metalworking interior decor along with his wife's glassblowing. He also made utility items such as axles, nails, and tools for all trades.

Mara watched as her and Kei's children ran off into the crowd to find their friends. In the center of the square, Zhira set up a booth with Tanen, who came to town for every festival to help Zhira with the extra loads of free potions that people enjoyed during the festivities. He looked up and waved at them before resuming his task.

"Still no sign of Dazel?" Mara asked.

Rylan shook her head. "I haven't been able to communicate with her for a few years now. Though, I did hear a rumor recently of a mysterious figure in the north, helping wayward travelers with what is claimed to be magic."

"You think it could be her?" Kei asked.

"Well it certainly isn't me. I don't have time to wander the northern territories looking for lost travelers, not with these two running amok," Mara said, nodding towards Keri and Gant, who were now looking for a hidden Karbalion.

"If she is helping others with magic, she must have retained some of her powers after all," Kei said hopefully. "Maybe you just need to be closer to her to talk to her."

"Perhaps one day I'll go in search of her, but I have a feeling that if Dazel doesn't want to be found, not even I would be able to find her," Rylan mused.

"Hey, speaking of absent people…no Mai this year?" Kei asked Rylan as they approached the already crowded square, which had been expanded three times in the last decade to accommodate the growing popularity of the festival.

"Not this year, she is off in the west helping a couple of towns resolve a trade conflict. Forbin is overseeing the capital in our absences, but I promised him I'd bring him back some floating potions," she replied.

Mara smiled. "I'll make sure Dad sets a few aside for him."

Outtakes

As I created the characters in this story, each took on a life of their own. I had arcs and plots foiled entirely by the organic way they developed in certain scenes, forcing me to rework the story as I went. They are amazing, natural, and incredible characters that were a joy to create. For me, a big part of writing is being able to visualize each scene as I am writing, meaning that I often thought of these characters as though they were filming scenes for a series or movie. Since this story is fairly serious, I decided it would be fun to include some 'outtakes' that hopefully provide a smile or two.

Inspired by the credit scenes in Pixar's 2004 classic *Monster's Inc.*, here are some 'deleted scenes and outtakes' of The Last Wizard & Kingdom's End for your entertainment.

Outtake One
The Last Wizard - Chapter 24

"It doesn't matter. You're too late," Gjanion said calmly, an unnerving smile spreading across his face.

Gjanion reached up and plucked the ruby from his crown. Horror-struck, Hearth looked up helplessly as the king took the ruby and secured it in the hilt of the silver sword.

"No!" Hearth exclaimed as King Gjanion turned to face Mara with all three relics.

"It feels so…strong. With these relics I will be the unstoppable, unquestioned, unequivocal king of—"

Pew pew! Pssshhhhhhh Pew!

The sounds interrupted Gjanion, who looked around, confused.

"Cut!" cried the director.

"What the hell is happening?" Gjanion asked.

Zhira, laughing, pointed to Gjanion's right hand. "Look at the sword!"

In his hand was not the prop of the relic sword he was used to wielding. Instead, someone had swapped it for a plastic toy sword complete with lights and a small speaker that provided very grainy and unrealistic sound effects. Realizing what had transpired, Gjanion roared with laughter.

"Who did this?" he asked, as tears came to his eyes.

Gant raised his hand slightly as he doubled over and nearly fell on the ground. He laughed so hard that no sound came from him until he gasped for air.

"That's too good," Zhira said, high-fiving his on-screen brother.

"Thanks," Gant managed to say between laughs.

After a few minutes, everyone got their laughter under control and the crew returned to their places to film the scene once again.

"From the sword! Action!"

"It feels so… strong. With these relics, I will be the unstoppable, unquestioned, unequivocal king of Kyros!" Gjanion roared.

At that same moment, the eclipse hit totality.

Or was supposed to. The lighting rig in the broken window shifted to imitate the moon going red, but instead it began flashing all sorts of colors. Somewhere, the sound system switched from the dark, haunting score being used to keep the mood of the scene to a mash-up of The Bee Gees performed by Weird Al.

"Gant!" Gjanion cried out, unable to hold back another fit of laughter.

"Weird Al. Nice touch," Mara said approvingly.

"I didn't know he did a Bee Gees mash-up!" Mai said, laughing as she danced along overdramatically.

"I am never going to get to record my scene," Dazel said from off stage, dressed in her silver and gold makeup.

Outtake Two
Kingdom's End - Chapter 8

"Kyra, come on. I'm breaking my back over here!" Kei exclaimed.

"Sorry, sorry. This choreography is hard."

As Kyra and Kei got reset to shoot their confrontation on the salt flats yet again, there was a startlingly loud sound from the rafters above Kei. He looked up just in time to see a lighting rig falling, but froze and did not dive out of the way in time.

"Kei!" Mara cried from off stage, rushing to his side.

"Ah…" Kei moaned, clutching his back. "I didn't mean literally breaking my back…"

"Wait, we can work with this!" Mara said, before turning to Tanen. "Get out here!"

Tanen rushed onto the stage. "What?"

"Let's film the healing scene! An actual heal will be so much more convincing."

"Oh, okay, yeah! Good call!"

The crew got set up quickly and Kyra scampered off stage as the lights dimmed.

"Action!" called the director.

"Heal him," Mara said, trying to sound commanding.

"Sorry?" Tanen put on a convincing look of confusion.

"Show us how you used your skills to help your people. We are your…people now. Give me…sorry, I forgot the line!" Mara called out.

"Cut!"

"Mara, this was your idea," Kei complained, still clearly in a great deal of pain.

"I know, I'm sorry."

"If you mess this up, they'll have to break my back again! Am I the only one here prepared today?" Kei asked, looking over at Kyra.

"Again, I'm sorry!"

"We have plenty of time," called the director.

"My back doesn't."

"Roll it again!"

This time, Mara nailed the scene. The director, happy to have gotten such an authentic shot, cuts the cameras.

"Thanks Tanen," Kei said, stretching his back. "Kyra, are you ready to give that fight another go?"

"Let's do it!"

Outtake Three
Kingdom's End - Chapter 11

"Zhira, what are you doing?" Eres asked, with a disapproving look on her face.

Zhira looked up. "Oh, gosh. Sorry I didn't mean…"

"My eyes are up here."

"Sorry, sorry. You're just so…shiny! I can see my reflection."

"That's a nice save, Z!" Gant called from across the stage.

"Seriously, I wasn't looking at her—"

"I'm going to call HR on you, weirdo!" Rylan laughed.

"I wasn't—"

"Eres, perhaps you should just take his ability to see," Dazel suggested.

Zhira began to sweat. "Can…can you do that?"

"You want to find out?" Eres said seriously, then suddenly burst out with laughter. "Relax, I'm only joking!"

Rylan and Gant broke into another fit of laughter as Zhira finally cracked a smile. "Well played. I am sorry though."

"Don't worry about it. Golden breasts are hard to ignore, I'm sure. I find myself looking down at them constantly!"

"You're the lucky one. Mine are only silver. Nobody looks my way," Dazel complained jokingly.

"Hang out with Narcissus here and you'll feel plenty flattered!" Eres said, winking at Zhira.

Outtake Four
Kingdom's End - Chapter 25

"So when do we get started on my origin story movie?" Radion asked. "Everyone gets an origin movie nowadays."

"Soon, I think. But we need a title," replied Phil, one of the producers.

"How about *Radion's War: The Story of Why There is Purportedly Only One Wizard in 'The Last Wizard'?*" Radion laughed.

"Oh man, or maybe *Slightly More Wizards Than There Will Be*," Phil replied, also laughing.

"Why not just make a whole series? Start with *Wizard*, then go to *Another Wizard*, which is followed by *The Next Wizard*, then *Wizards*, and *More Wizards*, but then things start to change and you get *Fewer Wizards*, and *Very Few Wizards*, and then finally we come to *The Last Wizard*," Radion could barely breathe while he rattled off his make-believe series.

Phil collected himself, then put on a mock-serious face. "I've got it. *Radion's War: More Wizards Than There Are About to Be*"

Radion and Phil couldn't stop laughing at all of the stupid names they came up with. They also invented a merchandise line and came up with alternate titles for the existing installments, such as *The Absolute Only Other Last Wizard (promise)* instead of *Kingdom's End*. They were so wrapped up in their string of comedic developments, that Radion almost didn't hear the director call for him.

"Oh now I have to go be all serious on camera. *Thanks* Phil."

"Anytime, Radion. Anytime."